Barbarians on an Ancient Sea

Barbarians on an Ancient Sea

William Westbrook

McBooks Press
Guilford, Connecticut

McBooks Press
An imprint of The Rowman & Littlefield Publishing Group, Inc.
4501 Forbes Blvd., Ste. 200
Lanham, MD 20706
www.rowman.com

Distributed by NATIONAL BOOK NETWORK

British Library Cataloguing in Publication Information available

Library of Congress Control Number Available
ISBN 978-1-4930-5136-6 (paperback)
ISBN 978-1-4930-5156-4 (e-book)

∞™ The paper used in this publication meets the minimum requirements of American National Standard for Information Sciences—Permanence of Paper for Printed Library Materials, ANSI/NISO Z39.48-1992.

Dedication

In memory of Little Eddie Phillips.
That generous provocateur.

Special Thanks

I am grateful to my able crew: Tripp Westbrook, Cabell Westbrook, Bob Westbrook, Kerry Feuerman and, of course, my loving wife Susan.

Preface

They change their sky but not their soul
who run away across the sea.

—Horace

One

The storm seemed to detonate the sky. The low growl of thunder turned to deafening explosions following the brilliant violence of lightning, continuously blinding the crew of the ship which tossed about on the sea like a twig—rudderless, mastless, helpless.

A series of mistakes had brought the ship to this X upon the ocean, far off course, disease having taken some of the crew to the bottom, poor sail handling having separated the ship from her mainmast when she rolled under a wave. It was a large ship that felt insignificant within the arms of the storm; lately from Boston, bound for Algiers and about to reach the barrier reef around the north coast of Bermuda.

The bulbous black clouds tumbled overhead as the ship at last grounded on the coral, several of the crew flung into the undulating maelstrom, avoiding one certain death for another.

The incessant sea pushed the ship farther over the reef, and then into *the reef, the jagged coral like a saw against the timbers. The ship began to fill with water. She lay on her side, her dirty bottom exposed to the waves as all manner of items floated free from her holds and out the hull into the dark air. Her precious cargo, however, was much too heavy to float. As the ship began to break open, the chest of gold coins slid along the edge of the reef and then down to a blackness even darker than the sky.*

Two

Ezra Somers arrived at his office on Aunt Peggy's Lane in St. George Town at the height of the gale, fighting to walk against the fist of wind that hit his chest and the rain that needled his face. He had work to do. He arrived sodden and flushed at his usual time, just past 8:00 am, and sat at his massive partner's desk, dripping upon the ledgers, correspondence, tally sheets, and shipping directions so necessary for the operation of the Somers Salt Company.

The windows rattled and a shutter banged like repeating shots, and it put him in mind of the recent spate of attacks on his salt ships by the French privateers and pirates in the Caribbean and along the east coast of the U.S.

Difficult times, difficult times, he muttered to himself. Most of the eastern ports of the United States were still clamoring for salt but, in truth, he had to admit that New England's orders had fallen off rather dramatically. Well, he thought to himself, add that to the million mysteries of the world.

He rose and limped across the room to look towards St. George's harbor, a favorite view for a man who made his living from trading by sea. But today visibility was limited to fifty feet outside his window and he could see nothing of the harbor. His foot hurt, for he suffered from gout, which he knew intellectually could be helped by reducing his nightly portion of wine but which he refused to do. *Stubborn* was a word often used when fellow Bermudians described Ezra Somers. In his mind, however, the trade-off simply wasn't worth it.

Somers' office was lined with books on all manner of subjects, for *knowing* was of particular importance to him. Well into his sixties, Somers fought old-ness; his mind raged against it. He was still as curious as he'd been as a boy turning over rocks or wading in shallow pools of water at low tide to study the creatures trapped there. He wanted to *question* the world, physically and philosophically, and beneath his wispy white hair was a fecund mind that never rested.

It was unusually cold for early spring in 1800, and a fresh gust of wind seemed to shake the building and might have moved his books a fraction of an inch. He thought of Nicholas Fallon, even now sailing home on his return from the Caribbean, and wondered at the day and perhaps night he would have to face battling wind and sea. Fallon was captain of *Rascal*, an American-made schooner that sailed for the Somers Salt Company to protect his ships, and also carried a *letter of marque* from the British Admiralty. This meant Fallon could legally attack Great Britain's enemies—notably French and Spanish—and not be hung as a pirate. He was free to sell his captured prizes to the Admiralty, and Somers, Fallon and the crew would all profit.

For the past two weeks Fallon had been patrolling north of Hispaniola in hopes of a prize or two. What he did not know was that his return to Bermuda would be brief, for Somers had, at last, received a substantial order for salt from New England. Given the dangerous situation along the American coast, Somers wanted *Rascal* to guard the salt ships to be certain they got through safely. One ship—*Lucille*—under Captain Pence, was in St. George's now and eager to be away to the south to pick up her load of salt at Grand Turk. The other—*Eleuthra*—under Captain Ashworthy, was already loading her salt in Grand Turk and would await *Lucille's* arrival. Thence they would both sail in company with *Rascal* to Boston.

Certainly *Rascal* was a well-found ship, and Fallon had an excellent crew of 90 plus the incomparable Beauty McFarland as first mate. With *Rascal* as escort, Somers had no concern for the convoy reaching the U.S., but as a roaring gust once again seemed to shake the floorboards under his feet he *did* have concern about Fallon making it through the gale. He said a silent prayer under his breath, turned from the window and limped back to work.

It was, indeed, an eventful day for Fallon at sea, with the gale keeping the crew occupied for twelve hours straight. *Rascal* was hove-to for most of it, lying some 200 miles southwest of Bermuda. Cully, *Rascal's* one-eyed master gunner, had double lashed the guns hours before the worst of the storm whitened the world with spume and blowing wave-tops, and none of the massive cannons had careened across the deck. A 3200 pound wandering cannon could easily crush a man or take him right through the side of the ship into the boil below.

Even hove-to, *Rascal* took a beating from the gale and Colquist, the surgeon, had treated several of the crew for contusions and concussions and at least two for broken bones. Colquist had come aboard as a temporary surgeon, initially borrowed from a ship laid up in ordinary in Bermuda, but he had become permanent. He was serious and moderate in his habits and had saved and treated enough men aboard *Rascal* to be respected by the crew and valued by Fallon.

Rascal had sailed south as far as Santo Domingo, but it had not been a successful cruise, for the privateers who normally worked around that island had apparently gone to ground. Once or twice the lookout had reported a sail, but nothing had come of it. So it was not a particularly happy ship that was currently riding out the storm, and every man aboard felt the loss of potential prize money keenly. And yet, they would not for all the world challenge Fallon on the subject, for he was a lucky captain who had always taken care of them in the past. He would again.

Rascal was a privateer of eighteen 12-pounders and a long nine in the bows, a fast and capable ship if handled with alacrity, at which Beauty McFarland excelled. She was a strong woman, short and roundish, with close black hair and black eyes that could look through a man bent on challenging her authority. Though women could be found at sea on occasion in menial work, Beauty was the exception in a position of responsibility. She and Fallon had been childhood friends on Bermuda, as well as ferocious competitors racing skiffs on St. George's harbor. Fallon had only occasionally bested her, for Beauty's mind was above all else tactical and decisive at that moment when the path to victory or defeat formed an imaginary fork on the water. She stood now lashed to the binnacle with her peg leg planted inside a ring bolt that had held it secure most of the day. Gangrene had crept into an infection when she was 16, and a mere coral scrape had resulted in a painful amputation. Fallon had held her hand throughout the operation, and in difficult times she could feel him holding her hand, still.

She looked at Fallon now, holding tightly to a shroud, his black hair tied in a matted club. He was giving the storm all he had, never going below to rest, reassuring the men that *Rascal* would hold them in her arms safe as houses. He was tall and lean, with green eyes that were kind when not in battle. His upper body was muscled, if scarred, and Beauty thought him handsome. Apparently, Elinore Somers thought so, as well, for they were to be married later in the spring. She thought of Elinore briefly, tall and blond and spirited, with the kind of spit that Beauty admired in a woman. Her own lover was demure and reticent and even fragile, and Beauty did her best to protect her from the prying eyes and gossip on the island. But their relationship was of course *known*, even somewhat tolerated, no doubt out of respect—or fear—for Beauty. Well, she *could* be ferocious in protecting those she loved; she had killed fighting for Fallon, of course, and would do whatever it took to protect young Ajani—Aja, as he preferred to be called, her particular favorite aboard.

Aja was just going around to the men, slowly and cautiously, checking each one with a word of comfort. He was lean and dark black and his arms were shadowed with muscle. But it was his eyes that held the men's attention, for they were bright with curiosity and concern. He was rescued from a sinking slaver as a boy and had taken to Beauty and Fallon over time, learning seamanship and navigation and the possibility of goodness in humanity. He became practiced in Fallon's ways, adopting his sense of caring and concern, and the men accepted him as one of their leaders. It was remarkable, really, but then Fallon insisted leadership was earned, not granted, as was so common in the Royal Navy. Aja had earned his place as second mate aboard *Rascal.*

The glass continued to drop throughout the day, and by the first dog watch, about 4:00 pm, the wind quite unbelievably increased. By the second dog the seas had grown truly monstrous and *Rascal* was constantly taking green water over the bows. It grew prematurely dark, the storm sucking the light out of the day, and it was a miracle that the lookout was able to spot a small light to the east, although only for an instant, and he hesitated to report it—but there it was again.

"Deck there!" came the call from above. "A ship off the starboard bow!"

Fallon had been wedged below in his cabin trying to eat his dinner when Aja came to get him. He quickly pulled on his tarpaulin and hat and made his way up the companionway. It was an angry sea by now, malevolent and black and grasping, and Fallon was struck by its power as it seemed to pull *Rascal* down into its troughs before suddenly releasing her. He could see Beauty by the binnacle next to Barclay, the white haired sailing master, all eyes to the northeast straining to see some sign of a ship. It was there, looming as a black shape, nothing more. It could be anything, of course, but it could also be an enemy. Battles had been fought in these conditions; in fact, Fallon had fought them.

There! A signal rocket! That ship was in trouble and had likely seen *Rascal's* stern light and was asking, begging more like it, for assistance. Fallon judged the distance to be two cables or more; it was difficult to tell in the dim light. He could barely see the ship's stern lantern.

"Nico!" Beauty called. "What can we do?" Concern was etched on her forehead as she stared at Fallon.

Clearly not much *could* be done. To approach another ship in this storm was impossible and might well prove fatal. Yet it was a ship in trouble, and to ignore a plea for help ran counter to every instinct in Fallon's body, not to mention the law of the sea.

There, another rocket!

The ships were arguably closer now; no doubt the other ship was making quite a bit of leeway, drifting down on *Rascal* with each wave.

Something would need to be done immediately. Fallon's mind said *sail away*, but his heart felt the pull of duty.

"Beauty, we must get alongside her!" yelled Fallon. "Get us underway and get your best man with a heaving line made fast to a hawser. Get us closer!"

Beauty nodded, astounded at the audacity of the order, for maneuvering in that sea and wind would be nearly impossible. And to get close enough to heave a line against the wind was doubly impossible. As *Rascal* began to slowly gather way the storm laid her over sharply and the men on deck fought to grab anything solid and handy to keep from going overboard.

"Nico!" yelled Beauty. "I'm going to try to get ahead and to windward of her. Do you hear? I am coming over top of her and then we'll throw a line!"

That was absolute madness. Fallon and Barclay and anyone save Aja, who had never seen such a thing, knew it would never work. But Beauty set her jaw, set her peg in the ring bolt and ordered the helmsman to head up as much as possible, though *Rascal's* double reefed fore and main sails seemed to barely move the ship. Harris, who had done some boxing in a checkered life, prepared the heaving line and brought it to the stern. The outline of the drifting ship could just be seen now, her stern light disappearing and then reappearing, noticeably closer each time she got on top of a wave.

Harris made his way aft with a monkey's fist, a small ball of rope tied around a heavy grapeshot at the end of a thin messenger line of about 50' to which was attached a much larger 6" hawser. The idea was to throw the monkey fist to the other ship's crew, who would haul on the messenger line, bringing the hawser across the water. Well, that was the idea.

Rascal was edging closer now, Beauty on the wheel with the helmsman; the timing of the thing was critical or the drifting ship might well come hurtling down onto *Rascal*, very possibly sinking them both. Fallon watched in amazement as Beauty seemed to run the calculations of drift and wind and boat speed in her mind, her face immobile as *Rascal's* bow rose higher and higher up the face of a growler and *there!* The drifting ship—Fallon could see she was a sloop—was almost on top of them. They were going to crash together! Yet Beauty held on, her eyes riveted on the sloop as she fell into a trough and *Rascal* just edged past her bow and up to windward.

"Now Harris!" Beauty shouted, her face now mobile and anxious as Harris threw the monkey's fist high into the air off *Rascal's* stern, well out to windward of the sloop. The wind shrieked and blew the line back across her bows. There were hands there to claw at the messenger line and Beauty called for *Rascal* to heave-to quickly as the line ran out. *Rascal* drifted down to leeward now, not quite matching the drifting sloop's speed but close enough so that when the thickest part of the line, the 6" hawser, was at last secured to the sloop's capstan the other end could be made fast to a bollard on *Rascal's* stern without pulling the deck out of her. Perhaps 100' of distance separated the two ships, tethered as they were, jerking and wrenching apart, drifting together, and jerking apart again.

Fallon had watched the whole thing happen in rapt amazement, astounded at Beauty's seamanship. But there was no time for wonder as both ships were now in peril and at any moment the line could break. Such was the strain on it that its 6" had been wrung tight to 3". Something must be done to relieve it quickly. The drifting sloop was now directly downwind of *Rascal* and Fallon staggered up the deck to the binnacle.

"Beauty!" he shouted. "Get Harris to throw another line if he can. We'll tie off on larboard, as well."

Beauty nodded and called for Harris to again prepare a heaving line and monkey's fist. Another 6" hawser was brought on deck from the cable tier and precious minutes passed with all eyes on the straining line running out from the stern. Harris worked methodically, judging the distance to the drifting ship against the strength of his arm—aided by the force of wind that shrieked in the rigging.

At last, he had his monkey's fist ready and stood on the stern, balancing carefully against the roll and plunge of the ship, watching the drifting sloop to leeward edge closer before sliding down a wave and backing away. Beauty ordered the mainsail eased to spill wind and Fallon could see hands aboard the sloop waiting in the bows but would not for all the world break into Harris' concentration. The man was stronger and better in this situation than Fallon would ever be.

Now *Rascal* rose up, and up farther still as a giant mountain of a wave rolled under her. And now the monkey's fist was in the air, lofted high into the wind, and it sailed—would it be short?—no! It was across, by God! The hands on the sloop quickly hauled on the line until the messenger's end was aboard and the 6" hawser could be brought across and was secured to the capstan with the other hawser. *Rascal's* hands then tied their end of the rope to a bollard on larboard, effectively splitting the strain with the other rope.

Now Beauty let the schooner fall off and the mainsail was brought in and *Rascal*, snugged down as she was, began to sail, however clumsily and slowly, off to the northwest. From behind them they could hear the sloop's crew cheer, and *Rascal's* own crew joined in, for it was very likely no one aboard either ship would ever see the like of it again.

Three

The ships fought each other all night with the feints and dodges of boxers, each jerk threatening to break a line or rip planking out of a ship. There was no sleeping in either ship as the motion was too rough and tumble and the imminent threat of disaster too present in each sailor's mind.

When at last the low gray light of dawn revealed itself the ships were miraculously still together and the wind—merciful God—was slackening. Fallon stood by the binnacle with Beauty and surveyed their tow, now very low in the water, a wreck of a ship, to be sure, for though her mast still stood her sails were in tatters. Barclay could only estimate their position; there certainly had been no stars last night, and it looked doubtful for a noon sight.

On the stern of the sloop stood a big man, blonde hair and beard blowing about in the wind, waving his hat at *Rascal* and now—what?—executing a deep bow of appreciation. Fallon nudged Beauty, who nudged Aja, and they all smiled at the big man's gratitude.

Fallon could see the sloop was pumping water over the side, and likely had been all night, yet still she was low in the water. Something would need to be done soon or she would sink behind them, threatening to take *Rascal* with her. The sea had lain down considerably, as had the wind, and in another few hours conditions would be better still. Fallon began making plans to take off the sloop's crew. It would be a delicate operation, though not as frightening as taking the tow last night.

One hour passed. Then three. The wind was down to a strong breeze and the sea had stretched out her rollers. Beauty ordered the ship to heave-to and, as *Rascal* settled, the momentum of the sloop carried her part way up to *Rascal's* larboard side. Hands on the sloop finished the job of getting their ship up to *Rascal*, using the capstan to winch the two ships closer. Fallon had coir fenders put over the side, as grappling hooks lashed the two boats together and the tow lines were cast off the sloop's capstan to be brought back aboard *Rascal*. The sloop's crew scrambled over the railings onto *Rascal's* deck, carrying bits of clothing and personal items as best they could, amazed and exhausted. The last to come was the big man with the blonde beard.

"Caleb Visser, captain," he said solemnly. "Or should I call you Jesus? For you have saved this poor flock in our hour of need."

"Nicholas Fallon, sir, at your service," replied Fallon with a slight smile. "Are all your men accounted for?"

"Yes, they are all here, sir," said Visser. "I think we had best cast off *Liberty* for she will be going to the bottom soon anyway."

In the event, the American sloop *Liberty* was cast adrift, sinking and forlorn, and as a reef was shaken out of *Rascal's* fore and mainsail, the sloop was very soon out of sight. Beauty brought the schooner about and pointed her bows for Bermuda at last, putting the night and the miles behind her.

Sometime later, when the hands had had their dinner and the wind had moderated even further, a quiet and exhausted Caleb Visser joined Fallon and Beauty in the great cabin aboard *Rascal*; well, *great* was perhaps an exaggeration, for *Rascal* was only a modest schooner. But Fallon's quarters were certainly larger than Visser's own cabin. Elinore had improved on the design immensely, adding damask cushions to the stern seats and insisting on a proper checkerboard floor of canvas. Fit for her captain, she'd said, and indeed Fallon loved her the more for caring about the floor under his feet.

"It is only by chance and a storm that we meet like this, Captain Visser," began Fallon, looking at the man closely as he settled in with his wine. He was about Fallon's height but heavier, perhaps twenty-five years old or so, his hair and beard a bit shaggy and he had the air of a sad boy about him. He did his best to smile, but it was a struggle, and both

Fallon and Beauty were immediately taken with sympathy for him, for the burden he carried at losing his ship was great.

"Yes, it was my lucky day, or rather night," replied Visser with quiet gratitude. "Without your intervention my crew and I would be dead by now. I am a fortunate man, indeed, and I apologize if I do not show it."

"Tell me, sir," began Fallon earnestly, "where were you bound?"

"That's a story in itself, Captain Fallon," Visser said with a weak smile. "I hope you have enough wine!" And then he paused, the facsimile of a smile leaving his face, as he seemed to grow contemplative.

"Call me Caleb, both of you please," he said to them, going immediately for the familiar, "for I'm but a fisherman on a mission of mercy. *Visser* is Dutch for fisherman, as you might know, and indeed my family has fished the waters of the Grand Banks for two generations for the *Gadus,* or cod which are so abundant off Newfoundland. Like many who fished those waters in all weathers for their whole lives, my father retreated at last to Boston and *bought* the cod instead of *fished* the cod, which was more profitable and easier. We had good years when our ships were protected by the Union Jack. But after the peace we lost that protection, and we lost the right to trade with Great Britain or her colonies, as well. My father pushed the boundaries in search of distant markets, and Southern Europe became our best by far. A quarter of all New England's cod went to the Mediterranean, by God. Until . . . until the Barbary pirates demanded the U.S. pay tributes to the rulers of Morocco, Algiers, Tunis, and Tripoli just as Great Britain and France did. Without tributes, the Barbary states would send their corsairs out to attack American shipping."

"I've heard stories about America refusing to pay tribute," said Beauty, the color rising on her neck. "How much did the pirates want?"

"Their demands were outrageous," said Visser. "It was millions of dollars a year. The U.S. had no money after the war, and was already deeply indebted to France, which is the source of the current enmity between our two countries. The government began paying the tributes, finally, but the payments are irregular and late and never enough. This angers the Barbary rulers, and no American ship that enters the Med can be sure of leaving."

Fallon watched Caleb closely and sensed that the American had arrived at the point in his story where good news tips to bad. All equanimity had left his face, replaced by a squinting worry that seemed to dull his blue eyes to gray. Fallon knew Beauty saw the same thing, for she reached for the bottle to pour them all more wine.

"As you will know," Caleb continued after a strong sip, "the Mediterranean is 4000 miles from Boston and it is normal for our ships to wood and water in Bermuda, at Hamilton. My own father left Boston nine months ago on a Visser ship to the Mediterranean but did not return. My older brother Alwin and I grew anxious, of course, and then two months ago we received word that his ship had been captured by the dey of Algiers' pirates, who demanded a ransom for his release. The amount was staggering: $10,000!"

"What about your government?" asked Beauty. "They should skewer the bastards! Your father is American!"

Caleb was momentarily taken aback by Beauty's reaction. It was doubtful he'd ever heard a woman speak so forcefully, and she won his respect in an instant.

"The government is in an argument between President Adams and those who want to pay for peace, and Thomas Jefferson and his followers who want war. While they argue in Washington, my father is a slave in Algeria. He is not a young man and . . ."

Clearly, the emotion in Visser's voice was real and desperate. Fallon wondered if his father was even alive at this point; after all, it had been almost a year since he was captured.

"So you are on your way to Algeria to negotiate for your father, I collect?" said Fallon sympathetically, anticipating where the story was going.

"Yes, exactly. I *was*, you mean," Caleb said dejectedly. "Alwin and I have mortgaged everything we have and called upon every friend and raised $12,000—in gold, as the dey demanded. We left Boston with two ships—the other is the schooner *Jocelyn* with Alwin in command—to bring home as many prisoners as we could. Our two ships were separated during the recent gale; we were supposed to rendezvous with *Jocelyn* in Bermuda but I decided to steer clear of the island, fearing for the shoals there. We attempted to run with the storm, and then tried to heave-to, but my vessel worked hard in the storm and sprung a plank, then another. We were taking on water badly and pumping around the clock. The gale blew out our sails when my helmsman was washed overboard and the ship was caught aback. We drifted, more or less sinking and out of control for some time, with no idea of our position. By yesterday afternoon I thought we were doomed. When one of the crew saw your stern light I immediately set off a rocket in hopes you'd see us. Thank God you did. And may I say that was as fine an act of seamanship as I have ever witnessed."

"It was all Beauty, sir," said Fallon to his blushing first mate. "But I fear your ransom is at the bottom by now. You did not think to bring it up when you came aboard?"

"Actually, there was nothing to bring up," said Caleb somberly, the worry dark on his face.

"How so?" Fallon asked, all curiosity.

"The gold is in *Jocelyn,*" said Caleb. "She was the bigger ship, and my older brother the better sailor, and we thought it would be safer in the event of bad weather or attack from pirates or privateers, for *Jocelyn* carries four guns each side, all 9-pounders. We were in sight of each other until the storm."

"I see," said Fallon with a note of caution in his voice. "Let's hope she came through the gale in good shape. That would have tested anyone, in any ship."

Beauty and Fallon both looked at each other, a brief glance of concern on their faces, which Caleb Visser hopefully did not see.

"And where are you bound, sir?" asked Visser.

"We are on our way home to Bermuda ourselves. You and your men will be our guests, and if this wind continues to move southeast I believe we will raise the island in two days."

"That is very generous of you, Nicholas," answered Caleb, genuinely moved by Fallon's kindness. "God willing I will find Alwin and *Jocelyn* riding at anchor at Hamilton wondering where in the deuce I've been."

Four

A LIGHT, MISTY RAIN LINGERED AFTER THE GALE AND SEEMED TO engulf St. George Town, glistening the homes and alleys, the carts and branches and cobblestones. Elinore Somers had awakened early to walk the beach, as was her custom, and hurriedly threw on her cloak against the wet morning.

The beach was her particular obsession and had been since she was a young girl dreaming daily of leaving Bermuda for—where? Anywhere, in truth. She'd envied boys, and Nicholas Fallon in particular, when they'd left to go to sea. She'd felt trapped; her mother was dead and she'd hated her father for nothing more than being her only parent.

The leaden sky was heavy on the sea, and even the shore birds were absent this morning, the day apparently being too somber even for them. Elinore bent her head against the wind, occasionally stopping to search the horizon for any sign of a ship. The ferocity of the gale had frightened her, and she didn't frighten easily. She knew rationally that *Rascal* would be coming from the south, yet fear was often irrational, especially when it was for someone you loved. Fallon was an excellent seaman, and Beauty was always concerned for the safety of the crew, but anything could happen at sea. And, as Fallon often said, much of it was bad.

Elinore was tall and lithe, with blonde hair and pale blue eyes that missed nothing. Today those eyes searched the distant sky for small, white patches of canvas. She had fallen in love with Fallon years before, had "set her cap" for him as the islanders would say; well, she knew what she wanted in a man. She closed her eyes for a moment and thought ahead to the not-too-distant future when they would be married in a small chapel by the sea, just as Fallon had promised her when he'd proposed marriage.

When she opened her eyes, she saw a small figure running towards her on the beach. In the distance, she thought it a foreshortened man, but it became a boy running at full tilt. It was Little Eddy, as he was known on the island, a clever boy always on the edge of mischief. Little Eddy was a beach forager, for Bermuda lay over 600 miles from the nearest land and all manner of items continually washed ashore. The coral surrounding the island, particularly the northern approaches, was a virtual graveyard for inattentive sailors. Their ships' cargoes were regularly salvaged by Bermudians. Little Eddy was a born salvager.

He had no father, and his mother had little time for him or, in truth, little affection. The boy's dream, like Elinore's dream had been, was to leave Bermuda and see the world. Perhaps, he reasoned, if he gathered and sold enough flotsam and ships' debris he could fund passage on a ship. At least he had a plan, which Elinore had to admit was more than she'd ever had.

"Miss Somers! Miss Somers!" said the breathless boy. "There's been a shipwreck at North Rock! You can see wood planks on the coral and there's clothes and things. It was that gale that did for her!"

Elinore's heart stopped for a beat, her mind going to Fallon's clothes, what he wore to sea, fearing the sight of a shirt upon the rocks that she knew.

"Little Eddy, please show me," she said as she took him by the arm. "Show me where."

When at last they reached the water's edge at North Rock the coral told its tale. Planks were indeed strewn about the shoreline and bits of ship were hung up in the coral heads: a chest, some pots and pans, clothing and empty tins, the remnants of a thing that lived and sailed. There were no bodies, for they would have been carried out to sea; hunting for survivors was out of the question.

Little Eddy hopped along the coral tops, picking up what he could, and hopping back to shore before a wave overtook him. He had an armful of salvage and a grim expression on his face.

"Here's part of the name board," he said to Elinore solemnly. He held up a piece of wooden plank with a single letter painted upon it.

Elinore held her breath, then breathed out slowly, for the ship that went down on the coral at North Rock could not have been *Rascal.*

Little Eddy held the letter "J" in his hands.

Five

In just over two days' time, for the wind dropped off considerably, Barclay had *Rascal* at the entrance to Hamilton Harbor on the southwest of Bermuda. Barclay was stooped and gray but his age was indeterminate. He seemed to have been born just as he was, for no one on Bermuda could remember him looking any other way except stooped and gray. He was a taciturn man who appeared and disappeared silently and, after Fallon, was the best navigator aboard *Rascal.* He had been particularly helpful in tutoring Aja in his study of the stars, and the two could be found talking on deck and looking at the heavens on many nights.

The coral clogged entrance to Hamilton was complicated, but Barclay had been there before, and soon enough they were inside. Clapboard buildings dotted the shoreline of the harbor, some with docks that reached into the water like brown fingers. There were ships at anchor or carrying on their business, loading and unloading cargo, ships from many countries except France and Spain. Caleb Visser scanned the harbor with a telescope, then with his bare eyes, then with the telescope again before finally lowering it slowly.

Jocelyn was nowhere to be seen.

Fallon and Beauty watched him quietly, not knowing what to say or do. But it was Aja who approached him from behind, putting his hand on Visser's shoulder in sympathy. Visser was grim, for he feared he had not only lost his ship but perhaps his brother and all their money and all hope of rescuing his father from a life of slavery. His shoulders sagged and his legs almost buckled under the weight of his failure.

Aja leaned closer, well acquainted with loss and hopelessness from his time as a kidnapped slave himself. Though *Ajani* meant *He who wins the struggle* in his native homeland, he knew a bleak future when he saw one.

"There is a proverb my father taught me, Caleb, sir," he said softly. "*The poorest man in this world is not the one without money. But the one who is without people.* You have people, Caleb, sir."

Quietly, Beauty and Fallon came up to join Aja.

"Yes, Caleb, you have friends around you," said Fallon. "And you have us *behind* you. The day is not over, and your mission is not lost. You are behind in innings, sir, but you shall have the match!"

And with that note of optimism they all put their hands on Caleb Visser's shoulders and he hung his head and set his jaw, for he wanted very much to believe them.

Later, after they had left word with a dock boy in Hamilton to ride like the wind to St. George Town if *Jocelyn* should sail in, *Rascal* threaded her way out of the harbor and sailed off on larboard up the northern coast of Bermuda. Visser understandably kept to himself at the taffrail, staring at their wake, lost in his own helplessness.

It was dusk when *Rascal* rounded up and let go in St. George's harbor. The little bay was virtually empty, the only vessel a Somers salt packet swinging slightly at her anchor. The sunset's light painted the shoreline cottage windows red, a flaming red to warm a returning sailor's heart. As soon as Fallon saw the ship secure, he and Caleb were rowed to shore in *Rascal's* gig.

Walking up the road from the harbor, Fallon could see that the candles still burned in Ezra Somer's office. That was no surprise, and he hoped he would find Elinore there, as well. They had been apart over a month, more than he'd planned for this last cruise but the sea kept its own calendar.

As Caleb and Fallon ascended the stairs to the office they could hear voices, one of which belonged to Elinore, and Fallon's heart leapt.

When he stepped through the open door of the office, however, he was unprepared to have her leap into his arms, sobbing. Somers was there, as well, along with Little Eddy, and they all crowded around Fallon, leaving Caleb off to the side, awkward and invisible.

"I was so worried, Nico!" Elimore cried. "But this is you! You're here! You're back home!"

"Safe and sound, back home," said Fallon softly into her ear. "We have a wedding to plan, remember? I always come back, love. Always."

"Welcome home, Nico," said Somers, slapping his captain on the back. "I never doubted it."

"Doubted what, Ezra?" said Fallon. "Why was everyone so worried?"

"It was the gale, Nico," said Elinore, wiping her eyes. "It was so horrible and we were so worried. For some reason it scared me this time, more than the other storms. It's not that I doubted you, or Beauty, I just became frightened because I knew you were sailing through it to come home."

"And there was a shipwreck, sir!" yelped Little Eddy. "At North Rock it was. There's lots of wood on shore!" Little Eddy, the scrounger turned newsboy.

"And who is this you've brought home?" asked Somers, ignoring Little Eddy's dampening outburst, and extending his hand to Caleb.

"Caleb Visser, at your service, sir," said Caleb tightly, the alarming news from Little Eddy's mouth having entered his brain and travelled to the pit of his stomach, where it was now forming a knot. "But tell me, if someone can, about the wreck?"

"Oh, I don't think it was a ship from around here," said Somers, trying to lighten the mood in the room. Elinore still had not let go of Fallon, and Little Eddy was rummaging in a sack he'd brought to Somers' office.

"I found this, sir!" said the boy. And he struggled to pull out the piece of name board he'd scrounged from the wreck, the letter "J" clearly visible.

Caleb Visser staggered as if he'd been shot.

"My God," said Visser, more to himself than anybody else. "My God."

There was silence in the room as every eye watched Visser take the "J" from Little Eddy and stare at it, then rub the letter with his hands. His mouth opened several times to speak but nothing came out.

"Ahem," said Fallon quietly. "Captain Visser is from Boston, a cod fisherman, and he and his brother were on their way to Algiers to pay a ransom for his father, also a cod fisherman, who was captured by corsairs working for the dey of Algiers. They left Boston in two ships, his brother was captain in the other one, and they were separated in the gale. We were able to pick up Caleb and his crew before their sloop sank. But . . . the ransom gold was in the other ship. Her name was *Jocelyn*."

There was a collective gasp in the room and, instinctively, hands went out to comfort Visser, who was fighting hard to hold back tears, his eyes down and closed.

"My God," was all he could whisper. And no one else could think of anything better to say.

Six

The gathering in Somers' office broke up in a sad way, with Little Eddy showing Caleb Visser the way to the White Horse pub, which had been in Fallon's family for generations, where the distraught fisherman planned to drink himself into a stupor. Ezra Somers headed home to go to bed and Fallon and Elinore walked slowly towards the fisherman's shack on the edge of the marsh, their secret place. Unfortunately, their excitement at seeing each other was inevitably affected by the plight of poor Caleb Visser and the utter hopelessness of his predicament.

They entered the shack with the key Elinore kept under a rock by the door and Fallon began building a small fire. It was a simple, one-room shack with a small table and chair on a circle of rug and, of course, a bed beneath the window where Elinore sat. The question now was whether they could set the world aside for a few moments and be the lovers they wanted to be.

As the shack heated up, the answer appeared to be *yes.* Elinore stood up as Fallon knelt and poked at the fire; she slipped off her coat and then her dress and undergarments, and when Fallon turned and looked up he gasped, for she was the most beautiful woman in the world, glowing white as an apparition, her blonde hair falling over her breasts, her legs slightly apart, the moonlight just peeking between them.

In moments he was beside her and her hands tore at his clothing with a fierce urgency that spoke of her fears for him and her need for this moment. All thoughts of the world's troubles vanished as they fell onto the bed, Elinore's hands and mouth finding remembered places and her tongue tasting the salt of the sea on Fallon's body. She guided his hands where she wanted them, and when he mounted her and began pushing gently she smiled a wicked sort of smile and rolled him over and sat astride him, still in command of this moment, breathing short gasps as she moved back and forth, holding him tightly inside of her. She leaned down over him, inches from his face, and began slowly rocking, then faster, until finally she sat up and arched her back and pounded her hips into him with a ferocity that came from someplace primal, undiscovered until that moment; and she screamed a scream of sexual release that filled the shack and perhaps the night around the shack.

Spent and wet from sweat, she collapsed.

Fallon held her to him and felt her heart pound his chest, her body relaxed at last, soft and tender again. He thought she might go to sleep just like that, on top of him. So he was surprised when she suddenly spoke.

"The bell," she said softly. "We need the Bermuda Bell."

Seven

Just before Christmas in 1613 an impoverished but brilliant young man named Robert Norwood set foot on the Somers Isles, before they were called Bermuda, and decided to seek his fortune diving on the many wrecks that littered the shoals. He had lately been a pirate, but found the pay lacking, from bad luck, perhaps, or lack of industry. So he was casting about for a new profession.

Salvaging seemed just the thing. His inventive mind devised a method of diving that was a first in the New World: he inverted and converted a wine barrel into a diving bell, hung weights about it and, with some help from a crew on the surface, descended upon the wrecks, breathing the air trapped inside the barrel. Thus, the Bermuda Bell was born. No written or oral history survived as to Norwood's success, but wags did say he failed at piracy when piracy was in full bloom, so there.

Over the next hundred plus years the Bermuda Bell was more or less continually put to use salvaging wrecks; albeit there were improvements made over time. The bell was enlarged, sheathed in lead, and a glass window installed. But the biggest improvement was the foot pump on the surface that continually pumped fresh air through a hose to the bell to replenish what the diver breathed. This latest incarnation of the bell was to be found in Tucker's Town, on the south coast of the island, in a salvager's barn.

So it was that Ezra Somers, Caleb Visser, and the ever present Little Eddy set out in a carriage the next day for Tucker's Town. Little Eddy seemed to have a particular liking for Visser, or at least felt badly for having found the letter "J" that sent the American into despair and thence to the pub.

The constant bumping and jerking over the rutted road was certainly doing Visser's headache no good. Fallon's father had finally put him to bed well after midnight in Fallon's old room, having heard the fisherman's tale several times over several hours at the bar. The senior Fallon wasn't surprised that he hadn't heard from his son last night; Elinore was first in line.

It was almost eight miles to Tucker's Town and it was the forenoon before they found the salvager's barn. He was a man in his sixties named Walker, a dour man who did not smile as he introduced himself. He led them into the barn and pulled a tarp off the bell and there it sat, a leaden mushroom that seemed to have grown out of the straw and dirt. After inspecting it, though no one knew what they were looking for, Somers asked when the thing might be delivered to North Rock.

"I have a contract at Bird Rock next week," said Walker. "Then the week after I could get the bell to you. Weather taken into account, of course."

Well, that was the best they were going to do, it seemed, but still it caused Visser to fret. Somers arranged a fee for Walker to bring the bell to the beach at North Rock in two weeks' time. He would be bringing it by wagon, along with the pump, of course. Somers would have to arrange for a barge to be at the beach with a mast and boom for raising and lowering the bell into the water.

"Tell me, sir," said Visser, rubbing his temples, "who will be diving on the wreck?"

"Well, not me for sure," said Walker. "You can dive on it yourself, of course. But it will go faster if you use someone who's done it before. You tell 'em what you're after, like money or jewels, and where in the wreck it is, or was, and it will go much better."

"Who would that be?" asked Somers, wondering whom he knew who had ever been in the bell. No one came to mind.

"Why, I would hire Indigo, of course," answered Walker, referring to one of his slaves. "But you'll have to pay him. He'll expect what I always let him have."

"And what is that, sir?" asked Somers.

"Whatever he can fit in his mouth and hands," said Walker, and for the first time he smiled, revealing he had no teeth.

Fallon spent his morning with his father, the best time to catch up before the pub opened, and thanked him for taking in Caleb Visser.

"He's a good man in a bad spot," said Fallon. "I can't imagine what I would do or how I would feel in his shoes."

"Yes," said the senior Fallon, kindly, "he's lost his brother and the gold they needed to free his father and he feels helpless. He's very grateful to you, I must say. Told me so over and over. And to Beauty; my God, how in the hell did she handle that ship?"

"I could never have done it," Fallon said modestly, but his father knew better. "It was a near thing; I could have reached out and touched *Liberty's* bowsprit, I think."

They sat in companionable silence for a while, father and son just feeling good being together. They were in Fallon's childhood home above the pub, where the family had always lived, and the hall clock near Fallon's bedroom ticked the time away. It was a remembered sound from his youth, constant and regular, a sound to be counted on to lull a young boy to sleep.

"Where is it for you now, son?" asked his father.

"Boston, it appears," replied Fallon. "Ezra said a big order for salt has come through, the first in a while. So I am to convoy two ships from Grand Turk to Boston. I saw one of them in the harbor when I came in last night; no doubt her captain will want to be off to Grand Turk as soon as possible to load his salt. There should be no problem getting a convoy through. The problem is that most of our ships aren't sailing in a convoy, of course, and pirates and privateers are always a problem. All our ships must be protected, and there is only one *Rascal*. I need a plan I don't have."

Fallon's father nodded. The clock in the hall seemed to tick louder.

"That's never stopped you before," he said with a smile.

It was late morning when Fallon climbed back aboard *Rascal*. There was only a small portion of the crew aboard, for *Rascal* was in a safe harbor. Beauty was out of the ship, no doubt at home with the woman she loved, and Fallon was greeted at the gangway by his second mate.

"Aja," said Fallon, "if Cully is aboard please ask him to come to my cabin. And you come too, please."

Aja went to fetch Cully, who was belowdecks taking stock of powder and shot, for they would need both before *Rascal* sailed again. Cully was a master gunner, the best shot Fallon had ever seen, in spite of having only one eye. He looked devilish with his black eye patch and wild white hair, but he was Fallon's right hand at the guns and was as loyal as a retriever. His Irish good humor always cheered the crew, and he was surprisingly well-read. He would scrounge for books in each new port, trading his well-thumbed copies for books from other ships' crews. Not many tars read, but some did.

In minutes, Aja and Cully stepped into the great cabin and found Fallon staring out the stern windows, deep in thought. He turned and bade them both sit at the desk while he ordered his thoughts.

"Cully, there is a veritable navy of French privateers and pirates who are stepping up the war on our packets, none of which has enough guns or manpower to fight them off. There is only one *Rascal*, and we can't protect all of them."

Cully nodded solemnly, as did Aja, both seeing the problem and turning it over in their minds. No one spoke then, for no good answer presented itself.

"Are the scantlings on the packets strong enough to handle more guns? Or bigger guns?" asked Fallon, getting to the heart of the matter and the reason he'd asked Cully to his cabin.

"Most of those ships are old, Nico," answered Cully, using the familiar with an old friend. "I'm afraid the big guns would rip the deck out of 'em. Well, anything more than a 6-pounder, say. Maybe you could reinforce the decks but . . ." And he let the thought drift off while he tried to work out the effort required in his mind.

The problem wasn't just guns, Fallon knew, but finding and training the crews to handle them. As well, the privateers were mostly sloops and the odd schooner, fore and aft rigged ships that were smaller but handier and quicker than the clumsy salt packets. Their goal was to cripple and board quickly, and they could overtake a salt ship from the rear with no danger of return fire, slipping unharmed under her counter no matter what armament the bigger ship carried.

Protecting all of Somers' ships seemed impossible, and for the life of him Fallon couldn't devise a plan to do it. *Rascal* couldn't be everywhere at once, but the damned pirates and privateers *could,* and that was the real problem. When the pirates got close enough to grapple, not even a packet's 6-pounders could depress enough to fire down into them.

Cully may have been thinking the same thing. May, in fact, have been thinking *exactly* the same thing, because a wide grin split his face.

"What if we *let* 'em get alongside, Nico?" he said. "We sure as hell can't beat 'em away, sounds like."

Fallon looked at his friend and master gunner a moment, trying to see where he was going with that idea. But Cully just kept grinning, and now nodding, and then he picked up an empty wine bottle from Fallon's desk, held it up a moment, and dropped it to the floor, where it shattered.

"And then we bomb the bastards!" shouted Cully. Aja jumped, but Fallon laughed out loud.

Eight

The next morning Cully led five crew mates to the doorstep of St. George's only farrier, a gruff farrier at that, named Wilton. He lived on the outskirts of the village in a hut of sorts surrounded by paddocks and several small sheds, one of which was where he worked trimming and shoeing horses' hooves. Out behind this shed was a midden, a refuse pile of bent nails and bits of metal that he was only too happy to sell. It was here that the crew went to work filling the canvas bags they'd brought.

Meanwhile, Aja led another five crewmen to the midden behind the White Horse where Fallon's father dumped the daily refuse of the pub, the food scraps and empty wine bottles and beef bones. The smell was extraordinary, and the men worked to gather bottles as quickly as possible, alternating between holding their noses and stuffing their bags. It was the first of many trips they would make to many pubs.

The meeting in Somers' office began before lunch and included Ezra Somers, Fallon, Cully, and Jeremiah Pence, captain of the salt packet *Lucille,* who was visibly agitated from having been at anchor too long, waiting on instructions to leave. The partner's desk dominated the center of the office, and was broad enough for Fallon to sit opposite Ezra Somers. In truth, Somers' side was messy with papers and Fallon's side was clean, for Fallon was rarely there.

"Captain Pence," began Somers, formally addressing the corpulent captain. "Your next cruise will take you south to Grand Turk, as usual, and thence to Boston. But we have an increasing problem getting our ships through from the Caribbean up the U.S. coast. French privateers and pirates are thick as thieves. I am not telling you something you don't know, of course, but what's wanting is a strategy to protect our ships no matter where they sail. And I believe Captain Fallon has something interesting in that regard."

"My strategy, Captain Fallon," snorted Pence, interrupting, "is to drive the buggers off! My men are more than capable of fighting back, I can assure you."

"I'm sure that is true," said Somers soothingly, "but you and I both know, Jeremiah, that even a brave packet is no match for a ruthless privateer bent on taking a prize. Or, worse, several privateers working together."

Pence's face fell a bit at that, for there was truth in what Somers said and he knew it. Pence had even been captured once by pirates off Curacao and sent to shore in a small boat, where kindly villagers kept him and his small crew nourished until he could be found and rescued. The pirates had been in a single sloop.

"I know you are eager to be away to the south, Jeremiah, but I wanted to wait until we had a chance to hear Captain Fallon's thoughts," said Somers tactfully.

There was silence in the office then, Fallon letting Pence work through his indignation to get to a place where he was ready to listen to reason. He could impose his plan on the man, but it was better to have him welcome it.

"Cully here has hit on an ingenious idea," said Fallon after the pause. "His notion takes into account the intent of the privateers to board quickly, with as little damage to the ships as possible."

It was on Fallon's side of the desk that Cully now placed a wine bottle filled with nails and a small packet of gunpowder, to which was attached a short length of fuse that protruded out of the top of the bottle, held in by a bit of cloth.

"This is a *grenado,* gentlemen," said Fallon. "It is a variation of those used by the notorious Captain Thompson when he fought off pirate hunters sent by the Governor of Jamaica over 50 years ago to capture his ship. Thompson used powder flasks, stinkpots, and all manner of grenados."

"You can't fire a bottle, sir!" exclaimed Pence, for he had apparently never heard of such a thing.

"No, you are very right, sir," said a patient Fallon. "I propose that, since you can't outfight the privateers at long range, you let them come close, by letting your sheets fly or heaving-to, appearing to give up. Then when they have grappled on and are preparing to board, your men light the grenados and drop them overboard onto the privateer's deck. We bomb the bastards, as Cully here would say."

Cully grinned broadly at the acknowledgement and nodded his head, Somers leaned back in his chair with his eyes alight, and Pence reacted as if he'd been bombed himself, with the stages of shock, consideration and, finally, acceptance playing out on his face.

"That is brilliant, Cully!" exclaimed Somers. "The nails and glass should work wonders on those buggers. It'll be the surprise of their lives, indeed it will!"

"We have made up 100 grenados for your ship, Captain Pence," said Fallon. "It really is the only way to beat off the privateers if your guns fail to keep them off your sides, don't you think? I will be leaving as soon as I can gather up my crew. If you can't wait until then to leave I suggest you take the grenados on board immediately and sail. I will catch up as quickly as I can or join you in Grand Turk."

In the event, a very skeptical Pence ordered the grenados to come aboard late that afternoon, for he planned to sail immediately. Fallon asked Aja to get word to the crew that they would be leaving in two days' time; it would take that long to locate them all. Beauty would need to get stores aboard quickly and, even if *Lucille* arrived in Grand Turk ahead of *Rascal*, it meant less time waiting around until her salt was loaded.

Then events would unfold as they would from there, for Fallon was a strong believer in the guiding hand of fate.

The afternoon sun warmed the air as Visser and Little Eddy walked the beach towards North Rock. Visser carried some dried flowers that Little

Eddy had somehow found, or scrounged, or stolen for the occasion, for Visser had planned a small service for his lost brother.

As they approached the cluster of coral where Little Eddy had found part of *Jocelyn's* name board the gulls swooped overhead, calling out with their high-pitched screams, their eyes fixed on the sea looking for food. Little Eddy led Visser out onto the coral heads as far as they could go, right to the water's edge. The waves were inconsequential today and the tide was on its way out as they both stared at the water.

"I'm very sorry, Caleb sir," said Little Eddy. "I wish I had never found that 'J'."

"No, no, Little Eddy," said Visser sadly. "I would rather know the truth than tell myself a lie that Alwin might still be alive. You didn't do anything wrong. But tell me, do you come here often to look for wreckage?"

"Well, not wrecks so much but things wash up on shore, particularly after a storm and the waves get high. Mostly it's something to do."

"Why aren't you in school?" asked Visser. "Does your mother know what you're up to?"

"Right here's where I always come," said Little Eddy, ignoring Visser's question. "I sometimes bring bread to feed the gulls, which is why they're making such a racket."

Visser looked closely at Little Eddy and saw a momentary sadness about him to match his own. The boy's hair was dark and unkempt, a hairless face with freckles and gray eyes.

"My dad is out there somewhere," the boy said. "He left when I was born, or near abouts. Mom said he sailed away and never came back. Thinks he's probably dead, you know. But you can't say for sure. Maybe he'll come back."

Visser's heart went out to the boy, for though he'd come to North Rock to bid his brother farewell he knew, in a way, that this was where Little Eddy came to find his father, on the rocks or on the sea. Thoughts of his own father inevitably intruded on the moment and he, too, wondered if he would ever be found.

Clouds obscured the sun as boy and man stood at the edge of the sea. The warm air was gone, replaced by a gray coldness that seemed to confirm their sense of loss. Visser held the flowers aloft a moment and then tossed them into the sea. The gulls swept down, pecked at the dried colors and then, deciding there was nothing to eat, lifted off the water to soar away.

Nine

Over 3000 miles from Bermuda, Achille Zabana sat on his haunches on a hill overlooking the rabble village below him. The sun was just coming up in the east and already a few villagers were creeping about, building cooking fires, and fetching water from the well located in the center of the small courtyard. It was there that he would call the villagers together to bear witness to the power of the dey of Algiers to deal with infidelity and rebellious behavior.

Zabana was a Frenchman whose mother was Turkish, his father unknown. The cruelties against a mixed race in Marseilles molded a young man in obvious and hidden ways, and he became unmoored, seeking revenge for the indignities heaped upon him by school mates, society and a religion taught but not accepted.

At twelve, he stowed away on a ship that was captured by corsairs sailing for the dey of Algiers. He was sold as a slave but offered freedom if he would convert to Islam. He accepted the offer, for Muslims could not be slaves. He quickly rose to become a clerk of sorts to the dey, speaking French as well as Turkish, and exercised the soft power of his office broadly, assuming authority he did not really have. He was despised for it, naturally, by those both above and beneath him.

At twenty-one he volunteered to quash a rebellion in a village in a far province, was granted the chance, and adopted the powerful strategy he had witnessed in Revolutionary France. Zabana had a portable beheading cart, or guillotine, built to be carried on his ship and landed ashore near the village. Then it was pulled by slaves away from the harbor and finally rolled into the village to the most public area he could find. He then sent spies to bring forth the wealthiest and most influential among the villagers; and they came, bewildered and trembling. Each of these unfortunates was forced to kneel before the cart and place his head on its cradle. Then the victim's arms were put through holes in the lower base of the cradle to hold his head. Next, Zabana ordered the terrible blade raised as all in the square looked on in horror. The victims' heads were cut off and fell into their hands, which surprisingly retained a momentary ability to hold them. Within a half hour the rebellion and disquiet were effectively over. Zabana loaded the beheading cart back onto his ship and sailed for home to an exultant dey.

Thereafter, Zabana was the man for the most difficult jobs, the most dangerous jobs, and he sailed with his beheading cart to many fractious villages, bringing them all under control easily. Finally, after so much success, he was named head of the dey's corsairs, those pirates who took any ships venturing into the Mediterranean from countries who did not pay a tribute to the dey for safe passage.

In this, too, Zabana was inordinately successful—and merciless. Hundreds of ships fell to his corsairs. Though they seized the ships and cargoes, of course, the most valuable cargo of all was human, the captain and crew and passengers who could be sold as slaves.

Today, as he looked at the awakening village below, Zabana felt strong and righteous. He would teach the lessons of power again, as he had so many times before. The village was fully alive now, and Zabana rose to signal to his men to roll the cart down the hill.

At that moment, Wilhelm Visser was awakening to another working day in Algiers, a day on the docks unloading lading from a recently captured prize with a handful of other slaves. He was 70 and had been in fair health when his ship had been captured. But the labor he endured and food he was given had reduced him and he'd physically shrunk under the weight of captivity.

Zabana had ordered his men to torture him into giving up his name and home; after three days of burning his skin with hot irons he would have given up his mother and God. Now he was a broken man, physically and emotionally, with no hope of escape.

Yet he knew his lot was better than most. He was being held for ransom and given lighter work than others faced each day. Most captives were sold in the *bedestan*, or slave market, and he'd seen Danes and Russians and Germans there, as well as Americans like himself. Apparently the dey's raiding parties extended to land as well as sea as his corsairs roamed Europe's coastline in search of slaves from all nations. Some of the slaves went to households, others to the quarries to break rocks for breakwaters around the harbor. The women and young children were pawed and leered at by old men who bid against one other to stock their harems or purchase *companions.* For many, rape was worse than death. It was disgusting and barbaric and Wilhelm Visser was totally incapable of preventing it.

He was lucky to be alive himself. He had been assured by other American merchants that, as long as the U.S. paid tribute to the Barbary rulers, it was safe to pass by Gibraltar to the Mediterranean. Either the dey had changed his mind, or the tribute hadn't been paid, or both. The explanation depended on whose lie you believed.

As he looked at the prize he was unloading—the ship appeared to be Venetian—he thought back briefly to his own ship's capture. His crew had fought valiantly but there was very little wind and the sweeps of the xebecs had brought the pirates right up to the side of his ship quickly. The heathens had climbed aboard, screaming and shouting and, in an instant, the ship was theirs.

The xebecs then took his ship in tow and the sweeps went to work, pulling him towards a future that he could never have imagined.

Ten

It was a tired captain who made his way back aboard *Rascal* just before dawn. The ship was dark and he dressed in his sea-going outfit by the light of a single candle in his cabin. He didn't wash himself, for he wanted Elinore's scent to linger on his body as long as possible.

The next two days were spent in addressing the endless tasks of getting the ship ready for sea. Fallon worked tirelessly along with the rest of the crew who came aboard in twos and threes. At night he was with Elinore, sometimes talking softly late into the night about their wedding, sometimes about nothing in particular. But, of course, it wasn't all talk.

At last, the ship was ready for sea. *Rascal* weighed in the morning after all the goodbyes had been said and the promises to return safely had been repeated again and again. Elinore and Ezra Somers were at the dock to see the ship off. Elinore had been stoic all morning around her father, with no outward sign that her last night with Fallon in the fisherman's shack had been memorable. For his part, it was an exhausted Fallon who waved from the taffrail until they were out of sight, his heart heavy as it always was at leaving.

The day turned into the night which turned into the next day and so on. The sailing was uneventful, the watches changing with regularity and the routine followed exactly by ninety men who knew their business, their ship, and their captain's ways. It grew warmer on the third afternoon out of Bermuda as *Rascal* pushed further south, eating up the distance between herself and *Lucille.* The ship seemed to grow happier as night fell, for the next day should see them in Grand Turk.

Then the stars.

Rascal was on a larboard tack, the reliable east wind full in her sails. Fallon and Beauty stood at the binnacle together staring at the magic overhead, aware that theirs was a special world that those who plied a trade on land would never know. The winter constellations, so familiar to them now, were like signs along the road, as reliable as old friends giving directions.

The talk, what there was, turned to old times and old friends and adventures and, inevitably, to the cruise ahead.

"Did you manage to set off one of Cully's grenados before we left, Nico?" asked Beauty. "Do they work as predicted?"

"Yes, Cully lit one and threw it inside an abandoned shack on St. David's Road, near the old pond."

"And?"

"And you wouldn't have wanted to be in that room," said Fallon. "Between the glass shards and the nails the wallpaper was destroyed. Unless the privateers are wearing armor, I must say I fear for their lives."

Beauty could see Fallon's teeth as he smiled, for he was an ardent foe of Frenchmen and could be counted on, in fact, *not* to care about their lives. Too many of his crew and friends had been taken down by French cannon and swords. Even if the war with France ended tomorrow he would be a long time caring about French lives.

Aja appeared out of the darkness and it was the three of them together, as it had so often been, standing at the binnacle balancing against the roll and heave of the ship without giving it a thought.

"Captain, sir," said Aja. "I think *Lucille* would have been safer if she'd waited to sail with us."

"Yes," said Fallon, "but I didn't insist. First, because it would only have frustrated Captain Pence to the point of unreasonableness. But, secondly, I believe the grenados will work—they must work if our ships are to protect themselves. Perhaps we'll find out."

"Aja," said Beauty, "you must know how ants go out in search of food. The colony sends soldier ants out to find food and, once they find it, they return to the colony to let the other ants know where the food is and lead them back to it."

"Yes," said Aja. "I have seen this many times."

"We're operating like the ants," said Beauty, winking at Fallon. "If Pence is attacked we want our pirate to go back where he came from with an ass full of glass and tell the rest of the bastards the food isn't worth it."

Ah, Beauty.

The morning began with a surprise.

"Beauty!" called Fallon. "All hands, all hands!" The lookout's report of a ship in the offing had brought Fallon out of his morning routine of walking the windward deck.

"Where away?" Fallon called as the ever-present Aja handed him his telescope.

"Southeast!" called the lookout. "A schooner, I make! Now two ships!"

Every member of the crew was now in action, and Cully's gun crews received shot and powder for the great guns. The decks were wetted and sanded so that the crew would not slip on bloody planks. In very little time slow match sparked to life in the sand tubs next to each one of 12-pounders and the long nine.

"Mr. Barclay," Fallon called to the sailing master, "take us down to those ships," and Barclay issued the orders that would bring *Rascal* into action as soon as possible. Here was Aja at Fallon's right hand waiting for orders as a hush descended on the ship and all eyes strained to see southward, into the future.

"Aja, have Cully stand by but not run out either battery yet," said Fallon. "Let's see what we see before we commit."

"Deck there!" came the call from the lookout. "Looks like t'other is a sloop! American or I'm a Chinaman!"

Now broadsides growled in the distance as *Rascal* edged closer, and Beauty planted her peg in the ring bolt and wedged herself against the binnacle. The set of her jaw said *Let's have it then.*

The scene could just be seen from the deck. Two ships were blasting away at each other, the smoke engulfing them in a cloud of gray. The closest ship was indeed an American sloop, with the stars and stripes at the gaff, and the other ship, a schooner, was pounding her at some distance, slightly to the south of the sloop, and the tactical opportunity was not clear yet.

"What do you think, Beauty?" asked Fallon, as his first mate raised her telescope.

"I think the schooner's French but I don't think she's navy; at least I can't see any flag flying. I'm thinking a privateer."

That didn't surprise Fallon, or at least completely surprise him. But it would call up a sense of excitement within the Rascals and make up for the disappointment of the last cruise.

The situation unfolding before them called for a decision soon. The two ships were sailing parallel lines to the southeast and were perhaps a mile distant from *Rascal.*

"Nico," said Beauty after lowering her telescope. "I think . . ."

"There!" Fallon exclaimed, still looking through his own telescope. A lucky shot had shattered the American's main boom and, with the wreckage dragging in the water, she slewed around up into the wind. With her boom acting as a sea anchor the sloop was hopelessly compromised to maneuver and fight.

"We'll drop down between the two ships, Beauty!" ordered Fallon. "Aja, up with the colors! Have Cully ready with the long nine!"

His mind was running the angles, time, and distance calculations so automatic to him now. Barclay ordered the sails trimmed just so and *Rascal* came thundering down on the battle, which by now was lopsided and hopeless for the American. The schooner was spilling wind to take off speed and edge closer, firing point blank into the sloop and obviously planning to board.

Rascal was less than a half mile from the scene when Cully's long nine joined the battle with a ranging shot that was just wide of the Frenchman's stern, upon which Fallon could now see *Loire* emblazoned through his telescope. The American's stern showed *Ceres.*

Beauty and Barclay conferred quietly and calmly, for it was almost time to harden up and cut between the two ships.

"Ready the starboard battery!" yelled Beauty to Cully, just as the long nine roared out a ball. Now no telescopes were needed as the stern quarter of *Loire* exploded in plain view and at least one crewman went down. A weak cheer went up from *Ceres* but there was no time to celebrate, for *Rascal* was very nearly up to the battle and Beauty had dropped down on *Loire* swiftly.

Fallon could see the French *capitaine* rallying his men to face this new threat, temporarily forgetting the helpless American. For an eerie moment, there was no sound as both ships waited for the hell they knew would come.

Beauty ordered the helmsman to harden up and Rascal passed between the sloop and the schooner.

"Fire!" Fallon screamed, and Rascal's starboard guns exploded a huge cough of iron balls at less than a hundred yards from *Loire*. The French ship seemed to stagger sideways with the impact and her crewmen were flung backwards. But her answer was immediate.

Rascal's starboard railing blew apart like brown dust in the wind as men were hurled from their stations by the impact of *Loire's* 9-pound balls into the hull, across her decks and into the ship's boats. The cries of the wounded were pitiful but, worse, some men did not cry and lay in grotesque positions of death. Colquist was down below, no doubt nervously waiting for the wounded who would be dragged and carried to him.

"Fire again, Cully!" yelled Fallon, already hoarse with excitement and fear. Here is where training and discipline paid off as *Rascal's* gun crews loaded and ran out in just over two minutes. *Rascal's* starboard guns threw their charges at *Loire* again, and again French crewmen cartwheeled over, some blown completely apart in red explosions of blood. Fallon could see the capitaine, sword out and pointing to *Rascal* as he exhorted his gun crews to fire again.

In a moment of silence Fallon had a clarifying thought.

"Beauty!" he called. "Slow the ship and cross behind her stern! Cully, ready the larboard battery!"

Beauty ordered the sheets be let fly and *Rascal* immediately slowed so dramatically that *Loire's* broadside missed her entirely and sailed out to sea. Quickly, the sheets were gotten in and Beauty let *Rascal's* head fall off as the ship fell across *Loire's* stern on a beam reach.

"Fire!" yelled Fallon, and *Rascal's* entire larboard battery burst through *Loire's* fragile stern, shattering the gallery windows and penetrating deep into the bowels of the ship, perhaps halfway through to the bows, killing anyone inside and exploding splinters up through the deck overhead into the feet and legs of the crew there.

"Now harden up again, Beauty!" ordered Fallon. "Come on the wind!" and *Rascal* came up on *Loire's* starboard side now, catching the French capitaine by surprise and, to his horror, here were *Rascal's* larboard guns being run out again before he could get his starboard battery loaded.

"Fire!" yelled Fallon. As the smoke blew past it was clear the damage was horrific, and Fallon could see no one at the binnacle of the schooner nor at the great guns on her starboard side.

"Ready boarders!" he yelled. But here was the capitaine rushing a man to the tiller as *Loire* had fallen off the wind and was almost upon *Rascal*. The two ships crashed hard together as Beauty ordered the sheets let fly and grappling hooks thrown over *Loire's* railing.

Fallon jumped to *Loire's* deck, only to slip in blood and go down hard against a cannon. Aja quickly helped him to his feet and the two joined the fighting, slashing at the French crew, thrusting and stabbing and pushing them back against their own railing. Pistols fired and jammed, bodies were clubbed and sliced open and the screaming of wounded men calling for help could be heard above the shouting. Men died where they stood, or crawled to the railings to try to stand, their bodies smearing a trail of blood behind them. At last, outnumbered, outfought, and out of able men, the capitaine approached Fallon, holding his sword in front of him with both hands to surrender. His face was ashen and his breath reeked of garlic and old cheese even from several feet away. It was over.

The remaining French crew fell down, or lay down where they stood in abject surrender, choosing life over death, gasping for air, some crying from fear or pain, many clutching at their wounds as their lives dribbled out between their fingers and onto the deck.

The non-wounded were locked below decks on *Loire* while the wounded would have to wait for Colquist to finish with *Rascal's* crew, which proved to take some time as there were many wounded and several would not see morning, no matter what Colquist did for them.

Now here was a hail from *Ceres*, which Fallon had quite forgotten about, and she limped across the sea on a now-dwindling breeze, her mainsail back aboard and her shattered boom cut loose.

"Ahoy, captain! I am Lieutenant Micah Woodson of the U.S. sloop *Ceres*," yelled a uniformed figure at the starboard rail through cupped hands. "Thank you, sir, for coming to our aid! Might we grapple onto your starboard side? You seem to be full up on the larboard! I will throw out fenders, although the wind seems to be moderating to nothing."

In the event, the three ships were tied together and the wind did, indeed, continue to die off over the next hour until the sea laid down to a ripple of wavelets. Fallon introduced himself to Woodson but suggested they meet in the morning to exchange news as all three ships and crews needed urgent attention at the moment.

Loire herself was the picture of devastation, with upended guns and fallen blocks and tattered sails and deep creases across the decks which were still filled with blood hours later when, the three ships still bound together, evening at last crept aboard.

Eleven

The next morning saw the crews at work on both *Loire* and *Rascal* and, after burying his dead crewmen, Woodson's crew was busy shipping a new boom for *Ceres*. There was a certain urgency in the air as an enemy ship could come upon them at any moment intending mischief and they were lying helpless, still bound as one, none prepared to fight.

Colquist had been awake all night doing all he could to ease pain and suffering or death, as the case might be. Fallon had spent much of the night with him, holding a crewman's hand like a wife or lover, talking softly and with all the encouragement he could summon that stopped short of a lie. He'd even spoken French to the most grievously wounded privateersmen, summoning feeling for men he had ordered mutilated by cannon fire hours before.

So, it was a weary Nicholas Fallon who welcomed Lieutenant Micah Woodson aboard for breakfast beneath the sound of mauls and the scrambling of feet overhead. Woodson was a gregarious man, not puffed up or proud but appealing in an everyman sort of way, with one eye which seemed not to follow the other. Before the American Revolution he had been a simple shopkeeper who knew little about ships but he'd joined the erstwhile American navy anyway. There were virtually no ships in the navy at that time but he'd found a berth in a merchantman-cum-privateer and served with distinction, seeing several engagements off the coast of South Carolina and rising to second lieutenant before the war ended. Instead of mustering out, he was offered a commission as lieutenant on *Ceres* assigned to Commodore Truxton's squadron who, within two years, would be on station in St. Kitts at Basseterre Roads.

"Captain," said Woodson between sips of steaming coffee, "I cannot begin to thank you enough for your aid in fighting off that French bastard. His second broadside snapped our boom or we would have made a better account of ourselves. But without your timely intervention I and what's left of my crew would be below decks on *Loire* at this moment, prisoners or worse, dying. As it is, my second lieutenant is mortally wounded and my master's mate not much better, so we are fairly mauled."

"It was indeed fortunate, Lieutenant Woodson," said Fallon, "but war is often unlucky as not so I am very happy we could be of service. I am very sorry about your losses, however."

"Yes, but at least we have a prize to share. I expect the closest prize court is Hamilton, is it not? I would think they would have some experience adjudicating prizes between our two countries? Or at least have seen it before? I confess I would just as soon give you the prize myself for all you have done but it is not within my power to do so."

"That is very kind of you, sir, to even consider it," answered Fallon. "I have enough men for a prize crew and could get *Loire* to Hamilton. Perhaps you would be so good as to write out a letter setting out the facts of the capture and I can see that the prize agent receives it along with my own account. Lord knows when any of us will see a farthing but it must be done correctly. My crew will do everything within their power to set the ship to rights before Hamilton, believe me."

"I do believe you, sir; in fact, I have no doubt of it. I will write my account immediately and you may be sure it will give you and your ship all credit. And sir," said Woodson, "unless you have plans for the prisoners which might bring you some reward for the trouble of transporting them wherever you are going, I would be happy to take them off your hands. The squadron at St. Kitts maintains contact with the French agent on Guadeloupe so that French prisoners may be exchanged for British seamen."

"Excellent, lieutenant," said Fallon. "I will have the prisoners sent over to you as soon as you are ready to lock them below decks. They would only be put in prison otherwise."

That really was a most satisfactory answer for the prisoners as Fallon had been fretting about transporting them in the prize to Bermuda.

Anything could happen carrying prisoners below decks, not least of which was an insurgency.

"But tell me, please," said Fallon, "of any news of French activity that might be helpful, for I am bound for Grand Turk and thence escorting a salt convoy to New England."

"Yes, of course," said Woodson, his wandering eye flicking to the side. "In general, pirate activity in the Caribbean is widespread, with the greatest danger seeming to be from Guadeloupe to Cayenne, and around the Bahamas and southern ports of the U.S. The situation is quite confusing, for island governments are recruiting so-called privateers and issuing false papers to obtain prizes. These ships are little more than pirates and the Caribbean is littered with them, many carrying *Letters of Marque* from several countries."

Fallon knew this was true, but he also knew that many American merchants sailed with false papers themselves so they could trade with British and French colonies—illegal for American merchants. He doubted if Woodson would bring the fact up, and Fallon certainly wasn't about to, for British colonies depended on American goods.

"If you are sailing to the U.S.," Woodson continued, "the greater danger is from the French navy I suppose, for they have a frigate near the Chesapeake Bay at last report. I sailed from Norfolk, Virginia, and did not see her but that is my latest intelligence. *Ceres* is bound for St. Kitts to bring dispatches to Commodore Truxton who will want this very intelligence. We are merely a dispatch vessel back and forth to St. Kitts, but my advice to you is to keep a sharp lookout once you are out of the Florida Straits."

Fallon, indeed, promised he would heed the advice. Woodson was the second American Fallon had met in two weeks and, like Caleb Visser, he seemed a good enough sort. Fallon was forming a very good opinion of Americans.

Soon enough, breakfast was finished and Woodson was back aboard *Ceres,* supervising the loading of prisoners belowdecks. It was a desultory group, with quite a few mulattos and blacks, a few Danes and Swedes, and at least one big Dutchman, in addition to Frenchmen, of course. The capitaine was the last to go below, his head down, a beaten man on his way to an uncertain future. Soon Woodson ordered the grappling hooks to be thrown off and the fenders hauled aboard. The breeze was finally showing some life as *Ceres* raised her sails and moved off to the southeast with a salute from Woodson.

Fallon surveyed *Rascal* with Beauty and then, with Aja, they walked *Loire's* decks as a group. Several repairs were being made on the French ship, which were enough to see her sail again.

"Aja, I want you to take *Loire* to Hamilton and the prize court," said Fallon. "You can choose your own prize crew, and do what you can to set the ship to rights before she's appraised. But Aja, I want to be sure you think you can handle command. What do you think?"

It was not a rhetorical question, for it would take several days to get to Bermuda and there was always the possibility of action whether the prize was fully manned or not. And while Aja had distinguished himself in battle and was a better than average navigator, he was still young for an independent command.

"Yes, captain, sir," replied Aja beaming. "I will be very careful with such a prize." And then he seemed to think better of it. "But I will miss sailing with you in the convoy to Boston."

It was doubtful Aja knew exactly where Boston was, but the prospect of missing a long journey aboard *Rascal* gave him pause. The ship was his home and the crew were his friends and Beauty and Fallon were something like his parents, such was the affection he had for them.

"Yes, I know," said Fallon sympathetically. "But it is your command if you'll take it, and I know of no one I would trust more to take it. You may release the crew when you reach Bermuda, for we will be some time in coming home. And Aja, do all that you can for poor Caleb Visser. You two have become friends and he will need all the support he can get if there is no gold found, which is very likely, I would think."

With that, Aja assumed command of the captured schooner, and within the hour he'd picked his crew and said his goodbyes and *Loire* was away to the north, Aja at the taffrail waving goodbye. Already the mauls were ringing out over the water.

Twelve

It took Ezra Somers the better part of a week to locate a barge with a mast and boom, but getting it to the beach at North Rock proved problematic as a strong east wind blew for the best part of a week, making the unhandy craft still more unhandy against the strong breeze. When the wind slacked at last the barge could make it around the southeastern tip of Bermuda, and the crew pulled it up onto the sand at a small beach. There it waited until Walker's contract was completed at Bird Rock—unsuccessful, as it turned out, the rumor of pearls on the seabed being unfounded. When Somers, Caleb Visser, and Elinore arrived at North Rock soon thereafter the Bermuda Bell waited on the sand with the slave named Indigo Jones standing patiently nearby with Little Eddy.

Slaves on Bermuda were generally more independent than most Caribbean slaves, and many masters allowed their slaves to hold jobs and receive wages if they had special skills that were in demand. Indigo's special skill was that he could dive in cold water as deep as three fathoms and survive.

With the barge on the beach, and the wind still cooperating, Somers' crew managed to get the bell onto the barge and get the awkward craft back into the sea. This took the better part of the morning to achieve, as the tide was ebbing and the barge was stuck with its heavy load. At last the barge floated free, and by the use of long oars as skulls the crew was able to maneuver it over the approximate location of the wreck of *Jocelyn* and get an anchor down.

On shore, Caleb Visser paced the sand thinking of his father; Elinore held her own father close and Little Eddy looked out to sea and *imagined* he had a father out there somewhere. The boy stuck by Caleb Visser, as usual, Little Eddy giving what support he could.

It was afternoon before the stout boom lifted the bell off the deck, the canvas air hose attached to the top, a signal line attached to the bottom so that Indigo could let the crew on the barge know when to bring the bell up. In a few moments, the bell swung over the side and was lowered into the water as a crewman began pumping rhythmically.

Indigo Jones stood on the barge as the bell hovered just feet below the water. He was wrapped in a blanket and was already shivering before he let the blanket fall to the deck. He slowly took a few deep breaths and, without looking around, jumped head first into the water and swam under the bell. The crew waited for a single tug on the signal rope and, when they felt it, began to lower the bell to the bottom.

Two tugs on the rope just before dusk and the bell was hauled to the surface, an exhausted and shivering Indigo Jones inside. He was shaking so badly he couldn't speak, having been underwater for almost an hour, and once the barge made it to the beach Elinore wrapped him in an extra blanket and led him to a fire that Somers and Little Eddy had been tending just for him.

There was very little wind, which was a kindness, and Caleb Visser rubbed Indigo's back and shoulders vigorously. Indigo kept his head down and his eyes closed, his fists clenched tightly under the blanket. The fire crackled and sent sparks swirling into the sky as the crew joined them within its circle of light and warmth.

"We'll try again tomorrow, Caleb," said Somers, trying to be encouraging. "We couldn't have expected to find anything the first day." Indigo nodded his head in agreement as his whole body shook with cold spasms.

Night was coming on quickly, as it did in the Caribbean, and soon the little group began walking down the beach towards the road which led away from the sea. There, the carriages and horses waited patiently to take them home and the prospect of a warm dinner and better luck on the morrow.

The next day was windy and the waves were breaking on the shore, preventing the barge from launching. The day after was no better and it was not until the day after that when the barge could be pushed off and the bell was made ready to launch over the side.

It went like that for three days of calm weather. The barge would maneuver into place and the bell would go over, followed by Indigo Jones, who would return in an hour empty-handed and beyond cold.

On shore, Somers, Elinore and Caleb Visser stood about each day waiting and making small talk. Little Eddy prowled the beach looking for this and that. The mornings were shifting shades of gray, and cold, and everyone kept returning to the fire throughout the day. The barge repeatedly tried anchoring in a slightly different spot off the shore, but the result was always the same. The little group fought to remain hopeful but each afternoon they left for home dispirited.

At last, the sun came out near the end of the week and, though the wind had picked up, the bargeman signaled he would go out. Indigo Jones had arrived, punctual as always, seeming no worse for wear for his daily efforts. After an hour of maneuvering, the bell went over, followed by Jones, and the little group on shore settled around the fire as usual.

The minutes dragged on and the air warmed slightly, the sun doing its best to cut through the chill. Gulls swooped and dove, and one alighted on the top of the barge's mast to keep sentinel over the goings-on. At last, the bargeman signaled the bell was coming up. Indeed, it was almost beyond comprehension that Indigo Jones had been below the surface for almost two hours, especially taking into account how cold the water was. From the shore the group could see no sign of any success, however, and spirits were low as the barge beached on the sand and Indigo Jones had to be practically carried up to the fire.

Once more Elinore put an extra blanket around the shivering figure and Visser tried to rub some life back into his shoulders. Somers put his arm around Visser's shoulders, as well, and even Little Eddy hung his head in sympathy.

"We'll find something eventually, Caleb," said Somers, as optimistically as he could, though he was feeling decidedly less optimistic by the day.

Visser nodded and managed a weak smile.

"Thank you, Ezra. Thank all of you. I don't know how I can ever repay you unless we find the gold," he said, and the futility of the whole enterprise seemed to overwhelm him as his voice cracked.

He only looked up when he heard Little Eddy shriek as Indigo Jones extended his right arm and opened his shaking hand.

Inside his fist was a gold coin, bright and like new.

Thirteen

Grand Turk came into view in late afternoon and, as *Rascal* entered Cockburn Harbor, Fallon could see the *salinas,* or salt flats where the salt was harvested. Closer on shore were women in wide-brimmed straw hats working in an open building packing 40-lb bags with salt. Ahead, *Eleuthera* was tugging at her rode well out into the harbor while *Lucille* was already low in the water, awaiting the small boats which would bring the last of the salt out to her.

Fallon's gig had been repaired enough to float and he sent a crewman with an invitation to both Pence and Ashworthy, captain of *Eleuthera*, to come aboard for dinner. In the event, they were both coming up the side just as dusk approached, darkness just behind them. Fallon welcomed them to his cabin and asked Beauty to join them, as well.

Ashworthy was a rotund man, obviously given to food and drink, with white mutton chop whiskers and a quite red nose. His puffy cheeks made his eyes seem rather small and piggish, but as they darted about the cabin he appeared to miss nothing.

"Tell me, Captain Pence," Fallon began, "how was your journey? I am all attention."

"You were right, by God!" Pence exclaimed. "It was the damnedest thing ever, I can assure you!"

"What was, sir?" asked Fallon, wondering what in the devil he was talking about, for he'd seemed to begin in the middle of his story.

"Why, the grenados, of course!" said Pence, acting surprised that Fallon was lagging behind. "We were set upon by a privateer not two days from Grand Turk. He came up under our counter and attempted to get under our guns. My men were ready, sir, and lit the grenados and threw them overboard."

"And what happened?" asked Beauty, catching the excitement.

"Why, they blew up, of course!" exclaimed Pence. "Glass and nails went everywhere, even into the side of my ship. I saw the buggers run below howling! They pushed away but we kept throwing grenados until they were out of range. Then we fired our 6-pounders at them. It was a glorious thing. Glorious!"

Pence looked around the cabin, beaming. Ashworthy, who had already heard the story when Pence had first arrived in Cockburn Harbor, burst out in laughter, slapping his big thighs at hearing it again.

"I want some of those things, those grenados," he said to Fallon. "Did you bring some along for me?"

"I did indeed," said Fallon agreeably, "and may I congratulate you, Captain Pence, on a wonderful victory. I take it none of your men were hurt in the battle?"

"Not a scratch, sir," said Pence. "But I daresay the Frenchies were scratched about and some of them might never sit down again."

"Excellent," said Fallon, smiling broadly. "God, how I love a lopsided victory!"

Ashworthy, who had already been in harbor a week, was quick to call attention to the fact and offer a suggestion that they leave that very evening since *Lucille* was now fully loaded.

"Thank you, Captain Ashworthy," said Fallon as diplomatically as possible. "But I would like to review our signals and, of course, our procedures for night sailing. I have made plans to leave at three bells in the morning watch to catch the first of the ebb. I believe that will be most satisfactory and give us the day to sail together."

What Fallon meant between the lines was: *let's see if you obey my signals during the daylight hours before we get to our first night together.* Fallon knew that packet captains were notoriously unwilling to heed signals and he wanted to be clear on the point that his signals had better be obeyed.

Ashworthy harumphed. Pence eyed Fallon with some small respect and Beauty only smiled.

"Now, let us review some elementary signals, gentlemen," said Fallon. "And Captain Pence, please help yourself to the lamb, for I believe you will find it as tasty as lamb can be aboard ship."

Sometime later the dinner was finished and Fallon had reviewed all the instructions he expected the packet captains to obey. As the little party broke up and Ashworthy and Pence made to return to their ships, Fallon added the *asterisk* he'd been saving for that moment.

"Gentlemen," he said, looking directly at the two men. "I have it on excellent authority that there is a French frigate operating off the coast of the U.S. This would be in addition to the privateers and pirates we know lurk in the Bahamas and, indeed, who scout the U.S. coast for British and American shipping." And then he leaned in closer to the two mens' faces. "If you do not obey my signals I cannot protect you. And in the event the frigate attacks, I *won't* protect you. I will not allow my ship to fall under a superior weight of metal while the ships I am trying to protect sail about stupidly. Do I make myself perfectly clear?"

He didn't wait for an answer from the astounded captains.

"Good," said Fallon. "Then I will bid you goodnight."

After seeing both captains over the side, Fallon retreated to his cabin to write a brief verse to Elinore. He kept his little verses in a drawer in his secretary and read them to her when they were together in the old fisherman's shack on the edge of the marsh. It was in that shack that they'd always made love, and he shuddered involuntarily at the thought of their last night together there.

All I ask is your arms around me now,
Your face next to mine,
Your breath the small breeze I need on my cheek,
The wind to guide me home.

It was a poor excuse for poetry; it didn't even rhyme. But Elinore always listened with her eyes closed, which was a good way to start the night.

Fourteen

Once again the wind was moderate at North Rock but mare's tails and mackerel scales began to push up from the horizon. As every sailor knew, weather was coming.

Thus, there was a sense of urgency as the barge was pushed off the beach into the shallow surf, with Indigo Jones in the bow and the Bermuda Bell just behind him. He had recovered from the devastating chill of yesterday afternoon and was smiling, no doubt anticipating a good day on the bottom.

The gulls were absent today, having apparently figured out that no one was fishing from the barge and thus there was no reason to be present.

On shore, Caleb Visser, Elinore, and Ezra Somers paced the sand once again, heartened by Indigo's find yesterday. Little Eddy was chasing shore birds, trying to stay warm. Today was not as sunny, so visibility would not be as good, but Indigo claimed to know where to go. He had brought along a large wire basket, fine meshed but strong, with a stout iron handle to which was attached a rope. He certainly seemed optimistic. From the shore Somers could see Indigo standing by the basket as the crew made the bell ready. The mast was swung into place and the rope attached to the top of it, the creaking of the block sounded clear and cold.

Once again, the bell was lowered over the side of the anchored barge and, once again, Indigo dove over the side and up into it. His basket was lowered next and he took it inside with him. A single tug on the line, and the bell sank beneath the surface.

Optimism is like the tide: it ebbs and flows. After an hour it had ebbed badly on the beach, and then after almost two hours it had gone out to sea entirely. The little group on shore busied themselves building a fire, trying to keep their spirits up, for if Indigo found nothing today it was unclear when he could try again. Already it was becoming cloudier, and the mares' tails seemed to be fairly galloping across the sky.

At last, a yell from the barge, which meant two tugs on the rope. Slowly the bell was retrieved from the bottom, coming up hand over fist, until the top broke the surface and Indigo swam out from inside. He had to be pulled out of the water and stood shivering uncontrollably as the bell was raised higher and finally swung over to be settled on the deck of the barge.

Those on shore could feel the bottom drop out of their hope, for there was no sign of any discovery aboard the barge. The boom was untied from the bell and there was some little effort to run the wire basket's rope through the block, and then the crew began heaving the rope down through the block with grunts aplenty.

Slowly the wire basket rose from the water and swung onto the barge, water running through the wires and onto the deck. Inside the basket were hundreds of what appeared to be bright gold oysters.

A great shout went up from the crew and was taken up by those on shore. As quickly as possible the barge weighed and one crewman used the skull to maneuver the unhandy craft to the beach, running it ashore on a breaking wave. Indigo was led off the barge onto the sand shivering in spastic movements. Elinore immediately wrapped him in a towel and began rubbing his back and shoulders.

Next, two men carried the basket laden with gold coins off the barge to where the group was standing at the water's edge. The basket was dropped onto the sand at Caleb Visser's feet, and at first he simply stared at it in disbelief, seeming not to comprehend the sight before his eyes. And then tears leapt from those eyes. There was the gold, a mound of it, as bright as the day he'd packed the chest. Little Eddy fell to his knees and dug his hands into the coins in amazement.

Elinore put her arm around Visser's shoulders, for the retrieval of the gold meant his dream was still alive. She only hoped his father was. Soon enough the moment was past and Caleb shook Somers' hand and pounded Indigo Jones' back and went to each of the crew and thanked them, as well. His eyes were dry and bright blue again.

The crew left to return the barge to Tucker's Town, for the wind was getting up as the weather moved in and would just serve to take them around the island. Meanwhile, Ezra, Elinore, Caleb, and Indigo loaded the basket full of coins into the back of their carriage and, with Little Eddy sitting next to the gold as guard, made off for St. George Town. To a person they were astonished by their good fortune, none more than Caleb Visser, of course.

Once back at Somers' office the gold was counted and the total was just shy of $11,500. It was remarkable, really, for almost all the treasure had been recovered and whatever was left, well, the sea could have.

Except that Indigo Jones stood by patiently, smiling. A really big, wide smile.

Fifteen

Wilhelm Visser lay in his cell looking at the stars and wondering, for the hundredth time or more, whether by some chance his sons could see the very same stars. It brought him comfort to think Caleb or Alwin were looking up, wondering how their father was doing, though in truth their father wasn't doing very well.

The old man's body ached terribly at the end of the day unloading ships, and his was considered light labor compared to what the other slaves did daily. The sun was relentless as always, and sores had developed on his arms and head that scabbed over and then bled and scabbed over again.

The elder Visser was a simple man who had always preached tolerance and pragmatism to his sons, and the twin pillars of his philosophy bore him up now. In fact, he bore no malice to his masters; they were human as he was. They could be wicked and cruel, to be sure, but all men could. The pragmatic view was to abide his situation as best he could, make the best of a very bad thing, and live to see tomorrow.

As he lay looking at the stars, the thought struck him that the rational, pragmatic thing for his sons to do was to continue on with their lives and refuse the temptation to try to free him. Lord knew they had enough to worry about just to survive the cod market. Whatever the pasha was demanding was too much for an old man who was not far from death, at any rate. He hoped and prayed his boys would see the situation as he did and he did his best to communicate his wishes to the stars, and thus to them.

Zabana entered the palace of the dey of Algiers, Mustapha Pasha, confident that he would be given an important assignment. After all, his corsair navy virtually ruled the Mediterranean and no merchant ship escaped his notice. He was shown into the Audience Hall, a long and magnificent colonnade with alabaster columns and intricate inlaid tile. Torches and candles set the hall ablaze with light, and a faint breeze wafted the smoke out the windows.

At the end of the hall the dey sat on a golden cushion, looking every inch the potentate. His thick beard seemed to cover much of his face and gave him a deeply sinister look calculated to terrify. He was dressed in flowing satin robes which disguised his considerable bulk.

Mustapha Pasha was appointed by Ottoman decree *ruler for life.* He was a master of intrigue, staying in power in the shifting political winds of the Ottoman Empire by pitting his enemies against one another, his friends against his enemies, and exerting control over whomever was left over. He received visitors in the Audience Hall under a painting he had commissioned showing him standing regally in robes and turban, his hand on the hilt of his sword, the severed heads of his enemies on the floor around him. If it was designed to strike fear into those who came before him it was inordinately effective.

All of Mustapha's political machinations were driven by a relentless greed for the sake of greed, for he already had more wealth than any of the deys who preceded him, a large harem of wives and concubines and countless servants and sycophants. Each week his income was reported to him by the Collector of Tributes and was mostly based on the activities of his corsairs against Mediterranean shipping.

Zabana led those corsairs and, after Mustapha, was the most powerful and cunning man in the regency of Algiers. Their relationship was mutually beneficial, but wary. It showed in the way the men looked at each other, their eyes dark and cold and suspicious.

"Zabana Reis," said the dey, addressing him as captain, "the tribute from the United States is late, as it always is, and when it arrives it will disappoint me, as it always does. Meanwhile, your corsairs take fewer prizes, American or otherwise, and that disappoints me, as well. I am disappointed, Zabana Reis, and growing poorer by the day."

Zabana said nothing, but anger flushed his face red.

"It is possible for a man to be too comfortable in his own house," said the dey, "tending his little garden every day, and never looking over his wall to the next world. I know this to be true. I hope you are not that man, Zabana Reis." The dey paused here to let the effect of his words sink in. "I think it is time to leave your garden."

The dey's words were not lost on Zabana. It was true that captures had fallen off, but most countries paid tribute and were safe, and the American merchants were wary of sailing to the Mediterranean. He was not to blame for that, except that he had taken so many ships already. Truth be told, he had also grown comfortable on land; his mistress found amusing ways to satisfy him.

"The British have not agreed to new terms, as well," continued the dey, "for their attention is directed towards the war with France. They must learn that it is not wise to ignore their important obligations here." The dey stared at his captain for a long moment of silence, hoping that he did not read the lie. Indeed, Great Britain paid over £1000 a year in tribute, an amount that would not go unnoticed by the Collector of Tributes were it not forthcoming.

"What would you have me do?" asked Zabana softly, for he thought the dey was being deliberately vague on the question of which ships were fair game.

"I want wealthy men and beautiful women, Zabana Reis," said the dey without emotion. "Leave your garden and find them."

Sixteen

It was the forenoon when *Loire* sailed into Hamilton's harbor and let go. There were random ships about at anchor, including Royal Navy sloops and a brig, but not much movement on the water itself. Aja had the newly patched gig lowered and the little crew pulled for government dock, where the Admiralty prize agent kept his office. Aja was understandably proud of sailing *Loire* to Hamilton; indeed, there had been no surprises and his small prize crew had done all they could with what they had available to make the ship presentable. There was still quite a bit of work to do but, yes, he was proud.

But, of course, life then pricked his pride. There was no prize agent in Hamilton at the moment, and might not be for some time. The word on the docks was that he had been recalled for scandalous behavior involving false appraisals and shoddy paperwork and missing funds that had ended up in the wrong pockets—his, apparently.

There was nothing for it. Obviously, Ezra Somers would have to decide what to do, for the prize partially belonged to The Somers Salt Company. The closest prize court was English Harbor, five days sail to the southeast. Aja climbed back down into his gig and, once aboard *Loire,* made ready to sail for St. George's to present the ship, and the problem, to Somers.

It seemed the prize money would have to wait because, as Fallon was wont to say, nothing was certain at sea.

Barclay worked out the distance to Boston from Grand Turk as 1500 miles, give or take, and laid a course which would allow the little convoy to pick up the fast-moving current that flowed up the east coast of the U.S. from the Gulf of Mexico to Newfoundland.

"Mr. Barclay," said Fallon, approaching the sailing master. "What can you tell me of the coastline of the U.S.? Have you been in those waters before?"

"Yes, a bit," answered Barclay. "I sailed the Chesapeake Bay as a young man, for my parents came from Bristol to Virginia, where they began raising tobacco. My youth was spent mucking around in boats in tidewater Virginia and, when I was older, I went to sea. I knew the farming life wasn't for me. I joined a ship trading up and down the coast as far as New York and worked my way up to second mate. I did that for a lot of years before the American Revolution. But the war put me in a quandary. I couldn't very well fight Great Britain, and I couldn't see fighting against the Americans, so I got a berth on a packet sailing for Bermuda to wait out the war. I've lived there ever since, except when I'm at sea, of course."

It was the most Fallon had ever heard the very private sailing master say about himself, or his family, and he chastised himself for not asking sooner, for Barclay had been sailing with him for several years.

"The stream next to the coast is about five miles off and moves quickly, maybe six knots," continued Barclay, getting back to business. "It's sixty miles wide in places and warmer than the water around it. Very strange, it is. And dangerous when the wind comes north. Many ships have been lost around North Carolina's cape and outer banks, in particular. We'd best beware in getting our ships around those banks."

And then Barclay ambled off to take a sight, for it was almost noon on a clear day and a good sight might not be possible for days.

Eleuthera and *Lucille* were behaving themselves so far, and Fallon was feeling a bit guilty that he'd been so harsh with their captains. But his experience told him that, often as not, packet captains went their own way. As dusk approached on the first day he met with Beauty at the taffrail as she made the evening signals to the merchantmen, which they both acknowledged.

"I must say you put the fear of God in those men," she said to Fallon. "Look how they are shortening sail and keeping station to leeward."

"Yes, so far so good," admitted Fallon. "But, of course, we have many miles ahead of us. We'll see if the fear holds."

They passed the next few minutes in companionable silence, two old friends who never felt the need to talk to fill in quiet gaps. They both instinctively looked west to catch the green flash, that mystical and magical flash of light that sometimes appeared just as the sinking sun dipped below the horizon. All sailors thought it good luck, but tonight they did not see it.

"Tell me, Nico," said Beauty in the gathering darkness, just making conversation, "how are the wedding plans coming with Elinore? What have you decided?"

"We'll be married in the little chapel at St. George's, by the sea, in the late spring," answered Fallon. "Ezra says this is our last cruise for a while, so I've promised Elinore I will be back to help her plan things, although I confess I am out of my depth with weddings."

"Yes, I expect you would be no help at all," said Beauty with a knowing smile. "You know, for as resourceful a captain as you are you are remarkably incompetent at some things."

"What else besides wedding planning?" asked Fallon, laughing.

"Remembering birthdays," Beauty said with a smile.

"Whose birthday did I forget, pray?"

"Mine, you dunderhead. Today is my birthday and I am terribly offended that you forgot it." Beauty laughed aloud in spite of herself, for she clearly meant no such thing.

"Oh, you're right, Beauty," Fallon said. "How could I have forgotten? Oh, wait, I didn't forget."

And he pulled a small package from his pocket. Beauty looked at him in surprise, looked at the package, and looked at him again.

"You didn't forget."

"Open it."

"You didn't forget!"

"No, now open it."

Beauty opened the package to find a necklace. A piece of rawhide strung through a small, hand carved wooden dog.

"*Sea Dog*," he said. "I kept a piece of wood from our old ship. Not my best carving, but, like you said, I am totally incompetent at some things. Many things, truth be told."

It was doubtful Beauty had cried many times in her life. But the memory of their old ship swelled up inside of her, that good and true ship that had battled a Spanish flotilla in a hurricane and paid the ultimate price, her bottom ripped out from coral, her shipwrecked crew using her timbers for rafts as *Sea Dog* looked after them at the last.

Those memories and more washed over her like the waves that had driven *Sea Dog* ashore, and she looked at Fallon silently for as long as she could see him through watery eyes, mouthed "*Thank you*" and then left to go below.

Seventeen

The skies were clear and the afternoon breeze moderate when the two pirates slipped from behind Lucayo on Bahama Island and glided out into the Atlantic. The wind was from the northeast and the two sloops bore off northwards, close-hauled on starboard tack, looking for whatever the day would bring. The ships were *C'est Bon* and *Jean Claude*, which attested to their French build but not their present ownership, for captured ships were commonplace in the Caribbean.

Pirate activity in the Bahamas was robust and had been for a decade or more, with little appetite by Bahamian authorities to drive the pirates out. Well, in truth the government in Nassau had no ships to fight pirates and petty officials took bribes to let them wood and water there.

Pirates like *C'est Bon* and *Jean Claude* were typical, their ships crammed with the dregs of Bahama's waterfronts like Nassau and Freetown, their captains elected by majority vote of the crew. They could be *un-elected*, as well, if they failed to bring their crews wealth. That could mean simple demotion or even hanging, or anything in between.

So it was that both captains were relieved when their lookouts reported that two fat packets were to the east, sailing northwest. They did not report the third ship, sailing to windward, for she was hidden by the bulk of the salt ships.

In moments, the lookout on *Rascal* yelled down to the deck.

"Deck there! Two sloops on larboard sailing northeast!"

It was the call Fallon had prepared himself for, because he knew well that pirates and privateers were thick in the Bahamas, in particular, and merchantmen were prime targets. He ordered Beauty to call the hands to stations and send a signal to Ashworthy and Pence to close up their positions.

Barclay and Beauty studied the oncoming sloops through their telescopes while shot and slow match were brought up from below decks, and Cully mustered his gun crews at their stations. Everything depended on how the sloops went about their business.

"The buggers are obviously working together," said Barclay. "How do you think they will attack?"

"Well, if it was me I'd stay to leeward and fire into the convoy," replied Beauty, "which they have the angle and speed to do. I'd try to draw *Rascal* down to leeward and then I'd cut through the line and try to separate the ships and get up to windward. That would put us at a disadvantage trying to claw to windward and engage them. Meanwhile the ships are all ahoo and sailing on their own. That's what I'd do."

Fallon had been listening to them as he studied the developing situation himself, judging the wind and shifts and calculating speed and distance.

"I think you're right, Beauty," he said, and as he looked at her he noticed the small wooden *Sea Dog* around her neck and he knew he'd done a good thing. "The question is whether they're as smart as you are."

Fallon watched as the sloops came for *Eleuthera,* firing from a distance of perhaps a half mile, not doing any damage but likely scaring Ashworthy to the soles of his feet. But *Eleuthera* was firing back gamely, her crew managing her larboard 6-pounders and doing their best. Both Barclay and Beauty eyed their captain, who did not take his eyes off the sloops. The ship was ready for action; gun crews waited anxiously for orders with the slow match coiled in a tub next to each cannon, little tendrils of smoke drifting upwards.

Rascal maintained her station to windward of the salt packets even as the sloops drew closer to *Eleuthera* and continued firing into her hull.

"Signal to both ships, Beauty," ordered Fallon. "The letter 'A'."

The letter 'A' was the signal to follow a plan Fallon had laid down for just such a circumstance, and Beauty ordered the signal sent aloft. Everything depended on the packet captains' courage.

Now the trailing sloop spilled her wind and dropped astern towards *Lucille*, firing her starboard guns as she came at the big packet, and Pence was firing back. Both packets had slowed imperceptibly, however, luffing their sails slightly as if the battle caused inattention to them.

"Beauty, I think the sloops will try to board as soon as they can," said Fallon calmly. "No doubt they are wondering what the schooner to windward is doing, or not going to do, perhaps thinking her captain a coward."

Beauty and Barclay both smiled. *That did not describe Nicholas Fallon.*

"Let's take way off as soon as they move to board," continued Fallon. "Duck *Lucille* and harden up to sail up her larboard side and rake the first sloop. Then, on to the second sloop. Have Cully ready with the long nine and the starboard battery. And raise the colors, if you please."

The sloops indeed appeared hesitant, perhaps confused that *Rascal* had not joined the fight. They edged closer to their prizes, feeling shielded from *Rascal's* guns. Both Ashworthy and Pence depressed their 6-pounders as far as possible and fired as long as possible until the sloops were about to grapple on.

"Now Beauty!" Fallon said with barely contained excitement. "Duck *Lucille's* stern. Cully, ready with the long nine!"

Now there were explosions of a different sort, smaller and irregular, and as *Rascal* sliced behind *Lucille* and quickly came up to the wind Fallon could see Pence's crew lobbing grenados over the packet's railing which were exploding on the deck of the sloop called *C'est Bon,* which was trying to board. Men were screaming in pain, likely not dying but wishing perhaps they could.

Plan 'A' was rolling out.

"Fire as you bear, Cully!" Fallon yelled, and the long nine roared its ball into *C'est Bon's* stern, shattering her small gallery windows and causing untold damage to the insides of the ship. Quickly Cully ordered the gun reloaded and ran to the starboard battery to order those guns run out, with a wave to Fallon.

"Low into the hull, Cully!" called Fallon, for it would not due to fire into *Lucille* by mistake.

"Fire!" Fallon ordered.

One by one Cully went to each gun, sighted it himself and ordered the crew to fire. Every shot told and blasted the larboard side of the sloop at the waterline. There would be water pouring through some of those holes into the ship even as the men on deck flung themselves about, trying to avoid those horrible bombs raining down on them.

"Reload the starboard battery and back to the nine!" yelled Fallon without another glance to *C'est Bon,* which had now disengaged and was trying to limp away from *Lucille.* Not a single shot had come aboard *Rascal.*

"Fire when ready!" he yelled to Cully. And once again the 9-pounder sent its ball towards the lead sloop—*Jean Claude*—and into her gallery, blowing out the windows and playing hell inside that fragile ship and no doubt killing anyone in its path. *Eleuthera's* crew were now throwing their grenados down on *Jean Claude*, as well, exploding nails and glass into the men preparing to board. Pirates were screaming like devils and some jumped below decks to escape. But there was no escape, and here was *Rascal* coming up beside them at less than half a cable and running out her reloaded starboard guns.

"Fire!" Fallon screamed, and one by one each 12-pounder thundered a ball into *Jean Claude's* waterline as *Rascal* swept past. Again, so total was the surprise between the hail of grenados and *Rascal's* sudden and swift appearance that the captain of *Jean Claude* managed to get only one shot off. Fallon was about to remark on it when he heard Beauty call Barclay's name and he turned to see him on the deck, his face twisted in pain, his left arm mangled and bloody. The single shot had found him, likely the ball's only damage, and even now men were bending to carry him below to Colquist. It was the kind of wound that could kill a man, as everyone aboard knew. At the least, he would lose his arm. But at the most . . .

Jean Claude appeared destroyed, with men lying about screaming and clutching their faces and bodies as the captain hacked at the grappling ropes with his sword in an effort to be away. At last the ship was free, sinking but free, and *Jean Claude* came before the wind to sail off to the southwest, back where she'd come from.

Now *Eleuthera* and *Lucille* hardened up their sails and began picking up speed on their old course, their crews cheering as they passed *Rascal*, which was standing by to leeward in case one of the sloops changed its mind and returned.

But Fallon couldn't enjoy the cheers. His mind was below with Barclay, fighting for his life this very moment. His arm was likely already off, lying in a tub.

Eighteen

Loire spent the night off the entrance to St. George's harbor, Aja not wanting to dare the channel on a black, moonless night. The ship was safe and secure and the breeze was light as the ship sailed back and forth. Aja stayed on deck, putting the ship about every hour to keep station and to look at the stars until they winked goodbye in the morning. The weight of the world was off his young shoulders, for he'd gotten the ship to Bermuda, albeit twice, and tomorrow would see *Loire* finally delivered.

At first light, with the sun coming up behind the ship, Aja crept into the channel. By the time *Loire's* anchor was down and her sails were furled and his gig was lowered, Aja could see Caleb Visser standing at the end of the dock. The American took off his hat and bowed, and Aja took that as a good sign that his spirits had improved.

But the news was better than that, far better as he soon learned. Upon climbing to the dock he was embraced in a big bear hug by Visser, who squeezed the very breath out of him and exclaimed that they'd found the gold.

"Mr. Caleb, sir," said Aja, once he'd gotten his breath back, "it is a wonderful thing to find your gold. I believe it is a miracle."

"Yes, indeed it is," said Visser. "But I was on my way to have breakfast with Ezra and Elinore when I saw you sailing in, and they will be delighted to see you and learn of your prize. I trust Nicholas and Beauty are well? Excellent, then pray come have a bite and tell us all about how you took that ship!"

They walked up the dock and down the small road to Somers' house, which sat on a hill facing the harbor perfectly placed to catch the sea breeze. Elinore met them at the door, welcoming Aja with open arms and questions about Fallon and Beauty. Assured that all was wonderfully well, she led them into the dining room where Somers sat drinking coffee. After Aja received another welcome and the same questions about Fallon and Beauty and, after an extra place was quickly set, the little group sat down to breakfast.

Aja related the events since *Rascal* left Bermuda for Grand Turk, the battle scene between *Ceres* and *Loire,* and the taking of *Loire* without a terrible price due to Fallon's decisiveness and Beauty's ship handling. He omitted anything to do with his own role; he had learned from Fallon how to give a report that gave credit to others.

"So you went to Hamilton and learned that drunken fool of a prize agent had been booted back to England, I take it?" asked Somers between mouthfuls of egg and fresh biscuit. "He was a thief, too, as I've just heard. We've been getting cheated for years."

"What's to be done with *Loire*, then?" asked Elinore.

"Damned if I know," said Somers, chewing contentedly. "Aja, what kind of condition did *Rascal* leave *Loire* in? She obviously got you here."

"Yes, Mr. Ezra, sir," replied Aja. "There are no holes below the waterline and the crew spliced the rigging, though much of it should really be replaced. The ships' boats need re-building, the railings still need some repair, the deck is gouged, the stern windows were blown out and there are shot holes we haven't gotten to. But I think she is a fine sailer, though the sails are old. I think she has bugs in the hold, however. The men would not sleep below decks."

Caleb Visser laughed loudly and the others joined him, for French ships seemed to often have cockroaches and bed bugs. The ship would need to be cleaned from stem to stern and probably smoked to kill them all.

The breakfast topic then moved on to cod fishing and days and nights spent on the Grand Banks in all weathers, for Visser had many stories of storms, tangled nets, and clashes with other fishermen, particularly Portuguese, who had fished the banks since, well, since cod. Visser was a good storyteller, with an easy charm and humility that kept his little audience enthralled, for they knew very little about fishing and even less about fishing the banks.

As the dishes were cleared at last, Somers brought the conversation back around to *Loire*, for it was obvious he had been turning the problem of what to do with her over in the back of his mind even as he listened to Visser.

"Obviously, we must get *Loire* to a prize agent to be bought into the service," he said. "Lieutenant Woodson was very good in suggesting she ship be appraised by a British agent; I hope his trust doesn't get him in trouble with his superiors. That said, I want to get *Loire* in the best condition possible for everyone's sake. I am thinking of sending her to English Harbor and the prize agent there. He will have to sort out shares but I daresay he will do the best he can. At any rate, it could be a long time before there's a new agent in Hamilton."

The incentive was obviously there to make *Loire* as fine a ship as possible so she would appraise for the highest possible price. Aja pictured the ship in his mind and the work to be done. He was still thinking when Elinore joined the conversation.

"That seems like a very sensible plan, father," said Elinore. "Assuming the ship is repaired, where will you get a captain and crew to sail *Loire* to Antigua?"

It was a good question, for most of Bermuda's men were already at sea, or preparing to go to sea, or on their way back from sea. Somers squinted his eyes in thought.

"Mr. Ezra, sir," said Aja excitedly. "I believe the crew and I could make the ship very good again within two weeks. And, Mr. Ezra, we could sail it to English Harbor for you." Aja smiled in his winning way, obviously anxious for a second command.

"Well," said Somers, thinking the thing over. "Nico will probably beat you back here, although you could take one of the trading packets back from English Harbor without any difficulty, so you shouldn't be gone too long. And I guess *Rascal* isn't going anywhere for a while once she's back, so I don't think Nico would mind."

Visser had been sitting with his head down for a few moments listening to the conversation. Elinore watched him, wondering what he was thinking. Suddenly, she found out.

"Do you think," Visser said raising his head and looking at Somers, "that I would have a chance to find a ship in English Harbor that could take me across the Atlantic? A better chance than here, I mean."

The question was logical, but startled the room. So intent had everyone been with finding Caleb Visser's gold that no one had really thought of what inevitably came next: getting to the Mediterranean with it.

"Well, I would think so, yes," answered Somers. "I am not aware of any ships from Bermuda trading with Southern Europe. But I believe the West Indies sends ships there with tobacco and sugar. The customs agent in English Harbor would certainly know more."

"Then may I accompany Aja?" said Visser, a hopeful expression on his face.

And Somers couldn't think of a reason why not, though no one really wanted to see Caleb Visser go.

Nineteen

Barclay's horrific injury cast a darkness over Fallon that blue skies and brisk sailing could not improve. Colquist had done—was still doing—all he could for the man but poor Barclay was slow to recover from surgery, his age no doubt a factor holding him back. That, and perhaps his general contrariness. Colquist had amputated his left arm above the shattered elbow and, so far at least, infection had been held at bay. The surgery saved his life, but war had collected its fee.

Beauty did her best to manage the ship and the packets while Fallon was below with Barclay, holding his lone hand and offering encouragement for hours on end. Gradually, the swelling in the stub of his arm began to recede and the stump was less inflamed. He would recover, it seemed, whether he was amenable to it or not.

Rascal caught up with the packets in very little time, sailing along without a care, the captains unaware of the price defending them had levied. Fallon asked Beauty to signal them to heave-to, for he wanted to review the charts they had and go over the signals once again if they should be attacked. What worked once might not work again, and they would no doubt want assurances that they were safe from other pirates now that they had left the Caribbean behind and were off the U.S. coast, assurance which he could not give. He wondered the same thing himself.

The meeting in Fallon's cabin went as well as could be expected, for both Pence and Ashworthy sensed Fallon's low mood. They were exuberant, however, in offering praise for the grenados and gave their first-hand accounts of the battle with the pirate sloops, which were remarkably similar. Each ship had some sixty grenados still aboard in case they were needed again, which both captains sincerely hoped they would not be.

Signals were reviewed once more, and both captains noted the effects of the powerful current just off the U.S., which they were now to ride up the coast to Boston. Fallon wondered if it would be that easy and, in his dark mood, knew it would not.

By some miracle, for it ran contrary to his contrariness, Barclay began to slowly improve. He was still confined to Colquist's care, and weak, but as his fever subsided he began making increasing entreaties to resume his old duties. Fallon would not allow it, however, for Colquist considered that the chance of infection and even gangrene were not past. A bump here, a scrape there, and things could be much worse.

As the little convoy approached Cape Hatteras, the air grew colder and the sky turned to leaden layers of gray. The fast-moving current continued to carry *Rascal* along with its silent force, but the motion was choppy. The lookouts reported a few sails, mostly fishermen, and the southern horizon remained clear.

Without Barclay and Aja, Fallon had taken over the navigational duties and Beauty managed the ship, and one of them was always on deck. Just now Fallon was down below studying the charts of the U.S., such as he had, particularly the area around North Carolina's infamous shoals and banks. In an hour he would signal the packets to move further out to sea, just to be safe. They were now perhaps a half mile north of *Rascal*, the ships easily seen even under the gray dome of cloud that seemed to engulf the world. It was unseasonably cold, and Fallon could smell a storm in the air.

He rolled up his charts and called for two cups of coffee to take on deck, for Beauty would no doubt be shivering and would appreciate something warm. He had been rather uncommunicative with his first mate for several days due to his time with Barclay and this was a small attempt to return to something approaching normal.

As he gained the deck and turned to look forward he saw a line of squalls in the distance. These could have freezing rain or even snow within them, and they could be carrying their own wind, as well. He heard Beauty prudently ordering the topsails furled and a reef in the fore and mainsail as he walked aft to hand the coffee to her at the binnacle. That's when the lookout yelled down.

"Deck there! Ship to the southwest!"

Fallon and Beauty turned quickly, spilling their coffee, but there was nothing to see from the deck. Even their telescopes showed nothing but low, gray clouds with dark ripples on their bellies. Neither spoke, for there was no point in conjecture until more was known.

Within half an hour the first squall was upon them, a snow squall that obliterated everything. The wind picked up within the squall, blowing the snow sideways. The packets could not be seen, of course; in fact, *Rascal's* bows could barely be seen for a few moments as the heavy flakes swirled and darted about the ship. It would have been delightful, a childlike moment of fantasy, but for the strange ship behind them.

Fallon and Beauty stood silently, deep in their own thoughts, both muffled up in their tarpaulins. *What was the damned ship?* Fallon wondered. He feared he knew.

The squall lasted for perhaps fifteen minutes and then moved on, taking the stronger wind with it, and Beauty ordered the reefs in the fore and mainsail shaken out. The packets could be seen again from the deck, still holding station and behaving like obedient children, shaking out their own reefs. Beauty was right, Fallon thought with a rueful grin, he must have put the fear of God in them.

It would be several minutes before the lookout could see more of the strange ship astern, for even though the squall was traveling fast it had yet to reach her.

"What do you think, Beauty?" Fallon asked, for he hoped she had thought of something he hadn't.

"I think we're not in a very good position, Nico, depending on who's back there," said Beauty with her usual honesty. No sugar on the words for her. "The ship's seen us and has probably seen the salt ships, as well.

And she will make much better speed through the water than we can behind those lubberly packets."

"I know," replied Fallon. "I'm hoping she's American, a merchantman or even navy."

There was nothing to be seen astern, the squall had seen to that. Fallon paced and stomped his frozen feet, occasionally looking over his shoulder at the dark horizon and wondering how to get out of the predicament he was sure would be upon them.

"Deck!" called the lookout. "She's a frigate! Two miles!"

The squall had passed over the distant ship and it was not the news Fallon had hoped for, though it was what he'd expected. *Damn and hell,* he thought. It was doubtful the Americans had many frigates. Micah Woodson had made it seem like his country was too poor to build them. But he *had* said there was a French frigate sailing the coast. *Damn and hell,* Fallon thought again.

The ship could still not be seen in the gloom from the deck as Beauty and Fallon fidgeted in the cold by the binnacle.

"What about asking Cully to bring the long nine to the stern?" asked Beauty, obviously searching for answers. They couldn't very well leave the packets and they couldn't change course. "If she's not friendly, we might at least get off a lucky shot."

"Yes, we could try that," answered Fallon, slowly thinking it through. "But by the time we manhandled the gun back to the stern and hacked away the taffrail and jury rigged a way to lash the carriage, well . . ." He let his voice trail off. They both knew that, even if successful, a rear action with a stern-chaser would likely only delay the inevitable.

Soon enough another snow squall was upon them, swirling and mesmerizing, as the ship sailed in a white cocoon, safe and quiet.

Now here was something, thought Fallon. The snow had given him an idea, or part of an idea, but he couldn't get it to fully form in his mind. What were the pieces to the puzzle? A frigate behind them. Packets in front of them. Snow about them. *What else?*

At last, *Rascal* sailed out of the squall and Beauty ordered the reefs shaken out. It was important to keep all the speed they could commensurate with the packets, of course. Fallon looked ahead and could see at least 2 more squalls on the horizon. He raised his telescope and could see the packets shaking out their reefs now, and he wondered if they'd seen the frigate.

"Deck! The frigate is French!"

Both Fallon and Beauty whirled around with their telescopes and yes, coming out of the last squall like an evil apparition was the frigate, proudly flying the tricolor. She was now something under a mile away, setting her topgallants, and Fallon was about to remark on the fact that she'd shown her colors so soon when there was a puff of smoke from the frigate's bow, and the sound of a cannon firing. *A bow chaser!*

"*Now* what do you think, Beauty?" asked Fallon, looking for the fall of the shot but seeing nothing.

"Well," she said slowly, "I'm trying to think of what we do next, you know, to get un-fucked."

Ah, Beauty.

Now the French were firing that damned bow chaser again, and again Fallon couldn't see the fall of the shot, but presumably *they* could, and they would keep firing until they found their range.

"It was about half a cable off starboard and short," said Beauty, filling in the blanks. "They're getting their gun hot."

Soon the situation would be untenable, Fallon knew. Surely the packets were aware they were all being followed, and that *Rascal* was being fired upon; the packet captains must be wondering about *Rascal's* fate—and their own.

Fallon looked the length of the ship at his men, some flapping their arms to shake off the snow or to stay warm. He thought briefly of Elinore, perhaps sitting by her fire reading, or having tea. It was a comfort to think of her thus, warm and safe, while at any moment he could he dashed to nothing by a random shot. His responsibility to the two lumbering packets weighed on him; he couldn't try to evade the frigate and save his ship while leaving the packets to be taken.

The last squall was almost upon them when he turned to take a bearing on the frigate once more. She was noticeably closer; he could pick out the gun crew on the bow as shapes moving to their task, which was to cripple the schooner sailing ahead of them. He heard Beauty order the log cast and the hail of eight knots in return; the stream was pushing them along nicely but pushing the frigate along nicely, as well. In fact, Fallon estimated the frigate must be making a good ten or twelve knots, for the gap between them was closing rapidly. Beauty was looking at the frigate with her telescope, no doubt estimating her speed just as he was.

Fallon looked at the oncoming squall, white and engulfing, and heard Beauty order a second reef in the fore and mainsail as the wind continued to pick up rather dramatically with each squall. In a very few minutes the world would be a swirling blur of white again. Fallon looked through his telescope at the frigate surging along behind them, seeming to get closer with each minute or each second. She rode high on her lines, no doubt light of stores after so long away from home.

Then came the familiar tingle on his arms as the hair raised to precede the idea that had not made it to his conscious mind yet. But now it came: *if this, then that, and then quickly the other.* But God it was risky, perhaps too risky, but was there a better plan?

He decided *no.*

"Beauty," he said hurriedly, "I have in mind to circle back and attack the frigate under cover of the squall. It's no good to continue like this. When the squall fills in around us I want to harden up to the east. Figure we sail a quarter mile or so, your call, then tack back towards the west, towards the frigate. You have to do this on instinct, Beauty, like racing skiffs on St. George's harbor."

"But Nico," interjected Beauty, trying to get some sanity into the conversation. "We won't exactly be able to see the frigate!"

"I know, I know," said Fallon. "But you've got the best instincts of anyone I know, Beauty. Feel when you should tack, feel it, and then bring us up to cross the frigate's stern if you can. You can do this, Beauty." He looked at her closely. "Plus, we don't have another option."

The snow was just starting to get heavy again as Beauty turned to study the frigate in her telescope, judging her speed and course once more just as the bow chaser belched a puff of smoke and sent a ball—*where?* A hole appeared in the mainsail.

That brought some urgency to the situation, and now Beauty looked at the oncoming squall in a different light, its snow a welcoming shroud of disguise if she could just get the tack right.

Fallon called Cully aft quickly, and the one-eyed gunner hurried to the binnacle. Something was up and he knew it, and the crew knew it, for Fallon would not stay long under another ship's guns without fighting back.

"Cully," Fallon began, "when this next squall covers us I want you to load the starboard battery, double-shot the guns, do you hear? We're going to harden up and sail east before we tack back towards the frigate. Cully, we'll get this one chance. She's high in the water, you see, and we're going to try to cross her stern and try to shoot her steering away. Make every shot count, go gun to gun and sight each one yourself. Right at the waterline, Cully. Blow her rudder to bits and cut her tiller ropes!"

In seconds the squall crept over the bows, bringing more wind as *Rascal* bore up close-hauled, Beauty still studying the frigate for as long as she could see it. She was all concentration now, not speaking, her eyes squinting, trying to see it all unfold. The starboard battery was being loaded, as Fallon had ordered, and then the ship slowly hardened up to the east, cloaked in snow.

Rascal sailed in a world of her own now, Beauty standing at the binnacle Sphinx like, rigid and white with the clinging snow. Fallon watched her as the ship kept her course away from the packets—God knew what Pence and Ashworthy would think when the squall cleared and there was no *Rascal* behind them. A minute. Then two. And then instinct took over and Beauty called for the ship to come about and all hands jumped to the command as *Rascal's* bowsprit swung through the wind and the ship kept turning, her speed slowing noticeably as her big booms were hauled out to leeward, totally in control, and *Rascal* settled before the east wind.

And now Fallon ordered the guns run out.

Still, there was nothing to see. Only the swirling snow zig-zagging like white motes to land on every surface, every rope and rail and every eyelash. The slow match hissed in the buckets beside the starboard guns as Cully stood at the most forward gun, peering to the west. Very soon now . . . very soon.

And then, just there! A shape off the starboard bow . . . was it? No. Yes! For a moment Fallon thought *Rascal* was too soon and would spear the frigate through her hull, but Beauty had it right. Damn! And even now Fallon saw that *Rascal* would pass the frigate's stern with yards—*yards!*—to spare.

Suddenly, they were so close Fallon could see men on the frigate's deck, their eyes open in surprise, mouthing French words of panic and confusion but it was too late to do anything. Even now Cully was standing up from the first gun.

"Fire!" he yelled. And then "Fire!" again and again as he went down the line of all the 12-pounders. Fallon stood at the starboard railing and watched the frigate's rudder explode at the waterline as 18 balls tore into her stern at such close range that chunks of wood came aboard *Rascal.* He looked up to see her name, *Josephine*—he knew where that name had come from!

And then they were by. Fallon ordered *Rascal* to come up on the frigate's larboard side as Cully loaded the guns again. The squall was moving well past by the time the starboard battery was ready and Fallon thought *Josephine* would be too far ahead for the guns to bear—*but wait!* The frigate was coming up into the wind, her bow facing east, the ship in irons, and now her sails were aback as the French crew desperately tried to control the ship. Spars snapped and rigging flew into the air and sails blew out before the wind.

"Bring her up, Beauty! Pass close on her larboard side!"

Rascal turned hard on the wind, gathering speed as she sailed up to windward and the floundering French ship. They were past her shattered stern and soon would pass her larboard side, for the frigate was turning away to the southward now, totally out of control.

"A broadside to her bows, Cully!" yelled Fallon, and *Rascal's* starboard guns screamed their shot into *Josephine's* larboard bow, obliterating her bowsprit and no doubt much of the interior heads of the ship. Now

Rascal was pulling away from the defenseless frigate, which was now drifting by the stern towards the southwest and the outer banks of North Carolina, that notorious graveyard of ships.

All hands looked towards Fallon, for their fighting blood was up now and it was time to finish off the frigate while she couldn't fight. But Fallon looked at Beauty and their eyes locked in wordless communication. The packets were now miles ahead and the coast was still dangerous and they must get back to their duty.

"Secure the guns, Beauty, and fall off towards the packets," said Fallon. A hard decision, but the right one. "And may I just say that was as amazing a thing as I will ever see. How did I ever win a race against you?"

Beauty smiled, the worry off her face now.

"It didn't happen often, Nico," she said.

Twenty

Over the next week and more Aja threw himself and the crew into getting *Loire* to rights; in fact, his goal was to return the schooner to the best condition since her build. The crew worked enthusiastically, as he knew they would. Caleb Visser would not be left out, for being a fisherman he was quite good with splicing ropes and committed himself to re-rigging the ship. Even Little Eddy jumped in, now always at Visser's side, and helped tar the rigging as it was sent up.

Paint pots were found below and brought up on deck and several of the crew began the tedious work of touching up the recently repaired railings and bulwarks damaged by *Rascal's* shot. The gouges in the deck were smoothed out as much as possible and the ship's boats thoroughly re-built. Holes in the hull had already been patched well enough to get *Loire* to Bermuda, but now the patches were gone over carefully and re-worked with fresh wood and paint until the ship was solid again and damage was close to invisible even to a careful eye.

Below decks, where the shot had come through the hull, the crew re-made furniture as they fought cockroaches and other vermin, for the cleaning and smoking would be saved for last. There was not an inch of the schooner that escaped attention, and each day saw the ship gradually come back to her old, original self. After two weeks, *Loire* was ready to leave Bermuda.

On their last night in St. George's harbor Visser and Aja paused at the binnacle proudly looking the length of the ship. In all respects *Loire* was ready for sea. It was a contemplative moment, for who knew what the future might hold? The lapping of the wavelets against the hull and the soft, dark evening that embraced the ship seemed to draw them closer.

"It occurred to me," said Visser to Aja, as the two of them stood together, "that of all the people I thanked for helping me bring my father home, I didn't properly thank you. You have been more than supportive, I must say. Thank you, Aja."

"There is no need, Caleb, sir," said Aja humbly. "I am glad you have a father, and I hope he is ready to come home. Because we are going to find him."

"How about your father, Aja?" said Visser. "Or, for that matter, your whole family? I'd like to hear more of you and where you came from, if you don't mind."

Aja grew quiet and looked at the stars, the blinking ones and the reddish ones and the bright whites, the same stars he had gazed at as a boy in Africa. He understood what they meant now, how they guided you when you were lost.

"My family were slaves before we were kidnapped into more slavery," he said quietly. "We worked on a white family's plantation in Senegal; I worked in the house, my mother and father worked in the fields. I learned English in the house and taught my parents to speak it a little. One night a group of men from a faraway village attacked the plantation and stole us, like you would steal cattle. I don't know what happened to the white family, but I heard screaming. We were taken to the coast of Africa, along with many other slaves on the plantation, to an island called Goreé. My mother and sister were put with the other women and kept separated from the men. I could hear my mother crying and calling my name and I called back but I don't know if she heard me. It was the worst pain I have ever felt. Sometimes I dream of her, and she is still calling my name, and I wake up crying."

"I can't imagine," said Visser tenderly.

"I was put on a ship with my father," continued Aja stoically, "and we were put with many men below decks. It was dark and I was very scared and men were crying and moaning. Some men seemed to die they were so scared. Every day the ship's crew came through the holds and took the dead men to throw overboard. There was no light, so I don't know how many days we sailed but it must have been many days and nights later that the ship was attacked by pirates who wanted to steal us. There were many men and women who tried to help the crew fight the pirates but they were all slaughtered. I hid behind some barrels and I could hear the pirates searching the ship but I made myself very small. When I couldn't hear anything else I came out from hiding and searched for anyone else alive but there was nobody. I couldn't find my father, so the pirates must have taken him."

"My God, Aja," said Visser. "How did you ever survive?"

"I ate some of the ship's biscuit and there was water in the casks," answered Aja. "Then two days later Captain Fallon found the ship and Cully found me hiding. I was taken aboard their ship, *Sea Dog*, but I was very afraid they were going to kill me or sell me again. But they didn't; they saved my life and became my friends."

"That is an amazing story, Aja," said Visser. "A miracle, really. And now look at you. Second mate in *Rascal*! But you have seen much, too much, of the baser side of man's nature, I'm afraid."

Aja was quiet then, his eyes looking forward towards *Loire's* bows, watching the men end the day talking amongst themselves.

"Yes," he said, knowing he could still be surprised.

Little Eddy walked home from the ship that night very tired and very dirty, with paint smudges on his face and hands but a jingle in his pocket thanks to Caleb Visser. He was nine years old, but somewhat small for his age, and most people in St. George Town put him at eight or younger.

When his father left for sea, Little Eddy's mother took in laundry and cleaned houses to make ends meet, but quickly tired of it. She was always good with advice to the women of the houses she cleaned, though, and became fascinated with tarot cards. The islanders knew of her and often dropped by to have their fortunes told, but no one really took what she said seriously. Well, until she read the cards for Nicholas Fallon's mother one night and turned into a legend on Bermuda.

For, unfortunately, Fallon's mother received the *Death* card, and a great depression came over her. She had spent a good deal of her life not feeling well and believing she was going to die, and she actually did pass on in three weeks after the card was revealed to her. Maybe it was a coincidence, maybe not, but soon after there was an influx of Bermudians wanting their fortunes read. Men were going to sea, a baby was to be born, a marriage proposal was about to be made—the usual stuff of worry. In very little time *Madame Pauline's Fortunes* opened in the English basement of a dry good's store in St. George Town.

Business was perhaps predictably good, for Madame Pauline had no real competitors on Bermuda for giving advice and telling fortunes. But her relationship with Little Eddy, never particularly close, suffered from loss of contact. He dodged school, scrounged the beaches during the day, and she worked at night. He was growing up mostly on his own.

Sometimes he snuck close by as his mother counseled various islanders on their life. He learned to understand the cards as his mother explained what they meant.

So he knew what he was doing later that night as he snuck out of his bedroom window, leaving what money he had along with the *8 of Cups* on his pillow.

The figure on the face of the card was walking away. It meant he was leaving Bermuda.

Twenty-One

As *Rascal* passed Washington the wind grew and came from the west, with warmth in it now. The ship bounded along energetically, pushed several knots faster by the remarkable stream of warm water under her hull. The crew chattered excitedly with every mile made good towards Boston, and their mood was contagious. Barclay was on deck occasionally, strapped into a chair, still pale and thinner than before surgery, trying to get used to having a missing limb. He complained, of course, and had every right to.

Even the packets made good speed, as if they were horses running for the barn and, indeed, in several days' time it could be imagined that the journey would be almost over. The only sails sighted now were American merchants and the odd American naval vessel patrolling the coast, for the quasi-war with the French had emboldened French privateers to all but enter U.S. harbors in search of prizes.

Fallon and Beauty studied the chart for the approaches to Boston harbor carefully; it wouldn't do to have come so far and run aground on the rocks at the entrance to their destination. Fallon noticed that Barclay was paying attention to their course and straining to overhear his conversation with Beauty, which he took as a good sign that the sailing master was gradually becoming more involved in the running of the ship. He could not use a sextant with one hand, of course, but Beauty took the sights and they conferred on their position and heading. Even that involvement was a milestone in his return to something like normal.

Boston harbor was chock-a-block with all manner of ships when *Rascal* came through the channel, and Fallon felt momentarily overwhelmed at the sight. Luggers and wherries and barges and hoys by the tens were crossing back and forth, and brigs, snows, and barques were anchored about. This was the business of a major port, the commerce of nations as goods and cargoes were loaded and unloaded by the ton, ships were re-supplied with water and provisions, livestock hoisted aboard cackling and lowing and bleating in fear and confusion and the inevitable bum-boats of small-time merchants selling tobacco and liquor and baubles right off the decks of their small craft.

Several hours after they'd gained the entrance to the harbor, a harbor pilot directed the packets to a wharf and *Rascal* dropped her anchor close by. If the crew was disappointed in not sinking the French frigate they didn't show it, for all knew the ship might well have ended up on the notorious shoals to the west, sunk and dismasted. One could always hope. And, besides, none of the crew had ever been to the United States, much less Boston, and all the hands were agape identifying ships from so many countries going to and fro or swinging to their anchors.

Fallon was a bit agape himself. He was about to call for his gig to take him to the wharf where the packets were off-loading when he saw a small boat coming within hailing distance. Indeed, there was someone rather official looking standing in the sternsheets about to speak.

"Ahoy, *Rascal*!" called the young officer whom Fallon could now see wore an unfamiliar uniform, one that was different from Micah Woodson's anyway. "Harbor patrol, sir! May I come aboard?"

In very little time the young officer was on *Rascal's* deck, informing Fallon that he was indeed with the harbor patrol, checking papers and manifests of all incoming ships. It was evident the United States was taking every precaution against her enemies, French or Spanish, as the case might be.

"And how long will you be staying in Boston, if I may ask, sir?" said the harbor patrol officer, handing *Rascal's* papers back to Fallon. "You are, of course, welcome to stay as long as you like."

Fallon had been considering the same question; his mission to escort the salt packets was effectively over the moment they tied off to the wharf. He could linger, of course, and see the famous American town where a protest over a tea tax effectively presaged the American Revolution. Or he could go home.

"I think we will load provisions and wood and water over the next two days and then be away," he said to the young officer. "Much as I would like to stay longer. But first I will call on our American agent if you will direct me to his office."

In the event, Fallon was soon away in his gig towards the quay where Pence and Ashworthy were offloading their salt, for the Somers' office was nearby. The docks were full of activity, and the gig had trouble locating an opening at the dock. At last, Fallon was ashore and in little time found the Somers agent in his office.

His name was John Dingle, an Irish-American, rotund man with bushy side whiskers and a shrewd look about his eyes, no doubt befitting a customs man. After introducing himself, Fallon got to the point.

"I have recently made the acquaintance of Caleb Visser, a fisherman who sails out of Boston. Do you know of him?" Fallon looked closely at Dingle, whose shrewdness seemed to vanish at the mention of Visser's name.

"Why, yes I know Visser," said Dingle. "And his brother Alwin and his father, Wilhelm, of course. Cod fishermen they are. Or were. Wilhelm Visser got himself captured by the damned Barbary pirates, I heard, and I have great fear he will never come back to Boston. Caleb and his brother Alwin have left to try to ransom him, but I can't imagine how that can happen. They are true bastards over there."

"Have you had other ships taken then?" asked Fallon.

"Oh, yes," answered Dingle. "So many that no one is sending ships there anymore. Well, no one but Silas McDonald, who is stubborn to the point of obstinacy. He is planning to sail *Mary of Dundee* for Malta any day and I don't expect we will see him back either. This war with the Barbary pirates is ruining the trade and ruining lives, sir. And the Vissers aren't the half of it, though I pray for them, I do."

Later, in the privacy of his cabin, Fallon settled on the stern cushions with a glass of wine and thought about what Dingle had said. He wondered what Caleb Visser would do without his gold, without his ship, without much of anything now. He genuinely liked the man, and he certainly understood his quest, quixotic as it was, to bring his father home. It seemed impossible now. Perhaps it had always been at least improbable.

Fallon was still musing when there was a knock at the door and Beauty entered.

"We should have stores aboard tomorrow, Nico," she reported. "Very cooperative, they are, here in Boston. Since we will be leaving so soon I decided not to allow the crew to have a run ashore. They'll be disappointed, but it might take a week to round them all up in Boston. Do you agree?"

"Yes, I want to be away for home as soon as possible. I have a wedding to plan, remember?"

"I do," said Beauty, fingering the sea dog around her neck. "I'm surprised you remembered it."

Twenty-Two

Zabana balanced easily on *Serpent*, a large xebec with twenty-four 12-pounders that served as his flagship. The ship had three masts with lateen sails and a bank of oars on each side for slaves. But the most distinguishing feature was the long bowsprit, around which was wrapped a carved wooden snake, its evil head at the tip. Glowing within the head were painted red eyes meant to terrify enemy ships.

The *janissaries*, however, were the corsair's secret weapon. These were the elite soldiers of the Ottoman Empire, swaggering and utterly fearless and seemingly immune from pain. Almost two hundred of them sat about *Serpent's* deck polishing their scimitars and cleaning their muskets. They were commanded by their *agha,* or chief, and some number of them sailed on all of Zabana's corsairs.

The janissaries wore tall red caps, with long, sashed robes and tight canvass breeches and iron-heeled, red slippers. Sometimes they talked with one another, sometimes not. Mostly they tended to their weapons or gambled, smoking and looking out at the passing sea with hooded eyes above drooping black mustaches.

Serpent's sailing complement was normally close to three hundred, but Zabana had rationed some of the crew to other ships. It was a constant management process to shuffle crews and recruit more, for he had over 60 corsairs at sea at any given time.

Zabana had contemplated the dey's orders, what was actually said and what was said between the lines. Though Zabana was powerful and wicked, the dey was more powerful and more wicked, and Zabana knew that, should his corsairs fail to bring in prizes, he might well be made to disappear. Though xebecs were not really suitable for open ocean, he decided to send his little navy far away, up the coast of Europe to Holland and Denmark and perhaps Sweden to raid villages where the women were fair and beautiful, and also west through the Strait to prowl off the coast of North Africa with orders to take ships at sea. If those ships were American, or even British, and could be taken quickly and easily, who would know? Things happened at sea. The ships could be sunk and the prisoners hidden below decks and brought secretly back into Algiers.

Taking the dey's hint, he'd decided to go to sea himself. *Serpent* had provisioned over the next several days and then weighed before first light, Zabana being anxious to be away from port, away from his *garden,* as the dey had said. In truth, it felt good to be at sea again. He had his beheading cart, and it pleased him to see the fear that it caused in the crew's eyes.

Zabana was neither short nor tall, with black hair and beard and the dark looks of a gypsy. His eyes were hooded, making him seem as if he was almost asleep. But, in fact, he was always alert, his mind constantly weighing options and risks and consequences, seeing life in three dimensions. He had a notoriously short temper and turned violent quickly, and yet he spoke in a barely audible voice, perhaps to conceal his lisp.

He said as little as necessary to command the ship; and those who did not strictly obey his orders were punished with the loss of a finger. A worse offense meant castration. And there was always beheading as the final punishment.

With luck, Zabana would return home with prizes in tow. He thought of the admonition he'd sent forth to all his corsairs: *don't come back without a prize*. He wanted his captains to be afraid for their lives. Or their fingers. Or something else.

Twenty-Three

First light saw *Rascal* move out of the harbor with a building sea breeze and a strong ebb, Beauty at the binnacle in her accustomed spot setting the course and calling for the tacks. *Rascal* was alive again, lunging and dipping and throwing off spray like a wet dog. Barclay was strapped to a chair on deck, his one sleeve pinned up, snug in a blanket. He was still weak and had to be carried to his chair by his mates, for he was much too unsteady to walk. Fallon considered that his balance might very well be thrown off due to the loss of an arm and he might have to learn to move about the ship again—but that would be later. For now, Colquist thought the sea air would lift his spirits.

"Mr. Barclay," said Fallon with a smile, "it is good to have you back again."

"Not in one piece, as it were," said Barclay. His personality was back, as well. "Beauty and I together make a whole sailor."

"Yes, I thought of that," said Fallon. "But you will be glad to know that you are still being paid in full, with no subtraction made for your, er, subtraction."

"I would not like to lose any more parts, Nico," Barclay retorted, "or you might change your mind. Pray do not put me in the way of another ball."

The morning and afternoon slipped behind them, the Atlantic rollers coming easily and regularly to lift the schooner gently up and set her down just as softly. The routine of the ship was reestablished after several days in port and the hands settled into their watches without a thought.

Moments of contemplation without a care were rare at sea, for every smudge or patch of white on the horizon could be an enemy, or an opportunity. Yet the cruise to Bermuda was uneventful, even peaceful, and each mile that passed under *Rascal's* keel and into her wake brought Fallon into the present in full appreciation of his ship's sailing qualities and his crew's abilities. Cully practiced his men at the great guns, loading and running out, until they reached two minutes between broadsides. That was an extraordinary time, and likely no ship in the Royal Navy could match it. Beauty sent men aloft to furl the topsails or strike the top masts day and night, for bad weather respected no hour or time of day. The crew seemed to delight in their exercises, not least because each man knew that their life or the lives of their mates might depend on their skill in weather or battle.

Fallon watched it all with a deep appreciation for the timing and sequence of tasks carried out so often that, at some point, routine became rule. There was both pleasure and security, he knew, in doing a thing the right way and at the right time. He stood leaning against the mainmast and thought of the ballet of battle as he watched Cully prepare for practice with the bow chaser, the long nine, the only cannon on *Rascal* not oriented to be perpendicular to the keel.

But Cully was about to start the dance.

A wet swab was pushed down the barrel to remove any salt or debris that might have settled there. Next, a canvas cartridge of gunpowder was pushed down inside and pierced by a metal pricker through the touch hole. A wad was then rammed home, typically a piece of canvas or old rope. Next, a ball was rammed in, followed by another wad of cloth to prevent the ball from rolling out in a heaving sea or if the muzzle was depressed. Then men heaved on the gun tackles until the carriage was run out against the ship's bulwark. This took the efforts of most of the gun crew, as the weight of the cannon and carriage was easily two tons. Finally, the touch hole at the rear or breech of the cannon was filled with finer gunpowder and, at the order of *Fire!*, was ignited.

Of course, the ball had to find a target. And in this, too, Cully's gun crews excelled. Cully's one good eye could sight the great guns with uncanny accuracy, and he was patient in teaching his men the technique—not so easy at all—of timing the match to the touch hole on a rolling and plunging deck. Nothing could teach the men about battle, of course, except battle. The explosion of a broadside in practice was exhilarating, but in battle it was frightening and could be paralyzing, with balls coming aboard, splinters flying and your mate turning into red jam next to you. No, only battle was battle, and Fallon's crew had the scars to prove it.

"Very good, Cully," Fallon said to his master gunner after the last shot was fired. "Secure the gun now and a tot of rum for the gun crew."

He looked at Beauty, who was grinning broadly. Even Barclay was smiling. No doubt they were thinking the same thing as he.

It was good Cully was on their side and not the enemy's.

It was barely thirty-six hours later that *Rascal* drifted to her accustomed anchorage at St. George's Harbor and Fallon stepped ashore on Bermuda once again. It was quite late and pitch dark as he climbed the hill up from the dock. The trip up the coast of America to Boston was behind him, the battles with pirates and the French frigate another story he could tell Ezra and Elinore, although he would attempt to minimize the danger to himself and his ship. In point of fact, he'd faced worse.

He walked towards the White Horse, more out of habit than intent; intuitively, he wanted to go home. The pub was closed, but a candle burned in his bedroom window as it always did when he was gone, the older Fallon still and always a father. He found the old man at the kitchen table reading, and after the warmest of greetings he sat down to join him.

"Tell me all about your trip, son," his father said excitedly. "Not the sanitized version you tell Elinore, either!"

And so the events of Fallon's trip poured out, like the reports he used to give his father when he came home from school. Somehow he was a boy again, looking for his father's approval, not a grown man who took part in great battles in far-away places. He was a son again, and he could see in his father's eyes that the old man was proud of him.

"And now you're home again, safe and sound, and I bet you haven't told me the half of what you've been through," said Fallon's father. "But I have news for you, as well. Caleb has found his gold! Or most of it, certainly. The damned bell was a wonder, Nico. It's unbelievable, is it not?"

Fallon was dumbfounded. He never thought in a hundred years that the gold could be found. And then it dawned on him that Visser would want to continue his quest to rescue his father. But before he could quite get it all ordered in his mind his father continued.

"And now Aja is gone with *Loire* to English Harbor. The prize agent in Hamilton was fired or recalled to England, so Ezra sent Aja to English Harbor and the prize agent there."

Fallon was surprised, but not surprised. It was common knowledge that the Hamilton agent was a drunk, and Ezra would want to divide the spoils from the prize as soon as possible. The men counted on prize money for a living.

"When did Aja leave?" asked Fallon.

"Just two days ago, Nico. He and the crew got the ship as good as new for the prize agent before they left. Caleb pitched in quite a bit, as well. No doubt to repay Ezra for letting him go along to English Harbor."

"Caleb went with Aja to English Harbor?" asked Fallon. "Whatever for?"

"To find a ship to take him to Algeria," answered Fallon's father. "He is determined to find a way."

That bit of news made Fallon sit up straight in his chair.

"Good God," he said. There was both fear and apprehension in those words.

Twenty-Four

The next morning Fallon found Elinore and Ezra in the Somers office and, after the embraces and kisses and handshakes and welcome homes, he listened raptly as they described how the gold was found by Indigo Jones and the Bermuda Bell. It was truly remarkable, unprecedented on Bermuda, and the island was abuzz. No doubt, the bell was now fully subscribed for months ahead.

In turn, Somers asked about the trip to Boston, and over coffee Fallon reported on everything since he'd left Bermuda. There was genuine relief that he had escaped injury from the pirate attack, though concern for Barclay's horrible wound, of course; and astonishment that *Rascal* had disabled a frigate, of all ships, without a shot coming aboard. It was something over an hour later when Elinore left, hugging Fallon home again and whispering a promise to meet him that night. He knew what that meant.

"Ezra," said Fallon, as they sat down across the great partner's desk they shared, "I understand Aja is off to English Harbor to carry *Loire* to the prize agent. And he has taken Caleb."

"Yes, I knew your crew and Woodson's crew would want to be paid off and Aja did a brilliant job of setting the schooner to rights, I must say. They will be coming back on the postal packet after, and since you have no upcoming cruise I didn't think you'd mind. Caleb seized the opportunity to go with him in hopes of finding a ship heading eastward to the Mediterranean. I could hardly refuse him, although it concerns me greatly to see him go."

"No, it was very right to send Aja to get the ship appraised," said Fallon. "The men will thank you for it, believe me. And I envy Aja having the opportunity to see old friends in English Harbor. Certainly, Harry Davies will welcome him."

Rear Admiral Harry Davies was in charge of the Leeward Station for the Royal Navy and a particular friend of Fallon's, having fought together against the French and Spanish as allies. Fallon briefly thought of Davies and wondered how he and the beautiful Paloma Campos were getting along, for Fallon had been instrumental in bringing them together.

But his mind then turned to Caleb Visser and the unknown dangers he would face in Algiers.

"Tell me, Ezra," he said, "what do you know of the Muslims of the Mediterranean, if anything? I don't believe I've ever met one, but in a month Caleb will likely meet plenty of them."

Ezra rose from the desk to retrieve a book from his vast library. He scanned the titles and selected the one he wanted before sitting down again.

"They are barbarians, Nico, barbarians on an ancient sea," said Somers, pushing the book across the desk to Fallon. "Oh, your average Muslim is no doubt a fine fellow, caring for his family, tending his garden and goats, praying daily and following the basic tenets of Islam. But extremists will find what they want to find in any religion to justify their base instincts and seize power and control. So often in history, wars are fought over religions. The Muslims and Christians have been at war for hundreds of years—*hundreds!*"

"How on earth do they justify that?" asked Fallon. "Do they even remember why they are fighting?"

"Well, the Muslims do, yes," said Somers. "Their leaders believe that Islam is the one, true faith and that Christians can and should be enslaved for not following it. They've been quite successful, I must say. The British government estimates that a million Christians have been enslaved between the states of Algeria, Tunis, Morocco, and Tripoli."

"Good God!" Fallon exclaimed. "How could France or Spain allow it? Or Great Britain, come to that?"

"That's a good question," said Somers. "The answer is that the great naval powers in Europe have bigger battles to fight with each other, I suppose, and feel the Barbary situation isn't worth a broadside, much less a war. It's easier to just pay the damned rulers what they want, a yearly tribute for safe passage. It's certainly cheaper than maintaining a navy just to fight the corsairs. And it has one other advantage: the nations who can't afford the tribute have their shipping attacked, which dissuades them from trading in the Mediterranean and offering competition to France, Great Britain, and Spain's own trading interests. By the way, this includes the Americans. Let's just say it is in Great Britain's economic interests if American merchant ships are taken by the Barbary corsairs. I believe British diplomats were actually the ones to inform the Barbary rulers that U.S. ships were no longer protected after the peace; in effect, *do what you will.* It was revenge, pure and simple, to my mind. Not a very pretty picture for us, I must say."

Fallon rose and walked to the window deep in thought. He had no great loyalty to Great Britain; most Bermudians felt the same way. But it made the truth no easier to hear.

"The Americans are the favorite targets of the corsairs these days, it seems," said Somers. "The U.S. has an *emerging* navy, shall we say, and can't adequately protect their shipping all over the world. So I pray Caleb will find a British ship to carry him across the sea. He has the ransom the dey demanded so I am hoping for his success."

"Yes, if he gets to Algeria," said Fallon. "And if his father is still alive. And if the dey is an honorable man. And if the corsairs don't have other ideas."

Ezra Somers' eyebrows went up.

"Exactly," said Fallon.

It was just after noon when Fallon left the office, Somers' book tucked under his arm. Soon he was back aboard *Rascal* and was engrossed in reading, by turns furious and frightened, but engrossed. Somers had given him *Remarks and Observations in Algiers,* the recently published diary of

Captain Richard O'Brien, a captured American seaman who, after many cruel years as a slave to the dey, had at last been ransomed by the United States government.

Certainly, Somers had read O'Brien's diary, as he'd probably read every book in his library, and summed up the major points well enough. But Fallon concentrated on the Barbary corsairs, learning they sailed in xebecs, for the most part. These ships were long, 80 to 130 feet wasn't unusual, with low freeboard and shallow draft. Xebecs were quite wide for their length, but the most notable feature was the giant lateen sails on two masts, with a smaller mizzen mast at the stern. This rig would make a xebec a witch on the wind, Fallon knew, and powerful, for they typically carried 18 or more guns. Between the gun ports were up to twelve sweeps each side for use when the wind was light. When the slaves were fresh a xebec could cover 4700 yards in twenty minutes for a speed of seven nautical miles per hour. No large vessel sailing close-hauled in a light breeze was faster or more maneuverable. In a windless chase, a fat merchantman would be finished as the xebecs could easily maneuver close by to board while the packet floated helplessly, dead in the water, her sails slatting and her crew no doubt praying hard for a flaw of wind. This is what O'Brien described happened to his ship, *Dauphine.*

Fallon's eyes fell on a passage from O'Brien's time in captivity:

> Picture to yourself your Brother Citizens or Unfortunate Countrymen in the Algerian State Prisons or Damned Castile, and starved 2/3rds and Naked . . . Once a Citizen of the United States of America, but at present the Most Miserable Slave in Algiers.

Fallon's mind went right to Wilhelm Visser, of course, for at least O'Brien had been treated rather well in captivity; no doubt better than the average sailor. God only knew what *they* faced.

A knock at the cabin door and Beauty stepped inside, a small crease of concern on her forehead. It was late afternoon and Fallon was surprised to see her, for she was sleeping out of the ship as he was.

"I thought you'd be here, Nico," she began. "I think you love this ship better than any house you will ever live in."

"Yes," said Fallon, throwing the book aside, "you are probably very right. But what brings you aboard?"

"I heard something in town that I thought you would want to know," she said. "It seems Little Eddy has run away to sea."

Fallon thought about the news for a moment. He knew many men who'd done that very thing at Little Eddy's age. The lure of the sea, of adventure, of seeing the world was powerful to a young boy.

"I guess I'm not totally surprised," said Fallon. "I don't think he had a wonderful life at home, but I'm sure his mother grieves."

"Yes, well," said Beauty, "the scuttlebutt is that he stowed away."

"Really?" said Fallon. "Then some captain will get a very clever ship's boy."

"Yes, Aja will," said Beauty. "My guess is he's probably aboard *Loire* this very moment."

Twenty-Five

It was twilight when a troubled Fallon made his way to the fisherman's shack on the edge of the marsh. He tried to put Caleb Visser's problems out of his mind, to compartmentalize his thoughts, for this was the special place where he and Elinore met to be alone, to talk and make plans and make love. It would not do to be preoccupied.

When he knocked and the door opened he gasped.

She was wearing nothing but a grin.

He slid his arms around her waist and kissed her softly, smiling through the kiss and then laughing out loud. Elinore giggled and began tearing at his clothes, throwing his jacket aside and pulling at his shirt to open it and feel his flesh against hers. She pulled him to the small bed and then down on top of her as he fumbled for the buttons on his breeches. When at last the two of them had his clothes off they kissed deeply, no laughing this time, only the quick breaths of anticipation that came like small gasps.

He began moving over her slowly, kissing her neck and moving to her breasts. She squirmed and reached down to guide him inside her, but he pulled back, back and down to the delicious scent below her waist. When finally he nuzzled her there, kissed her there, she gripped the bedcovers tightly and gave herself over to him, to whatever he wanted to do. In a moment she began crying softly in spasms of ecstasy.

And when she was sated and spent and almost incapable of movement, she moved. She turned over and presented herself to him and he mounted her from behind. They began a rhythmic back and forth that didn't end until he cried out in release and he collapsed by her side.

In minutes, they were both asleep.

The fire slowly began to die and the shack grew darker, the single candle on the table flickering its light off the walls when they awoke sometime later. It was now dark outside and Fallon rose to put some wood on the fire and light a second candle. Elinore had brought early spring flowers for the little table, a bottle of wine and some cheese. The fire made the shack warm and, obviously, romantic.

"Your backside looks good in candlelight, Nico, I must say," Elinore giggled.

"I bet you say that to all the sailors," Fallon said as he poked the flames.

"Only to the ones who promise to marry me," Elinore replied. "Speaking of which, perhaps we should open the wine and talk about the wedding."

This is the moment he'd been waiting for, dreading actually, a moment when the night could grow colder. He sat at the table and faced her.

"When are you thinking it should be, love?" he asked, and something in his voice put her on notice that the conversation could take a turn she wasn't expecting.

"When do you want it to be?" she asked, suddenly wary. "Do you want it to be later?"

"Maybe late June, I think," he said, trying to sound normal. "When it's warmer and the flowers are all blooming."

"Late June is fine, Nico. But something is on your mind that you're not saying. Tell me. Do you still want to be married?" She held her breath.

"More than anything in my life," he said, and said it like he meant it. She exhaled.

"But . . . ?" she asked.

"No, no *but*," he said, unconvincingly. "I'm just worried about Caleb Visser, I think. He's been on my mind a bit. That's all you're seeing."

"What are you worried about, Nico?"

"Ahem," he began.

"Ahem," again.

Then: "I have been reading quite a bit about the Barbary situation. It's very complicated and could be extremely dangerous. I hope Caleb knows what he's getting into, is all. He'll probably be fine and it will all turn out well, but . . . well, that's it."

There, it was out. He'd said it out loud and now he winced in the darkness, afraid to look at the woman he loved for fear she knew what was coming next.

"And . . . " she said. Wanting him to get it all out, whatever was bothering him, put it on the table next to the wine and cheese. *Come on, Nico.*

"And, I'm worried that he's a cod fisherman, really, and not prepared for what he might find over there. It . . . it could be beyond him, all alone like that."

"You want to take Caleb to Algiers to get his father, is that where this is going?" she asked, knowing that's *exactly* where it was going.

A silence. The fire glowed red and the wine stood unopened on the table.

"What about the wedding, Nico?" Elinore asked, barely masking her sadness.

"If I start now I believe I can be back in plenty of time for the wedding," answered Fallon, knowing full well that Elinore knew that wind and sea were unpredictable. But, in truth, he was worried about missing Visser in English Harbor more than he was worried about missing the wedding. Perhaps he shouldn't have been, and it was not something he wanted to admit to Elinore. But ships came and went from English Harbor frequently and Visser could get lucky and find one quickly and then finding him on the Atlantic would be difficult, if not impossible. As with so much at sea, there was not a moment to lose.

"Nico," said Elinore, a sadness in her voice now. Her mother was long dead and her father would be useless to help her plan a wedding. Fallon wasn't supposed to be going anywhere. "There are a million details to a wedding. I thought you would be here to help me. I always imagined it would be fun to plan it together."

There was nothing he could say to that, and he didn't try. Whether he would actually add anything to the planning or not was really beside the point, and he knew it.

"Tell me why, Nico. Why do you have to go?" she asked with full eyes.

It was a simple answer, and yet it wasn't. Fallon would be putting himself and his crew into danger, perhaps grave danger. He now knew enough to know that much. But the problem was that Caleb Visser didn't know what he didn't know. He could be innocently sailing into the maw of the lion on a noble mission to save his father, and everything in Fallon's body said that neither of them would come back alive.

"It . . . it's what I feel I should do," he said simply, knowing it was inadequate but absolutely true. "I promised Caleb when we rescued him that he would find his father. And that I would stand behind him. Frankly, I never expected he would find his gold."

Elinore stared at the ceiling. This is not how she imagined the next few months would go. Fallon had been away so much, and now he was choosing to go away again. And who could know if he would even be back by their wedding day? That sent her lower still and tears ran down her cheeks and into her ears. She was about to get up and get dressed to leave when she looked at him sitting at the table looking sadder than she'd ever seen him. Terribly sad, and naked.

In spite of her hurt and anger her heart went out to him. Perhaps he really could be back in time if he left right away. And maybe, in the scheme of things, planning a wedding didn't compare to what he felt he had to do to protect their friend.

"Perhaps I could wait a few days, Elinore, and we could begin plan–"

"No, Nico, you have a ship to get ready to sail," Elinore interrupted, raising up on one elbow. "So I have a better idea. I'm going with you to English Harbor. At least we'll have a little more time together and I can ask Paloma to help me plan the wedding. She's the one person I can think to ask." It was true that Elinore and Paloma were great friends. No doubt Paloma would be more than happy to help.

But . . . was all Fallon could think to say, and then he thought better of even saying that. Elinore was giving him what he needed, as she so often did, and asking very little in return. He looked at her with love and astonishment. He could see she was obviously disappointed, but she had fought for clear air, and instead of making it difficult for him, she'd made it easy. Somehow his deep appreciation and respect for her went deeper still and when he opened his mouth no words would immediately come.

"Don't," she said, holding up a finger. "I will never keep you from doing what you think is right. Just take me along on the way, please. Include me in your heroic ideas, Nico, if we're going to have a life together."

And then she opened her arms and pulled him back to the bed again and very soon Fallon couldn't imagine sailing to English Harbor or anywhere else without her.

Twenty-Six

Two days out of Bermuda Little Eddy stepped out from his hiding spot in *Loire's* hold and climbed up the ladder into the sunshine. He'd finished all the food and water he had brought aboard and was hungry and thirsty. He was also quite pale from sea sickness, but otherwise seemed none the worse for his time below decks.

Aja and Caleb Visser were thunderstruck.

"Little Eddy!" Visser exclaimed. "What on earth? You've been hiding below this whole time? Come here then!" Little Eddy walked rather forlornly towards the binnacle, his head down, expecting a tongue lashing or worse. But rather than berate the boy, Visser stared at the bedraggled youth a few moments, and then hugged him.

After getting past the shock of finding a stowaway on board his ship, Aja could only shake his head and smile. Not so long ago he'd hidden aboard a ship just like Little Eddy had done. He knew the fear of being found, the lonely blackness of the hold and the nibbling of rats as you slept, although if he'd been found he would have been killed. Or worse.

"Little Eddy," Aja said to the boy, who was still embraced by Visser, "how on earth did you get aboard?"

Little Eddy smiled brightly, for it certainly appeared he was not going to be punished, at least not immediately.

"I just swam out to the ship, sirs!" he said, relieved. And then he added, "My mum knows I've gone."

This was certainly true, as far as it went, so Little Eddy felt he was not actually lying. And then he quickly added, "I'm old enough to be on my own!" before anyone had a chance to question him about his mother. A clever boy, Little Eddy.

"All well and good, young man," said Visser, not unkindly. "But then why not simply *ask* to come along?"

"I was afraid you'd say no," answered Little Eddy in a flash. "I want to be a sailor!" Answering the question of *why* he'd left home before it was even asked.

Aja and Visser looked at each other, then at Little Eddy, and then back to each other again. Aja shrugged first. Well, what was to be done? It appeared they had a new hand on board to English Harbor.

Little Eddy was fed by the ship's cook and given a hammock to sling below decks. He already knew most of the men from time spent working on the ship, and they winked to one another when the boy came by, for many of them had gone to sea the same way. At the same age. For the same reasons.

"What do you think, Aja?" asked Visser as they walked around the ship together later that evening. "I assume you'll take him back with you to Bermuda?"

Aja was wondering the same thing. And, once again as he did with every situation at sea, he asked himself: *What would Fallon do?* He had no real answer, but his instinct told him to take Little Eddy back home. He couldn't very well leave him in English Harbor, alone. Meanwhile, the boy would be put to work.

Loire bounded along with a favorable slant of wind out of the northeast, day and night throwing up spray and making good her course to English Harbor. Aja felt he knew exactly where they were, for the noon sights were easy under a beautiful blue sky. Little Eddy worked into the ship's routine as a ship's boy, getting on easily with the crew and seeming to relish his adventure. If he was homesick, he didn't show it.

At last, *Loire* entered English Harbor under reduced sail and a British pendant, creeping to her anchorage at the head of the harbor near a ship Aja recognized easily, HMS *Avenger*, 74, Admiral Harry Davies. The last time Aja had been in English Harbor, Beauty had been in the naval hospital there, horribly wounded by a large splinter in her chest, fighting for her life. He had been a recently promoted second mate aboard *Rascal*, and now he returned in command of a ship! A temporary command, to be sure, but he was standing quite proudly as he pointed out the harbor's landmarks to Visser and the omnipresent Little Eddy.

He determined to get the anchor down as quickly as possible and then pay his respects to Admiral Davies. The admiral would want to know about Fallon and Beauty, of course, and Aja could make plans to introduce him to Caleb Visser, who would want to ask after a ship bound for Southern Europe.

He looked around at the little harbor, at the homes and shops and government buildings. It was all pleasingly familiar to him. He thought of Paloma Campos here, the beautiful Cuban loyalist whom Fallon had rescued from prison in Matanzas on the eve of her execution. Here, too, were Dr. and Señora Garón, without whose skill and prayers Beauty wouldn't be alive. So many memories of this place, all happy.

His eyes came back aboard and fell on Caleb Visser standing in the bows of the ship, searching the harbor for foreign flagged ships that might be leaving soon. The first leg of his journey to find his father was complete. He would be understandably relieved and nervous at the same time, for the next leg would take him to the other side of the world. He watched Little Eddy come up from below to see the sights—Little Eddy, who no doubt already thought he was on the other side of the world just being in a strange harbor away from Bermuda. Aja watched him and thought of his own journey to this place, his own wonder at each new harbor.

He ordered the sails furled and the ship drifted to her anchorage not far from *Avenger*. In very little time the anchor was down and his second independent command was over.

Twenty-Seven

Rascal plunged along on a bowline, close-hauled on larboard, for the wind had stubbornly come east southeast and remained there day and night. Since English Harbor was almost due south from Bermuda, putting the ship about to tack against the wind and sail on starboard took them further away from their destination. Barclay fretted about it but the wind was the wind and didn't care about his fretting, apparently. For his part, Fallon had already made plans in his own mind to sail through the Mona Passage between Santo Domingo and Porto Rico to get into the Caribbean Sea. They were making leeway to the west anyway, and they were sailing as fast as they could.

When Fallon had explained the situation on the Barbary coast to Beauty while still in Bermuda, at least as far as he knew or guessed it, she was in full agreement to leave at once. The ship was well stocked from their fast passage from Boston, and within twenty-four hours Beauty had everything else aboard that was needed.

Fallon and Elinore were to be found either walking on deck or, if thrashing to windward became too wet, snuggled on the stern cushions in his cabin. Elinore talked about the wedding often, trying to engage Fallon in planning, if just a little. But Fallon mostly nodded *yes* and was content to spend much of each day dozing in Elinore's arms. Beauty kept the ship moving without his help, knowing there was important business being done down below.

Rascal ate up the miles, always and forever on larboard, and the men grew accustomed to it and tended to lean a certain way, walk the decks a certain way and even eat and drink a certain way, for there was no tacking to relieve the angle of the deck. Still, the ship's routine was in full effect and the hands went to their duties with unquestioning obedience.

On the third day at sea Fallon took a stroll around deck to satisfy himself that all was well. Always alert for any unrest in the crew, he chatted amiably with those on watch and knew that everything was as it should be. Beauty seemed happy enough, as well, reveling in *Rascal's* performance as she continued to coax every ounce of speed out of the ship just as she had when racing skiffs on St. George's harbor. It was simply the way she liked to sail; in fact, insisted on sailing. And Barclay was allowed on deck more often by Colquist, walking with the aid of a cane to keep his balance, getting on well enough, it seemed. The carpenter had made a special wooden shelf and attached it to the binnacle to hold the slate so Barclay could write upon it with one hand when he was able to resume most of his duties. So it was a happy ship that bounded along like a hound after a rabbit.

"Nico," said Barclay after Fallon had taken a noon sight and they had conferred on their position. "I believe we will sight Porto Rico's western headland tomorrow morning and slip into the Mona Passage by noon. You are familiar with the Mona Passage, I know, having sailed through it a number of times."

"Yes," said Fallon. "I have been through it before. But no matter how many times I've sailed it I must say it has never been the same passage twice. Why I don't know."

"It is a strange body of water, without question," said Barclay. "Not always dangerous, but far from certain. The currents sometimes run against the wind in winter and produce high seas. And the wind can be northeast to southeast, or both in a day!"

Fallon had experienced the high seas in the Mona Passage and knew that, although it was ninety miles wide, it could be treacherous for an inattentive captain. He had known of sailors who said the land on either side of the passage shook on occasion, with coconuts falling from the trees. Whether from the wind or something else, they couldn't say. But *Rascal* had sailed through before without incident so at least part of the reports about the earth shaking and mysterious currents he put down to myth.

Late that afternoon Beauty joined him and Elinore for dinner and, as always, it was like family.

"Beauty," asked Elinore while the wine was being poured. "I would like to ask you a question, if I may."

"Anything, Elinore, as long as it's not about Nico. Because if you ask me about him I'll ask *you* about him and we both might end up knowing more than we wish we did."

They all laughed at that, not least because it was probably true.

"I want to ask if you'll be my maid of honor, Beauty," said Elinore with a smile.

Beauty was thunderstruck.

"Why, I've never been called a maid, or even a maiden," she said, smiling herself. "And yes, it would be an honor. So I accept, Elinore! Thank you."

A careful observer might have noticed the emotion in Beauty's voice and Elinore, of course, was a careful observer. For Fallon's part, he was just happy Beauty had said yes. It was another wedding detail taken care of, albeit an important one for Elinore.

The next morning Porto Rico lay off the larboard bow as Barclay had forecast. He was quite proud of himself, and accepted Beauty's and Fallon's congratulations for the accuracy of his navigation.

It was a beautiful morning, warm and clear, and a shout from the masthead directed the crew's attention to a pod of humpback whales sounding not a cable's distance away. It was a glorious sight, their bodies arching magnificently and the spray from their blowholes shooting fifty feet in the air. Everything seemed wonderfully right with the world as Fallon looked around the deck before going below to have breakfast with Elinore. Soon Beauty would be loosening the sails just a bit to bring them into the passage and he planned to be back on deck for that. He had just turned to go below when a hail came from the lookout.

"Deck there!" came the call. "Looks like a ship's boat off the starboard bow!"

Beauty and Barclay had just been conferring at the binnacle and Beauty reached for her telescope as Fallon joined them. Nothing was to be seen yet from the deck, of course, particularly a small boat on the water.

"Fall down to leeward, Beauty," said Fallon. "Let's see what we have here."

Elinore had been below but heard the lookout's hail and came on deck, standing unobtrusively off to the side. This was Nico's business and it wouldn't do to get too close. Besides, she enjoyed watching him do his captain's work.

After another quarter mile the bobbing boat could be seen from the deck, off to the southwest, but no one seemed to be aboard. It was not completely unknown to come across a ship's boat adrift; there could be plenty of explanations for that. But, of course, the fact that this was the Mona Passage added a layer of mystery which Fallon fought not to think about.

"Beauty, heave-to and have my gig lowered, please," said Fallon as the schooner drew closer. After the ship settled Fallon and a small crew climbed down into the gig and began rowing towards the open boat, a small knot slowly forming in Fallon's stomach which he tried to ignore. Things like this happened occasionally at sea, he told himself, and it could well be nothing. Or it could be something that wasn't good.

As the gig approached the boat Fallon stood up in the sternsheets to get a better view. It looked like something was in the bottom of the boat, and as the gig pulled alongside he could see it was a body laying face down on the floorboards. A body in uniform.

Fallon transferred to the drifting boat and held his breath as he rolled the poor soul over. The man's face was horribly bloated in death and sunburned a bright red. The lips were cracked with dried blood, and the man's tongue had swollen to twice or three times its normal size and forced his mouth open.

But, unmistakably, it was Micah Woodson.

Fallon gasped at the sight of the American officer and had to cover his mouth with his hand, for he feared he would be sick, so grotesque was Woodson's face. He steadied himself for a moment and then ordered the gig's crew to take the skiff under tow and row back to *Rascal's* side. He had seen many men die at sea, and horribly, but he had never seen death this way.

As the body was lifted from the skiff he glanced at Elinore, who looked as if she would be sick, as well, and she left to go below. He turned back to the small boat and saw something written on the floor boards underneath where Woodson had lain. Apparently, he had scratched out a word before he died.

Mona.

What did that mean, if anything? He had no idea beyond the obvious, for they had found Woodson at the entrance to Mona Passage. Fallon put that away to think about later as Woodson was placed on deck and Colquist bent over the body searching for wounds.

But there were no wounds.

"Micah Woodson died from thirst, captain," said Colquist sadly, "pure and simple. His body is shrunken from loss of water. I suspect he was put adrift to die in the sun."

Fallon and Beauty recoiled at the thought of dying of thirst. It was a wicked, evil thing to do to Woodson and it brought up a deep anger in both of them. He had been a decent man and he had been treated cravenly.

The American lieutenant was stitched up in canvas, the sack weighted with shot, and he slipped into the sea before noon with a prayer and a few words of friendship from Fallon said over his body. It was a dreary, sad business and left Fallon in a morose state of mind. Elinore had come on deck for the burial, but not even her comforting presence could rouse him from despair.

"What happened, Nico?" asked Elinore after the ceremony.

And then Beauty added, "What evil fucker would do that?"

"Pirates, I would think," said Fallon. "They have no use for prisoners. And they *are* bastards at their core, without rules or regard for life."

They were all quiet for a moment, each with their own thoughts.

"What do you make of *Mona* on the floor board beneath him?" Fallon asked Beauty.

"I assume Woodson was set adrift in the passage and was trying to tell whoever found him," said Beauty. "His last act."

"Yes," said Fallon, "that's what I suspect, as well. Perhaps a warning, too."

Elinore looked at Fallon and shuddered. Fallon's life wasn't all pretty skies and brisk winds; it was murder, as well. Horrible murder.

Barclay was standing nearby, rubbing his chin and staring into the passage. *Rascal* was still hove-to but would be falling off the wind soon to go inside.

"There's something else it could be, Nico," Barclay said. "The island dead center in the passage is called Mona. Rumor is it's a pirate haunt of late. I wonder at it."

They all fell silent, considering the possibility. Finally, Fallon seemed to make up his mind. He looked at the sky and felt the wind on his cheek and clenched his jaw hard.

"Set a course to bring us just to leeward of Mona Island, Mr. Barclay," he said firmly. "I want a very close look. If it's nothing, it's nothing. But I want to be close enough in case it's *something.*"

Soon *Rascal* fell off the wind and began sailing into the passage, the contradictory current throwing off choppy waves. Barclay gave the helmsman the course which would take them directly towards Mona Island, taking into account leeway from the east wind.

"You know, Nico," said Beauty seriously, "you have a look that's looking for trouble."

"I know," said Fallon reflexively. "And I hope we find it."

Twenty-Eight

The Mona Passage was a strait conceived by the Atlantic Ocean and Caribbean currents and, some would say, the devil. It was an area of shallow banks over which two great seas exchanged their waters. The fisherman along the Porto Rican coast knew it could be docile, in which case fishing was good; or treacherous, in which case they refused to go out. It was not unusual to see twelve foot seas and thunderous surf colliding with the shoreline.

The wind blew solidly from the east as *Rascal* drove past the headland of Porto Rico. As they sailed further inside the wind pushed the sea against the unpredictable currents and the resulting maelstrom threw *Rascal* this way and that, which caused Beauty to put two men on the wheel and furl the topsails.

Mona Island was well out of sight ahead, and would be until tomorrow morning, being about two hundred miles down the passage. From what Fallon knew it was uninhabited, although Barclay's rumor of a pirate haunt made him uneasy. He knew of pirate and privateer attacks in Mona Passage, of course, but the waters were so unpredictable and, to his knowledge, the islands so uninhabitable that he assumed no one would take up residence there. He had only ever seen Mona Island as a dot in his telescope, having always given it a wide berth. Now he wanted to sail closer, because now Micah Woodson was dead and whoever killed him might have some connection to the place.

The day proved uneventful after they entered the passage, but Beauty posted two lookouts against the possibility of action in the offing, for this was a major channel through which many merchant vessels and ships of several navies passed. But, today, nothing. It made the discovery of Micah Woodson stranger, and somehow sadder, for Fallon worried they would never find out why he died.

~

At one bell in the morning watch Fallon awoke with a start. It was still very dark outside his stern windows but his heart raced with expectation at what the day might bring. Worst case, today would see *Rascal* through the Mona Passage into the Caribbean Sea with English Harbor no more than three day's sail away. Best case, well, *what would best case be?* Fallon had to admit he was itching for a fight. He looked at Elinore, still blissfully asleep. What was he thinking, bringing her along? And then he remembered he'd made his own bed in that regard.

Beauty had the watch on deck and all was well. Her black coat made her mostly invisible in the darkness, but her teeth showed a white smile as Fallon approached the binnacle.

"Wind has dropped some during the night, Nico," she said. Indeed, the wind had moderated in the night but backed to the northeast, which would put Mona Island to windward when they got up to it. Fallon looked around the ship as the black shapes slowly greying in the coming light. In two hours' time they might well be in battle, the great guns booming out and shot screaming at them. Or they might simply sail past a lonely island in the middle of a turbulent sea, the mystery of Micah Woodson forever in the past.

"I've been thinking, Nico" she said. "The chart shows only one possible anchorage on Mona Island, up in the northwest corner. It's a poor anchorage and relatively shallow, looks like, but if a ship wanted to lay in wait in the Mona Passage that would be the place, in the lee of the island."

Fallon peered into the darkness and pictured the island in his mind, the anchorage against the steep wall in quiet water, a ship just waiting.

"You're right," said Fallon. "But if a ship is in that anchorage she would likely be anchored fore and aft with her guns trained on the entrance. It wouldn't be easy getting to her. Any ship that tried it would be a long time tacking against the wind and even poor gunners would have it easy." And then a pause. "It would be better to make her come out."

"I agree," said Beauty. "Assuming she's even there."

Fallon considered the options. One thing he knew: pirates elected their captain to make them rich. So, assuming a pirate vessel was even there, the crew would look to the captain to challenge *Rascal.*

But would he? Pirates attacked ships they could overwhelm by boarding quickly. *Rascal* would look well-found, well-armed and fast through a telescope, Beauty and Barclay saw to that. But . . . here came an idea now, raising the hair on his arms and working its way into his brain.

Make it look easy.

"Beauty," he said, trying to simultaneously give voice to the idea and interrogate it at the same time. "Let's assume there's a pirate anchored there. What if we scandalize *Rascal*? Hang laundry over the railing to hide some of the gun ports. Luff the sails. Let the ship wallow and drift about her course, like a yacht on holiday. And Beauty, we could make bunting out of signal flags to fly at the gaff. Something frivolous and merry!"

The bunting did it for her.

"If that doesn't get his attention, he's not much of a pirate," she said with a laugh. "Now we just have to figure out what to do when he gets alongside, for I assume you don't want to be too quick with the guns since he'll have the weather gauge."

"Right," said Fallon. If *Rascal* revealed the trick too soon the pirate ship could easily bear off or wear ship and be away. In the scenario Fallon was envisioning *Rascal* would be at the very disadvantage he liked to put other ships at, unable to head up to close battle on his terms.

"Call Cully aft and let's put our heads together," he said. "We need to bring the pirates close."

Barclay had come unsteadily on deck while Fallon and Beauty were conferring and he'd caught the gist of the conversation. In the dim light he could just see the familiar look on Fallon's face when an idea came to him, unformed fully but wicked in its mischief.

"How close do you want to be to the island, Nico?" Barclay asked.

"Close enough, Mr. Barclay," said Fallon, "for a ship to see my nightshirt."

Rascal sailed brightly along for another hour until the outline of Mona Island could be seen from the north side. A spur of land jutted out to the west, and it would be behind that spur where the anchorage would be found. The island itself was a high plateau, virtually flat on top with no distinguishing features save its sheer cliffs. Before the island could be seen from the deck, Beauty began *Rascal's* transformation.

Pieces of laundry were hung over the windward rail to flap in the breeze. Fallon, in fact, donated his nightshirt, much to the crew's delight. The carpenter brought up a strand of bunting his mates had made that stretched along the backstay from the stern to the mainmast. Both mainsail and foresail were drawing poorly and the helmsman was under orders to steer large, over-compensating for wind and wave as he tried to keep course. It was as poor a showing as *Rascal* had ever made, and Fallon was a trifle embarrassed, but only a trifle.

"Beauty," he said excitedly as the island came closer, "no telescopes from the deck. I want to appear like we haven't a care in the world. But have the lookout shout down what he sees the moment he sees it."

Fallon had considered ordering Elinore to stay below; well, an order was too strong for her. So he'd tried *asking* and, predictably, she'd only smiled and promised to stay out of the way.

The minutes crept by all the more slowly since *Rascal* was sailing so poorly. In fact, it was over an hour later that the ship came abreast of the spur of land protecting the anchorage. The crew was idling on deck on Beauty's orders, and some were even dancing on the bow with a fiddle—Cully's contribution.

"Deck there!" came the call that confirmed Fallon's instincts. "Ship at the anchorage! Wait—two ships! A schooner and sloop!"

That was what Fallon was hoping for, and he knew without knowing that the sloop was *Ceres,* Woodson's ship. The puzzle of his death was solved. It remained to be seen whether both ships would come out to fight, or just the schooner, or none. He asked Barclay to go below, much to the old sailing master's displeasure. But the fighting might be thick and the chance of Barclay being hurt or even killed was too great. Besides, practically speaking, a man with a cane would only be in the way.

"Deck! Ships are weighing!"

That was the news Fallon was eager to hear. The pirates would be sailing out of the anchorage soon, the wind behind them, aiming to cut off *Rascal* before she could get away. Of course, Fallon had no intention of *getting away*.

He looked at Beauty and smiled a maniacal sort of smile. Then he looked the length of his ship. He could see the cutlasses and boarding pikes and pistols assembled along the base of the windward rail. He could see the powder and slow match at each gun. And he could see the gun crews laying on their sides so as not to be seen. And, finally, he could see Elinore at the windward railing, her blond hair blowing about her face, and he realized with a start that she was doing her part to add to the picture of a yachting holiday. Certainly, no self-respecting pirate or privateer could resist a beautiful woman who appeared so care-free and within reach.

Now he could see the pirate ships sailing out of the anchorage from the deck, the schooner in the lead as was to be expected. She was about *Rascal's* size, but likely packed with almost twice as many men. Then came *Ceres*, a remembered ship, of course, and dangerous in a 2–1 fight if her captain was tactically minded. It was likely he was not, thought Fallon, having just been promoted less than a week ago when *Ceres* was taken. But, at any rate, Fallon would know soon as the ships were sailing free and getting closer with each second. Elinore casually gave him a glance, and a tight smile as well, and went below.

Barely two cables separated the pirate schooner from *Rascal* when she fired a shot across *Rascal's* bow. Immediately, Beauty ordered the sheets let fly and *Rascal* all but stopped dead in the water. Beauty stood by the binnacle watching the pirates come closer, no doubt smelling blood. She looked at Cully standing quietly behind the guns as if he was totally unconcerned over the impending fight. The crew was attentive, ready for orders, their weapons at their feet and the vision of prizes in their heads.

Now the pirate schooner was up to them and Fallon could see her burly captain standing at the binnacle, his cutlass in the air and a naval officer's hat on his head. Fallon assumed it was Woodson's, and set his jaw before nodding to Cully.

Quickly, *Rascal's* guns were run out, pushing aside the laundry hanging over the gun ports, and just as a mass of pirate humanity gathered to clamber aboard *Rascal,* Cully yelled "*Fire!*"

Grapeshot ripped through the boarders like iron spray as their blood spurted in all directions and they fell back on their mates to writhe their lives away. The pirates were stunned senseless as the ships came together, only it was the Rascals who threw out the grappling hooks and leapt over the railings. They screamed like Fallon had never heard them scream, like bloodthirsty wild things unleashed. Fallon was quickly over the side and began hacking with his sword, screaming like a madman himself, and turned towards the binnacle to find the captain. The pirate crew had recovered their wits and were fighting as if their lives depend on it, which was true, the Rascals giving no quarter and accepting no surrender. Fallon trampled bodies and slipped in blood until he reached the captain, who was swinging his cutlass in a wide arc to counter Cully's boarding pike. Fallon pushed past Cully just as the captain's cutlass clanged off the tip of the pike. Now Fallon's sword began an arc of its own but his arm was bumped by Cully and the slash went harmlessly high towards Woodson's hat. Suddenly, the captain raised up to bellow a primal roar of defiance and those few inches of new height meant Fallon's sword cut inevitably lower. Cut, in fact, the top of the captain's head off, his scalp flying with Woodson's hat to the deck. The captain looked stunned at the blow, and the blood had not even begun flowing down his face before Cully drove his boarding pike through his chest and out his back.

Beauty saw the captain fall and saw Cully pick up the dead man's cutlass and stagger to continue the fight, followed by Fallon. She also saw *Ceres* coming up on the windward side of the pirate schooner and clap on to join the battle. It was a natural instinct, perhaps, but a tactical mistake, for it failed to take advantage of *Rascal's* exposed starboard side. Beauty had held back part of *Rascal's* crew for just such an event, and now ordered them to leap to the schooner and cross the bloody deck to attack this new threat. They crashed into the fight and screamed the louder for being left impotent for so long. The other Rascals took heart from the infusion of manpower and surged against the pirates, who were dying in heaps, their pitiful moans unheard in the storm of shouting.

At last, the remaining pirates who weren't dead or dying gathered at the bow of the schooner for one last stand. But here was Fallon calling for them to surrender, surrender or die, and slowly they gave up and threw down their weapons. Fallon knew, however, that they were merely putting off death for a later time because they would inevitably be hung. Pirates always were.

The prisoners were locked below decks, with guards posted to be sure they stayed there. Already, wounded Rascals were being taken back aboard their own ship and down to Colquist, who would soon be up to his armpits in blood. Elinore was with him, as well, to help bandage the wounded under his direction.

Fallon slumped against the railing, exhausted. His men had fought like demons and surprise had been on their side, the pirate captain's greed overcoming his suspicion.

"Are you all right, Nico?" asked Beauty, who had joined him at the railing. "Are you hurt?"

"No, I'm not hurt," said Fallon. "I was glad to see the last wave of Rascals come over the side, I can tell you that. It was even odds until then."

"Deck there!" came the shout from the lookout. "Men on shore waving their shirts!"

And so they were. The remaining crew of *Ceres* were taken off the island just before evening, hungry and dehydrated after being put ashore to fend for themselves once their ship was captured. They had existed on iguana and rainwater for over a week. Fallon was looking forward to interviewing them to learn what had happened and how. But that was for later.

First, he searched the pirate captain's cabin but found nothing of significance. The schooner was *Céleste,* but there were no records and no log of her activities. It was the typical pirate way. He had the ship searched thoroughly but nothing was found—at first.

Then, in the deepest part of the hold, a chest. It was brought on deck and the Rascals gathered around as the carpenter took an iron bar and forced the lock off along with the hasp. Inside was a mound of silver specie that must have come off an earlier prize. It was not a fortune, but it was half a fortune, and the Rascals would be wealthier than they'd ever been as a result. Fallon resolved to give the families of his dead crewmen a fair share, and *Ceres'* crew a share, as well, for they deserved to have something for their ordeal.

Now there was a general buzz of excitement as Beauty allocated prize crews to the two captured ships. They each had enough stores in their holds to reach St. Kitts, for Fallon intended to call on Commodore Truxton to report Woodson's death and drop off *Ceres'* crew before sailing for English Harbor. He was taking a chance on missing Caleb Visser if the American got lucky and quickly caught an outbound ship, but St. Kitts was on the way and he didn't plan to stay long.

And, indeed, as the waves rolled into a blue evening the three ships were uncoupled at last and caught the freshening east wind to make their way south out of the Mona Passage. Colquist labored under a swinging lantern and against a heeling ship to save the lives he could. Elinore worked beside him, bandaging wounds and talking softly to the wounded. There were two Rascals dead and over twenty wounded, but the pirates had lost almost sixty men, most falling to the surprise broadside of grapeshot. Many more would die before Colquist could save them, and for now they were lying about *Rascal's* deck crying in pain or mercifully unconscious.

It was deep in the middle watch when Fallon went below at last, only to find Elinore dozing on the stern cushions, her dress a bloody rag.

He called for soap and water and she sleepily allowed him to bathe her before she collapsed in his cot. His last sight before falling into a deep sleep on the stern cushions was his nightshirt that had been returned to the back of his cabin door, blackened by gunpowder and shredded by grapeshot.

Twenty-Nine

Basseterre harbor on St. Kitts was not much of a harbor, more a roadstead several miles long and a half mile wide. It was here that a squadron of ships was assembled under Commodore Thomas Truxton, including his own flagship, USS *Constellation*, 38, a heavy frigate. Truxton's command extended throughout the whole Lesser Antilles and his orders were to subdue French privateers, most of whom were sailing out of Guadeloupe.

Fallon had entered the roadstead cautiously, *Rascal* flying the British ensign, with *Ceres* and *Céleste* trailing behind. Men from the *Adams, Eagle, Connecticut,* and *Baltimore* lined the railings of their respective ships to gawk somberly at the procession, for here was *Ceres* returning barely two weeks after leaving and no one could see Lieutenant Woodson aboard.

Fallon had ordered *Rascal* and the prizes to anchor and had immediately taken the gig to *Constellation,* for he could see the commodore's broad pennant flying there.

"Welcome aboard, sir," said Commodore Truxton gravely. "I confess I was startled when my lookout shouted that *Ceres* was sailing back into the harbor, and I am anxious to hear your story and how you came to have her. Who are you and what of Lieutenant Woodson, pray?"

"I am Captain Nicholas Fallon, of the British privateer *Rascal*, at your service," said Fallon. "And I regret to inform you of the death of Lieutenant Woodson at the hands of pirates in the Mona Passage."

Truxton's shoulders seemed to sag at the news of Woodson's death.

"I am aware that you gallantly came to *Ceres'* aid once before, captain," said Truxton sadly. "I must thank you again. But I grieve at the loss of Woodson, who was very popular with the men and an invaluable asset to me. Please tell me all you know."

And so the story of the discovery of Woodson's body in the small boat came out, and the clue he left pointing to Mona Island. Fallon made little of the battle with *Céleste,* for Truxton would know the scream of shot and cries of dying men well enough.

"I was able to interview several of *Ceres'* crew, sir, and they gave a good account of Woodson's bravery in the face of overwhelming odds. He was knocked completely unconscious in the fighting and the bastards set him adrift without food or water to die."

"His wife in Virginia will grieve to hear of his death," said Truxton sadly. "I will spare her the details, of course. He leaves behind two children, as well."

There was silence between them for a moment.

"I understand *Loire* is with a British agent to be appraised in Bermuda, is that correct?" asked Truxton.

"Actually, the Hamilton agent there was recalled and the ship has been taken to Antigua to the agent there. She has been returned to prime condition by now and should appraise well. Lieutenant Woodson's account of the battle will, of course, be turned over to the agent for consideration."

"I have no doubt of it, sir, and I commended Woodson for a wise decision," said Truxton kindly. "His crew was quite decimated and he obviously trusted you after so gallant a rescue. Meanwhile, I will buy *Ceres* back into the service, sir. We have an agent in Basseterre who will appraise her. I have constant need of a dispatch vessel. And I will take the prisoners, who will be given a fair trial. I have no doubt they will be hanged, however."

"Yes, *Ceres'* crew will testify against them, I'm sure," said Fallon, and then an idea struck him. "If you feel it appropriate, you might nudge the agent to give a high appraisal for the ship, for I would like to donate the prize money to poor Woodson's family. We have *Céleste* to take to English Harbor and the prize court there, as well as some specie we found aboard the schooner, and that will be quite enough for my crew."

"That is very generous of you, Captain Fallon," said Truxton. "Very generous indeed, for you paid a price in blood for *Ceres'* recapture. I will have a word with my agent ashore and give him a not-so-gentle nudge in the right direction with his numbers. And I will see that Woodson's family is the beneficiary of your kindness."

"And now, captain," continued Truxton, "how may the United States government be of service to you, for you have repeatedly been of service to us?"

"Well, sir," said Fallon, "any information you could provide relative to the situation with the Barbary states would be helpful. I intend sailing to those waters very soon and I am aware the corsairs have taken American shipping in the past, of course, but I believe a treaty has been signed. Is that correct?"

"Yes, we have a treaty with all the Barbary regencies now," said Truxton, but Fallon could see his skepticism. "However, I don't trust them for a minute, sir. Any pretext to declare the treaty broken will be used. Their demands are insatiable. But, if I may, you should have no trouble under a British flag, surely."

"Yes," said Fallon. "Hopefully, you are correct. But I will be carrying an American who is attempting to ransom his father."

He let his words hang in the air, and he could see Truxton's brow crease.

"That could be a difficult negotiation with those bastards, captain," he said, "for they always raise their prices. If I may, I might suggest you seek the advice of Mr. Richard O'Brien, the U.S. consul to the dey of Algiers, when you arrive. He was a prisoner of the dey's for some time and will know how to proceed."

"That is very good advice, commodore," said Fallon. "I have O'Brien's diary aboard, actually, but did not know he was back in Algiers as American consul."

"Yes, who better I suppose," said Truxton. "He knows their ways better than most, and trusts them less than most. I will write you a letter of introduction this instant and have it sent over to you."

With a few more words Fallon was seen over the side and rowed back to *Rascal.* He had made a quick decision about *Ceres* and could only hope Beauty and the crew would agree with it. He felt they would, given their great fortune in finding specie aboard *Céleste.* The news that Woodson had a family had never occurred to him.

Truxton's letter came aboard within an hour and by then *Ceres'* prize crew was back aboard *Rascal* and the bedraggled American survivors transferred to *Constellation*. It was a behemoth of a ship and no doubt Truxton could use the hands until a new commander for *Ceres* was appointed. Very soon *Rascal* and *Céleste* weighed and glided away from Basseterre.

Looking over his shoulder at the assembled American squadron Fallon's eyes fell on *Constellation*. He could see Truxton on the quarterdeck waving goodbye, and then saluting, which was a very unusual thing for a commodore to do.

Thirty

Serpent was two days out of Algiers and chanced upon a Baltic trader carrying mercantile goods to Italy. The packet was a small ship, easily taken without a shot, and the ship was searched eagerly for plunder or wealthy passengers who might be ransomed for large sums. Regular seamen or servants were destined for the slave market. Zabana had experience with captured passengers attempting to swallow their money, or even exchange clothes with their servants. Consequently, he personally examined his captives' hands and teeth, for these were the best indications of status. Sometimes he even had men beaten or given a saltwater emetic to force the retrieval of hidden or swallowed money.

Zabana knew all the tricks, and sorry was the prisoner who tried to fool him.

Serpent ranged into the waters south of Sardinia hoping for an American ship to present itself, a ship full of gold and beautiful women would be nice, he thought.

Though Wilhelm Visser received perhaps less scrutiny than slaves who had no chance of ransom, he also was at pains to do what he was told. He had witnessed what happened to those who disobeyed their masters; those poor wretches suffered indignities and all manner of punishments.

Algerians meted out punishments for even the smallest of transgressions. A Maltese slave who dared threaten his master with his fist had his arms and legs broken with an iron bar. A Turk was crucified for stealing an egg. And Visser had heard it said on the quay that two Moors who struck janissaries had their right hands amputated and hung from strings around their necks. So Visser was careful to do everything that was asked, and as a consequence he was allowed a bit of freedom to roam the city when he wasn't working. Even then he kept his head down.

But his eyes were open.

When the city of Algiers came under Ottoman control a wall was built to surround it on all sides, including along the sea. Five gates were installed in the wall, and five roads ran from the gates up the hill to the *qasba,* or fortification where the dey kept his palace. A major road ran north and south, bisecting the hillside into the upper city and lower city. The houses Visser passed gleamed bright white in the sun and the glare from the walls burned his eyes. Most were three stories tall, with open courtyards with fountains, tile floors, and a terrace on the roof. Oddly, the homes had few windows, but perhaps that kept them cool.

Each evening Visser returned to the *bagnio*, or prison by the quay, which used to house old Roman baths. Here is where the holding pens for captives were located, surrounded by stockade posts and open to the sky. New arrivals were given two thin blankets and a straw pallet for comfort; this was the sum total of their belongings until they were either ransomed or sold. At night, exhausted after a day spent working in the unrelenting sun, Visser could hear a flutist wander the twisting alleys playing something beautiful to announce the curfew.

One day a week Visser was set free to move about the city. He had earned that much for never giving the guards any trouble and, besides, how could he escape a walled city? He memorized the narrow streets and shrouded doorways, the door knockers and tiles, the smells of strong coffee and tobacco smoke. He walked the passageways and paused in the shade of broad-leafed trees that occasionally grew from a crevice of dirt.

The city, which once seemed so foreign to him, had become familiar.

Thirty-One

The entrance to English Harbor opened before them and *Rascal* and *Céleste* sailed in on an afternoon breeze that heeled both ships over on starboard ever so slightly. Elinore stood on the bow, a lovely, living figurehead, while Fallon and Beauty stood together by the binnacle as they passed the naval hospital where Dr. Garón had saved Beauty's life. As they glided by, Beauty fingered the sea dog necklace around her neck but said nothing, and Fallon wisely left her to her thoughts. Now they were past and on to the anchorage, where *Avenger* and *Loire* were both revealed drifting this way and that to their rodes in the breeze which had quickly gone light and fickle so far up the harbor.

Tentatively, Fallon raised his telescope and held his breath, willing Caleb Visser to appear in it. He could see Aja and—thank God—Visser waving their hats and arms and he and Beauty and Elinore waved back enthusiastically with both arms, Barclay with one, of course, a story to be told later. *Rascal* rounded up with a flourish and let go between *Loire* and *Avenger* and Beauty ordered the topsails backwinded to let the ship drift back and set the anchor. By the time *Rascal* had settled and *Céleste* had come to her anchor, Aja and Visser had come aboard to general celebration. Of course, they expressed surprise to see *Rascal*, surprise to see Elinore was aboard and sad surprise that poor Barclay had lost an arm.

While the hands went to work to coil down the lines and make the ship secure, Fallon asked Beauty, Aja and Visser below to his cabin. Elinore wanted to go ashore to see her good friend Paloma Campos and Fallon promised to meet her later.

"We couldn't let you have a great adventure to the Mediterranean without us," said Fallon, trying to be humorous, as the group settled around his desk. But it was evident that only the truth would do by way of explaining *Rascal's* presence in English Harbor, and he set himself to describe all that he knew and supposed about the Barbary coast. In particular, he shared what he had read in O'Brien's diary and even produced it for all to see.

"Nicholas," said Visser, "I am truly humbled at your offer to put yourself, your crew and your ship in danger for me. I don't know what to say to you, except to thank you with all my heart, and decline. I will find a ship and go alone, for I now know the risk is great and I cannot conscience you sharing it." He looked around the cabin in appreciation, but the faces that looked back at him seemed determined.

"Caleb, thank you for saying that," said Fallon. "But I don't think any of us could live with ourselves if we let you go alone. You've—"

"You see, Caleb," interrupted Beauty, cutting to the chase. "This isn't really a conversation about whether or not we're going with you. We're fucking going."

Ah, Beauty.

Fallon was on deck preparing to go ashore when there was a signal from *Avenger* requesting the captain come aboard and, of course, he couldn't refuse an admiral, even if he wasn't in the Royal Navy. Fallon and Aja dropped into *Rascal's* gig and were quickly rowed across to the flagship as the evening sky began its transformation from blue to pink to red.

"Ahoy the gig!" came the shout from Kinis, the flag captain. "Come aboard Captain Fallon! The admiral is anxious to see you!"

Kinis greeted both Fallon and Aja warmly, addressing Aja as second mate and shaking their hands heartily. Aja beamed, his eyes telling Kinis that his approbation meant the world to him, for Kinis was a by-the-book captain and would not countenance an officer who didn't deserve to be one. Kinis led Fallon below decks to be met by Davies in the great cabin, himself beaming and smiling broadly at the sight of his good friend.

Davies was tall, with blond hair worn in a traditional club, a throwback to an earlier custom in the navy. His face was tan and strong, and his blue eyes carried a mixture of cynicism and humor within them. His was a view of the world leavened by years in the Royal Navy, fighting enemies who were once friends, watching political boundaries change willy-nilly and learning to distrust what he couldn't see for himself. He had become deeply skeptical of so-called news; there were the facts, and then there was the truth.

Davies' friendship with Fallon had been tested by fire more than once as they had fought together in fair weather and foul, most foul, against France and Spain. Their random alliances were unusual but borne of necessity and opportunity. Davies lacked ships and manpower to fight all of Great Britain's foes and take advantage of every opportunity to harass them. And Fallon was an intrepid privateer whose letter of marque enabled him to take prizes—which Davies willingly bought into the service.

"I have of course spoken with Aja about his prize," exclaimed Davies, "and now I see that you have brought another one in! Do you never stop, Nicholas? I am all aback to hear of your derring-do but, first, how are things with Elinore? I hear she is aboard."

"She is very well, thank you," said Fallon. "She's gone ashore to see Paloma, something to do with wedding planning, if you can believe it. And how is Paloma? As beautiful as ever, I collect?"

Davies smiled and said softly, "As beautiful as ever, yes. I believe I will be following in your footsteps before the year is out. We have lightly touched on the subject of getting married at some point."

"That is wonderful, Harry," said Fallon. "I will let you know how it feels!"

A few more handshakes and at last they were ready for business. Fallon described the taking of *Loire,* though that seemed a lifetime ago and he was sure that Aja had reported most of it already. He described Micah Woodson, as well, as being a good American officer who was kind enough to take *Loire's* prisoners and suggest sending the ship to a British prize court to be appraised and sold into the service.

"Yes, that is remarkable," said Davies. "A good man, indeed."

"Yes, but I must save his fate for later, for it does not end well for him, I'm afraid."

Fallon then went on to describe the pirates' attack off the Bahamas and Cully's grenados that sent them scurrying back to their hole. Next, the snow squalls and the attack on the French frigate and Beauty's brilliant—for that was the only word for it—seamanship in bringing *Rascal* so close to *Josephine's* stern and Cully's enthusiastic bombardment of her rudder and tiller ropes.

Davies laughed in astonishment and clapped his hands.

"You are certainly the most intrepid captain I know, Nicholas! A frigate, by God!"

And then Fallon told him of his plan to sail with Visser to the Barbary Coast.

"You have met Caleb Visser, I collect?" asked Fallon.

"Yes, and I know about his father held in Algiers, as well. We'll talk more about that later, Nicholas. I have someone in mind who may be of importance, in that regard. But pray continue."

There was only the scene of Woodson's body in the boat now, his brave clue and finding the pirates at Mona Island, just where Woodson had said they'd be. Fallon described the battle briefly, touching on the laundry and bunting, and the taking of *Ceres* and *Céleste* at some cost to *Rascal.*

"But there was specie aboard, so that was a salve to the wounds we suffered," said Fallon. "And now I have a schooner to sell into the service, if you will have her."

"Yes, of course, for I am woefully lacking in schooners and will welcome her into the service, along with *Loire*, which I am sure will be appraised handsomely. The prize agent has been away to England and only returned yesterday or *Loire* would already have been appraised. Aja did a brilliant job getting her set to rights."

Fallon was not surprised at Davies' enthusiasm for more ships. He could imagine the great difficulty of communicating with Royal Navy ships throughout the Caribbean, there being some ninety or so, and knew that small vessels were much prized to convey critical orders and news to them. But the dispatch vessels had to be able to defend themselves, as well, which both *Céleste* and *Loire* had the guns to do if handled well.

"But tell me, Nicholas," said Davies, "will you have breakfast with me tomorrow so that we may continue our conversation? I fear I have kept you from your ship just as you've arrived. That will give me time to review my dispatches on the situation in Algeria and speak with someone who's recently returned from there. I might invite him to breakfast, as well, for he will have information that is only a few months old."

There was a knock at the cabin door.

"Come," said Davies, and his steward entered with the news that Samuel Jones 2nd, Captain of *Renegade,* 36, was about to be piped aboard. *Renegade* had been on the ways for weeks getting her copper bottom cleaned and was just coming back into service.

"You remember Jones, of course," said Davies. More a statement than a question, for who could forget the man's bravery in fighting *Coeur de France* in '98, a French ship-of-the-line many times *Renegade's* size in men and metal. *Coeur* was anchored in an unassailable position in the harbor at Port-a-Prince when Jones took *Renegade* in disguised as a Spanish ship and opened fire, luring *Coeur* out to do battle—and into a trap. *Coeur* was on the bottom now, burned to the waterline, and that single battle may have saved the slave rebellion on Saint-Domingue from failure. *Coeur's* sinking was famous throughout the Royal Navy, although the whole plan was Fallon's.

"I remember him well," said Fallon. "It will be wonderful to see him again."

In very little time Jones was piped aboard and shown to the great cabin to present himself to his admiral and rejoice at seeing his old friend and, truth be told, his idol, Nicholas Fallon.

"May I congratulate you on being made captain, Samuel," said Fallon. "Well deserved, I say."

"Oh, thank you sir, thank you," replied Jones, blushing in spite of himself. He was tall and gangly and fair-haired and blushing came easily.

"But it would never have happened but for your planning, sir. Begging your pardon, Admiral Davies."

"No, no, Jones," responded Davies, seeing Jones' embarrassment at giving credit elsewhere. "No, you are quite right. All credit to Captain Fallon for confounding the French."

Jones gazed about the room a bit starstruck. He had left home at 12 to join the Royal Navy as a ship's boy and never could have imagined that one day he would hold that most exalted of ranks, captain. His was a birthright of inferiority with humble beginnings, and now he was standing in an admiral's cabin with the two men he admired most in the world.

"Sir," he gathered himself to make his report to Davies. "*Renegade* has sent up the last of her yards and another five days should see us put back together and ready for sea." Of course, frigate captains would want to be at sea as quickly as possible. New frigate captains, in particular.

"Very good, Jones," replied Davies. "I will see to your orders shortly. Meanwhile, perhaps you will do me the honor of dinner aboard *Renegade* at your convenience. I would like to visit with your officers, some of whom I know are new."

"Oh, sir, that would be wonderful," said Jones. "The men will be excited and I will order the cook to lay on his best."

They chatted amiably a few more minutes and then Jones left to return to his ship and Fallon took his leave, as well. As he was rowed to shore to meet Elinore, he thought of the stranger Davies was inviting to breakfast the next morning. He hoped he would put his mind at ease but, even as that hopeful thought came to him, he knew it was false.

Thirty-Two

The next morning both *Loire* and *Céleste* made their way to the prize agent's dock where the ships would be valued and bought into service as Royal Navy dispatch vessels.

The *Cruisers and Convoys Act* had been enacted by Parliament in 1708 and it had survived, with minor modifications, to 1800. Privateers like *Rascal* generally operated under the same system, although Somers, being the ship's owner, had his own variation in play. All prize money was allocated by eighths. Two-eighths went to the Somers Salt Company; two-eighths to Fallon as captain; one-eighth was divided amongst the officers and sailing master; one-eighth between the surgeon, carpenter, and gunnery captain; and the final two-eighths divided among the crew. It was a system everyone felt was equitable, particularly since Fallon was a lucky captain and prize money seemed to follow him.

When the prizes sailed away to the prize agent, Fallon was rowed to Davies' flagship for breakfast. As usual, he was met cordially at the channel by Captain Kinis and escorted below to the great cabin, where Davies and a formal gentleman in waistcoat and shoes with gold buckles awaited him.

"Allow me to introduce Sir William Huntington-James, late of Gibraltar and the Levant," said Davies. "Sir William, meet Captain Nicholas Fallon, late of Bermuda and points west. Gentlemen, please be seated, for I believe I smell breakfast on the way."

Breakfast was indeed on the way and was served with all the silver dishes, goblets, and cutlery one would expect when dining with an admiral. There were fresh eggs in a cream sauce, a rasher of sausage, jams and marmalades and fresh bread and steaming coffee and Fallon ate as if he'd never seen food before.

"Nicholas," said Davies, "Sir William has recently arrived from the Mediterranean and I thought he might give us his point of view on the situation with the Barbary states. He tells me it is unstable, shall we say. Sir William?"

Fallon looked at his unfamiliar breakfast companion carefully as he spoke. He was unremarkable, really, having a pallid complexion and graying hair and limpid eyes that didn't often blink.

"I am employed as a trade representative, sir, and often find myself negotiating contracts for my clients in strange parts of the world. Mostly to do with shipping timber and coal. I am in Bermuda to evaluate the island's cedar supply, as it were. But I have lately been in the Levant, as Admiral Davies said. Perhaps I can be of some small service familiarizing you with particulars of the region."

Fallon looked at Davies, who lifted a small smile and held his gaze a moment while Sir William helped himself to more sausage. There was, in Davies' gaze, a message and this was what it said: *Sir William is not exactly who he says he is.* Which to Fallon meant he was a British spy.

"Thank you, Sir William," said Fallon. "I would be particularly interested in the harbor at Algiers and the fortifications there." Fallon, getting right to it and testing his theory about Sir William, for there would be no reason for a businessman to have so much as an opinion about harbor defense.

Sir William looked at Fallon appraisingly, no doubt coming to the opinion that this was a fellow not to be trifled with. He got right to the point.

"It is not a large harbor, captain," he said, "but it has a hook of land to the northwest called the Great Mole. The mole is over three hundred yards long and forms the letter J. At the tip it is well fortified, though most of the mole is only yards wide. I have counted the guns defending the city and believe there are close to 200 cannon, most 24 and 42 pounders. Ships are guided into the harbor by a pilot and made to anchor under the guns so that if there is any dispute with the dey they are, in effect, at his mercy. Since Great Britain has a treaty with the dey I don't expect you to have a problem, but one never knows with these fellows. Lately, there have been *incidents* with British ships that cast doubt on Britain's relationship with the rulers, to be sure."

Fallon was not surprised at Sir William's grasp of the harbor fortifications, for that was what spies were trained to do. He wondered at the man's life, slipping in and out of cities, carrying his secrets and perhaps an identity or two, never sure of his friends. Or his enemies, come to that.

They spent the next half hour discussing specifics of wind and weather in the Mediterranean, both unstable in the extreme. As for tides, there were none, at least not to speak of, for the inlet of water from the Atlantic Ocean through the Strait of Gibraltar was quite narrow.

Fallon's mind memorized every detail as Sir William related it. The guns of Algiers gave him pause, of course, but he had no intention of being intimidated or putting *Rascal* and her crew in danger. How that was to be avoided was a good question, however.

"What can you tell me of the prison, Sir William," Fallon asked, "and the prisoners."

"When the corsairs take white Christians at sea there is a great celebration when the ships dock. The prisoners are housed in the lower city near the quay and eventually brought to the slave market, or *bedestan*, where they may be sold to anyone. But if the dey wants a specific prisoner for ransom, or perhaps for his harem or personal attendant, or for manual labor for his government, such as mining stone for the breakwater, he has first rights and must meet the highest bid. Wealthy prisoners or officers are usually held for ransom and often given lighter work. Crews and ordinary seamen and passengers are sold into a life of hardship that cannot be imagined.

"Piracy is a hard business. These *reis*—the Arabic for captain—are excellent sailors with an obvious streak of brutality and a total ignorance or disregard for what we would call conventional morality. That is how they keep their power. And the unfortunate beneficiaries of their ways are the poor slaves they capture. These unfortunate souls are sold to a worse fate than can be imagined. I have no idea what your fisherman is doing, of course. But we should hope he is still alive, else you are on a fool's errand, I'm afraid."

Sir William did not say this unkindly and, in fact, Fallon knew it was a distinct possibility that the senior Visser could not bear up under hard labor.

"Where is the dey's palace?" asked Fallon.

"The dey keeps his palace and harem and courtiers in the qasba, a fortification at the top of the hill. The palace has a commanding view of the harbor and is heavily guarded, as well. The Algerians are great believers in guns."

"Yes, I would say so," said Fallon, thinking that it came from being at war for centuries on end, the "eternal war" against Christians, as he'd heard it called.

But he pushed the thought from his mind and turned the conversation, instead, to questions about the dey's corsairs.

"The dey has some 60 corsairs who are called pirates abroad but operate more like privateers, begging your pardon. They are licensed by the dey to plunder shipping and raid countries for slaves, with the dey keeping most of the money they bring at market or in ransom. The corsair ships are mostly xebecs or captured enemy ships and they carry soldiers called janissaries. They do the boarding and hand to hand fighting and all reports are they are quite good at it. Apparently, they are noisy and terrifying and utterly fearless. The corsairs are commanded by their so-called admiral, whose flagship is *Serpent,* a rather large xebec with many guns and oars. His name, incidentally, is Zabana. He is Turkish and French and completely ruthless. No other reis has had his success at sea, or on land, come to that. He is very powerful and perhaps feared by the dey, in some ways."

Fallon was thoughtful as he gazed past Sir William at the sea and sky beyond the great cabin's stern windows. The golden morning was giving away to a brighter, whiter sunshine that promised to be warm.

"Tell me, Sir William," he said at last, "what is the language in the Mediterranean? How does an Englishman communicate?"

"Ah, that is an excellent question," answered Sir William. "There are too many languages! Consider that the Mediterranean is sometimes called the *sea in the middle of the earth* and you will understand. Captain, there are over thirty kingdoms, republics, and principalities along its shores. But there is a common language, of a sort. It is *lingua franca,* a sort of perversion of Italian, with some Turk, Greek, Spanish, and a bit of Portuguese thrown in for spice. It is a language of many tongues, so to speak, and is spoken by sailors, brokers, traders, and slave masters all over the Mediterranean. If you speak Spanish you will be understood well enough, I assure you. I believe even the dey speaks lingua franca."

Davies had been quiet through most of the breakfast, but as the dishes were cleared by his steward he leaned into the table and addressed himself directly to Fallon.

"Nicholas, I am at a loss as to how to advise you, or help you in any way, which causes me great distress. And I am outraged that the British government permits these deys and sultans to rule the Mediterranean and take Christians as slaves. Why, Nelson himself was quoted in the Gazette as saying that it made his blood boil that his own country, the mightiest sea power the world has ever known, should pay a tribute to sail there. A tribute! From Great Britain! Were it up to me we would bombard Algiers until the dey surrendered and then go on to Tripoli and the rest."

"Indeed, Admiral, it may come to that one day," said Sir William cooly. "If Great Britain refuses to pay its tribute there will be war."

The breakfast concluded, Fallon thanked Davies and Sir William and left to return to his ship. His small ship, smaller still on a great ocean or in a far-away harbor surrounded by more cannon than he had ever seen in one place in his life.

Thirty-Three

The next day was Sunday and Beauty ordered a make and mend day, which allowed *Rascal's* crew to patch, darn, and wash their clothes and generally have the afternoon to themselves without having to be on duty. Fallon, however, had much to do and even more to think about.

At the top of his list was what to do with Little Eddy. The boy had been all but invisible since *Loire's* prize crew had come back aboard, no doubt hoping that he would be "out of sight, out of mind." But he was very much in Fallon's mind and he decided to speak with Beauty, Visser, and Aja and get their thoughts. Really, he was just putting off the decision.

In fact, here was Aja at his cabin door.

"A note from Admiral Davies, captain, sir," he said. "Just came by his gig."

"Thank you, Aja," said Fallon, taking the note and putting it aside for a moment. "I've been meaning to compliment you on your first independent command in getting *Loire* to Bermuda and then English Harbor. And your work on setting her to rights was truly impressive. I've no doubt the prize agent was astounded by your efforts. It looked like the ship was taken without a shot! But, truly, your abilities belie your age, young man. Well done."

Aja beamed, beamed like a child at Christmas seeing the toy he'd wished for, prayed for, appear with a bow. Nothing mattered more to him than Fallon's approval and he stood awkwardly smiling now before mumbling his appreciation and shaking Fallon's hand.

"Now, if you will be so good as to ask Beauty and Visser to join us here I'd like your collective guidance on a matter," said Fallon, returning to the business at hand. Aja left the cabin and Fallon turned his attention to Davies' note, which revealed an invitation to dinner aboard the flagship that afternoon. Besides he and Elinore, the guests were all friends: Beauty, Aja, Visser, Doctor and Señora Garón, and of course, Paloma. Now that was a dinner to look forward to, thought Fallon. There would be a vineyard's worth of wine poured and Davies could be relied upon to have his cook lay on his best.

But here was a knock at the door and his little meeting was about to begin.

"First, we are all invited to dinner on the flagship," he said to the group as they squeezed into the cabin and sat down around his desk. They all smiled in anticipation of the invitation and the sure knowledge that the dinner would be a feast, indeed.

"But I've asked you here for your counsel," continued Fallon, turning serious. "Something must be done about Little Eddy and I would like us all to be in agreement, if possible, as to what that something is. It is black and white, I'm afraid. He either stays aboard or he is sent home on the next packet ship to Bermuda."

Beauty looked at Aja. Aja looked at Visser. Visser looked at the floor. No one spoke, which Fallon took as a sign that they were all of the same mind and had likely already discussed the matter, leaving one of them to be the spokesman for the group. And, in fact, it was Visser who finally spoke.

"It's like this, Nicholas," he said, "Little Eddy made his decision to go to sea, which we all had to do at some point in our lives. He doesn't want to go home and I, that is, *we* think he could stay. I mean *should* stay. That is if you agree, of course."

Fallon looked at the three of them, none a parent. Of course, he wasn't either. But he thought of Little Eddy's mother losing her son, without so much as a goodbye, and felt a keen responsibility to her. Even more, he had to admit he didn't want the responsibility if the boy should be hurt or, God help, die under his command. Little Eddy might be doing no more than other boys did, perhaps, but at least some of the other boys had the blessings of their parents to go to sea. Little Eddy had stowed away. There was something in Fallon that couldn't abide taking him away from his mother.

"You are inclined to send him home, I believe," said Beauty, looking at Fallon's face closely. "I confess that was my first thought, as well. But Aja says he worked as hard as any man on *Loire* and the crew has accepted him as one of their own, so I guess I feel he's *earned* the right to stay. I will support you either way, Nico. I'm glad it's not my decision. I guess that's why you make the two-eighths!"

They all laughed at that, even Fallon. Responsibility on a ship eventually landed on the captain's lap, of course, else why was he the captain? Slowly the group broke up to get ready for dinner on the flagship, Fallon still at a loss as to what to do about Little Eddy.

There was nothing decided, but no decision to regret, either.

As Beauty made her way up the companionway and walked to the binnacle she wondered why Fallon was so against Little Eddy staying aboard. After all, boys ran away to sea all over the world. After Fallon had lost his mother even he . . . and then a thought struck her, a thought that was clear and true and so obvious she was surprised she hadn't had it before. Fallon had no mother as a child, which must have left a scar, and he wanted to spare Little Eddy the same wound. Even a mother as imperfect as Little Eddy's was still a mother. Fallon probably wasn't even aware of what he was doing, or trying to do, or why he was trying to do it.

We all keep secrets from ourselves, she thought, and turned back to her duties with the ship.

That afternoon, *Rascal's* gig clapped onto *Avenger* and the little party climbed through the channel to be welcomed by Davies, genial and gracious as always. He asked Fallon to wait a moment, however, while Beauty, Aja, Elinore, and Visser were shown below to *Avenger's* great cabin.

"You smoked our friend Sir William immediately, Nicholas," he said with a smile. "I could not but obey his request to keep his true occupation a secret from you. I hope you understand. When he's not a businessman he works for the government but is aligned rather closely with Lord

Keith who depends on him for information on French intentions in the Mediterranean. As you heard, he is a font of information on the Barbary situation, as well. I'm sorry for the deception, I am."

"Don't give it a thought, Harry," said Fallon. "I agree he certainly seemed knowledgeable enough about Algiers, which was truly helpful. In that part of the world, I'm afraid I will be lost."

Davies looked at his friend kindly. Not for the first time did he feel like they were brothers.

"If you become lost, Nicholas," he said, "you can always be found."

To say the dinner was a success would be to understate the evening.

The Garóns were very solicitous of Beauty, having grown close to her during her hospital stay on Antigua the previous year—had it been that long?—and since that time Señora Garón had had a baby girl. They all talked on and on, glass after glass, dish following dish until all the news was discussed and parsed and laughed at until nothing really mattered except that moment, that night with everyone together safe as houses. Paloma Campos was radiant, there was no other word for it, her black hair and brown skin seemed to gleam by candlelight, and the way she looked at Davies put Fallon in mind of his own feelings for Elinore, and several toasts were drunk to the joy of their engagement. At the last one Elinore cast a look to Fallon that said *you had better be back in time for the wedding.*

Only Caleb Visser seemed to hold back. Oh, he was engaged in the evening, to be sure, but he was new to the friendships. And he had to be forgiven for wondering what lay ahead, now that he had been fully acquainted with corsairs and slave markets and greedy deys. Fallon's heart went out to him, as did everyone's, for they had a hint of his despair, as well.

At last, the evening came to a close and they all stood on the deck saying goodbye and staring at the show of stars that seemed to have gathered just for them. It was a spectacular night, a night for fantasies and dreams. Indeed, as Fallon and Elinore climbed down into his gig to be rowed to shore and the Pegasus Inn, where Elinore and Paloma were staying, it appeared to them a hopeful sky. A lover's sky. And the very idea set them to thinking about what the rest of the night might bring.

That evening there was a candle by the bed in the Pegasus Inn and, though the window rattled a bit from the wind, it was peaceful and warm inside Elinore's small room. They locked the door and tried not to let the world's troubles inside.

Elinore was provocative and insisted on undressing Fallon first, slowly. She took off each bit of his clothing, taking her time, and when she came to his trousers she unbuttoned them *ever* so slowly, her fingers carelessly touching him as she turned the buttons one by one. By the time she'd released the last one Fallon was mad with desire, as she knew he would be.

When he was fully undressed she stood before him and began to undress herself. As each of her garments fell away her body's scent grew stronger and Fallon breathed her deeply, his eyes wide and alight with longing.

At last she wriggled free of the last of her undergarments and smiled a wicked smile at him, flirtatious and beckoning.

He gave into desire and put his hands on her and pulled her to him as she put her own hands in his hair. She closed her eyes and shuddered when he moved his mouth over her and then she began moving rhythmically, writhing, under his control now, the roles reversed, leaning against his face, her hunger building.

She pulled hard on his hair when at last she released, still standing, her body shaking and pulsing and vibrating uncontrollably. And then it was past; her hands relaxed in his hair and she reached for his shoulders to urge him up. She led him to the small bed by the table and there, by the light of the candle, she smiled that wicked smile again, inviting him to take her however he wanted.

Thirty-Four

The next few days were spent wooding and watering and provisioning *Rascal* to be ready in all respects for sea. A long time at sea, for who knew what stores they would find on the far side of the world?

Cully purchased shot from the magazine ashore to augment what *Rascal* had on board. Fallon had insisted on extra grapeshot for close work in case it came to that. Beauty and Aja were ashore arranging for a water hoy to come alongside and a barge to bring out beef and biscuit, Aja learning yet another aspect of command.

Fallon had turned the problem of Little Eddy over in his mind for several days and, when a packet bound for Bermuda had called at English Harbor he had made up his mind. The packet would leave for home the next morning carrying mail and a few passengers. He intended Little Eddy to be among them. The thought of a grieving mother, and his own fears for the boy's safety, had decided him. It didn't occur to him that there was likely something else at play, as well.

Fallon had informed Little Eddy of his decision and the boy had seemed to understand, accepting his fate with surprising stoicism. Visser and Aja seemed a bit taken aback but accepted Fallon's decision and even offered to escort the boy to the packet.

The next morning the sad little procession climbed through *Rascal's* gangway and down into Fallon's gig. It was a short row to the packet, which was bobbing idly at the quay. Beauty had asked Aja and Cully to go ashore for some last minute items from the chandlery once the packet was away. They carried a large duffel for the purpose which lay empty in the bottom of the gig.

Little Eddy waved goodbye to the ship with a brave face. The crew had all bade him farewell, sending him off with some gifts, a blanket and a tin of pudding, courtesy of the cook. All agreed he was a right shipmate. That was something to be proud of, thought Fallon, and hoped Little Eddy knew what he had earned in that praise.

Two days later, *Rascal* sailed out of English Harbor on the ebb and a light sea breeze. All the goodbyes had been said and, in truth, Fallon was anxious to be away. Elinore was stoic, for she had gathered herself and was resigned to his leaving and even his possible late return. There could be no knowing. She was on shore, waving, and Fallon could still smell her scent on his body, which would have made him smile if he was only leaving on an ordinary cruise. Admiral Davies was on the stern of *Avenger* and waved, as well. Who knew if they would ever see each other again? And then Kinis fired a single gun, which seemed to underscore the dangerousness of the cruise to Fallon, as if it needed underscoring.

Right, let's get this done, Fallon said to himself. The longer he stayed in port the longer he would be worried about the unknown. He thought of one of Ezra Somers' favorite Shakespeare quotes, something to the effect that *a coward dies a thousand deaths, a brave man only one*. It was time to be a brave man.

The course would take them northeast, making long boards against the trade winds until they could break free of them. The crew seemed delighted to be at sea and their humor was infectious, for they had all heard tales of the hidden delights of Algiers, veiled women with flashing black eyes and harems of concubines. It might all be fantasy, they knew, or it might not.

Barclay was on deck more often than not and clumsily attempted several noon sights for the first three days before clouds rolled in. Of course, he had every confidence in his dead reckoning and, beyond that, his instincts. But he was learning to use his stump and his good arm together, working as a team, and even his humor made an appearance at times.

So it was a happy ship that sailed into the Atlantic. All except for Caleb Visser, who often stood by himself at the windward railing looking apprehensively out to sea. Perhaps he was thinking of his own fantasy, of finding his father and bringing him home, of a life and a business they used to share, thought Fallon. His gold was below, the ransom he would need to buy his father's freedom—but who knew how it would go?

Odds were, not how they thought.

Later that evening at dinner, Beauty and Fallon discussed the broad outlines of a strategy based on what little information they knew, most from Sir William's account of the harbor fortifications in Algiers.

"Under no circumstances do I want *Rascal* under the harbor guns," said Fallon. "We would have virtually no leverage in the event the negotiation doesn't go well and we need to leave, perhaps quickly."

"What about the little fact that we're British citizens?" asked Beauty.

"Well, that should protect us, but Sir William's account made me uneasy on the point," said Fallon. "Any news of our capture would take months to get to London, I'm afraid. Diplomats would get involved, protests made and communiques sent back and forth. It might take months or even a year to settle it. Meanwhile, you're in a harem."

Beauty jumped at that, and Fallon burst out laughing.

"You do have a robe, I collect?" he asked, still laughing. "If not, they can—"

"*Fuck that,*" said Beauty, in her own inimitable way. And Fallon threw back his head and laughed some more.

A knock on the door.

"Come," said Fallon, still chuckling at his own joke. But his smile evaporated as Aja stepped into the cabin, followed by a small boy with a grin on his face.

Little Eddy was back aboard.

"Well, I guess it was meant to be, Beauty," said Fallon as they stood together at the binnacle the next morning. Little Eddy was in a circle of ship's boys with Cully, who was walking them through their duties in the event the ship went into battle.

"Yes," said Barclay, who was standing within earshot. "It's God's way of telling you you're not God."

"Only an insignificant captain, Mr. Barclay?" said Fallon with a smile.

"Your words, sir. Your words," said Barclay as he tut-tutted off.

"I wonder how he did it, Beauty?" asked Fallon. "You and Aja got him on the packet and it weighed almost as soon as he went aboard." He thought back over that morning, seeing in his mind Cully and Aja and Little Eddy climb down into the gig, the empty duffel lying on the floorboards, everyone with their heads down.

When they'd left, Beauty had asked to review the approaches to Algiers with Fallon below decks though he had already gone over what he knew in some detail. Consequently, he was not on deck when the gig returned from shore and the large duffel was hauled aboard *Rascal.*

The duffel.

It was a large duffel, he recalled, plenty big enough for a small boy to curl up inside. But that meant –

Beauty coughed under Fallon's gaze and left to check on some task of other that needed checking on, and Aja was nowhere to be seen.

Thirty-Five

The two xebecs sailed westward from the Levant, pushed along by a strong breeze from the south. Spring was coming sooner than usual to the Mediterranean and the two reis could feel it in the warm wind on their cheeks. That was both good and bad, for spring meant there was the possibility of early siroccos to worry about, that dry wind that came from the Sahara, sometimes carrying sand, sometimes at hurricane force, sometimes both.

Hasim Reis stood on the deck of his xebec, a re-capture from the Spanish named *Ruse,* appropriately named as it turned out, for Hasim was nothing if not clever. The other xebec's reis was named Rogers, a British renegade turned corsair who fled to Algiers and converted to Islam. It was that or be hung in Great Britain as a pirate. His xebec, *Gazelle*, was built in Algiers, captured by the French, and re-captured by Rogers in a pitched battle near Tunis.

There were a surprising number of European renegade pirates in Zabana's little navy. Some had been Royal Navy officers at one time who jumped ship for the better pay of a corsair captain, but there were Spanish, Dutch, French, and even Venetian captains, as well. All professed their devotion to Islam but what they really loved was gold, and the dey was generous when they captured Christians for the slave market.

Hasim and Rogers had sailed their ships in tandem before, but were only moderately successful and frequently provoked Zabana's ire as a result. On this cruise they had captured only two fishing boats near Cairo, netting six slaves. They had sunk the boats, along with their catch, because they really had no value. At last, low on food and water, they had sailed for their home port of Algiers.

Rascal plunged to the northeast on starboard tack, sailing close-hauled against the trades. With luck, they would reach Algiers in twenty sailing days, barring a turn in the weather which could leave them hove-to for days. *Rascal* sailed under full topsails and made all the distance she could, while she could.

At the end of the first week out of Antigua the routine of a ship at sea had taken hold firmly and the watches changed with monotonous regularity. A keen ear could gauge the strength of the wind by its octave in the ship's rigging. Flying fish were constant companions and each morning the deck was littered with flapping, silver bodies which had unwittingly flung themselves aboard in the night. These were cooked for breakfast, for some sailors would eat them, though not every sailor would eat fish. Then the deck was scraped of the scales and salt and Cully would exercise the gun crews or teach the youngsters the theory of gunnery.

The morning of the tenth day at sea found Fallon stepping over flying fish on the windward side of the ship to get some morning exercise. Barclay and Aja had gotten a tolerable noon sight the day before and thus there should have been nothing to trouble the captain. In fact, Fallon was remarkably calm considering he was going somewhere he'd never been to do something he'd never done. Well, as Fallon's father would say, *that never bothered you before.*

Finished with his walk, he leaned against the foremast and looked forward. Somewhere out there was Africa. He couldn't see it, of course, but in his mind a picture had formed of what he would find there. It was exotic and mysterious and dangerous from a distance. And maybe up close, he admitted.

"Captain, sir," said Aja, appearing at his side and interrupting his picture-making, "I have been thinking of Barbary people. I think they must be very strange to see."

"Yes, I suppose they dress and talk differently from us," agreed Fallon. "And their ships are different, of course."

"Are the people different inside?"

Fallon thought about this a moment, surprised and curious that Aja had asked the question and wondering exactly what he meant. Surely Algerian mothers and fathers loved their children. Surely they sat around their tables at night and told them stories that made their eyes go wide. Surely those children grew up and fell in love, to start the cycle all over again. But on the other side of the coin, Muslims bought and sold men, women, and children into slavery. They committed unspeakable acts of cruelty towards others based on righteousness and religion and greed. They robbed and murdered and plundered and kept slaves and made war on other nations.

"I think," said Fallon upon reflection, "they're more like us than we know."

The trip along the Mediterranean coast was uneventful, though both Hasim and Rogers kept a close eye on their provisions, which were dwindling fast. The slaves at the oars rowed mostly in the lulls, which was not often as the warm wind came reliably across the desert and pushed their ships along fast enough. The janissaries were bored, the crews were dispirited and all agreed the voyage was mostly a failure.

At last, Hasim and Rogers docked their ships at the quay in Algiers harbor and found that Zabana had left orders for them, threatening orders that would take them to sea again as soon as they could wood, water and provision their ships. They were to sail through the Strait of Gibraltar in search of prizes. It was unusual to order xebecs into the Atlantic, and it spoke of a certain urgency or desperation on Zabana's part. Their orders were vague as to when to come back, but crystal clear on what they were expected to bring back: Christian slaves.

The xebec crews were not allowed a run ashore; not even the married men could leave the ships to see their families. Wives and children came to the quay to exchange notes and gifts and to wail from the torture of seeing husbands and fathers but not touching them.

The night before they left Algiers, Hasim and Rogers met for evening prayers. The sun was sinking in the west as the men knelt on the deck of Hasim's ship to urge Allah to be kind to them. Both prayed for a merchant ship to appear on the horizon soon, even a small one, for they feared returning to the Mediterranean without a prize.

Each reis had but four fingers on his right hand as it was.

Hasim and Rogers sailed into the Strait of Gibraltar on a perfect afternoon. These waters were normally busy, but that day there was very little to attract their interest. So it came to pass that, at last, the xebecs cleared the Strait of Gibraltar and turned south along the coast of North Africa, into waters they had never sailed before. With the wind brisk from the northeast the sweeps could rest. There were thirty men chained to the oars, naked and burned from the sun, where they ate, slept, urinated, and defecated until they died. They were all infidels in the eyes of the corsairs, little more than dogs. And they were treated as such.

In addition to the ship's crew, each xebec carried one hundred janissaries and nine guns to the side, all 9-lb cannon, and each ship had skilled men to serve them. Years of fighting Christian navies and taking prizes had trained them well. Both Rogers and Hasim knew their mission to bring back Christian slaves was an important one and that they must not fail, thus each ship was driven by wind, oar and fear.

The small xebecs rolled and pitched and took on water occasionally, for their low freeboard and shallow draft were more suited to the Mediterranean, with its many bays and indentations and ports to run into in case of bad weather. But the open ocean was another thing altogether. Each reis would have to handle his ship in whatever conditions the sea offered them. Fortunately, the coast of North Africa offered shelter and safety at night, but each new day would see the ships ranging far and wide across the entrance to the Strait hoping to get lucky.

Lookouts scanned the horizon for sails as the first day outside the Strait closed but there was nothing to see.

Evening came aboard *Rascal* as a fog of darkness, settling about the ship in the empty spaces that were not wood or canvas or fiber or flesh. *Rascal* had her stern lantern lit and shortened sail for the night as Fallon had ordered. The wind and weather had cooperated beautifully and good luck seemed to be aboard.

Visser was at his customary place on the windward rail watching the world close off when Fallon approached him silently.

"Caleb, we will be half way to Gibraltar in another week if this wind holds, according to Barclay. Very close to your father."

"Yes," said Visser. "I will never be able to repay you for everything you have done and are doing. I pray it will not put you or your ship in danger. You don't know how I pray."

"That is good of you, Caleb," said Fallon. "I believe we will find your father and bring him home safely. But as to danger, there is danger everywhere, especially in a sailor's life. The men know that. Beauty knows that. At any moment a French squadron could come over the horizon and we would find ourselves in the gravest of dangers. Truth be told, we crave it a little bit, the danger, that is. I could not admit that to Elinore, but it is true. We chose this life, remember, and it has its rewards. The mornings at first light. Sailing through a storm safely. Coming home. Sometimes it is even noble, in its way. I can't think of a more noble purpose than freeing a person from slavery, Caleb. No matter who he is."

Visser thought of Aja's story, then, of how Fallon had rescued the boy and set him free. No doubt there were others, as well.

He looked at Fallon with fresh eyes. For the first time, Visser understood that, beyond the obvious friendship the two shared, something larger had set Fallon sailing into danger on the Barbary coast.

His own humanity gave him no choice.

Thirty-Six

Zabana was feeling better about life.

Two small American traders were taken without a shot. Zabana's janissaries stormed over their sides and, to add a touch of terror, blew a trumpet loudly before backing the frightened crews almost off the ships. Zabana placed thirteen of his own crew aboard each ship and ordered all but four of the Americans be locked below decks. Those four would be forced to work with the Turks to get the ships back to Algiers. If they didn't work hard enough, or if they tried to escape, they would be beaten and four more brought up. It was important not to kill slaves, or even wound them if it could be avoided, because wounded or crippled slaves were worth less.

Zabana kept to himself most of the time, alone in his cabin until called to come on deck. He still seethed at the dey's absolute authority over him and wondered how long the old man would stay in power. Deys had a way of dying prematurely, but Zabana would need a plan that couldn't fail and another plan for what to do when it did.

No ships were sighted in the next week; at least, no ships worth taking. Zabana reflected ruefully that he'd tried to explain the dearth of available prizes to the dey but his explanation had fallen on deaf ears. At this rate, he could anticipate more humiliation unless the raids on Europe's coast went well and his ships returned with golden-haired beauties and strong men. And there was always the possibility that Hasim and Rogers would capture a ship or two.

Zabana smiled, remembering when he'd cut off their fingers for some minor infraction. They weren't his best captains, but perhaps they were the most motivated.

Rascal made good time across the Atlantic; that often angry sea seemed to grant her a favor in her quest to reach the Mediterranean. The hands seemed happy enough. One of the jacks did find a flying fish wrapped up in his cot. And one of the ship's boys found his pant legs had been sewn together while he slept. It was the normal stuff of a mischievous shipmate, and Fallon thought he knew who that shipmate was. Little Eddy was aboard and up to tricks.

As *Rascal* approached the Strait of Gibraltar the hands grew tense, for the real adventure was about to begin. Fallon felt it, of course, and found himself looking into the distance ahead with a mix of dread and excitement for these waters were new to him, as well. Finally, quitting the deck, he went below to pore over a chart of the Mediterranean which Davies had kindly lent him. It was a large sea, almost a million square miles in surface area, and stretched from the Strait of Gibraltar eastward to the Levant, with several smaller seas and basins described on the chart. Sir William had said the weather could be unpredictable in the spring, with winds reversing direction seemingly in an instant. Fallon was still deep in thought sometime later as he rolled up the chart and went back on deck to join Barclay at the binnacle.

"Wind should be up soon, Nico," said Barclay. He had been studying the sky for some minutes while feeling the sea's gathering strength, and was sure of what he saw. Fallon agreed to a reef in the sails on the bet that Barclay was right.

Beauty was now on deck and thumped to the binnacle to join the others, having heard the shouted order to shorten sail. She immediately checked the slate and called for a cast of the log.

"We're sure about this wind, are we Barclay?" she asked with a show of skepticism.

"Perfectly sure, Beauty," retorted Barclay. "Within half hour or I'm an Irishman."

"Well, you may be part Irish, you know," said Beauty. "It wouldn't surprise me. Without the sense of humor."

Fallon smiled to himself at the verbal jousting between Beauty and Barclay. It was an everyday occurrence and both sides enjoyed it. He looked out towards the east and was still staring when the lookout's call came.

"Deck there," came the shout. "Two sail off the leeward bow!"

It could be anything of course, thought Fallon. Any ship from anywhere. But best not to take chances. They had sailed all these weeks without sighting a sail and now this.

Ruse and *Gazelle* had lookouts, as well, and they both reported a lone sail to the west. Hasim and Rogers had been on the verge of hauling their wind and heading back to Algiers when the strange sail had been sighted. *Allah be praised!* Food and water were short aboard both xebecs, but both captains hated the thought of returning to Algiers empty handed.

The janissaries on both ships were alerted and checked the priming on their muskets and the edge on their scimitars. They adjusted their hats and robes and the *agha* ordered them to be ready.

In truth, the janissaries were always ready. But they were not sailors, and they didn't notice the wind was increasing, but the helmsmen did.

Fallon climbed the rigging to see for himself what these two strange ships might portend. When he found them in his telescope he saw the distinctive shapes of lateen sails, and he knew instinctively he was looking at Barbary corsairs.

Quickly, he descended to the deck and walked aft to the binnacle.

"Beauty, call all hands to quarters," he said.

"Corsairs, Nico?" she asked after she'd given the orders and the crew jumped to their stations in disciplined motion. Little Eddy dove below to bring up powder and shot with the other ship's boys.

"I'm sure of it," said Fallon. And then added: "Or I'm an Irishman."

They both laughed, because of his name, of course. But Beauty felt the wind strengthening just as Barclay had predicted.

The corsairs were still several miles away and Fallon wondered what their strategy would be in the event they decided to attack. Perhaps they had already seen that the schooner in their telescopes was flying the British ensign. He wondered if that would make any difference.

Somehow, he thought it wouldn't.

Ruse and *Gazelle* were on larboard, edging down on the oncoming schooner. Both Hasim and Rogers knew their prayers had been answered, and they'd been ready to turn for home! Surely their faith had rewarded them with a ship full of Christian slaves.

"Seize the dogs!" yelled Hasim. And his ship's crew took up the chant.

Shot and powder were brought up for the guns, though neither Hasim nor Rogers thought it would be necessary to actually fight the ship coming towards them. They had the advantage in manpower, certainly. In their profession boarding was advisable, both to prevent their own casualties but most certainly to preserve the health of their future slaves.

The schooner could be seen from the deck now. Neither reis seemed worried that the oncoming ship was British. After all, they were all alone on the open sea.

The wind was goading the sea into a menacing thing. Beauty had her peg anchored firmly in the ringbolt next to the binnacle and the rest of the crew hung onto stays and the railings and moved about only with care.

"Nicholas," said Visser, having to raise his voice to be heard at the binnacle. "Great Britain has a treaty with these fellows, is that not correct?"

"Yes," Fallon shouted back. "But only if they honor it." The look on his face said he wasn't so sure they would. The look on Visser's face showed surprise, which Fallon knew was naiveté making an appearance. It only confirmed in his mind why he'd decided to convey Visser to Algiers.

The xebecs were about a mile away when the first warning puffs of smoke came from their bow chasers. Fallon couldn't see the fall of shot, but it certainly put paid to any question about a treaty.

"Ladies and gentlemen," he shouted over the shriek of wind. "I believe we are at war. Beauty, let's have Cully at the long nine to answer the call."

While Cully's crew went to work loading the cannon, Fallon and Beauty studied the tactical situation carefully. The wind was out of the south and blowing hard and it put the xebecs on larboard tack and *Rascal* on starboard with the weather gauge. It was a good question: which was faster, *Rascal* or xebec? Not knowing the answer pushed the idea of trying to outrun the corsairs out of Fallon's mind. No, it would be a fight.

Rascal's long nine barked, but with the plunge and roll of the ship it would be a miracle if Cully hit anything. Fallon looked for the fall of the shot but saw nothing. Puffs from the xebecs again, and now the corsairs split apart; the leeward corsair fell off to the northwest while the windward xebec held course, close-hauled on larboard and making directly for *Rascal's* bows.

"What do you think they're up to, Beauty?" asked Fallon. The xebec captains obviously had a plan in mind.

"I think . . . the windward ship is going to rake us," said Beauty, "aiming for the rigging I would guess. If they're after slaves they won't want to kill people. Then maybe the leeward ship hardens up and comes down across either our stern or bows to finish the job and board."

"Spoken like a true barbarian, Beauty," said Fallon with a grin. "Now, how do we lower the odds to one-to-one?" They both looked at each other a moment, then raised their telescopes to study the unfolding tactical situation again. The windward xebec was still coming on towards *Rascal's* bows and perhaps a half mile separated the ships.

Even now they could see a mass of men gathering at the xebecs' railings, their tall red hats making them visible through telescopes. There looked to be a great crowd of them on each ship, and Fallon surmised they were the famed janissaries that Sir William described. At all costs, they must be prevented from boarding.

The seas were rising up from the south, pushed by the steadily increasing wind, and *Rascal* swooped and dove like a swallow after a bug. The xebecs did the same, and Fallon was sure that water was coming over their low freeboard with each dive into a trough.

"Cully!" called Fallon. "Come aft quickly!" He was going to do something radical, even dangerous, in order to escape the untenable, uneven odds and prevent the xebecs' plan from unfolding. Beauty looked at him curiously as Cully approached.

"Beauty," Fallon shouted over the wind. "We're going to fall off sharply at the last moment and cross the first xebec's bows. Time it as close as you dare. Don't give him a warning or a chance to turn to follow us."

"Load both batteries with chain shot, Cully," he shouted over the wind. Aim for the rigging when we cross!"

Now a quarter mile separated the ships. Now less.

"The far xebec came about, Nico," said Beauty calmly. Fallon turned to see the far xebec sailing down close-hauled on larboard, her bows pointing towards the imaginary X on the ocean where the first xebec and *Rascal* should meet. The captains seemed to know their business, thought Fallon. He looked at Beauty, her eyes concentrating on the approaching xebec, which was now very close. Almost, in fact, close enough.

"Fall off!" ordered Beauty, and the helmsman turned the wheel sharply to larboard as the sheets were loosened and the schooner spun away from the xebec's bows at the last moment. Now Cully's forward gun roared, and then one by one each sent chain shot like bolas swirling in the air towards the delicate lattice work of rigging holding the xebec's foremast upright.

The effect was instantaneous as the xebec's forestay snapped and flew out to leeward like a vine blowing in the wind. Fallon could see several janissaries go down, their hats flying off their heads or perhaps their heads flying off their bodies. And now more ropes flew into the air as the xebec tried to fall off to follow *Rascal*, but the shrouds would not hold the mast. The big lateen sail billowed out, catching the full force of the wind as the mast groaned as it bent forward without any support from the larboard shrouds. Janissaries and crew were thrown about on deck and watched helplessly as the foremast snapped ten feet above the deck, carrying the sail and boom over the starboard side as seas broke over the ship's quarter.

But Fallon had no time to spare, as the second xebec was now very close, her guns run out on larboard. He could see Cully standing by his own larboard battery looking back at him, waiting for orders.

Hasim watched in shock as *Gazelle's* foremast snapped and went overboard and the big foresail seemed to blow off into the wind. *Gazelle* now sat dead in the water. Through his telescope he could see that seas were coming aboard the shallow-decked vessel and if he didn't help her she might well sink. This British captain was clever, he thought, but now *Ruse* was bearing down on him from the north and there would be no tricks. His guns were loaded and his men were ready. As soon as he boarded the schooner he would sail down to aid Rogers.

Now the British schooner's larboard guns were out, which was just what he'd expected. He looked at the janissaries on board his ship; they were ready to fight, no question. The guns were loaded. The scimitars were sharpened to a razor edge. The trumpeter had his trumpet in his hand.

"Nico," said Beauty quickly, "assuming we get by him in one piece, what's next?"

"We run for it," said Fallon without hesitating. "By the time that xebec comes about we should be over half a mile ahead. I figure he'll help keep his friend from sinking and we should be well over the horizon by the time they get sorted out."

"Good," said Beauty, "I was hoping you wouldn't do anything stupid like fight to the death."

Now the oncoming ships were a mere cable's distance apart, both twisting and dropping over the wave tops into troughs that seemed to swallow them. Fallon didn't need to remind Cully to fire on the uproll;

the old gunner knew his business and would fire his broadside all at once before *Rascal* could fall off a wave.

"Mr. Barclay," said Fallon suddenly. "Watch your parts!"

Barclay looked up and almost smiled at Fallon's dark humor.

But there was no time for a response, for the xebec was hurtling towards them and janissaries were already aiming their muskets.

Thirty-Seven

Rascal's BROADSIDE ROARED ACROSS THE WATER JUST AS *Ruse's* BROAD-side fired. Even in that hive of wind the sound was deafening, and the shudder of the deck under Fallon's feet told him something was wrong. The foremast was swinging wildly in the tempest, its shrouds parted and blown to heaven, the foresail beating like a marine drum, snapping and popping; its sheets were whips that could lash a man through his clothing. The xebec had aimed high, hoping to cripple *Rascal,* and the ship was indeed crippled.

But not finished.

Both ships dropped into troughs and, when they emerged again, they were past each other. Fallon looked the length of the ship and saw to his relief that all hands seemed to be standing. One ship's boy was down, and Fallon's breath caught in his throat. Visser was kneeling to pick up Little Eddy to be carried below.

"Nico," yelled Beauty. "The xebec is tacking!"

Hasim brought the xebec through the eye of the wind with care, for the rigging holding the mainmast aloft had suffered from the schooner's broadside and he had to be very careful. Luckily, the starboard shrouds were intact, only the larboard's were cut by the chain shot but he was still fortunate not to have lost his mast. The janissaries were not so lucky, and many were down and spurting their lives out on deck, their blood the color of their hats.

Prudence and loyalty told him to sail down to help *Gazelle,* which was clearly foundering in the heavy seas with her foresail over the side. He could see Rogers waving frantically and the water must be deep in the holds by now.

Hasim looked away towards the crippled schooner sailing eastward, towards the Strait. If the wind stayed out of the south his crew would have time to splice the larboard shrouds and *Ruse* should have no difficulty catching the schooner, whose name he could see was *Rascal.*

For a brief moment, Hasim wondered what to do. But only for a brief moment. Then he ordered a gun crew to the bow of the xebec to man the bow chaser.

Beauty sent men forward to take in the foresail and begin re-splicing the rigging. It was a harrowing job, for the foresail boom was swinging wildly and all the shrouds holding the foremast up had been cut except one on the windward side. That shroud was the only thing standing between hope and catastrophe.

Fallon looked over his shoulder and saw the xebec complete her tack and begin to gather speed. *Rascal* was almost a half mile ahead in the chase, but without the foresail it would be no contest. Even now there was a puff of smoke from the xebec's bow chaser. It would be very difficult to hit anything at that range in that sea, but it was always possible.

His mind went quickly to the chase off the U.S. coast by the French frigate, but there were no snow squalls here to hide *Rascal.* This chase would not end well, and he would have to face that fact. His mind raced for an answer, a forgotten feint or trick, but nothing came to him.

"What are you thinking, Beauty?" he said, hoping for something he hadn't thought of. "You get any ideas, you send them along."

And then he looked around at Barclay, who looked back at him without speaking. He looked at Aja, just returning to the binnacle with a report on Little Eddy. The boy had been felled by a block and Colquist reported that he would live, though his nose was smashed and his face would turn black and blue. Visser was with him, still.

Aja looked at the xebec, then at Fallon, then at the xebec again.

"We are not faster, captain sir," he said.

"No, Aja, we can't outrun them without a foresail."

The xebec fired her bow chaser again. And now the shot could be seen hitting the water not fifty feet from *Rascal;* the shots was getting closer as the xebec drew closer. Beauty coaxed every ounce of speed out of the schooner, but nothing would delay the inevitable and Fallon knew it. Now all hands were looking aft, at him. He looked at each one of them, for he knew most of them, knew their families even, and his eyes lighted on Cully, the Irishman who had lost an eye serving him, the loyal gunner who had dropped a wine bottle in his cabin and said *bomb the bastards.*

Suddenly, their last, best chance was clear to Fallon.

"Beauty," he said calmly, or as calmly as he could speak given that the xebec was doubtless preparing to fire again, "I'll want empty barrels hauled up and thrown overboard quickly. And have the long boat turned over and placed on deck. And call Cully aft please."

Barclay and Aja looked expectantly at their captain, looking for the old spark, the old gleam in his eyes that told them something was up, some idea was in his mind, and when he grinned at them they saw it.

"Cully," he said when the gunner approached. "I have a hypothetical question for you." Cully edged closer and smiled. "We have a problem with that xebec behind us," he said with dramatic understatement.

"Deck there!" interrupted the lookout. "Ship looks to be gaining."

Indeed, she could be seen easily from the deck now and seemed larger and more menacing and, what was the word? *Tenacious.*

"Yes," said Fallon, turning back to Cully, "as I was saying about the problem. Hypothetically, Cully, if we knew how fast we were moving, and we could judge how far the xebec was behind us, and if it was close *enough* behind us, but not *too* close mind, could we blow it up?"

Cully rocked back and Beauty jerked her head around.

"Blow it up? With a gun?" Cully asked, incredulously.

"No, a bomb," said Fallon, with a maniacal laugh. "Could we bomb the bastards, as someone once said?"

And then he told them about his crazy idea.

Hasim knew how it would end.

Ruse was gaining on the British schooner with each minute and soon his bow chaser would find the range. Even if the schooner's captain chose to fight—and he would if he had any idea what fate had in store for him and his crew—he had no chance of maneuvering without a foresail. The janissaries would overwhelm them once *Ruse* got alongside.

Hasim stole a quick glance over his shoulder towards *Gazelle* or, rather, towards where *Gazelle* had been. Now there was nothing he could see. It was a pity about Rogers, he thought, but now there would be no glory to share. The capture would be all his, the prize money all his.

And what was this? The schooner was throwing barrels over the side to lighten the ship. And he could see they'd started their water, pumping it overboard in an effort to go faster and escape the inevitable. They were frantic, these British, and they hadn't even heard the trumpet yet!

Fallon had ordered the empty barrels thrown overboard to give the picture of a desperate ship which, indeed, *Rascal* was. But also to judge how long it took for the barrels to float back to the xebec. And then he ordered the holds to be pumped dry to give his plan just that much extra time, for there was much to be done—and quickly.

The longboat was placed on deck as Fallon had ordered, then Barclay reported the speed measured by the cast of the log to Cully so he could measure the slow match accordingly. All Beauty's attention turned to getting every ounce of speed possible out of *Rascal*. The crew at the foremast were doing what they could, but in the tossing seas it was beyond a challenge to re-rig the mast. The foresail was down and inboard at last, however, so that was something.

"Aja," said Fallon to his second mate, "call the carpenter on deck and have him build a drogue out of old sailcloth. It should be weighted so when it's attached to the long boat it will hang below the surface and open up to keep the boat from drifting off course."

There was that damned bow chaser firing again. And as Fallon looked up he saw a hole open up in the mainsail. "Hurry!" he said to no one, and to everyone.

Here were two crew members carrying small barrels of gunpowder up from below decks, and powder boys behind with slow match and a tarpaulin, just as Fallon had ordered. The gunpowder was lashed between the thwarts of the longboat as the slow match was unwound. The crew moved deliberately, without panic. The thing had to be done right.

"What's our plan if this doesn't work, Nico?" asked Beauty.

"I don't have a second plan," said Fallon with a wink. "I barely have this one worked out."

Now Barclay was conferring with Cully on the length of slow match. The carpenter was attaching the drogue to the bow of the ship's boat and placing a 9-pound ball in a canvas sack to tie to the drogue to hold it below the surface where it wouldn't be seen.

Fallon looked back towards the xebec, now less than a quarter mile behind *Rascal;* well, perhaps more like 2 cables. It was time, for any later and the explosion could reach *Rascal.* And there would be an explosion, no question. The question was would it do any good?

Lowering his telescope, Hasim smiled at the agha, who ordered the janissaries to be ready for boarding. The schooner was even now putting her ship's boat in the water in a futile effort for more speed, but it was no use. Very soon the xebec would be alongside. Even from the deck he could easily count a hundred would-be slaves for the taking. Zabana would be very happy, wouldn't he?

When the longboat had splashed overboard, the drogue sank and opened like a large canvass basket to act against the push of wind and waves. The boat bobbed and dipped as the seas ran under her, the tarpaulin covering the gunpowder and slow match kept everything dry from the spray off the wave tops.

Fallon stood at *Rascal's* stern and counted the time in his head. Even with just the mainsail, *Rascal* was pulling away from the longboat quickly and the xebec was approaching even faster. Barclay had estimated time and distance as best he could and Cully had been precise in cutting the slow match, but it was an inexact science, of course. Perhaps the best that could be hoped for was that the explosion would shock the xebec's crew and momentarily create a diversion, allowing *Rascal's* crew more time to secure the foremast and get the sail up. But even as he thought those thoughts, Fallon knew he was hoping for the impossible.

On the xebec came, close enough that Fallon could see the brightly colored turbans on the crew and catch the glint off the curved swords he saw waving in the air. The longboat was a speck on the ocean now, sometimes there, sometimes not, and Fallon imagined the slow match doused by a wave, the plan fizzling out in a thin trail of smoke. He pounded his hand on the taffrail in exasperation.

And then the explosion.

A tremendous surge of thunder such as no man had ever heard. As loud as a volcano, or what anyone aboard thought a volcano would sound like. All hands turned aft to see a great fog of black smoke engulf the ocean and plume upwards towards the sky as ship debris whirled within it, visible and then not.

What emerged from the smoke was the sense of a ship without a bow; a gaping maw that seemed to eagerly drink the sea.

Thirty-Eight

The sun was lowering in the sky and, true to form in the Caribbean, it would be dark very soon. Davies' servant brought lit candles into the great cabin but did not deign to interrupt the admiral, who had thrown open the stern windows and was standing before them looking out to the harbor with a glass of wine in his one hand and a fresh Admiralty dispatch in the other.

The news was not good. British agents had intercepted a secret French communique describing plans for a siege of Gibraltar. There had been many attempted sieges of Gibraltar in the past, and none had succeeded. The last such siege had ended in 1783, unsuccessfully for the French and Spanish, but the British garrison at Gibraltar had suffered horribly. Davies had read accounts of starvation from want of fresh provisions, with fruits and vegetables in particular in short supply. Scurvy had been rampant among the five thousand troops stationed there, and in the villages nearby, as well. When at last the siege was lifted, the brittle bones of death remained on Gibraltar.

Now, it seemed Bonaparte was contemplating a fresh siege, for the Strait was of immense strategic importance. If the French could gain control of Gibraltar, Bonaparte could command all of the Mediterranean to the Levant, which was his avowed goal. That meant every military or diplomatic victory ever won by the British in that part of the world would be for nothing.

That was disturbing, certainly. But worse was that the intercepted communique was meant for the dey of Algiers. *What in God's name could that mean?* thought Davies. It seemed to signal that the Algerians would somehow play a role in the siege, perhaps to supply French ships, or perhaps there was something more dangerous afoot.

Clearly, the Admiralty took the threat of a siege of Gibraltar seriously. Seriously enough to order Davies to transport Sir William Huntington-James back to the Mediterranean as soon as possible, presumably to gather intelligence for Lord Keith.

Davies thought of the ships at his disposal. A schooner would do, no doubt, but all of his schooners were scattered throughout the Caribbean except *Loire* and *Céleste*, which he would buy into the service soon but for which he had no men yet. The obvious choice was *Renegade*, fresh off the ways with a clean bottom.

Davies stared out the stern windows and thought of the dinner he was to have aboard *Renegade* the next day. No doubt Jones would be anxious for orders, expecting perhaps to cruise against pirates operating out of Guadeloupe or look in at French activities at Port-a-Prince. But no, Jones's orders would take him far afield on a mission incredibly important to Great Britain and, it was not a stretch, the peace of the world. Davies sat down at his massive deck and began to draft orders to send *Renegade* into another, even more dangerous sea than the Caribbean. The same sea that Nicholas Fallon was no doubt about to enter.

By the second dogwatch *Rascal's* foremast had been saved. The wind had lain down somewhat and hands could go aloft to finish attaching the new rigging and, eventually, a new foresail with new sheets. *Rascal* had been hove-to for over six hours while the task was done, after first sending the gig back towards the xebec to search for survivors. There were none; the ship had gone down so quickly that all hands who hadn't been killed by the explosion had probably been knocked senseless and drowned. All that was recovered was a wooden sea chest of clothing floating forlornly on the sea, its owner gone to the bottom.

Planks and bits of ship flotsam had quickly drifted away and now *Rascal* came out of stays and become her old self again, gathering the wind to her chest and setting her bows to the east and the entrance to the Strait of Gibraltar.

Fallon went below to check on Little Eddy and found Visser sitting with the boy, whose face was, it had to be said, a mess. Already, his eyes and temples were black, his nose was splayed across his swollen face and his lips were both split.

"Good Lord, Little Eddy!" exclaimed Fallon. "You are the hero of the ship! How did all this happen?"

The boy tried to smile and speak but was so groggy from Colquist's ministrations that he couldn't really put sentences together just then.

"He told me he was looking up at the foresail when it blew away to leeward and a block dropped square on his face, Nicholas," said Visser. "Knocked him clean out."

"It's a wonder it didn't kill him, Caleb," said Fallon, reaching for the boy's hand to squeeze it to assure himself he was alive. "My God, what would I have told his mother?"

"I guess that he was the hero of the ship, Nicholas. But one day he will tell her himself, I'll wager."

Soon after, Fallon went back on deck satisfied that Little Eddy would live, though his nose and face would be awhile returning him to his original self. Beauty and Aja were checking the rigging at the foremast as the new ropes stretched into service, and Fallon found Barclay at the binnacle making notes on the slate.

"Mr. Barclay," said Fallon to the sailing master, "when Beauty and Aja are finished inspecting the new work I would like to invite you all to join me for dinner. Caleb Visser will join us, as well. We have much to talk about before we reach Algiers."

"Yes," said Barclay, "I expect we do. Barring any storms or attacking corsairs I believe we will be at Gibraltar within a week. This south wind is behaving wonderfully and we can only hope it will last."

In the event, Fallon welcomed them all to dinner an hour later. They all seemed to have gotten over the shock of the explosion that sank the xebec, though their wonder at Fallon's audacity was evident in their faces as they re-lived the battle.

"What in God's name made you think that would work, Nico?" said Beauty. "I mean, really, what were the chances?"

"I don't want to think what the chances were," said Fallon. "Or that it was our *only* chance. We were very lucky, this time. But we may not be so lucky the next. So I want us all to be very clear on the implications of entering the Mediterranean as a British privateer. I don't know what that gets us now, frankly."

"Is there a chance these were rogue corsairs, Nicholas," asked Visser, "maybe acting on their own?"

"Yes, I guess there's that possibility. But we should be extra vigilant all the same. I want to call at Gibraltar for the latest intelligence and report the attack before proceeding with a plan. Mr. Barclay, how far do you make it from Gibraltar to Algiers?"

"Between two and three days, captain," said Barclay, "if the wind is from the west or really from anywhere other than southeast. If it's a southeast wind at least five days or more depending on its strength."

"How do we proceed once we're there, Nicholas?" asked Visser, completely aware now that this whole adventure put him out of his depth and relying solely on Fallon for direction.

"We'll need to find Richard O'Brien as soon as possible," answered Fallon. "But how we do that I'm not exactly sure."

Thirty-Nine

Zabana returned to Algiers with thirty-four slaves. The last ship he'd taken, a Maltese trader, carried the captain's wife. Zabana had attempted to rape her the first night she was aboard, but the woman had fought back valiantly, even producing a knife to defend herself—whereupon Zabana figured she wasn't worth the trouble and had her chained in the hold. At some point the next night one of his crew had snuck below decks and raped her himself, as she wasn't able to defend herself because she was chained. *Serpent* eventually reached port and all the slaves were taken ashore to a pen in the bagnio to be held until they were sold. Likely, not long.

Mustapha Pasha personally congratulated Zabana on his good fortune and, indeed, on the good fortune of all the returning corsairs. Over 150 Christians had been taken by Zabana's fleet and not half the corsairs had returned from their cruises to Northern Europe. Zabana took his own tally, of course, and noted that Rogers and Hasim had not returned yet. He expected to see them at any time, however, as food and water would be a problem by now. He did not expect them to disappoint him.

After meeting Zabana at the quay, Mustapha's entourage slowly made its way up the bent streets to his palace. It was guarded day and night by palace guards he had handpicked for the job, not fully trusting the powerful janissaries. A coup had left his predecessor dead, strangled by those very elite soldiers.

The dey was a fatalist who knew he served as ruler at the pleasure of the sultan of the Ottoman Empire in Constantinople, and he sent monthly gifts to stay in the sultan's good graces. One of Zabana's corsairs had captured a timber ship, another a trader carrying ceramics, and both ships would be sent to the sultan to curry his favor. He'd noticed a woman among Zabana's captures, and he would send her as a gift, as well.

As he entered the gleaming qasba, the dey looked out over the rampart to the harbor below. His view overlooked both the upper and lower cities on the hillside and the homes of their inhabitants, a mixed group of shop owners and tradesmen, barterers, and merchants of all stripes who kept Algiers vibrant and teeming. Most of them owned slaves, from many to one, and they were a ready market for the new slaves just captured.

As he looked over the rooftops to the harbor he was hoping to see a French ship, perhaps a brig or frigate, but he did not. He was expecting a message from Napoleon Bonaparte himself to confirm an agreement long whispered but never enacted. It would make the dey wealthier than any dey had ever been; wealthier than even the sultan in Constantinople, perhaps. The dey rubbed his beard and smiled to himself.

At word from Bonaparte he would set Zabana and his corsairs on the British like hounds on a fox.

Zabana had not left *Serpent* to go ashore yet, for he had a punishment to carry out. He had learned through an informant of the rape of the Maltese captain's wife, and he was incensed. Truthfully, he might have also been embarrassed that one of his crewmen had accomplished what he hadn't. This was a serious assault on Zabana's pride and would require a serious punishment. He called for the beheading cart.

The quaking prisoner had to be forcibly dragged from below decks where he had been kept in chains. He was naked and whimpering and wailing by turns, pleading for forgiveness. But his captain was not a forgiving man.

The beheading cart stood ready, the evil blade high in the air, silent and cold. The man was led to the cart and placed in position before it on his knees while a sword tip pricked the back of his neck lest he pull away. Zabana's eyes showed no emotion as he raised his face to heaven.

In truth, this would be a lesson for all the crew to learn. One they would never forget.

Two guards held the poor man in position and pulled his arms behind his back. The man was crying and praying at the same time, begging for mercy and forgiveness—but none would be forthcoming.

At Zabana's nod the blade came hurtling down in a blur, smoothly and silently, past the prisoner's wincing face to cut off his testicles, which were lying in the cradle.

Forty

In the middle 1700s Gibraltar became a major trading port for goods from North America, Europe, and the Mediterranean, as well as a base for the Royal Navy and a garrison for British troops. Its strategic military importance was obvious, being the gateway to all of North Africa and the countries bordering the Mediterranean. Ships carrying wine, cotton, spices, tobacco, timber, and a host of mercantile goods regularly sailed into the port, there to be unloaded by immigrants from around the world seeking relief from poverty or war in their home countries. Gibraltar was at the head of the Mediterranean, the busiest international trading center in the world.

Rascal glided into the port of Gibraltar on a dying afternoon breeze to find hundreds of ships anchored there in various stages of loading or unloading. It was a breathtaking sight, and *Rascal's* captain and crew gawked at such a collection of shipping as they had never seen, not even in Boston.

Fallon could see two Royal Navy ships, the frigate *Mischief* and the brig *Helena,* anchored near the shore and, presumably, the custom houses and government buildings. To see only two Royal Navy ships surprised Fallon; the war with France and Spain was consuming much of the navy's sea-going arsenal.

"Beauty, please secure the ship and then have my gig lowered over the side," he said. "I want to row around the harbor while there is still light."

In the event, the gig was soon lowered and Fallon and Aja descended into it and cast off. The first ship they came to was an American merchant ship, *Margaret,* and her captain stood at the larboard railing as Fallon's gig glided up.

"Ahoy, captain!" called Fallon, "I trust you had a good voyage from America?"

"That we did, sir," replied the captain. "We are here waiting to offload our sugar and take dates and olives off a ship from Tunis. We dare not sail to Tunis just now so Tunis must come to us!"

"It is too dangerous, I take it, for Americans in the Mediterranean?" asked Fallon, though he thought he knew the answer.

"Aye, I'll not take a chance on becoming a prisoner and losing my ship. It's all I have in the world."

Fallon waved goodbye and ordered Aja to steer for a large trader lying more in the center of the harbor. A water hoy was alongside so perhaps the trader was soon to weigh, and go where? Anywhere in the world was possible. The hoy's crew were a mixed lot of immigrants, including some Muslims in their robes and caftans, all doing the work of the harbor.

A large man at the ship's waist was supervising the loading of barrels of water and looked up with curiosity as Fallon's gig approached. As the hoy cast off the gig took her place alongside the trader.

"I am Captain Nicholas Fallon of the British privateer *Rascal,* sir. I am seeking any information as to the situation in the Mediterranean relative to armed corsairs."

"I am Benetti, first mate of the Portuguese trader *Corfu,* sir, and I'm afraid the Mediterranean is aflame with unrest, captain. We are to pick up wine at Sanary-sur-Mer on the French coast but first we must get there, and the corsairs seem to be taking Christians where they find them. I spoke to a Dutchman off Cadiz and understand a Maltese ship was taken just last week and all aboard were taken off, including the captain's wife. I have heard nothing but disturbing news since we arrived here from London. Where are you bound, Captain?"

"I was planning to call at Algiers but after listening to you I'm not so sure," said Fallon. "I am hoping to get more information when I go ashore in the morning."

"Yes, the dock is full of gossip and captains trading it," said Benetti. "Have a care, Captain Fallon." And with that, the Italian disappeared into his ship.

Next, Fallon was rowed to *Mischief*, 44, and stood in the sternsheets and announced himself. Momentarily, a lieutenant's head appeared over the quarterdeck railing and invited Fallon aboard. He went up the side easily and was met by that same lieutenant, Gerard, who offered to show him below to Captain Elliot's cabin.

Captain Hieronymus Elliot was a middle-aged man, thin to the point of bones and tight flesh; indeed, his stiff uniform seemed to hold him together. He coolly welcomed Fallon into his cabin and bade him sit while he hailed his steward for some wine. Fallon studied the cabin which, like its occupant, was spare and unprepossessing. He wondered at his host's financial circumstances, or perhaps he was merely penurious.

"What can I do for you, Captain Fallon?" asked Elliott, sitting down behind his desk. "I was made aware you had sailed in on a schooner and I've been expecting you, frankly."

"I have on board an American," replied Fallon, "who was notified almost a year ago that his father had been captured by the dey of Algiers' corsairs and could be ransomed. The American is a fisherman and has raised the money the dey demanded but lost his ship in a storm. I offered to bring him to ransom his father but was attacked by two corsairs several days ago. We were flying British colors quite plainly, so I am obviously wondering if Great Britain's treaty with the dey is still in effect."

Captain Elliot smiled a rueful sort of smile and leaned forward in his chair.

"What of your battle with the corsairs?" the captain asked, a hint of suspicion or disbelief in his voice. He had heard of no corsairs taking British ships.

It would not do to gloat over sinking two corsairs, so Fallon answered matter-of-factly that, indeed, both corsairs were sunk in the battle, but that the wind had helped dismast one of them. He did not mention that the other one had been bombed, fearing Elliot would think it fantastical.

"I see," said Elliot, but his blank expression suggested he did not see at all. He knew the corsairs to be wily fighters and could not imagine how a lone schooner could defeat two of them. However, it was fair to say imagination was not his strong suit.

"Well, Great Britain has a treaty with all the regencies," he said with a sniff, "so I can see no reason why you should have been attacked." This was the same to Fallon's ears as: *You are lying*, and it made him furious.

"Sir, the fact is we were attacked by two corsairs, and we are most certainly British," said Fallon defiantly. "I came to you to ask for protection getting into Algiers." Fallon was quite aware that he was sitting on a frigate and a brig was at anchor nearby.

"Admiral Lord Keith is supporting the Austrians against Masséna at Genoa," said Elliot with a sigh. "My orders are not to leave Gibraltar undefended until the fleet returns. Until then . . . " He spread his hands in the universal sign of *What can I do?*

"You seem quite capable, captain," he continued condescendingly, "I have no doubt you'll manage to get your man out of Algiers."

Fallon could only stare at the floor in anger. He rose, his wine untouched, and with a few words left Elliot's great cabin. He was none the wiser for having come.

As he dropped into his gig it was clear to him that he was on his own.

Forty-One

In a matter of days *Renegade* weighed, carrying four months-worth of supplies: over five hundred barrels of beef, pork, flour and meal; seven hundred bushels of beans and potatoes; some forty tons of rice, fish, cheese, candles, soap, bread and butter; eighteen hundred gallons of molasses, vinegar, and lamp oil; and over six thousand gallons of rum. All this plus every orange, lemon, and pineapple that could be crammed into whatever space was available, which was quite a lot.

The big ship plunged into the Atlantic under a dome of blue sky fringed with puffy clouds like the white hair around an old man's bald head. Jones had *Renegade* carrying every sail consonant with the eighteen knot breeze. He ran his ship according to the book. It was a taut ship, a good ship, not too harsh, not too lenient, a model Royal Navy ship. Admiral Davies had no worry for the men's health or happiness on *Renegade* with Jones in command, for they seemed cheerfully accepting of their lot as underpaid, overworked, prone-to-death by broadside sailors. It was a remarkable testament to the average jack that he could find comfort in tedious routine, cheer in harsh conditions and endure ship's fare that the average British citizen couldn't stomach, hot or cold. In fact, Royal Navy tars could withstand almost anything, any deprivation except the loss of their tot of rum. Harsh captains who stopped a crew's rum had been known to face mutiny.

Sir William Huntington-James had come aboard in the forenoon and Jones had seen him settled in his cabin—the first lieutenant's quarters being made available for him—and invited him to dinner that evening. Jones was naive to intrigue and curious about what exactly Sir

William *did.* And how he went about it. He didn't expect to learn much but perhaps something would come out over wine.

Davies had shared the dispatch from the Admiralty with Jones, though he noted it hadn't stated when the siege of Gibraltar was contemplated, or whether the dey of Algiers' role was crucial. Davies expressed that it probably wasn't, but it would certainly make things more difficult for the Royal Navy. Sixty corsairs turning their attention to British ships would make resupplying Gibraltar virtually impossible by sea given the scattered forces under the Admiralty's command.

It took all of Great Britain's armed cutters, sloops, brigs, frigates, and ships-of-the-line just to maintain blockades along the French coastline and bring pressure to bear on Bonaparte at sea. One more theatre of action would likely prove too much and stretch Great Britain too far. One had only to look at the outrageous treaties with the Barbary regencies to realize that if Great Britain had the ships to control the Mediterranean it would never pay to purchase peace. Every corsair would be sunk without quarter and every palace bombed to the ground.

The thought of Great Britain's acquiescence to the Barbary pirates confused Jones, who knew nothing of world affairs, particularly a world so alien to his own. But perhaps he would learn a great deal at dinner with Sir William.

He paced the windward side of the ship and thought of his friend Nicholas Fallon, weeks ahead of him and perhaps even now through the Strait. No doubt Sir William would want to know exactly what Fallon intended in the Mediterranean.

The thing was, Jones had no idea.

Several days spent in Gibraltar getting provisions on board and Fallon knew little more than he'd already learned. The customs official seemed as confused as everyone else as to the dey's intentions, but that was not unusual. *The dey depends on the day,* he'd said without humor. At a question about Zabana the customs official stiffened. He was, the official said, *rapacious,* literally living on prey.

Beauty was able to procure a longboat to replace the one blown up and Cully restocked the shot locker. Barrels of water and sacks of biscuit had also come aboard. In all respects, *Rascal* was ready for sea, except that the sea in question was the Mediterranean and Fallon had not yet settled on a plan for entering Algiers.

After a great deal of pacing the deck he decided to leave *Rascal* hove-to off the harbor's entrance, flying the tricolor, and go ashore in his gig as a French privateer capitaine; well, being British was certainly no guarantee of safe passage. As far as he knew, the French were on good terms with the Barbary regencies and he spoke French well enough to fool all but a Frenchman. Once ashore, he would endeavor to find O'Brien or even the British consul and seek their advice. At all accounts it seemed wise to keep their mission a secret until he had the lay of the land. If the dey knew there was a fortune in gold aboard a ship outside his harbor Fallon's options would considerably narrow.

He reviewed the plan with Beauty, Aja, Barclay, and Visser at dinner and no one had a better idea. Visser was noticeably quiet, and it seemed to Fallon that now that he was so close he was losing his hope, or perhaps he was just overcome with apprehension at what they would find in Algiers.

In truth, Fallon hadn't a clue.

Zabana grew impatient for the return of Hasim and Rogers. They should have already sailed into Algiers with slaves, or at least with excuses, but the fact that they were not back didn't worry him as much as it made him angry.

He was not alone. The dey's good humor had vanished after the first corsair successes and the subsequent auction and he now sent a messenger to *Serpent* daily to ask when Zabana was going to leave his garden again.

So Zabana had gotten his ship ready for sea once more. Stores had been brought aboard and the beheading cart's blade was polished and sharpened in full view of the crew as an instructional aid to discipline.

At last the ship was ready to leave Algiers again and Zabana left his mistress's warm bed and walked down the zagged streets to the quay. He stood for a moment judging his ship's lines. She was full of stores and would need to be balanced just so to sail her best. Satisfied that *Serpent* looked ready for sea he boarded the ship from the quay and called all hands to make sail.

Zabana walked the deck as *Serpent* slowly gathered speed and soon sailed west into the morning, towards the Strait, for he wanted to see if there was any sign of his two missing corsairs.

Forty-Two

Rascal weighed and left Gibraltar under lowering clouds. The dark, heavy sky looked troubled enough to moan or perhaps cry soon. It was still early and there was very little wind and the air was humid and heavy. Several crewmen looked astern at Gibraltar, and safety, receding into a blur of masts and mist and mountain.

Fallon watched Aja put the ship's boys to work polishing the brass and copper fittings about the binnacle and deck. Little Eddy fit right in and seeing him at tasks with the other youngsters was a natural thing not to be wondered at. He was recovering from the falling block and had only purplish bruises to show for it. He seemed to be back to his old self.

His old self meant tricks and pranks; yet somehow whatever mischief he caused, and there was believed to be a lot of it, never led back to him. A rat in a sea chest, a loose tie on a swinging cot that mysteriously came undone, a wet nightshirt. These incidents and more amused the crew and kept them guessing what would come next. Fallon thought back to his own beginning as a ship's boy but couldn't remember being as clever as Little Eddy, particularly at not getting caught.

Beauty had all sails up and drawing as best they could in the light airs and the ship crept along through the desultory morning. The crew was edgy with the knowledge that they would be sailing to a land exotic and mysterious and dangerous, the very home of the corsairs who'd attacked their ship.

There were no other ships to be seen under the low horizon as *Rascal* sailed slowly into the Mediterranean. It was not lost on Fallon that the great navies of the world, and the great naval commanders, had sailed into these very waters for hundreds of years. Nelson had entered the Mediterranean several years before and gained fame at the Battle of the Nile, defeating the French navy and Bonaparte's aspirations in Egypt while being wounded. Davies had said Nelson was outraged that Great Britain paid a yearly tribute to sail in the very sea he had conquered.

As Fallon stood at the taffrail he could hear Beauty's wooden peg thumping towards him and he imagined the gist of the conversation they were about to have. He'd heard rumors and concerns among the crew and guessed what was on Beauty's mind. He was not wrong.

Beauty looked at their slight wake, no more than a trifle really in the light breeze from the west, and then at the dark sky that seemed to engulf the world. She wasn't concerned for the weather, for she saw no thunderheads that could come crashing down on them. The ship was fine, but she wasn't.

"Nico," she began tentatively, "the men know that the Muslims want white Christians as slaves in Algeria. And they've heard they can be *perverse* with their slaves, if you know what I mean. No one wants that, Nico, and the men would rather die fighting than be taken. They wanted me to tell you."

Fallon was about to respond when there was the sound of the sky moaning in the distance. Or was that a cannon?

The American packet *Mary of Dundee* had cleared the Strait without incident and was plodding along towards the east. She had enough in her holds to make the year for the captain and crew and their excitement at selling their cargo was only tempered by the wild stories they'd heard about Barbary pirates. Everyone was on edge and anxious for a slant of wind.

It was late in the afternoon when the lookout reported what they all feared: a big xebec to the southeast crawling towards them. In the light air it couldn't be told if she would reach them before dark, however. The xebec was sailing northwest, *Mary* sailing east with the light and fickle wind behind her. Captain Silas McDonald paced the deck deep in concern, but not outright panic, though he repeatedly asked his first mate when it would begin to grow dark.

Perhaps it wouldn't matter. Even now the lookout reported the xebec's sweeps had turned their ship's head directly towards *Mary of Dundee* and she was gathering speed.

Zabana paced the deck of *Serpent* in anticipation of the coming battle. His sweeps were rowing powerfully, the janissaries were massed along the railings and at the bows of the galley and he could see no reason for failure. At a mile he ordered the gun crew to load the bow chaser and fire a shot across the American trader's bow, the signal to heave-to. It was a massive blast, landing well off the merchant ship's bows, but it apparently lacked the desired effect for the ship sailed slowly on. That put Zabana in a quiet rage, and he urged the helmsman to bring the big xebec to the side of the prize.

He intended to board her.

Every sail aboard *Rascal* was up and she was sailing wing on wing, with the main out to starboard and the foresail out to larboard. Nothing could be seen yet from the deck, but the lookout had reported an American trader under fire from a large rowed ship flying Algerian colors.

Fallon walked to *Rascal's* stern and looked out to the west for wind. There *might* be something on the water in the distance, but he couldn't be sure. He reached into his pocket and pulled out a guinea, gave it a quick kiss and threw it overboard. *Bring me a flaw of wind,* he said under his breath. Barclay watched him and smiled to himself, for he had done the same thing many times in his life. It was an old sailor's superstition.

Fallon turned back to the binnacle where Beauty and Aja waited for orders. As he opened his mouth to speak he felt something on his neck, just a little something to move the hairs, and he quickly turned around to see cat's paws creeping across the sea in *Rascal's* direction. *Wind!*

"I swear, Nico," exclaimed Beauty. "You are the luckiest fucker in the world."

"Better lucky than smart," said Fallon with a grin. "Let's ride this for all its worth! Aja, have the colors sent up and ask Cully to stand by the long nine."

Rascal rode the leading edge of the small breeze, making just a few knots as the wind pushed the ship along to the east. Fallon was just reaching for his telescope to see what could be seen from the deck when the lookout's call came.

"Deck there! The Arab is going to cut her off!"

Yes, Fallon could see the big xebec rowing on a converging course to the slow moving American. In his telescope he could see the xebec had a large, protruding bowsprit that seemed to be . . . he adjusted his telescope, yes, it had a snake wrapped around it.

So, Serpent*!*

Now Cully signaled he was ready, and *Rascal's* bow chaser thundered out its nine 9-lb. ball just wide of the xebec. *Rascal* was coming down towards the big merchantman and bringing the breeze with her, but Fallon knew *Serpent* would get there first.

Two minutes. *Whump!* went the long nine again and all hands looked for the fall of the shot. Fallon and Beauty both shrugged at not seeing a splash, when suddenly *Serpent's* larboard oars stopped momentarily. The ball had come aboard in the center of the sweeps and several oars were out of commission. But just as quickly the rest began rowing and *Serpent* drew ever closer to the American.

"Good shooting, Cully! By God!" yelled Fallon. "Reload!" He was in a fever to join the battle now, oblivious of the odds that awaited him not a cable's distance away.

But something new.

Fallon could hear wild shouting and banging and a trumpet blowing across the water as the janissaries beat on the side of the their ship, a tactic that no doubt scared the wits out of *Mary's* crew. But *Mary* fired her small 6-pounders as rapidly as she could and kept it up until the xebec was expertly brought alongside the merchantman. Janissaries carrying muskets and swords were over the side in an instant but the Americans were fighting back and the sound of musket pops could be heard across the water.

"Beauty!" yelled Fallon. "Lay us along the xebec's starboard side! Boarders ready!"

And then a quick thought.

"Cully!" called Fallon. "Load the larboard battery with grapeshot and run out! Fire when we're alongside!"

Beauty deftly brought *Rascal* up towards *Serpent's* side as Fallon had ordered and the grappling hooks were about to be thrown out.

Suddenly, *Rascal's* larboard battery thundered its nine guns in unison and the janissaries that seconds ago had massed along *Serpent's* starboard railing went down like pins in a child's game, their bodies punctured by hundreds of iron balls at point blank range. Fallon saw red hats blown away and bodies fly backwards and swords and muskets tossed in the air. For a moment he thought he saw a guillotine on the xebec's deck behind the janissaries—was he mistaken?—but in the smoke it was impossible to tell.

Now the ships were lashed together but before Fallon's crew could leap aboard the xebec the janissaries were on *Rascal's* deck and taking the fight to them. Fallon jumped into the fighting and cleaved a janissary's head almost in half, his hat falling away in two pieces. Above *Rascal* on the American ship's deck the fighting was hand to hand, as well, but Fallon had his own men to worry about. Blood and bodies caused both sides to trip and fall as they lunged and hacked at each other. Cully's broadside had decimated the dey's elite fighters but pride and fury drove them to attack and attack again.

Fallon and Aja fought side by side and covered each other's backs as they hacked and cut their way into the center of the fighting aboard *Rascal.* The Rascals screamed as loudly as the janissaries and it seemed to give the smaller American crew heart as they fought nearby. Then, a trumpet blew and it appeared to swell the janissaries' pride for they surged and attacked even more vigorously. But here was Cully swinging a musket in a roundhouse and driving the trumpet through the back of the trumpeter's throat. Fallon heard Beauty rally the men and he knew he was in danger of losing *Rascal* if they gave any quarter. He saw Aja stab a janissary in the stomach with his dirk, the man appearing surprised at the pain as he raised his scimitar but Fallon plunged his own sword into the man's neck. The fighting was vicious and Rascals were flailing and falling and blood was leaking over the sides of all three ships.

Now it was growing darker and starting to rain. Zabana was beside himself with fury but he knew in the logical part of his mind that the tide had turned and he must quit the fight. The British broadside had killed too many janissaries and his own crew were getting hacked to pieces, as well. It was better to escape with some slaves than to lose his ship, and he signaled for the agha to recall his men. The agha screamed for his soldiers to capture anyone they could and get back to the ship. The crowd of red caps fell back, clawing at the Rascals and the American crewmen as they retreated and tried to pull men down into their xebec. Fallon threw himself after them, slashing at first one janissary and then another, swinging his sword so fiercely that he cut off both hands of a big brute of a man who was reaching for Aja. A final push at the last of the boarders and now only one was left to scream in defiance on *Rascal's* deck, scream until Beauty thrust a boarding pike through his belly, his eyes opening in astonishment that a woman, a *woman!* had done this to him.

Zabana watched as several captives were dragged aboard and he ordered the grappling lines cut and the oarsmen pushed off *Rascal* and *Mary* to get clear. The xebec began to creep to the east with the wind behind her.

Zabana saw a man he took for the British captain run to the bow of the schooner and look at him as *Serpent* pulled away. *Who was this?* he wondered. A few more musket shots into the heavy rain and darkness and *Serpent* had gathered way downwind towards Algiers.

"Beauty!" A weary Fallon called as he walked back to the stern after getting a good look at the xebec's captain. "Let's get alongside *Mary* so we can get the wounded aboard *Rascal*. Aja, get a prize crew ready!" It was all he could do to stand.

By the time *Rascal* had grappled onto *Mary of Dundee* and the wounded Rascals got aboard and down belowdecks it was dark indeed. The American crew was small, and most were either taken by the janissaries or dead. Unfortunately, Silas McDonald was found with a bullet hole between his eyes, staring sightless up towards the raining sky. Aja took command, for *Mary's* second was dead, as well, and ordered the ship to wear and make for Gibraltar.

At last, Beauty wore ship and settled *Rascal* on her course back to Gibraltar, as well, her decks littered with heaps of dead janissaries. They would need to be given a decent burial in the morning, though Fallon was not sure what a decent Muslim burial should be. He debated simply throwing them overboard but thought better of it. He looked over his shoulder and could sense, if he couldn't see, the merchantman behind him, making the best way she could.

It was eerily quiet except for the creaking of blocks and the gurgle of water past the hull. But Fallon knew there would be moaning aplenty below decks as Colquist bent to the wounded and he left the deck to go below and offer what comfort he could. He was met by the surgeon who pulled him aside to give his report.

"Captain, we lost twelve men, though I have no idea how many are on the deck. I have seventeen here wounded, most with lacerations, although one man had an ear shot off. I expect all of them to live. But captain, Caleb Visser is one of the wounded and he has asked to see you repeatedly. I'm afraid it is bad news."

Fallon found Visser laying on a cot with his left shoulder oozing blood through a bandage. He looked half-mad with pain and anxiety.

"Oh, Captain," he said through clenched teeth. "Thank God you've come. Nicholas, I was fighting the heathens on *Rascal's* deck and was slashed to the bone. As I fell I saw Little Eddy . . ."

"Don't tell me he's wounded?" Fallon exclaimed anxiously, fearing the worst. But it was worse than the worst.

"No, he's gone," said Visser. "They took him, Nicholas. They took Little Eddy."

Forty-Three

The rain slacked at last and *Rascal* and *Mary of Dundee* tacked against the light westerly all night and it was the first dog the next day when the two ships at last glided into the shadow of Gibraltar. *Rascal's* decks had been holystoned back to their usual whiteness and the dead crew and janissaries had all been given a decent, though Christian, burial at dawn. It was all Fallon knew how to do and if the janissaries didn't like it they could complain all they wanted.

There was a pall over the ship, a dreadful something beyond melancholy, palpable and sad and fearful. Little Eddy had become the ship's favorite, and now he was gone, taken for a slave, and the crew feared they knew *what kind of slave.*

Little Eddy's kidnapping had raised the stakes, raised them to the moon, and every man vowed to do whatever was necessary to get him back. Fallon considered re-visiting Elliott to ask for help, but just as quickly re-considered, for it would do no good. Elliott would not be leaving the safety of Gibraltar if he could help it.

Aja anchored *Mary* near *Rascal* and Fallon decided to send him ashore to enquire about an American representative in Gibraltar. The ship and cargo could be sold and the proceeds sent to the captain and crews' families, for Fallon wanted none of it. He was now after bigger game.

After his own ship was secure Fallon retreated to his cabin to think through the situation. He was wracked with anxiety and fear himself, but he needed to consider what options he had. The more he thought about it, however, he couldn't think of one. At least, not a good one.

So, a dinner. Somber and grim.

"I think we all know we have to go to Algiers, no matter what it takes," Fallon began after a sip of wine. "Now more than ever." He was addressing Beauty, Barclay, and Aja in his cabin over lamb stew and vegetables, the dinner barely touched. Poor Visser was below decks recovering from his wound which, Colquist confirmed, had gone right to the bone.

"The French masquerade might have been a good one but now it won't work," said Fallon. "Zabana knows we're British. And if we go near the harbor and he's there who knows what will happen. Great Britain's treaty with the dey is obviously rubbish. Two hundred guns could shoot us to splinters very quickly."

"Goddammit," was all that Beauty could say. And everyone nodded, yes, *Goddammit.*

No one had anything else to say as the dishes were cleared and the pudding was brought out to sit patiently on the sideboard.

Fallon ordered more wine on the chance that it would spur conversation and ideas and take the stale air of desperation out of the cabin. He also laid out a chart from Gibraltar to Algeria and began studying it. The coastline of Algeria was indented here and there with natural harbors protected from all but northerlies. But the coastline was shallow, hence the xebecs and galleys favored in this part of the world.

Aja had been looking at the chart closely, watching Fallon's finger trace the coastline between Tangier and Tunis. It was almost perfectly designed as a hunting ground for pirates, with an endless succession of small bays and coves. He excused himself for a moment and left the cabin and Beauty rose to stand at the open gallery windows. The air coming into the cabin was dry and hot, the breeze coming from an unseen desert many miles away. Gibraltar was bustling with late afternoon activity as cargoes were loaded and unloaded and the hoys and luggers sailed in and out of the anchored ships delivering passengers, supplies, crews, and captains.

A brief intake of air, perhaps a gasp from Barclay, and Beauty turned around and Fallon looked up. For Aja had returned to the cabin dressed in a white, flowing caftan with a swirl of cloth on his head like a turban. He stood before the group barefooted and unsmiling, but his eyes danced.

No one said anything at first. They all just stared at Aja. Fallon stared, as well, for what he was seeing was a plan to get Little Eddy and Wilhelm Visser out of Algeria.

At that moment Little Eddy was chained in *Serpent's* hold, exhausted from crying and calling for help. A rat had scurried past his feet in the darkness and terrified him and he had drawn his legs up as far as the chain would allow to form a human ball.

Two decks above him Zabana paced his cabin in cold fury. His janissary contingent was totally decimated, the American merchantman had escaped, and all he had to show for it was a few Christian men and a boy in the holds where a hundred slaves should have been. Zabana wanted to hurt the boy because he had come from the British ship, or even torture and kill him in blind anger but even one slave was worth something, and a boy would be worth more than something to the right bidder.

He had forgotten all about Rogers and Hasim and turned his attention to the British schooner which had thwarted his plan to take the American merchantman. That was the real problem, not any failure of his own. Why was she here in the Mediterranean?

He would see the British captain who had mauled his ship and killed so many of his men beg for mercy before his cart. But there would be no mercy. He would cut off a limb at a time, then castrate him, before finally cutting off his head.

He would order his men to work day and night to repair his flagship and he must replace the slaves and janissaries he had lost to the British broadside. Then he would set off again, hunting, particularly for a certain ship.

He came out of his revenge induced reverie with a start, for first he would have to see Mustapha Pasha and report on his failure to take the American packet because of the intercession of the British schooner.

He did not expect the interview to go well.

The plan was coming together now in Fallon's mind and his finger stabbed at the chart as the little group in his cabin tried to see what he was seeing. Algeria lay on the southern side of the Mediterranean, with the port city of Algiers some little way beyond the Strait itself. There were indentations in the coastline aplenty, particularly past Tipasa, an ancient city several days' walk from Algiers.

"Beauty," said Fallon, a new determination in his voice, "I want you to land Aja and me here, just past Tipasa." He pointed to a small cove on the chart. It was shallow but the ship's gig should have no trouble landing there. "Aja is an African, to all accounts, and I am his Christian slave, head down, weary, dejected. We should be able to make our way to Algiers in two days or so. Meanwhile, Beauty, return here to Gibraltar. Give us two weeks, then sail back to pick us up at the same spot. We'll find O'Brien or the British consul or somebody who can tell us how to get Little Eddy and Wilhelm Visser back." And he said it in such a way that everyone in the cabin knew he would not be taking no for an answer.

"And if you're not there, Nico?" asked Beauty. "What then?"

Fallon looked at the chart of the harbor. The fortifications. The mole. And he remembered Sir William's words: *no one ever knows with these fellows.*

"In that case, I think you'll be getting a ransom note unless I am very much mistaken."

That brought everyone up short, but they could see that Fallon was committed to the idea now and, really, what else could they do? The thought of Little Eddy being sold in a slave market was more than any of them could bear and it brought a certain urgency to the room. It was not lost on any of them that they now felt what Caleb Visser had felt all along.

That night Fallon lay on the stern cushions with a glass of wine and thought of everything that could go wrong with his plan. Once ashore, he and Aja would be on their own and would have to make the most of any situation they faced. He had no fear for Aja's quick wit and could trust him to act decisively.

The problem, of course, was that Aja couldn't speak Arabic or whatever the language was that Muslims on the Barbary Coast spoke. He might look the part of a Muslim but he couldn't speak the part. Fallon would have to rely on lingua franca if it came to speaking. He decided they would both carry a dirk and a pistol under their robes in case there was a misunderstanding they couldn't mumble their way out of.

Forty-Four

Rascal crept towards Tipasa under a moonless sky as Aja and Fallon got dressed in Fallon's cabin. The sea chest which had been salvaged after the corsair attack had yielded caftans and headwear and a pair of sandals. The carpenter had been able to replicate a second pair of sandals from tanned leather he'd purchased in Gibraltar and sew the caftans to fit. When they were finished dressing, Fallon and Aja came on deck to be gawked at and admired, for the transformation was really quite complete.

An hour before dawn *Rascal's* gig was lowered over the side as the ship lay hove-to some thirty-five miles past Tipasa in a small, shallow cove. Fallon had said goodbye to Caleb Visser below decks and Visser's eyes had been full of gratitude. The American promised to pray every night for Fallon's safe return, for he knew without knowing how dangerous the coming days would be.

On deck, Beauty pulled Fallon aside for a last word.

"You know, Nico," she said, "you are the only family I have and I love you like my brother. You be sure to be here when I come back or these Muslim fuckers are going to get the full wrath of the McFarland clan." And then she opened his hand and put her necklace with the rawhide string in his palm, the wooden sea dog that Fallon had carved for her. "Wear this for good luck, Nico. *Sea Dog* brought us back together once before. Bring this back to me and put it in my hand just like I am putting it in yours. Then I'll know you're safe."

"Thank you, Beauty," said Fallon gratefully as he tied the necklace around his neck. "I'll need all the luck I can get."

With that, Fallon and Aja climbed down into the gig and were rowed away to the shore of the Barbary coast. The gig beached easily and master and slave stepped ashore, the slave carrying a canvas bag with food and water on his back. They set off towards the east, towards Algiers and an unknown world.

Once they moved more inland the sand became packed and they stumbled upon an ancient track that headed eastward, no doubt travelled by Arabs for hundreds of years or perhaps thousands. Fallon and Aja said little, both acutely aware they were strangers in a strange land and they had better get used to not speaking English. The first travelers they saw were headed west towards Tipasa and, as they approached, both Aja and Fallon held their breath. This was the first test, and Fallon kept his head down while Aja held his high. But the travelers paid them no mind and continued on their way. The first test was passed and they began to breathe normally again.

That night they camped some little ways from the trail, gathering dead twigs to build a small fire. They ate their dinner and lay down next to each other for warmth, for the spring night was chilly.

"How are you doing captain, sir?" asked Aja in barely above a whisper. "Is the load very heavy?"

"I'm fine, Aja," said Fallon, also in a whisper, though he thought it probably not necessary. "I think we might reach the city by tomorrow evening. And then the real test begins."

They drifted off to sleep under a starry sky full of old friends, the planets and stars of a hundred passages on distant waters. They had perhaps slept for several hours when suddenly there was a sound, a padded kind of *thump*, then another, and as they raised up they saw a camel walking towards them. Riding the camel was a large man dressed more or less as they were, except most of his face was covered by a scarf, and leading the camel was another, smaller man dressed and covered similarly. Fallon suspected they were Bedouins, desert dwellers who were said to be the original Arabs and who travelled by camel across Africa in a nomadic existence.

O'Brien's diary had described Bedouins as clannish, keeping to themselves and the desert and only occasionally visiting cities like Algiers to trade camels or goats. Fallon remembered O'Brien's description of their fractious loyalties. One Bedouin aphorism captured the complexity: *I am against my brother, my brother and I are against my cousin, my cousin and I are against the stranger.*

The Bedouins were approaching two strangers.

As the larger Bedouin on the camel dismounted Aja stood up. Fallon thought it best to remain seated in subservience, but he slid his hand into the slit of his caftan and found his pistol. He noticed that both men carried small, curved swords in sashes around their waists.

Aja took the initiative to speak first, in his native African dialect, and opened his arms in welcoming friendship. Fallon could see it surprised and confused the Bedouins, who likely did not understand, and they stepped closer to the fire.

The larger Bedouin spoke to Aja in what Fallon supposed was Arabic. Aja looked at Fallon quizzically, wondering what to do. It was clear that no one understood anyone so far.

And then the other, smaller Bedouin stepped closer and looked at Fallon carefully; it was obvious Fallon was not Arabic and was probably Christian.

"We are curious if we are among friends or enemies," the smaller Bedouin asked in lingua franca. "Do you understand me? Who are you and where are you going?"

Fallon froze at a question he had not anticipated, but he understood it at least.

"I am Armand," Fallon said, thinking quickly. "My master is from Senegal, to the south, and we are traveling to Algiers." He hoped that would explain Aja's language. The larger Bedouin remained stoic, unmoved, never taking his eyes off Aja. Fallon remained on high alert, sensing a dangerous moment.

"Why do you go to Algiers?" asked the Bedouin facing Aja.

"I am to be sold there," answered Fallon, as if the question had been directed to him.

The Bedouins were unmoved. They studied Aja's face, and then Fallon's face carefully, as if trying to make up their minds about what to believe, or do.

"Do you know *Bisha'a?*" said the small man to Fallon with a sneer that Fallon didn't like.

Fallon shook his head no.

"*Bisha'a* is how we know if you are lying," said the Bedouin, lowering his scarf to reveal a smile. And then as if on cue both men pulled their small swords from their waistbands and the big man pushed Aja down beside Fallon.

Fallon's hand was still on the butt of his pistol under his caftan. He had no idea what the Bedouins intended to do, or what the test they called *Bisha'a* was, but he had no doubt they would fail it.

The larger Bedouin retrieved a knife from a satchel on the camel, which had lain down and was watching contentedly. Then he thrust the knife into the hot coals and waited patiently by the fire, his sword back in his waistband, his hands hanging at his sides.

"*Bisha'a* is a test of deception," said the smaller Bedouin, waving his own sword in Fallon's face. "A truthful man has nothing to fear." He looked at Aja, who was looking hard at the knife in the fire. "Your master will lick the blade of the knife three times. If his tongue does not burn it will mean you are telling the truth."

"What if it does burn his tongue?" asked Fallon, as casually as he could.

"Then we kill you," said the Bedouin matter-of-factly. "A simple test. Speak to your master."

Fallon's head snapped back involuntarily, but he leaned over to Aja and whispered: "They want you to lick the knife to see if we are telling the truth. Use the big man's sword when the time comes to act."

Aja nodded, cool and unblinking, trying to project a confidence he did not feel. Once again Fallon appreciated his presence of mind under pressure.

Slowly, the knife's blade began to glow a bright red. A few moments more, and the larger man withdrew it from the ashes and beckoned Aja to stand. The knife was brought up to Aja's face and the Bedouin said *Bisha'a* softly, his eyes widening in anticipation of the coming pain.

Aja bravely moved closer to the knife, as if he had nothing to fear, but he glanced to the big man's belly and the sword in his waistband. The smaller Bedouin watched raptly as Aja slowly opened his mouth and stuck out his tongue. It was then that Fallon saw his chance and lunged forward to grab the smaller Bedouin's arm that held the sword and pull him down. The big man's attention went quickly to the fight and Aja reached for the man's sword and quickly withdrew it. The Bedouin still held the hot knife in front of him but Aja sliced downwards with all his might and almost severed the man's arm. An upward thrust to his belly, a gurgling scream, and the Bedouin staggered and fell backwards on top of the fire.

Now a shot, muffled. Aja turned as Fallon rolled the smaller Bedouin to the side and stood up, the man's caftan turning red around a small hole near his neck.

"Good job, Aja," said Fallon. "But I guess we're not as convincing as we hoped. Let's get this one out of the fire and get their clothes and scarves and weapons off of them. Then we'll get them buried."

Without another word they laid the two Bedouins next to each other wearing only their wounds. The camel had not risen but merely watched the scene with a certain insouciance common to the breed.

They had no choice but to dig shallow graves by hand and sword and this took the better part of the night, for they continually stopped to listen for anyone approaching. The sand was softer off the path but not so soft that the work was fast or easy. When at last they had two graves dug they rolled the dead Bedouins into them and covered the bodies with sand. By morning some brush had been found to lay loosely on top to help provide cover. They rousted the camel to stand and Fallon boosted Aja up on it. He looked down at Fallon and smiled, then they both laughed, for it was a totally incongruous situation they'd gotten themselves into.

And there was still a whole day to go.

Forty-Five

It was dawn when *Serpent* reached the quay inside Algiers' harbor and a deeply humiliated Zabana ordered the captives to be off-loaded and taken to the slave pens. There were several ships at the quay being unloaded and *Serpent* was the farthest from the gate. That suited Zabana's mood, for he had no wish to be seen by the dey until he was ready.

He would sail the world if he had to in order to find the British schooner that had stolen his prize from him. Resentment seethed inside Zabana as he looked longingly at his beheading cart, imagining everything he was going to do to the schooner's infidel captain.

First, he would have to confess his loss to the dey. He would lie about the attack and claim he fought valiantly against a bigger ship, perhaps a large frigate.

And she would be British, of course.

Wilhelm Visser was on the quay as usual with a bag of wheat on his shoulder when he saw wounded and bedraggled sailors and janissaries being led off Zabana's ship. He saw new captives being marched towards the pens, and among them was a young boy. He looked to be about eight, and Visser was immediately gripped by fear for him. He would no doubt be sold at the slave auction with all the other prisoners that Zabana's corsairs had captured, and he knew that certain Arabs liked young boys for pleasure.

What could he do?

He thought of his own sons at that age, young and full of life and *trusting*, and he thought he would be sick. The boy looked at him as he was led away and Visser looked back, a promise in his eyes that he had no idea how to fulfill.

And then, an idea. There was nothing to lose by trying, he decided.

After so long in captivity and constantly acquiescing to their demands, the guards on the dock had come to know Visser and trust him more than most slaves. In truth, he had never given the guards any reason to mistrust him.

So it was not unnatural for him to approach the head guard overseeing the other slaves on the quay to ask a favor. With all the wickedness he could summon in a smile he asked if he and the boy could have a pen to themselves.

The head guard smiled back wickedly, as well. Then the other guards joined in, smiling knowingly.

It could be arranged.

Fallon and Aja slowly crossed the desert and no one stopped them or paid much notice. To all accounts they looked like Bedouins, or hoped they did, and their faces were covered with scarves to present only their eyes to the curious. As they drew closer to Algiers the travelers they met grew more numerous and, if anything, paid even less attention to them. It grew much hotter in the middle of the day, and though Fallon longed to remove the scarf covering most of his face he dared not. Aja repeatedly asked if he would please ride the camel, but Fallon refused. His role was to be Aja's slave and he would trudge on; the more tired he became the more he looked the part.

The camel was a sturdy beast and easily followed Fallon. The Bedouins were known to be excellent camel trainers and the camel Aja rode proved the point. When they reached the edge of the city, however, they would set him free and go ahead on foot.

Algiers was not far away now. The track veered closer to the sea; Fallon could smell it close by, but without climbing a tree he could see no boats or sails. As the light began to fade in the late afternoon a small, hot breeze began blowing from the south. Out there somewhere was the fabled Sahara Desert with its miles upon miles of arid sand. It was said that all of Africa's myths and mirages originated there.

They decided to stop short of the city and make camp early, off the track as before, but without a fire. Fallon wanted to enter the city fresh the next morning, with his wits about him should quick thinking be required, which was more than likely. He calculated that Algiers must be only a few miles away. He tried to sleep, but all he could do was fret about how easily they had been found out by the Bedouins. There were so many cultural clues, he decided, that no amount of disguise could cover. Perhaps the way they held their heads, or met a gaze, or perhaps something just hadn't seemed *right* about them to the Bedouins.

As he thought ahead to what the next day would bring inside the city, he felt a cold shudder of fear. And it wasn't the cooling desert air he was feeling. He had a premonition of failure as powerful as any feeling he had felt in his life. And it was made all the more powerful by the knowledge that there was no turning back.

The long rollers of the Atlantic held moonlight as Jones took a turn around *Renegade's* deck. He stood at the taffrail and stared at the ship's wake, flecked with light that disappeared and reappeared. It seemed to stretch all the way back to Antigua.

Jones was the most junior on the captain's seniority list, but he was still a young man and the war and old age created vacancies on the list so he had no worry about moving up. He lived in the present; well, most of the time. And the present meant seeing his ship and his important passenger safely to the Mediterranean.

Sir William had said little at their dinner that first night to enlighten him as to his role in the events of the Mediterranean or his particular relationship with Lord Keith. Secrecy was apparently the watchword and, to that end, Sir William had kept more or less to himself since that dinner, no doubt to avoid unwanted conversation and prying questions. Jones had no real experience with men like Sir William, men who kept to the shadows and revealed a false front to the world. Perhaps Sir William sensed his curiosity and that made him all the more reclusive.

Admiral Davies had confided in Jones only that his passenger was an acquaintance of Lord Keith's, who relied on Sir William's insights gained as a businessman who moved more or less freely between nations in the Mediterranean. To Jones, even with his limited world view, that said *spy*. Jones' orders were to call at Gibraltar, ascertain Lord Keith's exact whereabouts, and deliver Sir William to him.

That, along with a letter entrusted to him by Admiral Davies.

Forty-Six

Fallon opened his eyes just before dawn. It took him a moment to focus but then he sat bolt upright, for he and Aja had been joined by a stranger in the night. The man sat cross-legged and looked at Fallon kindly with something like a beatific smile on his face.

Fallon shook Aja awake and they both stared unspeaking at the stranger. He was perhaps middle-aged or slightly older, round under his tunic which, even in the darkness, didn't appear to be traditional Bedouin or Arab dress. He still smiled under Fallon's appraisal, his hands folded on his lap with no weapon apparent. Nor any ill intent.

"Do you speak English?" said the man in English. "Or do you speak French?" said the man in French. "Or should we speak in Spanish?" said the man in Spanish.

"I speak all three languages," said Fallon without thinking. "But I would prefer to speak English."

"Excellent, good sir," said the man. "I am Friar Orturo, sometimes called *la blanche Friar*, or White Friar in some parts of Algiers. I apologize for giving you a fright, but I thought it best to not wake you unexpectedly in the middle of the night, for I saw you were armed and I did not want a misunderstanding. I suspected you were not Arab by your skin. Although your companion might well be."

"His name is Aja, and he is from Senegal," replied Fallon, at least telling that part of the truth. "He is my master."

"I see," said the Friar, without a hint of skepticism. "I was a slave myself once for two years. The corsairs took a Spanish trader I was on and imprisoned all of the crew and myself. We were sold at auction in the marketplace."

"How did you become free?" asked Fallon, immediately absorbed by this strange man's presence.

"I was always good at sketches, and one day my master asked me to draw his likeness in charcoal. I did, and he liked it so much he allowed me to draw others whom he knew, which I did. And they paid me. Instead of keeping the money himself, my master allowed me to buy my freedom a little at a time. Until one day I was free."

"And now?" asked Fallon, intrigued. "How can you be a friar in a Muslim country?"

"I don't try to convert anyone, certainly," said the friar. "My order was always passive and itinerant, anyway, created to wander this earth and help others through kindness. It was always my intention to live God's will in this way. I was always good with languages and I managed to pick up lingua franca within a year. I minister to those who need help finding their way in the world, no matter who they are. I often venture outside the walls of the city to seek out travelers. That's how I came upon you."

And then he resumed his smiling.

Fallon looked at Aja, who gave no expression back, and then looked at the friar again. He seemed to be who he said he was, and Fallon could not sniff an imposter or spy. But could he be trusted to help them?

"You are wondering, perhaps, if I can be trusted to be of some service to you," said the friar softly. "If it is God's will I will help you. If it is not, I will leave you."

Fallon was taken aback, even shocked, that his thoughts were so transparent. They had always been so with Elinore, but with a stranger? Was his face so expressive?

"I think we should ask this friar for guidance, captain, sir," said Aja suddenly, giving Fallon and the Friar a start. "He seems to read our minds anyway."

And so the story of Wilhelm and Caleb Visser came out as the sky lightened to the east. The attack by the corsairs, the taking of Little

Eddy, leaving out the encounter with the Bedouins and the lie detection test and ending with their hope to find Richard O'Brien, the American consul, and seek his advice for freeing Visser and, now, Little Eddy. Friar Orturo listened with his kindly mien, nodding at points along the way, but never interrupting. Fallon apologized for claiming to be a slave, genuinely sorry for lying to a holy man, his Anglican upbringing making him feel guilty.

"I am sorry to tell you that Captain O'Brien is not in Algiers at present," said the friar, waving away the apology, "but on his way back to America, where he goes periodically to consult with the government. I know him well; he is a good man. But I also tell you I know Wilhelm Visser is alive, but weak from overwork and poor food and has all but given up hope of going home. As to the boy, I'm afraid it will be impossible to rescue the boy as it is a deeply unfortunate circumstance that young boys and girls are highly prized as slaves here and the dey will not interfere in the auction of them. I'm sorry."

Most of the news, with the exception of Wilhelm Visser being alive, crushed Fallon and Aja. Any semblance of a plan was gone with O'Brien, and Little Eddy seemed doomed to slavery or worse.

"You are wondering what is to be done now, I believe," said the friar, once again a mind reader.

"Yes," admitted Fallon sadly.

"No one has ever been rescued from the prison," said the friar. "And, if I may, any attempt to interfere with the auction will result in the worst punishment. You will be caught and killed, probably horribly. Sometimes they throw prisoners who try to escape over the wall, a symbolic escape I suppose, except that I am told there are hooks placed there to receive the poor souls and they are impaled. Those who don't die immediately are left to twist on the hooks until they do. I suspect that would be your fate. Both of you."

"But what are we to do, friar, sir," asked Aja, whose eyes were now wide with fear and worry.

"Sometimes, my brother, we cannot interfere with life," said the friar, reflecting his avowed passivity. "Especially life in a country not our own.

They have customs and ideas here that seem strange to outsiders, even hostile or barbaric, but not to them. To them it is just life."

"There has to be a way," said Fallon, with determination and conviction he didn't really feel. "I don't plan to leave Algiers having done nothing."

Friar Orturo studied them both carefully, their faces now fully illuminated by the risen sun. Their apprehension was clear; well, they had come across an ocean to do something brave only to discover it was impossible.

"There is a belief in our order," he said, "that I know you will understand because you are sailors. If you are in a howling wind and you try to capture the wind in a box, what have you done? For now the wind in the box is just air. Similarly, if you stand by a fast-moving river and try to capture it in a bottle, what have you done? Now the fast-moving river is just water in a bottle. The parable is meant to describe our need to control life, which cannot be controlled. If we try to master it, we fail."

There was a noise, the rustle of the camel in harness as the beast shifted position.

"I understand the parable, friar," said Fallon quietly. "Perhaps as you say I am trying to control life. I am certainly trying to save a life. Two, actually. Does your faith allow you to help us in any way?"

"What is it you would have me do?" asked the friar.

"Is there a guard at the entrance to the city?" Fallon asked.

"Yes, there is a gate on this side of the city and it has a janissary to guard it. He looks very carefully at all who enter," replied the friar.

"Would you help us get inside then?" asked Fallon. "That's all we could ask. Just to get inside."

The friar thought for a moment. It was getting lighter now, the morning coming softly in the desert. The night's chill would soon be another memory.

"Yes," said the friar with a sigh, "I believe I can get you through the gate. But you will have to be good actors."

Fallon looked at Aja and they both laughed.

Forty-Seven

Friar Orturo led the way with Fallon and Aja trailing behind. The camel had been left at the campsite. It was a valuable animal and a Bedouin or passing traveler would count themselves lucky to find it.

They talked of many things as they walked, always silent, however, when passing fellow travelers. Friar Orturo was a learned man, and he put Fallon in mind of Ezra Somers, with the exception that Somers had a short fuse and was anything but passive, being prone to anger and even violence on occasion.

As they approached the city the friar suggested they throw away their weapons, which they did. Well, the obvious ones anyway. Up ahead a white wall stretched left and right as far as could be seen. In the middle of the wall was a black gate through which travelers passed. A tall janissary stood guard with a musket, carefully eyeing each person who approached.

As they drew closer, Friar Orturo whispered their cue, and Fallon and Aja began moving around in circles, laughing uproariously. The friar was gesturing with his arms, becoming animated as he spoke in Arabic to the guard.

Next, Fallon and Aja began picking imaginary flowers, laughing when they found a pretty one, moving about the desert picking and picking until they each had an imaginary bouquet. Then they placed the flowers one by one in each other's turban and went back to picking flowers. Slowly they found more flowers next to the gate and then there were some lovely ones just inside the gate within the city and they moved inside to pick those.

The janissary stared at them hard, but heeded the friar's pleas and let them pass, looking away in disgust as he did so.

Once inside the wall, Fallon and Aja continued picking flowers along the narrow path until it wound around to their right, out of sight of the gate.

"You are indeed wonderful actors, my friends," said the Friar, smiling benevolently. "The guard was compassionate and willingly let you pass."

"What did you tell him, pray, that convinced him to do so?" Fallon asked incongruously.

"Why, I told him the truth as I saw it," said the Friar mischievously. "I told him you were both crazy."

Fallon and Aja both smiled broadly.

"In the Islamic faith," the friar continued, "all diseases are trials and tests from Allah, even diseases of the mind. I told him you had weak minds and came to the city to pray and be cured."

"Thank you, Friar," said Fallon. "You have saved us a great deal of trouble getting into the city."

"No, my brothers," said the Friar, not unkindly. "Your trouble will be getting out."

And then he ambled away.

A group of janissaries came down their little path and Fallon and Aja kept their heads down, but they could see the red slippers of the janissaries as they marched past them. Once the soldiers were out of sight, they began walking slowly, Fallon behind Aja, to explore the city.

The sun glistened the white walls and the heat already shimmered off the rooftop terraces above the bright houses they passed. They wound their way along narrow streets and alleys barely wider than they could reach with their arms outstretched; the buildings seemed to almost lean over the streets and touch. In these shadowy passages, or *ruelles,* pirates and thieves had found easy anonymity for hundreds of years, slipping in and out of the safety of darkness unseen and unheard. Fallon and Aja halted next to an arched door with a black knocker in the shape of a fist to get their bearings, which proved quite impossible. A tiny passage, or *impasse*, wound away into shadows and they slipped along it until it opened in sunlight to a *souk*, or marketplace. Merchants called out to them, hawking their wares, but they dared not look up. Out of the corners of their eyes they could see bolts of silk and damask for sale on long tables next to crates of chickens and tables of jewelry and thrown vases. The day's business was in full swing.

As they came to an intersection of sorts they looked to their right up the hill and could see the qasba above a dense sea of houses broken by domed mosques and gold-topped minarets. And, above that, a blindingly white sentinel—the palace of the dey. Turning next to their left they could see a bit of the harbor, spectacularly blue in the clear light. Fallon counted a score of xebecs and feluccas, light galleys with oars, and all manner of smaller vessels. He moved his scarf a bit to get a better view but he could see no sign of Zabana's ship. That was good.

"Let's take this road down to the harbor," he whispered to Aja, who nodded and turned left. It was always the sailor's way to head to the sea; the water pulled at the heart. But this was not for sustenance, but recognizance. The road was made of cobblestones worn smooth by hundreds of years of foot traffic and in very little time they were through an open gate at the base of the lower city and stood on the quay. To their left, the long arm of the Great Mole that Sir William had described. It curved in a hook inward several hundred yards from the quay. Fallon could see a ship sailing near the mole that was festooned with banners and flags, which he took to be the pilot boat on patrol for ships wanting to enter the harbor. He knew from the chart the harbor was quite shallow in many places and a pilot would be needed to guide approaching ships to their anchorages.

To their right were various packets being unloaded by men in ragged clothes whom Fallon took for slaves. The ships looked to be Russian and Italian and could have been captures, but who could tell? A small knot of guards hovered near the slaves, fingering their scimitars or muskets as the men worked dutifully under their gaze. One slave seemed less vigorous, even bent and frail. Fallon wondered if this was Wilhelm Visser, but he dared not stare. A moment more, for they were afraid to stay longer, and with a murmur to Aja they turned and retraced their steps up the hill.

Now they could see up the road to the magnificent white palace with its tall walls pierced by the black circles of cannons. It was certainly in a commanding position to defend the city and, along with the cannon situated on the mole, made Algiers unassailable by sea by all but a fleet bombardment. To Fallon's mind, it made the decision to come on foot as opposed to sailing into the harbor the correct one.

The houses on either side of the road were like cubes of salt or sugar stacked on top of one another, marching up the hill towards the qasba. Fallon tugged Aja's sleeve and they turned left down a narrow path, across the steep hill, towards another busy marketplace. He hoped an opportunity would present itself in one of these souks to find someone European, hopefully British, anyone who could counsel them and give them the lay of the land.

The merchants were set up under porticos around a square, within which was an elaborate water fountain surrounded by low stone pedestals. Suddenly, Fallon knew this was the auction site for slaves; indeed, chains with manacles were attached to the pedestals. Fallon closed his eyes, imagining Little Eddy standing on the highest pedestal, the bidders surrounding him, touching his body and feeling his arms and legs and perhaps more. Fallon winced at the image and turned to look at Aja, whose eyes were glowing fiercely. They had both come to the same conclusion about the market and for Aja, in particular, the pedestals were a grim reminder of his own auction into slavery.

They pushed on through the square and found a bench against a tree upon which to rest. Their heads down, staring at their sandaled feet, they dared to talk quietly.

"Aja, what do you think so far?" whispered Fallon.

"I saw some men look at us strangely back in the market," said Aja softly. "I don't think we should stay here too long."

"Yes. But I wish we could find the prison where the slaves are held," said Fallon quietly. "Sir William said it was just above the harbor somewhere. Let's take another look and then we can find a spot in the shadows to consider next steps."

"I understand, captain, sir," said Aja. "I will lead the way as we walk."

But they were to have an escort. Just as they were about to rise more feet suddenly came into their downward view. Four pairs of feet with red slippers. A deep voice asked them a question which they did not understand. But what they knew was that their freedom was over.

Renegade had every sail up and drawing in the warm southerly as she bore the breeze to her bosom, taking all the wind's power for her own, her ropes straining with the great effort of driving a ship at full force under sail. Occasionally an unlucky sailor took a wash of green water over the bow to the jeers and laughter of his shipmates, and porpoises ran alongside for great stretches of time, easily keeping pace with the ship. It was glorious sailing, glorious enough to forget about the poor food and hard labor and meagre pay that was the lot of Royal Navy tars. A man could forget all his troubles on a day such as this.

The big ship was its own city. And each man had a job to do to make the city work efficiently. Any slacking was immediately felt throughout the ship and dealt with by the bosun or any of the lieutenants before word of the miscreant reached Captain Jones's ears. Jones had been aboard ships with loose captains who rarely came out of their cabins and barely took an interest in the running of the ship or the scuttlebutt on the lower decks. He had seen the lethargy that brought to a ship's company, and how rumor and mischief followed. He vowed if he ever had his own ship he would be a firm but compassionate captain and nothing would escape his notice. Of course, he expected every man to do his duty no matter the conditions or situation. The men were drilled and drilled again, and Jones delighted in the cries of the men racing each other aloft and the creaking of the big guns running in and out, in and out. He knew that repetition brought disciplined action in battle, when smoke and thunder could overwhelm the senses.

Renegade was just over a week from Gibraltar, her passage aided by the favorable slant of wind from the south that seemed constant day and night. The lookout had reported no other ships in sight since they'd left

English Harbor and it was easy to be lulled into a soft, easy sense of security, so easy that Jones worked the crew at exercises aloft and with the great guns to keep the men on their toes as they pushed further across the Atlantic and closer to Southern Europe.

It was just in the forenoon when all Jones' attention to preparation, all the sail changes aloft and practice with the great guns ceased being pure exercise.

"Deck there!" came the lookout's call from on high. "Ship off the larboard bow! I make her five miles away!"

That single report set every man on alert and Jones was called from his cabin to come on deck at once. Nothing could be seen from the deck yet, and a ship coming from Southern Europe could be from any country, but Jones wisely called *Beat to Quarters* and the drums rat-a-tatted as the men went to their stations. Shot and powder were brought out of the locker and the gun crews stood ready at their charges. The bulkheads were struck before the mysterious ship was four miles away.

"Lookout!" called Jones from the quarterdeck. "What do you make of her now?"

"A small frigate by the looks of her!" came the answer. "French or I'm damned!"

That sent excitement through *Renegade's* crew; to a ship so long in harbor on the ways the prospect of a prize was beyond welcome. The tension onboard was palpable and Jones felt it, as well, and he longed inexpressibly to command a ship in battle again. It had been a year since *Renegade* had been in action.

The ships were growing closer and Jones ordered the British colors to be hoisted to see if that would flush the same action from the oncoming ship. It did, the French capitaine showing unexpected spunk in the face of a bigger foe. On the ships came; on their present courses they would pass within a quarter mile of each other. Jones ordered the helmsman to fall off to leeward so as to close the gap and attempt to force the capitaine's hand before he had to show his own. *Renegade* had the weather gauge, though the French actually preferred to engage from leeward, a position that left them in a position to retreat before the wind. In fact, at a mile and a half the French ship bore off northward, the capitaine's spunk having evaporated, and ran before the wind in an attempt to outrun the big British ship. *Renegade* quickly fell off, as well, and followed.

"Deck there!" came the lookout's call. "She looks to be a Venus class!"

Jones knew immediately that he was chasing one of the class of small frigates favored by the French. He knew them to be lightly built, not from any want of good design or materials, but because of intent: French ships were not built to be away from port for any great length of time and thus the need to carry a great store of shot and supplies was limited. Jones pictured the ship in his mind and knew that she carried twenty-six 12-pounders and was probably a good sailer.

But not, as it turned out, as fast downwind as the much larger *Renegade*. Within two hours the British ship was up to her and her name could be read: *Honneur*. It was soon after that Jones had stolen the Frenchman's wind and forced the capitaine to accept the inevitable. This was a race he would not win. Without firing a shot he hauled down his colors and hove-to.

Renegade had her first prize in a very long time. After he had sent a boarding party across to *Honneur*, Jones began pacing the deck deep in thought, smiling to himself as he walked. It was not every day that a French prize could be taken without a shot. He wondered how it would look in the Gazette, and then he chided himself for caring.

Here was his gig coming back, hopefully carrying the capitaine's orders, assuming they hadn't been thrown overboard. At word that the French crew were locked below decks, Jones breathed easier and ordered *Renegade's* guns secured.

This battle, such as it was, was over.

It was much later when Jones sat in his cabin and pondered the interview with the French capitaine of *Honneur* which, to his mind, had produced little in the way of useful information. He had invited Sir William to sit in on the interview and translate, for he spoke many languages, including French. *Honneur* had been on her way to Martinique to take off several officials and return them to France, no more. Jones and Sir William had reviewed the capitaine's orders and concluded he was telling the truth.

Jones and the crew of *Renegade* were delighted that the French ship had been taken without a shot, for that meant it was not necessary to repair damage—shot holes and shattered spars and the like—before taking her to the prize court. Jones ordered a small prize crew aboard *Honneur* to follow *Renegade* to Gibraltar and the prize agent there.

If Lord Keith was not there, his orders were to proceed on to Genoa to find him.

Forty-Eight

Clearly, the game was up.

What exactly about their appearance had tipped off the janissaries was hard to know. But Fallon was sure that the failure to understand the questions put to them didn't help their cause, and no amount of Senegalese did either. Obviously, Fallon was a white Christian they'd never seen before and that made the janissaries curious, as well. Aja did his best to confuse the situation but in the end they were both roughly rousted up, searched and their weapons taken. Then they were made to walk down the small, steep road through the lower city to the bagnio by the quay and the holding pens that waited there. Well, Fallon thought ruefully, it had been his idea to see the holding pens and now they would.

Just outside the pens was a squat building and it was into a room there that Fallon and Aja were led and told to sit on two wooden chairs. A third chair, behind a wooden table, was empty. Two janissaries remained to guard the prisoners and stood behind them, stoic and silent.

Some minutes passed, then a short, swarthy man in a green caftan and golden turban entered the room from a door on the right, conferred briefly with one of the janissaries and sat at the table opposite the prisoners. A gold necklace hung around his neck and a jeweled cockade was fixed to the front of his turban.

"I am Doruk, and I am in charge of the dey's prisoners," he said in lingua franca. "Who are you and what is your business in Algiers, may I ask?"

Fallon considered him carefully and wrestled with how to answer. He was at once afraid to give too much away and, on the other hand, his mind searched for an answer that would free them. In the end, he went for the truth. Well, most of it anyway.

"I am Captain Nicholas Fallon, Captain of the British privateer *Rascal*, and this is my second mate Ajani. We are British subjects come to arrange a ransom for an American prisoner," said Fallon. "His name is Wilhelm Visser. Our ship is in Gibraltar because we were attacked by an Algerian corsair once we were through the Strait and had to turn back. In light of the attack we felt it was too dangerous to enter the country as British citizens outright, so we adopted these disguises in order to find Richard O'Brien, whom we were instructed to contact in order to arrange the payment of the ransom. I have a letter of introduction to Mr. O'Brien." Fallon reached under his tunic and found the letter and handed it to Doruk.

If Doruk was surprised in any way by Fallon's statement he didn't show it. He simply studied his two captives closely, eyes going from one to the other. The letter meant nothing to him, not least because he couldn't read English.

"Where is the ransom money now?" he asked finally, and now his eyes seemed to flicker in anticipation, for if the story of the gold were true it would be most welcome news to Mustapha Pasha.

"It is on our ship in Gibraltar," said Fallon. "We have only to see Visser alive and be sure our ship can enter the harbor safely with the ransom. Then we can exchange the gold for the prisoner."

Fallon watched the emotions play out on Doruk's face. It was a dark face, thinly bearded, pockmarked and oily and Fallon couldn't imagine anything truthful coming out of his mouth. But he was determined to play the hand out and hope for the best. Really, he knew, he had no other choice.

"British ships are always welcome in Algiers," said Doruk with all innocence. "Perhaps you are mistaken about the attack. Or perhaps our corsair could not see your flag."

Here Fallon decided to go on the offensive, this in spite of the fact they were prisoners at the moment.

"There was no mistake," he said angrily. "We were clearly flying British colors. Janissaries boarded us but we repelled them. Not, however, before they kidnapped one of our ship's boys. We want him back immediately, as well, or there will be no ransom for Visser. We will take our gold and sail back where we came from."

That outburst produced a silent stalemate. Fallon hoped his improvised attempt to tie the gold, which Doruk so obviously coveted, to Little Eddy's release as well as Visser's would work. Doruk's face was a mask of oily blankness. There was no recognition of Little Eddy's capture or signal that Visser was either alive or dead, and Fallon's fear of failure began to gnaw at him. Aja fidgeted in his chair, as well, aware that suddenly things were at a crux.

"I don't think you're going anywhere for a while, Captain Fallon," said Doruk with a little smile. "You see, I don't know whether you have gold or not. I don't even know if you are a real captain. What I do know is that we have two new prisoners who are in Algiers under suspicious circumstances, secretly armed. You have told a very strange story. It may be true or not. But I must consult with Mustapha. He is a wise and beneficent man and will know what to do, and I believe he will want to talk to you himself."

"Tell me this, then," Fallon said to Doruk in as insistent a tone as he could muster. "Are Visser and the boy even alive? If they aren't I swear on my mother's eyes you will never see a piece of gold."

Doruk only ignored the question and smiled. Then he rose to leave and had a word with one of the guards, who nodded in understanding.

"Captain, if that is what you are," he said as he turned back to Fallon, "you will be our guests for a while. Please put any thought of escape out of your head. It is a thin line between brave and foolish, is it not?"

Fallon and Aja were led outside to the holding pens. They were stockade built, open to the sky, in a line like open air cells with wooden poles for bars. Most of the pens seemed empty, or nearly so. Perhaps there had been a recent auction, thought Fallon ruefully. But some prisoners came forward to call to them in a polyglot of languages as they went by, and some of them spoke English. Fallon paused once to ask about Wilhelm Visser and Little Eddy but the janissary behind him pushed him forward roughly.

At last they came to a smaller pen whose gate was quickly unlocked and they were pushed inside. The harsh sun threw a shadow to the back of the cell but the pen appeared empty except for several straw pallets covered with blankets that were on the floor. One of the janissaries reached into a chest outside the cell and produced two more blankets which he threw inside onto the floor. Then the gate was closed and locked with a click that seemed final.

As Fallon and Aja stood adjusting to their new home one of the pallets seemed to move as a prisoner sat up under his blanket and let out a yell.

Little Eddy struggled to stand, sobbing and smiling at the same time.

Forty-Nine

Just before curfew in Algiers the prisoners from the work crew on the quay were led the short distance to the bagnio and the holding pens where they were housed. Visser had been thinking all day of Little Eddy, as the boy called himself, and the fantastic tale he'd begun telling last night before the exhausted boy had fallen asleep in mid-sentence. Could it be true that Caleb had come to ransom him and was aboard a privateer in Gibraltar? It was almost too much to believe but here was Little Eddy and the boy clearly knew his son. To think of Caleb so close made the longing to see him inexpressibly painful, but he dared not be overly optimistic. The Algerians were not to be trusted to negotiate in good faith.

As he stepped inside his pen, Visser's eyes widened in fear as he saw Little Eddy talking to two new prisoners whom he recognized as the two men he'd seen on the quay earlier in the day dressed as Bedouins. They hadn't fooled him and, apparently, they hadn't fooled the janissaries who patrolled the city either.

"Who are you?" he asked suspiciously in lingua franca. The new prisoners' robes were gone and they were in ship's slops now.

"I am Captain Nicholas Fallon," said Fallon in English. "And this is my second mate Ajani. Would you by chance be Wilhelm Visser?"

Visser was momentarily stunned at being found and recognized. Fallon watched him closely and could see surprise give way to comprehension.

"I am, by God!" said Visser.

"Then we are in the right place," said Fallon with a smile. "Everyone we're looking for is here."

Visser, Little Eddy, Aja, and Fallon began talking excitedly, each contributing to the narrative of how they came to be together. *Rascal's* rescue of Caleb Visser's ship tumbled out, and Wilhelm nodded in appreciation of the seamanship required to take a ship in tow in a gale, for he had certainly faced storms aplenty fishing off the banks.

"There were two ships from Boston in that storm, Wilhelm," said Fallon solemnly. "The other carried the gold for your ransom. I'm sorry to have to tell you that your other son, Alwin, commanded the second ship which foundered on the north shore of Bermuda. I expect with the loss of all hands."

Visser looked stunned. It was a part of the story that Little Eddy had omitted. Tears shot from his eyes as he pictured his oldest son cast upon the shoals, dying in a vain attempt to rescue his father. Fallon let him be, motioning Little Eddy and Aja to the far corner of the cell while the old man worked through his grief. When the elder Visser's chest had stopped heaving, Fallon approached him softly and placed a hand upon his shoulder.

"I know you are grieving for your son, Wilhelm," he said, "and you are no doubt taking all the guilt for his death upon yourself. But it is only what any son would have done. Or any father, come to that. It is what you would have done for Alwin. He delivered the gold to Bermuda, and Caleb found it, and at this moment it is aboard my ship in Gibraltar. And if Alwin were here to know it he would be pleased that he had helped, believe me. I know that is small recompense for the loss of a son, but it is the truth."

Fallon backed away and left Wilhelm Visser alone with his memories and his sadness. He had said all that he thought to say and it would be up to Visser to work through it and come back to this time, this moment and what would come next.

Later that night, Wilhelm Visser called out to Fallon and the others to come closer to talk. He was still immensely sad, but he had found pride in his son and determination to escape to be with his other son, Caleb. He wasn't through grieving, but he was at least looking forward.

Now Fallon told him about Caleb's wounding in the battle with Zabana, assuring him that Caleb was in no current danger. Visser stiffened at the mention of Zabana, for he had witnessed the corsair admiral's ruthlessness first hand.

Suddenly, the door opened to their pen and one of the guards entered and put food down on the ground while a second guard stood by. Their dinner consisted of stale bread and vinegar and water. Just enough to sustain life, more or less.

"I am feeling overwhelmed that you both are here," Visser said solemnly after the guards had left. They were all four crowded together on the floor looking at their pitiful dinners. "First, because you have brought my son, Caleb, to try to rescue me. There is no more generous and selfless act I could imagine. And second, because you are now a prisoner just as I am, and for that I hate myself for bringing you here. It is the end of the story for you, I'm afraid. They will work you hard until they auction you, and then you will work like a dog for the rest of your lives for someone else. Or the dey might buy you and send you to the mines. If you are most fortunate you will be ransomed, but as you can see that can take a very long time. I am beyond grateful that you have come so far and risked so much for me. But I am beyond sad that it has been for nothing. I fear I am not worth the price you will pay. Or that Alwin has already paid."

There was a sudden silence in the group now. Little Eddy squirmed and looked with wide eyes at Fallon and Aja.

"Do you think we can escape this place?" he blurted out. "I want to go back to the ship."

It was a child-like, innocent question and Fallon smiled with understanding. He wanted to go back to the ship, too, but at that moment there seemed to be no way that was going to happen.

"Tell me about what your life is like here, Wilhelm," he said. "Tell me about the guards and when you leave for work and everything you know about the streets and quay."

Wilhelm Visser had an eye for detail and he poured out everything he knew about Algiers, the janissaries and what it was like to be a slave in that walled city.

"After work they feed us, as you have seen," he said. "A single guard patrols the pens at night, checking the locks around midnight. I have never heard of an escape. Or even an attempt to escape. In the morning they come for us at first light. I go to the docks to unload ships they have captured or friendly ships who are trading with the Arabs. I don't know what they will do with you. I hope it will not be too strenuous."

Visser continued talking while Aja and Fallon listened raptly and absorbed every aspect of his narrative, interrupting occasionally to probe or ask a clarifying question. But the more Visser talked the more Fallon could see no way to escape their fate. They were about to be slaves, worked and used until they were ransomed or they died.

⁓

Mustapha Pasha listened to Doruk's description of the new prisoners with satisfaction, not least because of the possibility to have their gold as well as slaves. Doruk told him that he had ordered Fallon and his second mate to be held in the same pen as Visser and the boy to prove that they were alive. He hoped that would convince Fallon to cooperate, and the dey nodded sagely.

"I believe we might send a note to Fallon's ship, called *Rascal,* to make it plain it is safe to enter our harbor," said Doruk.

"But it must be an excellent message, most convincing, and it would be best if it came from the British captain himself," said Mustapha. "Have him brought to me tomorrow morning and I will speak with him."

"I don't think he will write the message willingly if he smells a trap," said Doruk delicately.

"He might smell the trap but he will write the message, I assure you," replied Mustapha. "Did you not say that Fallon seemed anxious about the ship's boy that we captured?"

"Yes, your highness," said Doruk, smiling broadly.

"Then have the boy brought to me, as well," said Mustapha. "I will give the captain something to be anxious about indeed."

⁓

Late that night, after Visser and Little Eddy and Aja were asleep, Fallon lay on his straw mat and stared at the blinking stars in the constellation above him. The ancient sailors of the Mediterranean saw in those stars a great ship gliding silently on an endless voyage across the sky. They called the ship *Argo Navis.* It appeared low on the horizon in spring skies and seemed to be sailing westward. Fallon looked at this apparition of a ship, seeing her poop deck, sails, keel and even her compass. It did indeed seem to be sailing to the west. He imagined he was aboard, for staring at the ship inevitably put him in mind of sailing home.

His interview with Doruk had unnerved him; his boast about sailing away with the gold had been embarrassingly weak. The question he wrestled with was what would happen next?

The longer he lay awake the more he was sure that the dey would try to lure *Rascal* into Algiers' harbor where he would have the ship at his mercy. The dey would have the gold, the ship and some ninety crewmen as slaves for market. Fallon involuntarily clenched his fists at the thought.

He could trust Beauty to be too smart to believe the dey's promises of safe passage. Unless . . . unless they used him or Little Eddy for bait somehow.

That thought threw him into a paroxysm of guilt and gripping fear for Beauty and the crew. His mind fought for a way to resist the paralysis that he felt creeping over him; he must think of *something.* He fingered the sea dog around his neck, unconsciously hoping for luck. He was still hoping for it just before dawn when he closed his eyes, not to sleep, but to wonder if the only plan he'd imagined had any chance of success.

He decided it did not, but it was the only plan he had.

Fifty

The next morning the janissaries came for Fallon and Little Eddy and they were led up the hill through the upper city. The houses seemed to tumble upwards in clusters of white, while against the bluing sky the dey's palace seemed majestic, shining, unassailable.

The pair were shown into the columned Audience Hall, the marble floors stretching to where Doruk stood and, there, seated on a golden cushion, was the dey himself.

"I am Mustapha Pasha," said the dey to Fallon, his dark eyes penetrating and unblinking. "You call yourself Captain Fallon, I understand, and claim to be in Algiers to ransom one of our slaves, Wilhelm Visser. Am I correct?"

"Yes," said Fallon warily.

"Further, you claim your ship was attacked by an Algerian corsair inside the Strait and thus you decided to enter our country on foot, in disguise, without the ransom. Is this correct?"

"Yes," said Fallon, waiting to see where the dey would take the conversation from here.

"You have stated your ship, a privateer named *Rascal,* is at this very moment in Gibraltar with the ransom."

"Yes," said Fallon again, shifting his eyes to Doruk, who smiled.

"How much money did you bring?" asked the dey.

"We brought what we understood the ransom for Wilhelm Visser to be, which is $10,000," replied Fallon coolly. "In gold."

The dey rubbed his beard, appearing to be deep in thought. Fallon had watched his eyes carefully when he'd said *in gold* and saw them flicker.

"Very well," said the dey at last. "You may send a message to your ship stating that it is safe to enter our harbor. We will then exchange the prisoner for the gold and you will be free to go on your way. I will even allow your ship's boy to go free, as well. This is a sign of my good faith, Captain Fallon."

"I have stated to Doruk that my ship will not move without my command," said Fallon firmly. "I will return to my ship with the boy and my second mate and bring the ransom back myself. You will still have Wilhelm Visser and we can arrange an exchange at a mutually agreeable time and place."

The dey's eyes squinted.

"Captain, you are in a poor position to demand anything," he said harshly. "I can have you killed in an instant, and your second mate. I would kill the boy but he is such a fine young man that I have other uses for him."

A pause. Fallon's stomach clenched.

"Doruk, take off the boy's clothes."

Little Eddy had been oblivious to the proceedings until now, not understanding lingua franca. But Doruk made a move towards him and he instinctively broke free of the guard and ducked behind Fallon who, in any case, had stepped between the boy and Doruk.

"Your resistance is useless, captain," said the dey. "If you are dead who will protect the boy, eh? Such a delightful looking boy. He will be loved by someone when you are dead, captain. Oh yes, *loved.*"

Little Eddy grasped Fallon's waist tightly, and peeked around him to see Doruk, who was smiling broadly.

"No!" Fallon shouted through clenched teeth. But he knew he was in a poor position to protect Little Eddy, and as Doruk took a step forward he could feel the boy shaking behind him.

"I will send the message," he said with resignation.

"Excellent, captain," said the dey condescendingly. "My scribe has pen and paper and he reads and speaks English, I might add. Because he is English! You will write your message and he will know if you are practicing deceit. I wouldn't do that if I were you, captain. There will be no second chances. For you or the boy."

The dey clapped his hands once and there appeared from behind one of the columns a short, slight man carrying pen and paper.

Apparently, the dey was quite confident in the outcome of the interview, thought Fallon. He had been totally outflanked.

Doruk peeled Little Eddy away from Fallon and held his arm tightly, still smiling. "Now you will write the best letter of your life, captain," he said. "But no tricks."

The scribe led Fallon to an alcove overlooking the upper city that was flooded with light and placed the pen and paper on the ledge.

"I am Howard," he said, "personal scribe to the dey. I must warn you not to try anything devious with the letter. Make it straight forward and utterly convincing."

"How did an Englishman come to be the dey's scribe?" asked Fallon contemptuously.

But Howard brushed the contempt away. "It was that or lose my balls, my friend. What would you have done in my place?"

The two men stared at each other a moment before Fallon took the quill pen and dipped it in the jar of ink.

And then he turned to Howard with a question.

"How will my ship enter the harbor? I understand it is quite shallow in places."

"That will be no problem, captain," said Howard. "There is a pilot boat that will meet the ship and guide her in to an anchorage."

Whereupon Fallon seemed to accept the answer and began writing.

Dear First Mate McFarland,

I have the dey's promise that Algiers is safe for British ships. Upon receipt of this message you will take aboard any additional crew that

you need in Gibraltar and prepare to be off the mole at the harbor in 10 days' time. That's where a pilot boat will meet you. Good luck.
Nicholas Fallon, Captain
May 8, 1800

Finished writing, Fallon looked at Howard as he read the message.

"Convincing enough for you, Howard?" Fallon asked bitterly.

"It had better be, captain. If your ship is not here in ten days the dey will . . . well, let's just say he keeps his threats."

Fallon stared at the letter in the alcove, and then reached behind his neck to untie the necklace Beauty had given him for luck and tossed it on the note.

"So McFarland will know the letter is really from me," said Fallon. "Now let the boy go!"

Howard looked at the note, then the necklace, and then Fallon. Apparently, the dey's threat to the boy had worked rather well. The necklace certainly seemed to prove Fallon wanted the note to be believed. It was a good touch.

Howard signaled to Doruk that the letter was approved and the boy was released to run to Fallon's side. As the two were led away down the Audience Hall Fallon turned to look back at the dey, but the gold cushion was empty. He was gone.

As Fallon and Little Eddy were marched back down the hill towards the bagnio, Zabana was emerging from a darkened doorway of a cafe on a side street. Having finished his small coffee, he was leaving to go back to his ship to supervise the repairs caused by his battle with the British schooner. What he saw from the shadows astounded him, confused him, and angered him, for there was the wicked British captain who had attacked him! And the boy he had captured from the captain's ship! Doruk and two guards were leading them down the hill from the dey's palace. How did the British captain get here? And, most importantly, why was he meeting with the dey? The questions flooded Zabana's mind as he watched the little procession proceed towards the quay.

As he stepped out into the street behind them, Zabana was struck by another thought. A better kind of thought that almost made him smile. The British captain was in prison less than one hundred yards from his ship.

Zabana would have him!

Fifty-One

The xebec left the quay immediately with the message for *Rascal,* the ship's name written clearly on the outside of the packet. There was a good breeze from the southeast and the galley slaves could rest easy as the ship sped along westward. Coming back against the wind would be another story, unfortunately. The slaves were naked and chained to their oars in the usual custom aboard galleys and they sat in their own excrement, their skin peeling in blistered layers from sunburn. They appeared to sleep and perhaps some did, but one man was actually dead and had not been discovered yet.

The reis knew he had nothing to fear from any nation or any ship as the dey's treaties protected him from attack from the larger countries' navies. And, who knew, perhaps he might even take a prize.

But no ships were sighted all day and by late afternoon the next day he was off Gibraltar. He ordered the big sail taken in and the sweeps to begin, which is when the dead slave was discovered and thrown overboard. Slowly the xebec entered the harbor under the precaution of a white flag and the reis looked at each ship they passed to find one whose name matched what was written on the packet.

Beauty saw the xebec rowing towards the ship and immediately called all hands. Though they were in a British harbor, the recent battle with Algerians was fresh in her mind and she was taking no chances. Rascals stood at their stations with cutlasses, muskets and pistols and Cully had the gun crews ready, as well.

As the xebec approached closer the tension aboard *Rascal* was palpable as every hand fingered a weapon or stood by a cannon. Here was the enemy bearding the lion in its own den.

The xebec slowed and drifted. As it drew closer one of the janissaries stood on the bow and extended a long pole with the packet tied to the tip across the few feet of water separating the two ships. Beauty caught her breath in fear and concern, knowing without knowing that Fallon was in trouble, perhaps even dead, and that the message would not be good.

She ordered one of the hands to grab the packet and bring it aboard. No words were spoken between the ships. It was doubtful anyone could have understood anyone anyway. His mission accomplished, the reis ordered the slaves to begin rowing away from *Rascal* and the harbor and he did not look back. Soon the lateen sails were hoisted, the white flag hauled down, and the xebec slanted southeastward for Algiers.

Beauty held the packet in her hands, fearing to open it and fearing not to. She looked at the retreating galley, mystified that the British would allow the ship to enter the harbor without blowing it to bits. What kind of treaty did Britain have anyway? It only applied one way, certainly. Just days ago they had been attacked by Algerians, and now one of their ships sailed blithely into a British harbor and away again without consequences. It infuriated her, but her attention was brought back to the packet, for something must be done with it and she took it below to her cabin after first ordering the crew to stand down. They relaxed but didn't move and watched her as she left the deck.

In the privacy of her cabin she opened the packet and her necklace immediately fell out. She gasped and stared at it, trying to imagine what it could mean, and then turned her attention to the note.

She read it through once. Then read it through again. Then picked up the necklace and squeezed it tightly. It was obvious Fallon was up to something, but the question was *what?*

Firstly, Fallon had never called her McFarland in her life, so she knew he was trying to send her a message within the message. Secondly, she had implored him to bring the necklace back and put it in her hands so she would know he was safe. But he'd sent it to her. Her conclusion: he wasn't safe. In fact, he was likely a prisoner along with Aja. Those things seemed solid to her, but as to the bones of the message she wasn't so sure.

> *Upon receipt of this message you will take aboard any additional crew that you need in Gibraltar and prepare to be off the mole at the harbor in 10 days' time. That's where a pilot boat will meet you.*

He had been clear that she was to be off the mole in ten days from the date of the letter. He'd stated that the Algerians would send a pilot boat out to guide *Rascal* to an anchorage, but Fallon had insisted more than once to her that he would never allow *Rascal* to anchor under the harbor's guns. What the devil was he up to?

It was a riddle, and the more she read and reread the note the more obscure it became. Yet everything depended upon her figuring it out.

A knock at the door and Barclay entered.

"The hands are worried sick, Beauty," he said. "What can I tell them?"

"I don't know what to tell them, Barclay," answered Beauty. "I believe Nico and Aja are alive but in what condition I don't know. The note orders us to be at Algiers in less than 10 days' time. To do what I'm not entirely sure."

She handed him the note to read for himself. She could see Barclay read it through several times and shook his head.

"It's straightforward enough, it seems," he said. "But Nico would never write this note this way without a reason. What is he trying to tell us do you think?"

"That's the thing I have to figure out, Barclay," said Beauty. "And I've only got a few days to do it. The thing to do is to think like Nico, if I can."

"How are you ever going to do that?" asked Barclay.

"I've got to think of the normal thing a normal person would do," said Beauty. "And then fucking do the opposite."

Fifty-Two

Rascal rode easily at dawn under the looming shadow of Gibraltar. Beauty paced the deck deep in thought. The decks were holystoned and the crew went about their duties, splicing ropes and blacking rigging and chipping shot. Except that few could concentrate knowing that Fallon and Aja were in a desperate situation—and desperate was the right word.

Barclay had leveled with them, not sharing the message exactly but letting them know Fallon and Aja appeared to be alive, though probably prisoners and even slaves, and *Rascal* would be going to Algiers to get them. They were all anxious, jumpy, and eager for the time to pass. And, in truth, feeling more than a little guilty that they were doing nothing while Fallon and Aja were in such a precarious situation. And Little Eddy, what of him? No word, Barclay had said.

Beauty had shared the note with Caleb Visser, as well. He was up and about now, still convalescing from his shoulder wound, but the note sent him into despair. Not because there was no word of his father, but because it appeared his worst fears had come true. Fallon and Aja had been captured.

The rhythmic thump of Beauty's peg leg on the deck went on all day. Back and forth, bow to stern and back, her mind in a wrestling match with itself. Her considerable capacity for anger was in search of an outlet. First, the corsairs had attacked them, a British ship on the high seas. Then the janissaries had attacked them and taken Little Eddy. Now Beauty wanted to attack someone. Fallon's note might give her the chance if she could figure the damn thing out.

What did Fallon mean by *take aboard any additional crew?* He knew *Rascal* had almost a full complement already. The ship was ready for sea and ready for battle, though fighting hand to hand against janissaries might be beyond the pale.

Then suddenly she stopped. Every hand looked up from whatever small task or mindless work they were doing. They saw Beauty looking across the harbor, past the ships at anchor or moving about. Perhaps what she was thinking of doing wasn't exactly what Fallon was implying, but it was certainly counterintuitive enough that it could be.

At eight bells in the morning watch Beauty called for the gig to take her ashore. Her visit would either take a long time or no time, but she was determined to do something that would aid their chances against the corsairs. Once ashore, she asked a dockhand for directions and set off for the army garrison.

As might be expected, it was a long walk up a very steep hill. The army would want a strategic position in the event of an attack on Gibraltar, and the fort was well placed with a commanding view of the harbor. Beauty climbed the track as best she could—thank goodness the ground was hard—but it was some time before she got to the gate of the fort and she had to compose herself and catch her breath.

The garrison was laid out in a quad with a center courtyard, barracks surrounding three sides with administrative offices, stock rooms, and the powder room immediately opposite the main gate. In the center of the quad perhaps five hundred soldiers were drilling, commanded by a full-throated sergeant. Beauty skirted the drill field and made for the building on the far side. Seeing a door marked "Colonel Bisanz," she knocked.

Colonel Bisanz was a tanned, fit, be-medaled man with a spectacular handlebar mustache that curled just so at the tips. At Beauty's entrance he rose from his desk, took off his wire glasses and looked at her curiously.

"Good morning," he said formally. "Pray be seated, Miss . . . ?"

"I am Beautrice McFarland, Colonel Bisanz. My friends call me Beauty but we'll wait on that."

If Bisanz was taken aback at the challenge in Beauty's words he didn't show it.

"I see," he said. "And what is your business here, may I ask?"

"I am first mate on the British privateer, *Rascal,* which is sitting in the harbor just below us. Her captain is Nicholas Fallon, who went on foot to Algiers with our second mate in an attempt to rescue an American and British subject from slavery."

A frown creased Bisanz's face.

"Your captain is either very brave or very foolish, I believe," said the colonel flatly. "By foot you say? Why did he not just sail his ship into the harbor? Are you aware we have a treaty with the dey of Algiers?"

"We were attacked by two corsairs before we even made Gibraltar, Colonel Bisanz," answered Beauty, the heat coming in her words. "We sunk the bastards in open ocean. Then we sailed through the Strait where we found a third one—a big xebec—attacking an American merchant ship. We came to the American's aid and the fucking janissaries snatched one of our crew. We were lucky to survive. So the treaty isn't worth a damn, colonel."

"Hmm," said Bisanz. It was likely he'd never heard a woman with Beauty's particular vocabulary. And the news of corsair attacks on British ships took him aback. He had no idea of it. He hesitated to speak, for it was clear Beauty's color was getting up.

"I am sorry for your troubles, but I fail to see why you are here, madam," he said as solicitously as he could. "Perhaps the Admiralty . . ."

"No, the Admiralty is in London. You're here and I'm here to ask the army for help because the fucking navy is no help," said Beauty and, indeed, her face was growing redder. "We took casualties in the last attack and now I've got to get four people out of Algiers in a week and if the janissaries get at us again I don't know how it will go this time. I'm working on a plan but I need soldiers, maybe a hundred of your best fighters, to come with us to Algiers. I'll feed 'em and pay 'em but I need their help. I need *your* help."

At that, Bisanz's eyebrows went up and he blustered "That's quite impossible," and "No, no, no," until Beauty rose and stood over his desk and looked down on him.

"Colonel Bisanz," she said quietly, "one of the people we're trying to save is an eight-year-old boy who was snatched off our ship. He's going to auction."

At that, the colonel closed his mouth and set his jaw tightly. His entire body seemed to grow rigid and tense. He was well aware of the fates of many young boys and girls sold as slaves at Barbary auctions. He rose without a glance to Beauty and walked to the window to look out at the soldiers drilling in the center of the quad. What this woman was asking, of course, was unrealistic in the extreme and in no way comported with his orders. What she wanted was also beyond his authority to grant. Only court martial could come to an officer who dared consider stepping beyond his command. He knew Admiral Lord Keith was away and that the meek Captain Elliott would be no help if this woman approached him, which she probably had. So, no doubt in desperation, she'd come to him. She couldn't have known he had a young son in England himself, could she?

A minute went by. Then more.

Bisanz continued his meditation by the window. The chances of Fallon getting into Algiers and out again alive were basically nil, much less getting out with two slaves. Algiers was a heavily guarded, walled city. This Fallon fellow was on a hopeless mission. But, Jesus, he kept coming back to the boy, picturing his own son's face on the little fellow.

The sergeant outside was still shouting, the soldiers were still drilling, everything was as it should be except this fierce woman was in his office likely drilling holes into his back with her eyes, no doubt wondering if he was the kind of officer who could be bound by a higher code than his orders. *God in heaven,* he thought.

He was still looking out the window when he bowed his head and closed his eyes and whispered *yes*. He was exactly that kind of officer.

And then a voice behind him said softly: "Thank you, colonel. And please call me Beauty."

Fifty-Three

Fallon and Aja had been led away at dawn towards the mole to carry stone by cart to the curved tip. The breakwater was being enlarged, presumably so even more cannons could be placed there. Fallon and Aja were in chains, their legs bound together.

The manacles on Fallon's ankles rubbed the skin off in very little time, and a quick glance at Aja's ankles showed they were bloody, as well.

It was still early morning.

Fallon looked at the city of Algiers rising up the hill to the south, and he could make out men and women walking in the narrow streets. The sounds of camels braying and goats bleating floated down to the jetty, and he thought he could even smell strong coffee.

The pilot boat was on station outside the harbor, its flags and ribbons in full force in the stout breeze. Fallon recognized it as a French galiote, or something very like it, a smallish ship with four crew and four sets of oars meant to carry light cargo in its relatively shallow holds. At the tip of its lateen sail a red streamer blew off to the sky. At night it berthed at the quay and was tied down snug before curfew but, like the slaves, it was up working at dawn.

As surreptitiously as he could, Fallon scanned the harbor and counted the ships anchored there. There were quite a few corsairs mixed in with the fishing vessels, while at the quay a Turkish flagged vessel was just leaving. It was massive, easily one of the biggest merchant vessels Fallon had ever seen. No doubt it traded throughout the Mediterranean carrying livestock and lumber and all manner of mercantile items from Tangier to the Levant. As it was warped away it revealed a ship lying beyond it at the quay, and Fallon involuntarily jerked his head back in surprise and nudged Aja to have a look. It was a large xebec with a distinctive snake's head at the bow.

Serpent!

Fallon could see stores being brought aboard the ship even as repairs seemed to be in progress on the starboard side, no doubt due to Cully's broadside. There was no sign of Zabana that Fallon could see, but the ship was quite far away. He would be around.

Fallon wondered momentarily if the presence of *Serpent* would change his nascent plan to escape. Only if Zabana discovered he was a prisoner, he decided. He thought of the guillotine on board the ship and wondered idly how often it had been used, but before he could dwell further the overseer grunted and Fallon turned his attention back to the rocks.

"Zabana Reis," said Mustapha Pasha, "you have brought back slaves for me, which is good. But you have lost half your janissaries, which is not good. How did this happen?"

Zabana had to be careful how he answered, not knowing what the British schooner captain had already told the dey. He could not take a chance on a lie.

"We came upon an American merchantman near the Strait. We were both becalmed so we rowed to intercept her. But a British ship was riding the breeze down to us and came to the American's aid. There was a huge battle and we took what slaves we could, but the wicked British fired grapeshot into our janissaries and killed many of them in one broadside. We took several Americans and one British boy."

"Yes," said the dey contemptuously, "if you had known the British schooner carried gold perhaps you would have fought harder."

Zabana felt the venom in the dey's words. *Gold!*

"I have interviewed the British captain," continued the imperious dey, "whose name is Fallon. He entered Algiers with his second mate on foot after your battle and was found walking around the city. Reason has convinced him to send word to his ship to bring the gold to us." Here the dey smiled; it was one of the few times Zabana had ever seen his teeth.

"You must order your corsairs to let the ship pass. Then when it is in the harbor you will have your second chance to take her. It should not be so difficult then."

Zabana felt his face burn at these last words, but he could say nothing, make no excuses, so he remained silent, his eyes blazing. This was the basis of the dey's power, he knew, manipulation and humiliation.

Seeing Zabana's face the dey added one last stab.

"Zabana Reis, I will send you more janissaries. Use them wisely and carefully. They are not inexhaustible, nor is my patience. And do not think to harm the British captain, if it is in your mind to take out your own impotence on him. He may be important in some way to lure his ship into the harbor. I want him alive and willing when the time comes."

Zabana's body clenched in embarrassment. The dey's insinuations and humiliations had wounded him deeply and he vowed he would have his revenge.

But first, Fallon. He would protect him, yes. But then he would kill him in the worst way imaginable.

Fifty-Four

The available charts, maps and written accounts of travelers and explorers to North Africa showed Algiers was surrounded by the largest hot desert in the known world, the Sahara. At three and a half million square miles it was over thirty-two times the size of Great Britain. And considerably warmer.

As Fallon and Aja worked on the breakwater each day the breeze off the desert felt increasingly warm, such that the air seemed to burn their noses and throats. Sweat poured from their bodies and they stopped often to drink copious amounts of water supplied by their guards.

Fallon could still see *Serpent* across the harbor but the repair work seemed to have been completed for there were no actual work parties about. He had yet to see Zabana.

Each day was the same as sleds of rocks would be brought from the mines, dragged by scarecrow slaves to the quay where Fallon and Aja would drag them out to the breakwater and tumble them to the edges and down into the water to gradually make the mole wider. Sled after sled, rock upon rock. Fallon and Aja spoke very little, for they needed all their strength just to get through each day. At night they were returned to their pen to be reunited with Wilhelm Visser and Little Eddy, so tired they could barely move.

As they ate dinner near the end of their first week of captivity Fallon knew, tired as he was, he had to work on the plan for their attempted escape. Beauty should be off the mole in a few days. *If she had gotten his message. If she had understood it.*

He paused for a moment. Would she arrive on time? And then he smiled a tired smile. Of course she would.

"Let me tell you what I have been thinking," Fallon said as they nursed their little dinners. He told them about his note to Beauty with the hoped-for secret message and his idea to steal a boat, providing they could escape from their pen.

Aja, well familiar with Fallon's ways, managed a wide smile. "I watched you watch the harbor, captain, sir," he said. "I have been waiting for this moment."

Visser looked visibly afraid. "We will only have this one chance, captain," he said. "If we don't succeed I can't imagine what they will do to us. These people know how to torture people until there is no will left to live."

"I believe you, Wilhelm," said Fallon earnestly. "I know what we are risking. But hopefully we have a plan of sorts in motion and we must do our part to see it through. It is our chance to be free, *your* chance to be free and to see your son. Are you willing to try Wilhelm?"

Visser looked at Fallon and slowly nodded. "Maybe I can help," he said. "The guards don't concern themselves much with me on the docks. Tell me what I can do."

"Well," said Fallon, "can you bring back anything under your tunic that we can use?"

"What are you looking for?" asked Visser.

"I don't know," answered Fallon with a smile. "A knife or a musket would be nice."

"How about a cannon?" asked Aja, also smiling.

"I'll see what I can do," said Visser with a grin. "But a cannon will be difficult, though worthy."

"Bring anything you can that you think we can use to lure the midnight guard inside, Wilhelm," said Fallon. "Now, Little Eddy, let me ask you a question."

Little Eddy's eyes got wide and the boy sat upright, anticipating a role in the escape.

"You were the fastest boy up the mast on *Rascal*," said Fallon. "Like a monkey you were. Tell me, can you climb these walls?" He nodded towards the stockade walls of the pen. They were long poles, set inches apart and perhaps fifteen feet tall.

Little Eddy stood up and walked to the wall with the door. He stood with his back to the group, staring at the poles. Finally, he approached the wall more closely and began trying to insert his hands into the cracks between poles. He was a small boy for his age, with small hands and arms, and he found a pole with enough space on either side that he could push his hands through.

Suddenly his feet were off the ground and on the wall, his toes wrapped around the pole pushing him up and up. He struggled once, getting a hand stuck, but managed to free himself and then he was at the top. Little Eddy, the acrobat.

The little crowd below him wanted to cheer but dared not. Instead, Fallon whispered as loudly as he could, "Well done!"

And Little Eddy scampered down.

Now it all depended on what Wilhelm Visser could fit under his tunic.

At dawn the next morning *Rascal* weighed under a sky that came with violent streaks of red. Barclay commented on it, mumbling the sailor's aphorism: *Red sky at night, sailor's delight. Red sky at morning, sailors take warning.* He knew what they were seeing was dust in the eastern sky and that dirty weather was coming.

The wind had come east southeast, and Beauty's decision to sail sooner rather than later to Tipasa seemed prescient, for it would give the crew a chance to rest before the final push to Algiers. In truth, the crew couldn't have waited another day in Gibraltar. They were more than anxious to be away.

Colonel Bisanz had shown up last evening with one hundred of his finest soldiers, all volunteers, each man equipped to fight a small war.

Beauty had welcomed each soldier aboard as *Rascal's* boats brought them out and, at the last, she had gone ashore to personally thank Bisanz. She found him standing by himself on the dock in the twilight, his men gone, alone.

"Colonel," she began, "I don't know how to thank you for your support and these volunteers. God willing we won't have any trouble, but I pity the poor devils who try to stop us."

"I pray you won't need to fight to free your people, Beauty. The corsairs are ruthless; but I don't have to tell you that. All I ask is to bring my boys home with yours, if you can. But remember, they volunteered for the mission. It's them to thank, not me."

She studied his face in the dim light, a face with bright eyes and that spectacular mustache, and smiled.

"I thank God and you, colonel. And then the boys. In that order. Goodbye." And then Beauty did something she'd never done before in her life.

She kissed a man.

Renegade's progress had slowed considerably as she was forced to tack against the building easterly. In consequence, they were a day later than Jones had predicted arriving in Gibraltar.

He scanned the harbor for any sign of *Rascal* but she was nowhere to be seen. That was not surprising, just disappointing. What was surprising was seeing Lord Keith's flagship, *Artemis*, 74, riding at anchor in the crowded roadstead.

Renegade had barely found a spot to anchor when her number flew from the flagship with the signal: *captain repair onboard.* Jones went below to quickly change into his best uniform and alert Sir William to make himself ready to be rowed across to *Artemis.* At the last he remembered Admiral Davies' letter for Lord Keith and then, checking himself in the small mirror and brushing his unruly hair, he pronounced himself as good as he was going to look. Back on deck, he waited while Sir William's dunnage was lowered into his captain's gig, along with Sir William, and in very little time they were approaching the massive hulk of the flagship and being hailed to come aboard.

Jones went up the side, his heart in his throat at seeing the famous Lord Keith, the hero of Saldanha Bay for capturing an entire Dutch squadron, and now commander-in-chief of the Mediterranean station. He and Sir William were shown to Keith's great cabin by a rather bent first lieutenant and found themselves in a room of glittering gold from the epaulettes of several captains already there.

Jones and Sir William were introduced to the flag captain, Burrell, and Captain Elliott of *Mischief,* who looked pale and nervous, and finally Lord Keith himself, resplendent in his Royal Navy uniform and shock of white hair. He had an erect bearing and strong jaw but his eyes were wise and wide.

"William, it is good to see you again," said Lord Keith, obviously well-acquainted with the British agent. "There is much to talk about and I confess making sense of it all gives me a headache. At least the Austrians are giving a good account of themselves against Masséna. I believe we will see the French defeated in the coming months, which has allowed me to return to Gibraltar. Poor Burrell thought we would run out of rum if we stayed longer! We only arrived on station this morning and the rum will come aboard before the water casks!"

At this everyone in the great cabin laughed, for all knew the average jack could do without anything, face any deprivation except the loss of rum.

"May I pay a special compliment to Captain Jones, sir?" said Sir William. "He not only brought me safely across the Atlantic but he took a prize on the way. And without a shot!"

"Good Lord, Captain Jones!" exclaimed Lord Keith. "I am all aback to hear how you did that! Pray let's have a glass so you can tell the story." And with that the steward brought out several bottles of claret as Jones told the story of capturing *Honneur* as modestly as he could.

"Well," said Jones a bit timidly, "we chanced upon a small French frigate and were able to run her down easily, for *Renegade* has a clean bottom. The prisoners are located below decks and well-guarded. Sir William was kind enough to help me interview the captain and review his orders since he is fluent in French. I brought them with me and, oh, and this is a letter from Admiral Davies for you personally, sir."

Jones withdrew the papers from his breast pocket and handed them across the massive desk to Lord Keith who looked a question at Sir William.

"The capitaine's orders concerned bringing back French officials from the Caribbean to Paris, no more," responded Sir William to the unasked question. "I doubt if he had the imagination or courage for mischief."

At this Lord Keith relaxed and put the French capitaine's orders aside for the moment.

"Captain Burrell, will you please see that the prisoners are removed to the prison ashore?" said Lord Keith. "They are a damned nuisance but the prize is worth it, no doubt." And then he addressed himself to Jones.

"Captain Jones, I will gladly buy *Honneur* into the service, of course. The prize agent is fair-minded and you and your crew should profit handsomely as there was no damage to the ship."

Jones blushed radiantly.

"And now gentlemen, if you will excuse me a moment while I read this note from Admiral Davies I would be grateful," said Lord Keith, rising to go to the stern windows where the light was better. "Pray help yourself to more wine."

The steward went man to man and poured the claret carefully, refilling the Admiral's glass which sat upon the desk half empty. Jones was careful not to do more than sip, wanting to make a good impression on these exalted figures. He stole a glance at Elliott, who seemed to recede to the edges of the room.

After a few moments, Lord Keith turned from the stern windows and took his seat again. His face was still kind but his eyes had narrowed a bit.

"Captain Elliott, Admiral Davies tells me that a privateer named Fallon should have entered these waters from Antigua and I am wondering if you spoke to him at all."

Elliott looked startled to be called upon but, gathering himself, he sniffed before answering. "Yes, I welcomed him aboard the first time he entered Gibraltar. I can only report that Captain Fallon told the most fantastic story of sinking two Algerian corsairs just days before and I immediately took him for a fabulist. He was only in a schooner, after all, and we all know too well the reputation of corsairs. At any rate, he asked for my help and protection to Algiers, but of course I refused based on my orders from you to remain on station. I must say I found Fallon hot-tempered and rude."

"Did Fallon mention that he was attempting to ransom an old man from slavery?" asked Keith, his eyes squinting a bit more. "As for sinking two corsairs, Admiral Davies gives Fallon his highest approbation and claims that he is as clever a captain as they come. Perhaps the captain's story was not as far-fetched as it sounded."

At that, Elliot blanched. He was none too tanned anyway, preferring to spend most of his time in the Royal Navy in his cabin.

"You said Fallon returned to Gibraltar again, Captain Elliot?" continued Lord Keith without waiting for an answer to his last question. "Did you endeavor to find out why?"

"I did not, sir," mumbled Elliot. "I was very busy with affairs on board ship. The word on the lower deck, however, was that *Rascal's* crew claimed they fought *another* corsair to the east. Fallon also had a prize crew aboard an American merchant vessel, *Mary of Dundee.* Surely that beggars explanation, as well. At any rate, within a day or two he had left again. When the ship came back a third time it stayed for a week, I suppose. I was told the captain was no longer aboard but I can't vouchsafe for that. Then, two nights ago, Colonel Bisanz brought troops from the garrison to the shore and they were loaded onto the privateer. The next morning she sailed away. Why Bisanz did that I couldn't say, but it was highly irregular."

Lord Keith took a moment to digest this information, tapping Davies' letter on the desk and looking squarely at Jones.

"Captain Jones," he asked, "are you acquainted with Captain Fallon? I realize the Caribbean is a large sea but I am curious."

Jones didn't blink, for Captain Elliott's description of Fallon as a fantastic liar had infuriated him. "Yes sir," he answered as evenly as he could, "I have served alongside him with Admiral Davies and can attest to his bravery and . . . and cunning. He is the cleverest captain I know." Here Jones shot a quick look to Elliott, whose face had recovered its natural color and now moved on to red.

"How was it you served alongside a privateer, may I ask," said Lord Keith with a hint of skepticism in his voice.

"Captain Fallon was an informal advisor to Admiral Davies, sir," said Jones. "He looked at situations from a privateer's point of view and I believe Admiral Davies valued his opinion in the highest. It was Fallon's idea to trick *Coeur de France* into leaving Port-a-Prince to fight. The plan was all his." Jones had tactfully left out his own role in luring the ship out. But he knew that the sinking of the French flagship was well-known throughout the Royal Navy.

"I heard *Coeur* went down with all hands, is that true?" asked Keith. "I believe she carried 100 guns?"

"All true, sir," replied Jones quietly. He fidgeted in his chair, his wine untouched, fearing he had been too forthcoming with praise for his friend in an effort to defend him from Elliott's slur.

"Sir William," asked Lord Keith, "do you have anything to add to this conversation?"

"Only that I met Captain Fallon once at Admiral Davies' invitation and endeavored to acquaint him with what I knew of the Barbary situation." A pause. "I found his questions insightful and direct. From what Davies told me beforehand, I can believe Captain Jones' account. I realize we have a treaty with the dey, but it seems to be unravelling."

This seemed to slam the door in Elliott's face and he found he could say nothing in response except, "I was only following my orders, sir."

Lord Keith looked at Elliott sadly. He really was a dolt of a captain and Keith knew it and had known it for some time.

"Quite," he said at last, and endeavored to swallow his disappointment in one of his officers.

The topic turned to lighter subjects at last, the best clarets ever taken from a French prize, the peculiarities of a folluca's sailing rig, the increasing difficulty of pressing men to man Great Britain's many ships. At last the little meeting came to a close and the captains rose to leave to return to their ships.

"Captain Jones," said Lord Keith, "may I ask you to stay a moment, sir?"

Jones could only stay behind, of course, though he feared a reprimand for crossing swords with one of Lord Keith's captains. Sir William lingered, as well, but of course he was staying aboard.

As Burrell closed the cabin door behind him, Lord Keith bade his two remaining guests to sit again as he picked up Davies' letter and seemed to re-read at least parts of it.

"I don't know Admiral Davies personally, you understand," he said as he looked at Jones. "But I know of him, to be sure, and I know he is held in high regard in Whitehall. So I am inclined to believe that what he says in his letter is true. He is saying, to put it succinctly, that Fallon is his irreplaceable ally in the Caribbean and should the opportunity arise to render him assistance in his quest to ransom an Algerian slave he hopes we will do so. It is a glowing letter, to be sure. He admits to Fallon's unorthodox ways and ideas that at first seem far-fetched. And Davies said something striking: he said that Fallon was his *imagination.* I am not used to modest Admirals in the Royal Navy."

It was then that Lord Keith looked at Sir William and smiled a knowing smile.

"I keep my own imagination close at hand," he said quietly.

Sir William barely nodded to acknowledge the compliment. "If I may, Lord Keith," he said, "what else did Admiral Davies say that has you so interested in Fallon's well-being?"

Lord Keith looked down at the letter in his hands and then up to Sir William. It was a good question, and Sir William was right to ask it. After all, the two of them had much to discuss about the Mediterranean as it was.

"Admiral Davies said that if there was one man who would have ideas to disrupt any potential alliance between France and Algiers it would be Fallon. He staked his reputation on it. Which would seem to make Fallon a very valuable asset, indeed, given the Admiralty's concerns."

Sir William leaned back in his chair. Jones sat rock still in his, not deigning to speak or even move.

"Captain Elliott said that Colonel Bisanz had loaded troops onto *Rascal* before she sailed, and that Fallon was not aboard," said Sir William. "I am wondering why, and what it all means. And I am wondering if a conversation with the colonel wouldn't tell us more than we know now if, indeed, you have the opportunity to intercede on Fallon's behalf."

Sir William, serving up some imagination to Lord Keith.

The three men arrived at the quay after a bumpy row in the Admiral's gig, for the harbor was feeling the beginning of unsettled weather. Lord Keith was well acquainted with Colonel Bisanz and liked the man, as did Sir William, but both were quite in the dark about his actions and wanted to get the full picture of what had gone on with *Rascal* and some account of why Fallon was not aboard any longer. For Jones' part he was honored to be in their inner circle and kept his mouth shut.

They arrived at the quad and then proceeded immediately to find Colonel Bisanz who, as he had with Beauty, welcomed them formally. It was odd for a Royal Navy admiral and British army officer to ever be in the same room with each other and the meeting began tentatively.

"I understand you brought troops to the shore two nights ago to be loaded aboard *Rascal*, a British privateer," Lord Keith began. "Can you tell me why, pray? I am not here to challenge your actions in any way, colonel. But I am developing a personal interest in *Rascal*."

"If you know the ship, Admiral," answered Bisanz, "then you might also know her first mate, Beauty McFarland. If she had asked for a thousand troops I might have given them to her."

At that Jones laughed in spite of himself, then quickly settled, embarrassed.

"I don't know the ship itself, colonel," said Lord Keith with a smile. "But somehow I am not surprised that she carries a woman as first mate. I imagine she is formidable. Captain Jones?"

"I know Beauty very well," said Jones. "And I wouldn't refuse her anything either. I fear I would be in danger if I did."

Bisanz related the story Beauty had told him in great detail, knowing Lord Keith would want the full picture. At the news of the kidnapping of a ship's boy named Little Eddy Jones involuntarily recoiled, as did Lord Keith, for they both knew the tales surrounding children sold at auction. Next, the story of Fallon and Aja's capture was on the table, with Jones interrupting to describe Aja for Lord Keith. After that, the admiral rose and paced the small office while Bisanz told of the meeting with Beauty and how she'd asked for volunteers to sail to Algiers based on Fallon's message and instructions.

"Instructions, you say?" asked Jones. "Captain Fallon was specific?"

"Yes," said Bisanz. "Beauty said he was quite specific about when she was to arrive off the mole at the harbor's entrance."

For the first time since hearing the story Jones smiled. Lord Keith noticed.

"Fallon has a plan, admiral," he said. "I don't know what it is but I will wager my pay that Beauty has tipped to it and knows what she's doing."

Lord Keith shook his head in something like wonder. He was beginning to understand Admiral Davies' respect for Fallon's ingenuity. But it seemed he'd gotten himself captured, along with his second mate, and now his first mate was off to help him with a ship full of British soldiers and it seemed to Lord Keith that nothing could be done further.

He didn't see Sir William's glance to Jones, and the nod from Jones in answer.

Fifty-Five

Rascal tacked eastward, then made long boards south for most of the day, making what distance she could against building wind and seas. Barclay estimated they would be off Tipasa past midnight the next day, whereupon Beauty planned to heave-to until it was time to leave in order to be off the mole at dawn. On time per Fallon's note, but for what was unclear.

The volunteers were all sitting on deck cleaning their muskets and sleeping after the cook had served up a sailor's feast of stewed pork with vegetables and, to top it off, duff pudding. The pudding had been Barclay's idea, for he was a particular pudding aficionado.

As evening approached Beauty checked the course and speed, noted the increase in wind, and retreated to her cabin for a late dinner of her own and to read, for perhaps the hundredth time, Fallon's message. She had not looked at it since leaving Gibraltar, preferring to put it out of her mind and concentrate on things at hand so as to see it again later with fresh eyes. She poured herself a glass of wine and sat at her desk, the message open before her. As she touched the sea dog around her neck her eyes fell on the oft-read passage:

> *Upon receipt of this message you will take aboard any additional crew that you need in Gibraltar and prepare to be off the mole at the harbor in 10 days' time. That's where a pilot boat will meet you.*

She had certainly taken aboard all that she needed, at least to her own satisfaction, by getting the colonel's volunteers.

From what she could see, all that was left was to meet the pilot ship and be guided into the harbor. How the hell was that going to rescue anybody? What was supposed to happen after that?

And then, as she read the passage again, her hand froze as she raised the wine glass to her lips.

The last sentence didn't say anything about being guided into the harbor.

Morning found Fallon and Aja working side by side on the mole, Fallon straining to see Wilhelm Visser laboring on the docks across the harbor. But he was not to be seen in the glare of the sun or the shadows cast by the big ships. For the past several days Visser had been unloading only grain, so there had been nothing to smuggle back to the pen. Fallon prayed that he would bring back something useful that night that they could build a plan around. If not, they would have to try to overpower the guards at dinner, a risky move because one guard stayed back, outside the pen, while the other guard delivered the dinner inside. Visser said the outside guard always held a cocked musket.

Dinner was the only time the pen was unlocked in the evening; the guard who came around midnight just looked inside through the stockade walls to see that all was well.

The wind began to strengthen in the afternoon and the flags and bunting on the ships at anchor stood out stiffly. It was a furnace of a wind, blown across hundreds or thousands of miles of desert, full of dirt and grit. It became untenable to work with bare faces and eyes closed against wind. The guards came for them early and they were taken back to the pens.

It was not much better there. The wind came hot and dry through the stockade walls, and Fallon, Aja, and Little Eddy all huddled with their heads down and their eyes closed to keep the debris at bay. But they could hear the lock snap open and squinted to see Wilhelm Visser being shown into the pen by his guards.

He entered the pen with his head down. Fallon looked closely at him, hoping for a hint of success, but the old man's bearing didn't change even after the guards had walked away.

"I have brought very little from the docks," Visser said dejectedly. "Today there was much work to do and the guards were unusually vigilant with us. We were unloading some gifts to the dey from an Italian merchant."

He reached under his tunic and brought out a cloth sack. From within it he withdrew a wooden ladle used to serve out shipboard gruel, and a silver urn with curved handles.

"It was all I could scrounge from the holds of the ship we were unloading," Visser said softly. "It isn't much to work with, I know."

Fallon looked at what Visser had smuggled from the ship and his heart sank. He didn't know what he was expecting, but it was more than this. Whatever disappointment he felt, however, was doubled on Visser's face, and he forced himself to smile.

"It's perfect," he lied, and then in spite of himself he laughed out loud.

The little group looked down at the purloined objects, the dust swirling around them, and they all laughed, laughed like madmen in a mad world. Then Aja stopped laughing and picked up the wooden ladle. He looked at it a moment, and then broke it over his knee. The wooden handle snapped off with a sharp, splintered tip.

"I have an idea, captain sir," he said. And Fallon and everyone else leaned in to hear it above the shrieking wind.

Just after midnight the guard made his rounds of the pens, holding a lantern aloft, checking the locks and looking in at the sleeping bodies. Most of the straw pallets had blown apart and the prisoners were asleep on the dirt floor. The guard counted them as best he could in the shafts of light thrown through the stockade walls before going on to the next pen.

At Fallon's pen the guard paused, for near the middle of the floor, just a few yards inside the gate, the lantern's light seemed to glint off something silver. Something like a vase or urn. Yes, an urn, and one of the prisoners seemed to be praying over it, or chanting something unintelligible. The other prisoners seemed to be asleep along the sides of the pen. This was all very strange to the guard, and he debated with himself over what to do. *How could the urn have come here?* he wondered. If it was silver it was worth more than a thousand days of working!

Now Aja, who had been chanting, lifted the urn into the air, into a shaft of light from the lantern, seemingly ignoring the guard. He said a few more words, put it back on the floor and backed away to the rear of the pen.

The guard hesitated, but greed was a powerful emotion. He decided it would do no harm to open the gate to see better. The lock snapped open and he stepped inside, the lantern held high in one hand, his scimitar in the other.

The urn glowed brightly in his lantern's light.

The guard stood still a moment and looked around the pen, but no one moved. One of the men seemed to be snoring, in fact. Three more steps and he could reach the urn.

He took the first step before Little Eddy dropped out of the sky onto his back and he stumbled to the ground. Immediately, Fallon rose and leapt on top of the guard and drove the ladle's splintered handle into his neck.

It was over so quickly that Fallon and Aja were momentarily speechless. It was Wilhelm Visser who pounded on their backs and brought them around to reality. Little Eddy whooped before they quieted him. Slowly they dragged the guard to the rear of the pen and wrapped him with a blanket. Then, with a last look around, they locked the gate behind them.

Once outside the holding pen area they bent low and crept along the quay to where the pilot boat was tied. The slaves were all ashore, presumably exhausted from rowing back and forth all day at the mouth of the harbor, and the crew would not return with them until just before dawn. The full force of the wind could be better felt on the quay and Fallon wondered briefly if the pilot boat would even go out past the mole in those conditions. Indeed, it felt like a gale had blown up since yesterday, but pilot boats went out no matter what the weather around the world, he decided. He knew Beauty would be on time and the dey would expect *Rascal* to be shown into the harbor. That put his mind to rest and he led the little group aboard.

It was so dark he had trouble locating the hatches that opened to the holds. The boat was shallow and the holds were not deep, but they were empty. There were two hatches on the centerline of the boat, fore and aft, and he motioned to Aja to open the forward one.

"Be ready to come up quickly when you hear me yell," he said as quietly as he could and still be heard above the shriek of wind. "Put Little Eddy in first and you go after."

Next he asked Visser to climb into the aft hatch and Fallon climbed in behind him. Both hatches were closed and the four of them lay uncomfortably in the darkness on the floorboards to await dawn.

The boat jerked at her lines and pitched like a tethered wild thing yearning to be free. The air in the hold was stuffy and hot and Fallon thought at least one of them might be sick; he only hoped it wasn't him.

By his estimate there was still several hours before dawn.

Barclay brought *Rascal* a mile from the mole well before daylight in the early morning, and Beauty ordered the ship to heave-to for an hour. Cully had loaded both batteries with grapeshot and the hands were at stations armed with pistols, muskets, and cutlasses. The volunteers were glad the ship had settled down as many had been retching in the scuppers for some time. They held their rifles and looked into the blackness.

And still the wind continued to rise, black and malevolent, picking a fight. Beauty had ordered the topsails furled and then the topmasts struck altogether. Barclay had been right, there was a dirty day ahead. The dust was beginning to coat the decks with fine grit, and the volunteers put their hands over the ends of their rifle barrels to keep the sand out.

Barclay approached the binnacle and handed Beauty her favorite weapon, a boarding pike.

"You might need this," he said. "I expect you will."

"Thanks, Barclay," she said. "As Fallon would say if he were here, we're about to see what we see."

Barclay nodded, though she could only see his white head moving up and down.

"I think we're getting a sirocco," he said in a raised voice. "It's a sandstorm they get in this sea. Comes off the Sahara. I wonder what kind of visibility we'll have at dawn. Might not be much."

Beauty gave an unseen nod of her own. She'd heard of siroccos; every sailor had. But few sailors had ever experienced one. The tales she'd heard said the winds could reach gale or even hurricane force. As much as her face was stinging from the sand now, she wondered what in God's name would that feel like?

The alarm was raised just before dawn when the guards came to get the slaves from the holding pens for the day's labors. The gate to Fallon's cell was locked but clearly no one was there. Well, excepting the dead guard with the splinter in his neck. How could that be?

The word went up and down the narrow streets and a general search of the town was begun immediately. Zabana was in his home near the palace in the upper city and was awakened by the trumpeting janissaries and hurriedly dressed. What was this? Prisoners had escaped!

He knew immediately who it was.

As he stepped outside, the wind almost blew his door off its hinges. The sirocco was building to its full force and it seemed it had brought all the sands of the Sahara with it. No one was outside except the janissaries, and each one of them had his face wrapped more or less completely.

At first, Zabana assumed the British captain would try to escape the city the same way he had entered it, through the gate to the west. But as he turned to rush towards the gate a new thought struck him. *The sea.* Fallon was a sea captain, after all. He would try for a boat.

Zabana reversed direction and began running to the harbor, calling to the janissaries he passed to follow him.

The pilot boat lurched more than usual, and Fallon could hear the crew come aboard. They were yelling above the wind but their words were unintelligible. Then more feet on the deck with a softer step, barefooted slaves no doubt. The hatches groaned and creaked over Fallon's head as the men on deck moved around, and he could hear chains being handled. He figured the slaves were being chained to their oars. *Poor sods*, he thought. If they were naked as usual he could only imagine the sting of the sand on their bare bodies.

Fallon found himself praying that the crew didn't have anything to stow below decks. He hadn't thought of that. There was more yelling, and probably cursing in Arabic if he could have understood it. The prospect of taking a shallow draft boat even a hundred yards off the dock in that wind and sea must be daunting, thought Fallon. But they had probably seen it all and sailed it all before.

Now a different motion, steadier, and Fallon supposed the slaves were rowing. The pilot boat was still swooping but he could feel the thrust through the water with each pull of the oars. He had no experience with lateen sails but he wondered if a reef or two could be taken, and how, and whether they could be taken before the sail was raised. He was working out the complexity of the maneuver to keep himself occupied in the closed black world of the hold. He could hear Visser breathing behind him, labored and wheezy. *We'll only get this one chance,* he'd said.

It seemed like a long time, perhaps an hour, before the motion of the boat changed and Fallon suspected they'd been able to get some sail up. Now he could feel the heel of the boat as it rolled him back onto Visser. It was impossible to tell which direction they were sailing, but as the wind was out of the southeast and they were heeling to starboard he figured they were heading west.

Was Beauty out there somewhere?

He tried to imagine *Rascal* sailing close-hauled towards them. The ship would be on starboard, the men at their stations, the sails deeply reefed. In his mind he could see Barclay at the binnacle shielding his eyes against the blowing dust, with Beauty beside him, her peg planted securely in a ring bolt to hold her steady.

And she *would* be steady.

Rascal had been underway for half an hour when Beauty saw the pilot boat sailing towards them, dipping and plunging in the sea, her streamers blowing stiffly off the tip of the raked mast and long boom upon which the lateen sail was gathered in a deep reef. She'd ordered the soldiers to sit or lay down hours ago as a precaution, for there was no way of knowing how this was going to play out.

"Barclay," she yelled above the sandblast of wind, "let's heave-to again, please. Then we'll see what the next move is."

The schooner turned into the wind as if to tack and then intentionally stalled, the foresail backwinded and the mainsail brought to centerline, where the motion died considerably and the ship went neither here nor there.

The pilot boat was now about a half mile away and still swooping over the seas like a gull. The sky behind her was brown, a rusted wall of air and sand that abraded everything it touched. Beauty squinted into the wind; it looked to her like there were four crewmen as well as a number of slaves at the oars in the small boat. At two hundred yards one of the crewmen, no doubt the captain of the pilot boat, began waving his arms for the schooner to follow.

Damned if I will, thought Beauty.

At a hundred yards the captain was still waving, this time more insistently, and yelling. Beauty looked at Cully standing by the larboard battery, the slow match sizzling in a bucket next to each cannon. The soldiers were still hidden on the deck as ordered. Now the captain of the pilot boat steered directly towards *Rascal,* and Beauty saw he would have to veer soon or he would run aboard the schooner.

At that moment there was confusion on board the pilot boat as it spun around on its axis and nearly capsized in a breaking sea. Beauty could see ragged men fighting and two of the crew were thrown overboard. Then three. A scuffle near the stern and now four! The little boat was nearly swamped and after the sail was taken in completely the remaining men began bailing furiously—and the rowers began rowing for *Rascal.*

The air was so thick with dust that it was nearly impossible for Beauty to look into the wind, but standing at the tiller was someone who looked an awful lot like Nicholas Fallon.

You fucker! Beauty said under her breath. *You did it!*

Fifty-Six

Zabana boarded *Serpent* and immediately ordered the hands rousted out of their hammocks. There wasn't time to bring the slaves down to the quay so he would leave without them. The janissaries who tumbled aboard could row if it came to that. He looked around and could see no boats missing from the quay; only the pilot boat was out as usual; the weather never kept it at the dock.

The pilot boat!

This was the day the pilot boat was to meet the British schooner off the mole! The ship with the gold! He knew in an instant who was aboard that boat.

Zabana's crew made fast work of the lines and as the wind was blowing *Serpent* away from the dock they raised the big sails while they were somewhat in the lee of the quay and moved away quickly towards the harbor's entrance. They wore ship while still in the harbor, less risky than outside, and double-reefed the sails. The pilot boat was nowhere to be seen as they passed the mole but on instinct Zabana ordered the helmsman to bear west.

Fallon expertly guided the pilot boat to the lee side of *Rascal* and then, with the schooner blocking the worst of the wind and sea, he motioned to the slaves to edge closer to the side of the ship. Eager hands were there to jump into the smaller boat to secure it. First, Wilhelm Visser was handed up into the arms, or rather the good arm, of his son. Both men broke down in tears and had to be led away from the gangway. Next

Little Eddy went up to the general delight and cheering of the crew. Fallon located the key to the manacles in a box at the stern of the pilot boat and unlocked each of the slaves from their oars. Then he and Aja began handing up the poor, naked men. One by one the bewildered slaves gained *Rascal's* deck and were led below to Colquist to be examined. They all seemed to be Turks or North Africans but that could be sorted out later. Now they were all free men.

Then, at last, Aja and Fallon came through the channel and were swooped up into the arms of Beauty and Cully and the rest. The soldiers were gathered around, as well, and Fallon was trying to ask Beauty about them when the lookout's call came down to the deck and froze everyone momentarily.

"Deck there! It's that snake xebec to the east!"

Fallon jerked his head around and squinted into the sandstorm. He could see nothing from the deck; he was frankly amazed the lookout had seen anything either.

"Beauty, head north quickly! We'll try to outrun him downwind!"

The Rascals leapt to their roles in the stinging wind, their bare feet crunching the sand that covered the deck and was piling up in the crevices and corners. The sirocco had gained strength in the last hour and was now a gale at full force and Beauty called for a reef in the main and foresail and still *Rascal* bounded northward on a broad reach with a bone in her teeth. Shot and slow match were already on deck and the soldiers crowded the center of the ship to be clear of the gun crews.

There, the thunder of a cannon! Fallon looked past Aja to see Zabana's ship in the distance, its deadly snake's head lunging towards them.

Serpent's big sails were double reefed but her relatively light weight and shallow draft made her extremely fast in a big wind and the sirocco was certainly that. The seas were growing, as well, but Zabana was confident he had the ship to catch the schooner. It was only a matter of time.

At a mile and a half away he'd fired his bow chaser and would keep firing it to get the barrel hot as they drew closer. He was mad with the chase, the humiliation at Fallon's hands burning his skin more than the sand.

He nodded to the agha to ready his men.

~

Fallon and Beauty watched as *Serpent* fell in behind them sailing northwest and continuing to fire her bow chaser, though in that heaving sea at a mile it would be a lucky shot indeed that found its mark.

"What do you think, Beauty?" asked Fallon. Both ships were on starboard tack, their sails well out in conditions where they should be hove-to.

"I don't know what he's planning," said Beauty as she looked over her shoulder. "That ship is a handful, though. It's amazing it's even upright. But if we're going to make a move we'd better make it soon. Anything can happen in this damn wind and I don't want it to happen to us!"

Fallon kept his eyes riveted on *Serpent* and judged the distance between the two ships to be less than a half mile. The red grit was in his eyes and mouth and nose and it was hard to breathe looking back into the wind.

"Here's an idea you won't like, Nico," Beauty shouted. And she was right, he didn't like it.

Yet Fallon immediately saw the strategy for what it was: their best chance. He nodded to Beauty to come about and yelled to Aja to have Cully stand by the long nine and have the gun crews stand by the larboard battery and double shot the guns with chain and shot. If even one of those guns found a stay or sheet or, please God, a spar—*Serpent* could be mortally wounded in this wind and sea. One could only hope.

But now Beauty was focused on picking the trough she wanted to turn into as the waves rolled under *Rascal*, lifting her stern high into the air before the ship hurtled down the face of the wave and buried her nose in the base of the wave ahead. The waves were coming fairly regularly, but there was some variation and Beauty wanted the greatest distance between waves she could find.

The helmsmen—for there were two of them on the big wheel—were looking forward awaiting her order to come about and Beauty was looking astern, not at the xebec but at the sea. At last a monster wave lifted them up on its shoulders and she yelled, "Now!"

The schooner slid down the face of the wave at an angle, the hands bringing the big sails in slowly as the helmsmen guided *Rascal* smoothly and turned just quickly enough to keep her moving under control as the wind moderated in the trough. Her bow came around just as the next wave reared up and *Rascal* climbed up, and up, her sails coming in tighter and filling as the wind came over the top of the wave. Here's where the drills and discipline paid off and when Fallon tore his eyes away from the maneuver and looked ahead there was *Serpent* charging towards them, caught fully unaware by Beauty's maneuver.

Now Cully opened fire with the long nine and the crew cheered. The ships were closing very quickly, with *Rascal* on larboard tack now, diving into the troughs and climbing up the face of the next wave in line. *Serpent* now had a difficult choice. Since her larboard rail was buried with the heel of the ship, her larboard guns would be useless. She could attempt to fall off to bring her starboard battery to bear, but she risked wearing ship, which could be catastrophic in that wind and sea. Now the xebec's usual advantages were nullified or worked against her: her oars were useless and her light ballast made her unhandy and extremely dangerous in these conditions.

And events were unfolding quickly.

Zabana lisped a curse and watched as *Rascal,* for he had seen the schooner's name, had come about and was now sailing back towards him. And now her bow chaser was firing! His own cannon fired again, but he could see the odds had shifted away from his favor. No matter what he did *Serpent* would be raked and, even if he could exchange fire gun for gun, his ship was far more lightly built and would likely suffer the most damage. A broadside exchange could prove fatal.

Here came the British ship, her sails as hard as knife blades. She would pass well within broadside range and Zabana could imagine her cannons loaded with chain shot to shoot away his rigging. *Rascal* had the steadier platform, for *Serpent* was yawing and rolling in the quartering seas, water often coming over her larboard rail. She would be lucky if a single cannon could fire and Zabana knew it.

The realization that he had been outfoxed brought bile to his throat and something in his mind refused to accept another humiliation. His rage and malevolence took control of his reason and his thin grasp on reality slipped away. *Two could play at surprises!* he exclaimed out loud. Quickly he ordered the crewmen to loosen the sails and, laughing maniacally, he pushed the helmsmen away and took the tiller himself. He knew his idea was brilliant and he became focused on executing his plan perfectly.

Rascal was charging down and he wanted all the satisfaction of ramming her himself.

"Aja," yelled Fallon, "tell Cully to stand by the larboard battery. For the rigging lads!"

As the ships approached one another Fallon could see the snake's head clearly at the end of *Serpent*'s bowsprit. It was turning towards him now as *Serpent* appeared to be falling down to pass closer to *Rascal.* The snake's head was mesmerizing and detailed with eyes that were painted red and seemed to glow like embers.

Suddenly, the snake turned hard to larboard and began to cross directly into *Rascal's* path. Beauty saw what was happening and called for the helmsman to fall off but it was too late. Zabana was driving the snake's head into *Rascal on purpose!* As Fallon and Beauty watched helplessly the burning eyes plunged into the bow of the schooner and stuck fast.

Everyone on both ships was thrown to the decks; some were knocked unconscious and others lost their weapons and their wits. *Serpent's* masts went by the board and her sails fell over the side with them. *Rascal's* foremast snapped half way up and her mainmast came crashing down over the side in a tangle of rigging and sail and lumber that no doubt killed anyone under it. The ships were locked together, both severely wounded and helpless as the sirocco screamed overhead and threw waves as tall as small houses at the ships.

Fallon gained his feet and helped Beauty to hers as Aja tried to sort out the soldiers and crew who had been thrown against the cannons and bulwarks. Barclay was holding onto the wheel with his only arm and trying to stand while Cully's face was a mass of blood from a brutal meeting with a gun carriage.

Suddenly, a trumpet's call rent the air above the roar of the wind.

Fifty-Seven

The janissaries were massing to climb along the snake's body and onto *Rascal's* deck.

"Rascals! Soldiers! To me!" yelled Fallon and he charged towards the bows of his ship, his sword out and held high.

The first shot rang out and a janissary fell to Wilhelm Visser's hand, his musket borrowed from an unconscious soldier. More shots followed as janissaries fired from *Serpent's* deck before climbing aboard *Rascal*. Several soldiers fell wounded but then their comrades fired a volley that sent janissaries tumbling into the sea.

Fallon jumped into the thick of the fighting, yelling furiously and lurching forward on the heaving, twisting deck. He slashed at a man's neck, almost decapitating him, and took a slash of his own across his chest from collarbone to gut. It wasn't deep, but the cut immediately began oozing blood. Aja was beside him, as usual, yelling at the top of his lungs and fighting to protect his friend and captain. But he was down! A janissary had swung his musket and caught Aja on his arm and was now raising his weapon above his head for the final blow when Beauty thrust her boarding pike through his spine, sending him to the deck, instantly paralyzed and dying.

Now Aja was up, his left arm hanging uselessly, but hacking with his right arm at the boarders. And the British soldiers were surging forward, their bayonets fixed to their rifles, their drills on the quad coming to the fore as they fired their muskets on the lurching ship and then thrust their way through the knot of janissaries at the bow, stabbing and plunging with their bayonets at anyone and everyone in a red hat.

But the movement was chaotic under their feet. The ships were locked together but the snake's head was twisting and pulling back and forth into *Rascal's* rigging with each sea that swept under the ships. The xebec slammed into the schooner and jerked away, only to be thrust into *Rascal* again, the sea working each ship independently, corkscrewing them this way and that, their timbers groaning at being wrenched in such an unnatural way.

The agha was aboard *Rascal*, calling *Surrender dogs!* in English and slashing with his scimitar; he drove one of the Rascals to the deck with a half-severed arm before Cully, rising up from beside a cannon, pushed his pistol against the agha's side and fired, the ball passing through both lungs and out the other side of the man's body.

As the ships were pushed to the northwest the sirocco began picking up moisture from the sea and mixed it with the dust high in the atmosphere, only to send it downward in what the Italians called *blood rain,* large red drops that splattered to the decks and began to mix with the blood already soaking the sand there. Now faces were dripping blood rain and every man looked to be bleeding.

The Rascals closed ranks around the wounded Fallon and Aja, fighting all the more furiously as a great mass of janissaries charged. But it was the soldiers, Bisanz's volunteers, who stood against the Muslim elite and evened the odds, giving no quarter, not backing up an inch and then, with a renewed push, they now began forcing the janissaries backwards. Fallon sensed the fighting was at a crux and he cheered the men on with all the voice he could muster.

At last, the xebec's snake head began to work its way loose from *Rascal*, the seas releasing *Serpent's* grip on the schooner's side. Zabana saw it from the deck of his ship and called for the janissaries to leap back aboard *Serpent* but the ships were suddenly free from each other and it was too late. Some of the janissaries leaped overboard in a desperate attempt to swim for their ship but the seas were too large and they disappeared in the valleys between the waves. The xebec pulled free but was helpless without masts and sails and the swells pushed her stern around to *Rascal.* Now the ships crunched together again, side against side.

"Grappling hooks!" yelled Fallon weakly, not wanting *Serpent* to drift away on the next wave, wanting to finish what Zabana had started. Most of the Rascals were fighting in the bows of the ship but Cully and two men rushed to lash the two ships together. Now *Serpent's* crew were bystanders no more as *Rascal's* crew jumped to the xebec's deck and began stabbing and cutting at them. Fallon climbed unsteadily over the railings and fell to *Serpent's* deck and had to struggle to his feet, the front of his shirt a bright red from both his own blood and the rain. Zabana saw his chance and hatred and humiliation shone in his black eyes. He held a sword in each hand and whispered Arabic phrases that the wind took away as he pushed into the fighting to get to Fallon.

Fallon saw him and stood gamely to his charge, holding onto the guillotine with one hand to steady himself and holding his sword in the other.

Zabana saw his moment and lunged, but Fallon backed up and parried the thrust and then brought his sword down with every reserve ounce of strength he possessed. Zabana's right hand was severed completely, though it still held a death grip on his sword as it fell to the xebec's deck.

Zabana looked at it stupidly as Fallon raised his foot and kicked him in the groin, knocking him backwards and through his beloved guillotine. He looked up at the steel blade dripping blood rain and then at his executioner. His eyes were wide as Fallon swung his sword with both hands towards the side of the guillotine and severed the restraining rope. The falling blade gained extra impetus by the lifting deck and in one seventieth of a second it plunged into and then through Zabana's body.

Whereupon Fallon fell to the deck unconscious.

Seeing their leader fall gave *Serpent's* crew nothing to fight for, or be afraid of, and they threw their weapons overboard and fell to the deck in surrender. The Rascals on the galley rushed to Fallon and hoisted him up as gently as the surging deck would allow and passed him over the railing to Wilhelm and Caleb Visser who immediately carried him below to Colquist, Little Eddy running ahead shouting to clear the way.

On board *Rascal* the slaughter was almost complete as the dey's finest soldiers were decimated by Britain's finest and *Rascal's* crew. Those janissaries left standing threw down their swords and some leapt into the roiling sea rather than become prisoners of the Christians they had sworn to kill or enslave.

Suddenly, there was no one left to fight. But there was a ship to save! *Rascal* had a gaping hole in her bow and the top of every wave slapped water inside the ship. She had no sails up and only part of the foremast and the seas had her at their mercy.

The rest of the Rascals on the xebec leapt back aboard the schooner, leaving *Serpent's* crew lying on her deck. But one of them had hidden a sword beneath his body. He lunged at the railing and began hacking at the grappling lines that held the two ships together. At last they came apart, the xebec drifting down *Rascal's* side and away behind her trailing rigging and spars.

Now Beauty took charge and began issuing orders to attempt to set *Rascal* to rights as quickly as possible. The carpenter reported four feet and rising in the well and the ship was yawing badly and utterly out of control as the sirocco raged around it. It suddenly occurred to her that her sea dog's luck had run out, that the ship couldn't survive the awful storm as battered and broken as she was.

Then a cannon!

Beauty jerked her head around in wonder that the crew aboard *Serpent* were still fighting but they had drifted far behind.

No! Out of the brown gloom was an apparition as beautiful and welcome as anything she could imagine she'd ever see—*Renegade! How in the world?* she wondered. The big ship was coming down from the north under a scrap of sail and already there were men gathering on the bow with a messenger line. It was just what *Rascal* had done to save Visser, and in just such a storm—minus the blood rain.

Renegade was rolling up the larger waves and moving fast in spite of carrying so little sail. The thing would have to be timed just right and Beauty hoped they had a strong hand with the monkey fist. She was about to find out.

Jones stood calmly next to the helmsman as he guided the ship closer to the desperate *Rascal.* The schooner's bow faced north and *Avenger* would be passing as closely as possible on her starboard side so the messenger line would be thrown into the middle of the ship. *Renegade* would need to quickly heave-to as the line was walked up the schooner's deck to be tied off at the bow. Then *Renegade* could come out of stays and slowly take up the slack on the tow line. That was the plan, anyway.

In the event, the plan failed.

The monkey fist landed in the sea just short of *Rascal* and Jones was obliged to sail by and come about for a second approach closer to the dismasted ship. After some anxious moments maneuvering to get closer, and closer still, the line was heaved again and landed at the startled Barclay's feet and a crewman reacted quickly and gathered the messenger in and walked it forward to be tied off on the capstan at *Rascal's* bow. *Renegade* immediately hove-to while her big hawser was then winched aboard *Rascal*, both ships dipping and rolling and falling down the steep seas. The whole process seemed to take an eternity, but once Jones saw everything was secure he ordered the ship out of stays and the helmsman to proceed west and slowly the frigate and her tow clawed their way towards the Strait of Gibraltar. Jones could see Fallon's crew hacking at the rigging that was hanging over the side to free the ship from the enormous drag it created. They would be at it for some time.

Beauty ordered a detail to begin patching the giant hole in *Rascal's* bows and within two hours they had done a fair job of keeping the water out. The carpenter sounded the well again and Beauty set the hands to pumping six feet of water back where it belonged.

Jones anxiously walked to the stern of his ship and looked back towards *Rascal.* The schooner was following like a disobedient puppy fighting its leash and trying to go its own way. He saw Beauty and thought he could see Aja but he couldn't see Fallon.

As he stared into the brown air, he wondered why.

Fifty-Eight

Fallon wasn't going to die, but he wasn't going to be his old alive self for a while. He'd lost so much blood his face and lips were pale, and Colquist immediately set to stitching the long cut closed. Fallon was in and out of consciousness and the laudanum helped keep him quiet.

He was the least of the medical problems below deck. Several of *Rascal's* crewmen and Bisanz's soldiers were fighting for their lives down there as surely as they had fought above decks. The cuts from scimitars were wicked, the curved swords sharpened as they were to a razor's edge by patient janissaries quietly preparing for battle. The tub holding amputated limbs began to fill up.

Wilhelm and Caleb Visser came below to be with Fallon, who was gingerly placed in his cabin cot. They both looked at the man who, along with Aja, had risked his life to unite them. Wilhelm, overcome with emotion, held onto his son's hand and wept.

After receiving a report from Little Eddy on Fallon's condition, Beauty's spirits rose and she began to see progress in getting the ship set to rights. A scrap of sail was rigged to the broken foremast and it gave the helmsman more steerage. The carpenter reported only three feet in the well, and no more water coming in. Relieved, Beauty ordered rum piped up and that one order cheered the men enormously. Barclay estimated the ship was making three knots and would likely make more once the well was pumped down even further.

The dead had been piled along the railings for burial as soon as possible and Beauty deemed it time. After a brief service sailor and soldier alike slid into the sea, stitched in canvass weighted by shot. Beauty said a

Christian prayer over the dead janissaries and they, too went overboard. The battle had been a bloody business, and Beauty was doubly grateful to Colonel Bisanz for she knew in her bones the fight would have gone the other way without his men.

When at last she allowed herself to pause, Beauty wondered how in God's name *Renegade* showed up when she did, out of the gloom, to come to their rescue. Beauty wasn't one to look a gift horse in the mouth, *but what the fuck was Jones doing in the Mediterranean anyway?*

Jones stood on the stern of *Renegade* and watched the work being done on *Rascal.* She had a bit of sail up now and that had prevented her yawing this way and that. It had also taken some of the strain off the huge hawser that served as a tow line. The ship looked a wreck, and as he watched the bodies slide into the sea he wondered at the battle she'd fought and won. Victory had come at a terrible cost, as it usually did. *Rascal* had been lucky to survive.

But, of course, it wasn't luck that *Renegade* had found her. Sir William had had a quiet word with Lord Keith after the meeting with Colonel Bisanz and, later that day, orders had arrived that set *Renegade* sailing towards the coast of North Africa. Lord Keith's orders were necessarily vague, but they involved ranging as far as Algiers and looking into the harbor. Not close enough to provoke the Algerians, but close enough for a lookout to identify any British ships inside. It was left to Jones to use his discretion if *Renegade* was challenged.

Of course, the sirocco was a surprise, but *Renegade* was a well-found ship and could handle storms of that size. The wind was slowly dying off now, and the seas would eventually lay down. Jones fretted about Fallon's absence on the deck and feared the worst. He had seen the burial service and wondered if his friend was among those who had slid into the sea.

It was almost two days later when *Renegade* and *Rascal* reached Gibraltar and let go their anchors in the shadow of the huge headland. The harbor was partially deserted as ships were slow to return after putting to sea during the sirocco, not wanting to be caught on a lee shore. The harbor itself was roughly thirty square miles and quite deep for much of its center—almost 1300 feet down at its deepest, though holding the bottom anywhere in the harbor in such a storm would worry any captain.

Beauty was surprised to see a flagship flying an admiral's pennant at anchor. She wondered what it all meant: *Renegade*, the admiral, all that. But she was about to find out as she saw *Renegade's* gig immediately lowered and Captain Jones climb down into it and the gig's crew begin rowing feverishly towards *Rascal.*

Jones was met at the gangway by Beauty who, after thanking him profusely for saving *Rascal,* proclaimed Fallon alive but wounded from a slash down his belly and resting in his cabin. Jones immediately went below and encountered Aja with his broken arm in a sling coming up the companionway. After the briefest of greetings Jones continued to Fallon's cabin and knocked softly. To his surprise, Fallon greeted him through clenched teeth, and Wilhelm and Caleb Visser backed out to leave these two friends alone.

"Now what have you done?" asked Jones with a forced smile to comfort Fallon. "I promised Admiral Davies that, if I crossed your hawse, I would look after you on behalf of Elinore and I seemed to have broken my word."

"I must apologize, Samuel," said Fallon gamely. "But if the cut had gone lower it might have indeed caused Elinore distress."

At that Jones laughed and Fallon managed a smile.

"But why in God's name are you here, Jones?" asked Fallon. "Beauty told me you came to our rescue during the height of the sirocco and I confess I couldn't believe it. That was a very brave thing to do, Jones. We were in rather desperate shape after the battle with *Serpent*, I'm afraid. But surely you're a bit far afield from Antigua?"

At that, the story of Jones' orders to convey Sir William to Lord Keith came out and the subsequent taking of the prize and the meeting with Lord Keith and, later, Colonel Bisanz.

"Yes," said Fallon. "Beauty told me about the colonel's volunteers. They made all the difference against the janissaries. I'm afraid we lost some of them but, God, they were brave! But how did you come to find us, Jones?"

"It was Sir William having a talk with Lord Keith, I believe," replied Jones. "Next thing I knew I had orders to approach Algiers and look into the harbor for you. But I found you rather sooner!"

With that Jones could see that Fallon was growing tired and he bade to take his leave. Fallon did not object, for he had much information to digest and his eyes were growing heavy.

Jones was barely in his gig when he saw his number go up on *Artemis'* yard. Lord Keith wanted to see him.

Fifty-Nine

"I must say you are a very poor patient, Nico," said Beauty. "Colquist tells me you are getting up and moving about against his expressed orders. He's very afraid you will pop your stitches."

It had been several days since *Rascal* had anchored and Beauty had seen Fallon's condition improve significantly over that time, though he had no business getting up.

"Yes, he's being a bit of a nanny," said Fallon with a smile. "But I am feeling stronger and I'm quite bored out of my mind."

"Well, perhaps this will relieve your boredom," she said. "Lord Keith would like an audience with your highness. He sent word this morning and will come to you to talk."

"What do you think that's all about?" asked Fallon.

"You won't have too long to wonder," said Beauty with a grin. "Unless I'm mistaken I just heard his coxswain call out so the admiral's gig must be alongside."

Beauty left to thump up the companionway and welcome Lord Keith aboard. The work was going full tilt on deck to return *Rascal* to her usual condition but the masts were still out of her and would be until the yard sent word they were ready to swing two new ones aboard. But here was the famous Lord Keith coming through the channel.

"You must be Beauty McFarland, first mate on *Rascal,* I believe," he said warmly. "I have heard wondrous things about you, not least your ability to charm crusty army officers into doing your bidding. But that is our secret and should stay in Gibraltar."

Beauty smiled and blushed simultaneously.

In moments she led Lord Keith down the companionway to Fallon's cabin and found him sitting upright—against Colquist's orders—in a chair by the stern windows.

"Captain Fallon," said Lord Keith, "don't attempt to get up I implore you. Your surgeon would have both our necks if those stitches I hear you have should open. I am content to sit on the stern cushions and I promise I will only be a few minutes."

With that, Lord Keith sat down and Beauty discretely left the cabin.

"It is a pleasure to meet you, my lord," said Fallon. "I have heard so much about you over the years. Your exploits reach Bermuda, where I am from."

"And I have heard a great deal about you, captain," said Lord Keith. "Admiral Davies speaks very highly of you, as does Sir William and, well, everyone seems to have something interesting to say about you."

Fallon laughed and shifted uneasily in his chair.

"No doubt Captain Jones has filled you in on his trip across the Atlantic to return Sir William to the Mediterranean. He even took a French frigate on the way, and without a shot! Now, I will take you into my confidence as to why that trip was necessary. The Admiralty believes Bonaparte is attempting to enlist the dey of Algiers in a scheme to blockade Gibraltar. Presumably the siege would mean Bonaparte would have free rein over this sea that he seems to covet. Sir William is now endeavoring to find out how far along the plans are but the threat is real. Sir William's sources tell him that the dey is supportive of the idea, if only to enrich himself, though he has demanded proof of Bonaparte's sincerity. I believe there is to be a down payment to show good faith."

Fallon took a moment to absorb the information Lord Keith shared. It didn't take much imagination to visualize Gibraltar under siege from French ships-of-the-line and the dey's corsairs, with Britain unable to muster a strong defense.

"How many ships do you have at your disposal, my lord?" asked Fallon, getting right to the nub of the matter.

"I have four frigates and my flagship, captain," said Lord Keith, and he thought he could hear Fallon's mind working. "Two of the frigates are on station in Genoa to help the Austrians and the other two are here. I believe you met Captain Elliott of *Mischief?*"

Fallon only nodded, not wanting his face to give away his feelings about Elliott. Lord Keith watched him closely.

"I am here because Admiral Davies sent word that you might be helpful in this situation," continued Lord Keith, "and now perhaps doubly so since I understand you were a prisoner of the dey's before making a remarkable escape. The story is up and down the waterfront."

If Fallon was moved by Lord Keith's flattering words he didn't show it; instead, his eyes were fixed on an unseen horizon beyond the stern windows. Lord Keith looked at those eyes now, and they seemed brighter than when he'd first entered the cabin. What Lord Keith couldn't see or, obviously, sense was the hair standing up on Fallon's arms, as well.

"Lord Keith," Fallon said softly after a few moments, "you know what I would do if I were you?"

Sir William sat at Fallon's desk with quill and paper as Fallon dictated, in French, from his chair by the stern windows. Fallon chose his words carefully; they needed to be firm and utterly convincing and, hopefully, hidden between the lines, a hint of outrage. As Sir William wrote, a thin smile crossed his face.

For a Bermuda privateer, Fallon was really very good at this sort of thing.

Sixty

One week later the French Venus class frigate *Honneur* arrived off the mole in Algiers harbor at twilight. The dey had been alerted and clapped his hands in anticipation, for this was the sign he'd been waiting for—he was soon to be the richest man in all the Ottoman Empire.

The crew of the pilot boat—the new pilot boat—sailed out of the harbor to guide the frigate inside to an anchorage. Because darkness was closing in, they could not see *Renegade* lurking out of sight barely a mile away. Barclay and Beauty were aboard, having sailed in these waters before, and the sailing master aboard *Renegade* was glad of it as he trembled at the thought of navigating so close to the Barbary coast.

Meanwhile, in the qasba, the dey sent for his prettiest concubines and ordered a private feast to be prepared for the French capitaine. His eyes were alight with greed and seemed to burn as brightly as any torch in the Audience Hall. He had not mourned Zabana's death because he knew him to be wicked and grasping and, ultimately, disloyal and a threat to the dey's health. But he had grieved the loss of gold when that pernicious Fallon had escaped. Now, however, that was forgotten. The dey had demanded that Bonaparte pay him a fortune; no, two fortunes for his help in blockading Gibraltar. He'd also demanded a token payment in advance, and now came a frigate carrying it. Surely, reasoned the dey, Bonaparte would not have sent a ship if the answer was no.

The pilot boat approached *Honneur* with all flags and banners flying and if it seemed odd that the frigate trailed her ship's boats behind her no one on the pilot boat remarked on it. Obviously, the French capitaine was anxious to go ashore, and who could blame him?

The twilight was giving way to darkness as *Honneur* sailed past the tip of the mole behind the pilot boat and, at the order from Jones, opened fire with a robust broadside at the harbor fortifications. The frigate's bow chaser joined in with a clean hit on the pilot boat, not over 100 yards ahead. Quickly, Jones ordered the small crew aboard *Honneur* to reload and run out and get off another unanswered broadside, the bright flashes from the muzzles lighting up the side of the ship.

The leadsman called out the depths and Jones took note that it would soon be time to abandon ship. A minute passed, then two, and now there were bright flashes from the mole as the Algerians collected their wits and their gun crews and fired back.

"Fire!" yelled Jones and again the frigate's broadside roared out, though where the balls landed was not clear in the darkness.

Jones found a moment to smile at the thought of the false orders Fallon had so carefully dictated and Sir William had so beautifully written and which he had secreted in the capitaine's desk drawer.

But there was not a moment to lose. He called for the men to lash the wheel and abandon the ship. The shore batteries fired again, and he could feel *Honneur* stagger from several hits. Looking around, he gave the order to unlock the hatches over the holds before following the last of his men overboard into the waiting boats.

The French prisoners clambered on deck to a barrage of fire from the shore batteries and, bewildered and confused, they rushed to the familiar guns where they found shot and powder and slow match waiting. They had no idea where they were, of course, but what they did know was they were under fire and all their training said load the guns and fight back. The capitaine wasted no time in ordering his men to fire into the blackness.

Which they did, right up until the time that *Honneur* ran aground and they found themselves boarded by hundreds of soldiers in red hats.

For the second time in little more than a month, the French capitaine surrendered.

Sixty-One

Fallon sat in a chair at the stern of his ship nursing his coffee and trying not to stretch the tender scar across his body. It had been two weeks since *Renegade* had returned from Algiers and, during that time, *Rascal* had gotten her masts in and rigging sent up. He had Lord Keith to thank for the dock yard's sense of urgency. Thanks to the Admiral, Fallon should be back to Bermuda just in time for his wedding. *Thank God for that,* thought Fallon.

The sky was a solid blue globe and the sea reflected the color but flecked it with whitecaps. *Rascal* was racing towards Bermuda, towards an imaginary finish line which was off St. George's harbor. The wind was coming southeast and was pushing the ship along like it knew speed was important. He glanced across the sparkling water towards *Renegade* bounding along, as well, keeping pace under reduced sail.

The Vissers were gathered on the starboard rail, still using every moment to catch up with each other's lives. They would be awhile doing it, for there was much in the details that would be thought of in random moments over time.

Little Eddy skylarked in the rigging with the other ship's boys, demonstrating the resiliency of youth and the ability to live in the present. He never knew what likely lay in store for him in Algiers and thankfully he never would. Aja watched him with a smile on his face, his arm still in a light sling but almost healed, according to Colquist.

Beauty bantered with Barclay at the binnacle as usual, each giving as good as they got on every topic from weather to waves. She wore her sea dog necklace with more confidence in its powers than ever before. It had been tested.

Down below decks was Caleb Visser's ransom money, the gold that had been salvaged and never spent. Well, not all of it anyway. Visser had insisted on paying Colonel Bisanz's soldiers handsomely and Bisanz had at last relented and allowed it. Caleb and Beauty had gone to the garrison to thank him on behalf of the ship and Fallon, and mourn with him the loss of fifteen of his finest men.

Sir William and Lord Keith had come aboard before they'd weighed with the welcome news that the dey was apparently furious with Bonaparte for *Honneur's* random act of violence against his nation. Sir William's sources reported that the fake orders to attack Algiers which Fallon had dictated had quashed any thoughts of believing the capitaine's quite fantastic story of being duped by the British.

Fallon sat in the sunshine and summoned the past few month's experiences, one by one, to parade past his mind. Not so much to relive life, for there were too many moments he had no wish to relive, but to put them indelibly in his memory so as not to forget what he'd seen and felt in a world far away and so alien to his own.

He had received help all along this journey, certainly from Davies and, at the last, Jones. But earlier from poor Woodson to Dingle to Truxton and Colonel Bisanz and, of course, the good Friar Orturo who helped him and Aja get into Algiers.

He recalled the Friar's words about the wisdom of letting life come to you and accepting it without trying to control it. He'd said it was futile to put a howling wind in a box. Fallon could understand the point as a matter of philosophy, but letting life have its way had never been his way. Events weren't inevitable in his world. If they were, he'd be dead several times over and Wilhelm Visser and Little Eddy would still be slaves in Algiers. He shook his head at the thought.

It was never easy, but sometimes you could let the wind back out of the box. And, as Beauty would say, let the fucker howl.

Afterword

In 1805, Mustapha Pasha was assassinated by one of his own janissaries.

In 1816, a combined British and Dutch fleet bombarded Algiers in a successful attempt to free 3000 slaves.

In 1847, the taking of Christian slaves by Algerian corsairs finally ended when France conquered Algeria.